KARAOKE RAP

KARAOKE RAP

LAURENCE GOUGH

M&S

Canadian Cataloguing in Publication Data

Gough, Laurence
    Karaoke rap

ISBN 0-7710-3403-2

I. Title

PS8563.08393K37   1997   C813'.54   C97-930857-7
PR9199.3.G68K37   1997

The publishers acknowledge the support of the Canada Council for the Arts and the Ontario Arts Council for their publishing program.

Typesetting by M&S, Toronto
Printed and bound in Canada

McClelland & Stewart Inc.
The Canadian Publishers
481 University Avenue
Toronto, Ontario
M5G 2E9

1 2 3 4 5   01 00 99 98 97

This one's for Mrs. Audrey Rogers Boates, AKA my dear mother

1

The light was green but it had been green ever since Marty first started watching it, from more than a block away. If his timing was right, the light was going to turn red any second. In his professional opinion there was no way they were going to make it through the intersection. He eased his black size-ten Florsheim off the gas pedal. The Bentley immediately began to lose momentum. Steve, sitting bolt upright in the front passenger seat, glanced anxiously around. In the back, Axel stirred restlessly. Beside him, Jake continued to read his *Financial Times*, unperturbed.

Steve and Axel were muscle. Axel was paid by the week but Steve, in a family that seemed to go on forever, was a distant relative who'd landed on Jake's doorstep.

Steve was new to the job, had been lifting and dropping things for Jake for less than a month. Most of the time he stood idly in a corner, his narrow brow furrowed as he tried with the limited tools that were available to him to grind his attitude into an appropriate shape.

Axel was worse. He insisted that he was a mournful expatriate Austrian, but Marty had gotten him drunk on schnapps one morning, and Axel had let it slip that he was from Zwickau, East Germany, where he'd worked at the Trabant factory.

Axel's father, Heinz, had been a low-ranking member of the Stasi, the East German secret police. Axel, quoting his mother, described him as stolid, acned, clumsily furtive. For these reasons and many better ones, none of his friends had liked him. Heinz had been murdered the day the Berlin Wall tumbled. He'd been lighting a cigarette when he was run down by a long-oppressed-but-finally-free G.D.R. citizen driving a brand-new Trabant.

Heinz was picked off in a narrow cul-de-sac located at the bottom of Zwickau's steepest hill. The Trabant has a cruising speed not much faster than a brisk trot. But the murder car, aided by gravity and a strong tailwind, hit him at nearly one hundred kilometres per hour, as he attempted to scale a ten-storey-high wall of sturdy German brick. He was instantly turned to something akin to mortar. The Trabant's driver, who happened to be Axel's mother, was also killed.

Little orphan Axel fled his doomed country that same evening, eventually making his way to Canada via Chile and Mexico. "I haff got so extreme high resistance to pain!" he'd proclaimed to Jake, and promptly butted his cigarette in his mouth to prove it.

Jake had hired him, but not before giving him fair warning that capitalism was a risky business. Screw up while doing business for Jake, he might chain you to that post in the basement, cut slices off you and feed them to the trio of Dobermans that ran wild in his backyard. Vivisection, Jake called it.

Axel knew all this. It had been explained to him in great detail during the employment interview. But it wasn't easy, being a neophyte hoodlum. He was never sure where he should carry his switchblade – in his pants or a jacket pocket. His pistol, spare magazines and matched silencer weighed heavy on him. His leather shoulder holster chafed his skin, and gave him a rash he couldn't seem to get rid of. With every step he took, the extra bullets he carried loose in his pocket rattled like a fistful of snakes. That very morning, Marty had humiliated him by publicly criticizing his chocolate-brown suede Hush Puppies as being insufficiently lethal, should he be required to kick the shit out of somebody.

Worse, he couldn't get his hair to stay slicked back and flat.

Even worse, he kept misplacing his mirrored sunglasses. He hated it when everybody stood around waiting for him, rolling their eyes and cursing and sighing with exasperation, while he hunted those damn glasses down.

What Axel wanted was to be like Marty. He wanted to look just like Marty and think just like Marty. He wanted nothing less than to *be* Marty. He wanted to wear Marty's clothes, tip Marty's barber, drink at Marty's favourite bar and make crazy passionate love to Marty's girlfriend, once he found out who she was.

Steve said, "Why're we slowin' down?"

"Red light," said Marty.

Axel said, "I haff excellent vision but I don't see no red light."

"Me neither," said Marty.

Jake's low chuckle was the sound of a raven being roughly asphyxiated.

Marty wore mauve-tinted sunglasses, an undertaker's suit, crisp white shirt, plain black tie, and a chauffeur's cap with a shiny black peak and gold badge, that Jake had special-ordered from a supplier in New York.

From the Bentley's backseat came the abrasive sound of Jake rattling his *Financial Post*. Jake cleared his throat. He spat a shred of tobacco down at the thickly carpeted floor, and Marty made a mental note to get the Dustbuster out of the trunk before he picked up Melanie.

Jake said, "What're we slowin' down for, wassa problem?" He had a voice, the old man. His words seemed to have been fired out of a churning cement mixer filled to overflowing with cigar smoke, booze, flakes of rust. Whenever he said anything out loud, which was rarely, people turned and gawked. Jake could put the fear of God into a man just saying hello.

Marty glanced in the rearview mirror. "Light's gonna change, Jake."

Jake raised his bony, withered head. His teeth gleamed yellow, but he wasn't smiling.

The light turned amber, then red. Marty feathered the brake pedal. The Bentley came to a full stop with the white-painted crosswalk line reflected in the gleaming chrome bumper. Marty automatically glanced left and right, checked the traffic backing up behind him and saw nothing unusual. Not that he felt vulnerable. The Bentley had been fitted with armour plate in the doors and roof and in front of the firewall and behind the backseat. The thick, aquarium-green glass was bulletproof, the door locks were heavy-duty, the bumpers reinforced with sturdy bars of titanium. The car had been built for a Kuwaiti who didn't much care for the genuine pigskin upholstery. Jake had traded him straight up for a Harley-Davidson Road King with zero clicks on the odometer and a gas tank full of uncut cocaine.

Marty shifted in his seat. To his left the ocean moved restlessly, big rollers heaving themselves up and bashing themselves to smithereens against the granite seawall. The wind hurled flecks of foam into the trees. A couple of women about ten years younger than Marty, both of them in their early twenties, strolled past the windshield. A blonde with a buzzcut, a ponytailed brunette. Model types, leggy and thin, wearing more makeup than clothes. Marty believed that, if he were given half a chance, he could fall in love with either one of them, or both simultaneously. The wind played with their skirts. He caught the smooth curve of a white thigh, a flash of black silk. He blushed, and looked away.

Jake said, "Ya see dat, ya see all dat leg? What a fuckin' miracle a fuckin' genetics! Ain't she a beauty?"

Steve said, "Yeah!"

"Hübschen Mädchen," observed Axel. He smiled. "Pretty girls. Roy Orbison."

"Pretty *Woman*," said Steve.

"Shaddup da bot' a ya!" Jake powered down the window, spat shreds of cigar into the wind, powered the window back up. He said, "I seen racehorses with shorter legs. Man oh man, how I'd like ta . . ."

Marty glanced in the rearview mirror. Jake was staring stolidly at his lap. Either he'd forgotten what he was talking about, or he'd had an orgasm. Marty would've bet his precious life at twenty to one on the former.

There were a few sailboats out there, goofing around. Not many. Little ones, with mini-spinnakers and red dots on the mainsails. Fireballs, playing tag between moored freighters long as a city block.

Axel said, "Look at the pretty sailboats!"

Steve twisted in his seat and gave Axel a look that was equivalent to a gentle poke in the eye with a switchblade knife.

The light turned green. Marty pressed down on the gas pedal. The Bentley eased through the intersection. Eight miles to the gallon. He might have been driving a smallish cruise ship, for all the sensation of movement that he felt.

Jake said, "Base metals, dat's where da money's gonna be made."

"Yeah?" Marty checked the rearview but the old man had his nose buried in the paper.

"Steel an' aluminum."

"What about gold?"

"Diamonds," said Jake. "Ya got any, get rid a dem. T-bills would be excellent, a person could explain where dey came by da cash." Jake fell to peering out the window at the new highrises that had sprung up like so many aroused mushrooms in front of the Bayshore Hotel. The past few years, Jake had taken to spending most of his time at home, dreaming and scheming. But at least once a week, rain or shine, he liked to crawl into the Bentley and go for a ride, check out the city's ever-changing landscape and ogle the city's women. He'd talk about parcels of land that had been worth thousands and were now worth of millions. He'd spot a shapely redhead and start talking ten miles a minute about the dozens of redheads he'd had carnal knowledge of, in one way or another. Of all the world had to offer, Jake's top three were murder, women and the stock market.

They were in the park now, the remains of the zoo coming up on Marty's left, Coal Harbour to his right. A flock of hunch-shouldered Canada geese with heads as black as balaclavas moved like cloned gangstas across an expanse of patchy, anaemic grass. Not too far ahead of them, the road split left and right. Marty said, "Hey, Jake, wanna go past the aquarium or take the long way around?"

"Take a right," said Jake.

Marty nodded, relieved that he didn't have to drive past the aquarium. It was a complicated world. People sometimes went crazy, had to have terrible things done to them to bring them under control. But animals were different. All they wanted was to be left alone to live out their lives as best they could. So what happened? Whales got stuffed into pools the size of a hot tub, and civilized people made money off them.

Jake said, "Pull over."

Marty eased the Bentley up against the curb. There was a guy down there by the seawall, beating a Rottweiler with a big stick. Marty powered down the window. The dog made shrill yelping sounds that were completely out of character, not the kind of sounds you'd expect a dog that large and powerful to make. Marty was reminded of John Madden, the television sports announcer. Madden was a huge man, the size of a bus, but he had the shrill voice of a guy who made his living selling high-end English bone china.

The dog lover lifted up on the dull black toes of his Doc Martens. Marty figured him for six-foot-something, maybe two hundred and twenty. He wore a studded black leather jacket, ragged jeans, those stylish boots. His wallet was chained to his belt. The chain threw off sparks of light as his arm came up, and metal flashed all across his tight-clenched fist. The length of wood bounced off the Rottweiler's skull. The dog winced, and turned its massive head towards Marty. Its smouldering coal-black eyes zeroed in on him.

Axel said, "I think that great beast is in love mit you!"

"Shaddap!" yelled Jake.

Marty glanced around. Nobody. Not a soul. Except for the four men and the dog, the park was empty.

Jake said, "Whatta ya see?"

"Not a fucking thing!" said Axel.

"Not you, dimwit."

"Nothing," said Marty. He took another look around, his eyes cutting through all points of the compass. He said, "There's just him and us, Jake."

"Fuckin' act a God." Jake's cigar glowed red as his eyes. He spat tobacco at the carpet. He leaned forward in his seat, bounced his knuckles off the back of Steve's shiny hair. "Whatta ya waitin' for? Go get 'im."

"Let me do it!" said Axel. He clapped his hands together. "I promise to be efficient!"

Marty shifted the gearshift into park.

Steve thought, *Go get 'im*. What did that mean, exactly? He popped open the glove compartment and got out his leather gloves and wriggled into them finger by finger. Behind him, Jake worked on his cigar, rattled his newspaper. Axel stared at Steve, with eyes full of jealousy and venom. Steve unfastened his seatbelt and pushed open the door, got out of the car, eased the door shut and pulled his pistol, a Beretta, out of his pocket. He'd checked the weapon that morning and he could tell by the weight that it was loaded, but he ejected the magazine anyway, just to be on the safe side.

Wood crashed on bone. The dog whined piteously.

He slammed the magazine back into the gun. Metal clanged on metal, the sound plenty loud enough for Jake to hear it, if he wanted to. Steve pulled the Beretta's slide back a quarter-inch, what the cops called a push-check.

His mind slipped away. He wondered where the leggy, racehorse-type women had gone, what they were up to. He imagined them perched on stools at one of the dozens of Starbucks that littered the city, slurping cappuccinos. Or maybe buying clothes at one of those expensive little shops on Robson. He watched the blonde step into a changing room and shut the door behind her. Alone, or believing she was alone, unaware that Steve's overheated imagination had slipped in there with her, she lifted her skirt and . . .

At five-eight, Steve was two inches shorter than Axel and six inches shorter than Marty, barely tall enough to look over the Bentley's glossy roof at the dog basher, who was still hard at work, but starting to tire.

On the far side of the harbour there was a building going up, another highrise. The construction crew was the size of ants. Steve reasoned that, because of his diminutive physique, to anyone over there who was looking at him he'd be even smaller than an ant. In a lineup, who could distinguish one ant from a bunch of other ants?

He screwed the noise-suppressor onto the pistol's snub nose as he worked his way diagonally across and down the grassy slope to the asphalt pathway that ran along the seawall all the way around the park.

The dog lover heard him coming, turned and gave him a hostile stare. Steve held the pistol by his side, close up against his thigh, the gun hidden by his unbuttoned sports jacket. He made it to the asphalt, walked directly towards the man. The guy had a gold earring in each ear. He accurately read Steve's posture and the look in his eyes. The chunk of wood he was using on the Rott was about eighteen inches long. Oak, by the look of it. The guy pointed it at him and said, "Shove off, buddy."

Steve kept walking towards the man. He waited until the piece of wood bumped against his chest, then lifted his pistol and squeezed the trigger three times. The gun huffed and puffed, spat fire and lead. A look filtered into the man's eyes. Surprise. Dismay. Steve reached out with his left hand. He gave the leather jacket's zipper a savage yank. Beneath the jacket the man wore a peach-coloured sleeveless T-shirt. He looked down at the three small holes, his bloody chest. Steve used the pistol to lever up the man's chin, so he could look into the shattered windows of his soul.

Meanwhile, the dog panted feverishly, tongue hanging loose. A furry eyewitness to the mayhem as Steve pulled the trigger and a killer bullet raced up through the dog owner's soft palate and into the heart of his brain.

The dead man's legs went out from under him. He fell, face up and heavily, onto the asphalt. Steve leaned over him and unhesitatingly shot him twice in the forehead, in that narrow span of barren ground between the bushy black eyebrows and prematurely receding hairline. The copper-jacketed bullets drilled through bone, pulverized grey mush. The head snapped back, bounced and rolled. The muzzle blasts speckled pasty skin. Dead eyes bulged, and sank back.

In the Bentley, there was nothing but consternation.

Jake said, "Ya see dat?"

"Pow!" sang Axel. "Pow! Pow! Pow!"

Marty nodded.

Jake said, "He squibbed da guy, din't he?"

Marty nodded again.

"Squibbed him, what, five a six times?"

"Eight!" said Axel, holding up seven fingers.

"Six," said Marty. But really, what difference did it make?

"Jeez, what a asshole. Fa kickin' a fuckin' mutt. Jeez." Jake chewed on his cigar. He said, "Should I mention I'm surprised?"

"Me too!" said Axel.

"Shaddap!"

Down on the seawall, Steve turned towards the dog, his heart pumping, more than ready to do whatever had to be done. Blood oozed thickly from a deep cut on the animal's skull. It's big brown eyes held steady on Steve's, seeing all of him, watching. Steve vaguely remembered reading something in a newspaper or magazine about a killer who was identified by the victim's dog. He believed the snitch was a sheepdog, but it might've been a border collie. He aimed his pistol at the Rottweiler. The dog sat up a little straighter. It woofed at him, as if introducing itself, then got busy licking itself clean.

The thing was trying to make itself presentable. Pathetic. Steve thought about what Jake might do to him if the beast bloodied his car. Painful things, for sure.

But Jake had all those Dobermans out there in the yard, so maybe he liked dogs. But anyway, there was no way he was gonna smoke this particular dog, not unless he got a direct order. He went over, bent and caught up the cobalt-blue anodized aluminum tag on the dog's spiked collar.

MARILYN. No way. He unscrewed the noise-suppressor and slid it into his pants pocket. Jake's supply of suppressors came to him via UPS or one of the other carriers, from a small factory in Texas. Suppressors were only good for a few shots, but could easily be repaired by packing them with steel wool or fibreglass. On the other hand, pistols lasted forever but were cheap and easily traced. Steve tossed his gun into the harbour. He unfastened the dog collar and threw it away, took a moment to look around. The coast was clear. It was just him, the dog, and the bullet-riddled corpse. He picked up the spent shell casings and flipped them underhand into the ocean. He rolled the corpse over to the edge of the seawall and gave it a good push.

Too late, he noticed that the tide was out. The dead man hit the mud and lay there, face down. He'd left a smear of blood on the pavement, but what was Steve supposed to do, call Molly Maids? He slapped his thigh. "C'mere, Butch."

The dog stuck close as his new master made his way back to the Bentley. Steve opened the front passenger-side door. He laid his sports jacket down on the floor, pointed at the car and told the Rott to climb aboard. The dog jumped in, curled up on the jacket. Smart. Agile, too, when you considered its bulk. Steve got in, shut the door. He rested the heels of his shoes lightly on the dog. Butch stared up at him. The look in the Rott's eyes was warm and affectionate, tinged with doleful. Steve reached down between his legs and massaged a neck thick and unyielding as a tree.

Marty shifted into drive and pulled away from the curb.

Jake said, "I never seen nothin' like it."

"Und me neither!" said Axel.

"In all my days," said Jake.

"Six shots," said Marty. "Pop pop pop."

"That's only three," said Axel. "*Drei.*" He held up three fingers.

Marty glanced at Steve. "Was the guy so dumb he had to be shot to death to get your point? You wanted to pass judgement on him, why didn't you kick him in the nuts like any normal person would?"

"Good question," said Jake. He viciously sucked at something caught between his teeth. He spat. A soggy chunk of cigar smacked into the back of Steve's neck, and crept slowly down inside his shirt. "What's wit da fuckin' mutt?"

"She's a stray," said Steve.

Axel said, "You could buy a saddle, und charge for horsy rides."

Steve said, "Her name's Butch."

"You don't fuckin' clean up afta' her, her name's gonna be Butchered." Jake spat again. Steve flinched, but it was a clean miss. Either Jake's aim had deteriorated, or his mood had improved.

Jake lit a fresh cigar as Marty made a left onto Pipeline Road. Twenty years ago, Jake and Marty's father had buried a guy not far from the limestone footpath that circled Beaver Lake. Marty had been a tiny little kid, back then. The stiff had never been found. Not that it mattered. Jake was and always had been and always would be a *que sera* kind of guy.

But that wasn't to say he was reckless.

Decisive, yes. Ruthless, no doubt about it. Willing to take chances, for sure. But at the same time, he was extraordinarily vigilant, and cautious.

In 1927 Jake had ridden a train to New York in search of Prohibition. He'd partied it up into the thirties, made enough dough to go home a rich man. Back in Canada, N.Y. accent intact, he'd dived headfirst into prostitution, gambling, drugs. Now, in the twilight of what was by any standard a fabulous career, he was starting to wind down a little. With Marty and Steve and Axel for company, he kept in shape by paddling around the indoor pool for an hour or so every day, and by drinking moderately and eating wisely and not to excess, by restricting himself to a dozen cigars a week, and by getting laid every third Saturday morning by an expensive young woman with a clean bill of health. He still enjoyed these little dalliances, mostly.

He continued to dabble in the vices, mostly because they were lucrative, but also because he liked to maintain a certain presence in the industry, keep an iron in the fire. But much of his time and energy was spent flipping real estate or playing the stock market. He liked the market because it was riskier than the rackets.

Marty's father, who'd logged a couple of hundred thousand miles on the odometers of a fleet of Jake's automobiles, and helped Jake bury more guys than both of them together could count on all their fingers and toes combined, was dead of natural causes. Jake missed him. He'd been a good man, steady and dependable. Marty had all the right genes. The kid had no family, except for Jake.

In fact neither of them had anybody, except for each other. But now, suddenly, there was someone new and interesting in Jake's life. Butch. He called softly to the dog, and it scrambled up on Steve's lap. Jake gently scratched the Rott behind its floppy ear.

Steve said, "Easy, now." Butch growled low in her throat. She turned her massive head and curled her upper lip, warned Steve off with a razor-sharp incisor. He fell back as if he'd been shot.

Jake said, "Thassa girl!"

The Rott surged over the seat towards him, licked skin from his face with a tongue like a rasp. The animal's breath might have come straight from a forge. It tried, all hundred and forty pounds of it, to crawl into Jake's lap.

Axel's eyes, as he watched the exchange, were cold and bright. Brighter by far than Axel.

Jake tried to push the creature away. Butch wriggled in a paroxysm of pleasure. She purred raggedly, as if she mistakenly believed she was a great big pussycat.

Jake said, "I t'ink Butch likes me." His voice was bleak. The words rattled off his teeth like stones.

Marty knew how Jake's mind worked, could see clear as if an airplane had written it in the sky what Jake was thinking as he'd watched Steve squib the dog owner.

Jake was thinking that Steve was an idiot and the first thing they had to do was dig a hole for him and the last thing they had to do was drop him into it and cover him over for all of eternity.

But Steve had lucked out. He'd brought back the Rott, and because Jake and the Rott had a lot in common, they were getting along just fine.

Jake said, "Marty, when we get outta da park, stop by one a dem pet-food places ya shop fa' da Dobermans."

Marty said, "Okay, Jake."

Jake said, "We gonna need a couple a big bowls, one fa water an' one fa food. An' a bag a dem fake bones fa chewin' on, a new collar an' leash, powders and whatever for da fleas . . ." Jake ran out of steam. The cables of loose flesh beneath his jaw swayed slightly and were still. His face was horribly distorted. What was wrong with him? Marty realized he was smiling.

The old man, as he wiped viscous strings of doggy drool from his face, appeared to be happy as a bucketful of clams.

2

Earlier that same day, a Supreme Court jury had filed in, milled around uncertainly, sat down. A hush had settled over the courtroom. Willows had leaned forward expectantly. Claire Parker had shut her eyes and clasped her hands together. She might have been praying.

The Supreme Court judge, a doddering halfwit named Jimmy Morrison Sutherland, cranked up his hearing aid and inquired of the jury foreman as to whether the jury had achieved a decision.

The foreman said, "We have, Your Honour."

The defence team of McRae, Fawell, and Fuller were three of the sleaziest and wealthiest lawyers in the entire city. Jane Fuller was a generation younger than her partners, and she was the sparkplug of the team. Some had it that McRae and Fawell were living on their reputations, that McRae's intellect was receding as rapidly as his hairline, that entire mountain ranges of cocaine had so thoroughly cooked his brain that he was incapable of stringing together more than two or three short, borderline-literate sentences. Fawell, who had a weakness for the bottle, was awaiting his third kidney transplant.

"Will the defendant rise . . . ?"

Jane Fuller gave the defendant an openly saucy wink, and motioned him to get up off his ass and give the court its due. Jimmy "Fatboy" McEwen was a twenty-three-year-old upper-echelon

drug dealer and coke addict who, while dim-summing at a Chinatown restaurant, had pulled his Glock and calmly told the ninety-
year-old Chinese waiter he was going to kill him, then done so.

Then, mostly because he enjoyed the racket his pistol made
when he pulled the trigger, he'd riddled the restaurant's several
huge saltwater aquariums full of delicious live rock cod and crab.
Several patrons had been injured by flying glass, crab and fish
parts, panicked fellow diners. When McEwen paused to reload his
weapon, a cook named Benny Lee bounced a dull meat cleaver off
his skull, and knocked him unconscious.

McEwen's initial defence had consisted of the unarguable fact
that his dim sum order had been royally screwed up. Inordinately
cheerful cops patted him on the shoulder and told him they didn't
blame him one little bit, offered him a ballpoint pen and pad of
lined paper and invited him to describe the entire disgraceful incident in his own words, as best he could. They advised him not to
worry about sentence structure or spelling or the cheapness and
commonality of his sentiments. The key to a successful confession, they assured him, was to keep everything nice and simple, so
anybody with basic reading skills could understand what he was
saying. They bought him a Coke and cigarettes. They told him to
take as much time as he needed.

But the carnage and attendant publicity had lured the public-
ity-hungry defence team of McRae, Fawell, and Fuller to McEwen's
cell. When McEwen told them he'd have no problem coming up
with their criminally outrageous fee if they didn't mind suitcases
full of small-denomination bills, a deal was swiftly struck. A
sample of McEwen's blood was taken and analysed, and it was discovered that McEwen was a walking pharmacy, that he'd ingested
so many varieties of drugs that it was a wonder he was able to
function on even the lowest plane.

The prosecutor's case was further eroded when a number of
witnesses abruptly embarked on lengthy vacations in Eastern
Europe or the Caribbean. Other witnesses suddenly became proud
owners of a shiny new car or light truck or power boat. Benny

Lee, who was considered a crucial prosecution witness, vanished unexpectedly. He was located three weeks later, when a city works crew was dispatched to investigate a plugged storm drain. For these and many other gruesome reasons, McRae, Fawell, and Fuller expected the prosecution's case to fizzle. The defence team oozed confidence.

Addressing the jury foreman, the judge said, "Would you please read your verdict to the court."

The foreman cleared his throat. "Your Honour, we find the defendant, Jimmy "Fatboy" McEwen, not guilty."

There were at least three dozen cops in the courtroom. Most of them had attended on their own time. McEwen had been a career criminal since age eight, when he'd started boosting and crashing cars. He'd been in and out, in and out. Willows and Parker had him pegged for three previous shootings, all fatal. A sneering McEwen had strolled each time, when the Crown witnesses had faded.

Now, unbelievably, he'd walked again. Willows exhaled with a rush, and realized he'd been holding his breath. His stomach churned sourly. He stared hard at McEwen until McEwen finally sensed that he was being watched. Their eyes locked.

Grinning, McEwen gave Willows the finger. Jane Fuller playfully slapped at his hand. McEwen grabbed her bejewelled fingers and raised her hand aloft in a victory salute.

Willows kept staring at him. All his life, McEwen's temper had led him around by the nose. Willows told himself that, sooner or later, McEwen would take a heavy, heavy fall. In Kingston, or whatever maximum-security hellhole they eventually sent him to, the personality traits that served him so well on the street would betray and swiftly kill him. The kid was a murderous, halfwitted hothead punk. It would only be a matter of minutes until he leaned into the wrong con, took a shank in the gut and died in a fountain of blood.

Willows' eyes, as he stared at McEwen, read the kid his whole pathetic story, from first page to last.

McEwen was there, but he wasn't there. His fate was signed and sealed and about to be delivered. He was, whether he knew it or not, a goner.

Fatboy blew Willows a kiss. He turned to Parker, lewdly cupped his crotch, and blew her a kiss too.

Willows flushed. He could still hear the echo of Fatboy's laughter long after he'd walked out of the courtroom.

3

Ozzie fed quarters into the machine, pushed buttons. Two frosty-cold cans of Coke and one can of Pepsi thumped into the dispenser. He scooped up the cans, tossed the Pepsi to Dean as he crossed the faded linoleum of the lunchroom floor.

It was eight minutes past twelve by the big electric clock on the wall above the door. Ozzie straddled the bench seat. Dean sat hunched on the far side of the table with his brown paper bag in front of him. The situation, the way the lunchroom was laid out and furnished and the way they were sitting, it was like being in the slammer. All that was missing was a whole lot of cons and a whole lot of noise. Ozzie popped the tab on his first Coke. He sipped, examined a cracked, dirt-packed fingernail, scratched idly at a dime-size callus on his palm.

Dean plucked a sandwich from the bag. His teeth cut through floppy white bread, lettuce, a solid inch of tinned meat. Spam, maybe. His jaws rolled. A glop of yellow mustard dribbled out of his mouth, ran slowly down his chin and went splat on the table. Ozzie sat there, enjoying the show.

Dean gulped down the mouthful of sandwich, wiped his chin with the back of his hand. The reason they were in the yard, they'd just finished a job. Dean said, "Charlie got anything for us, or we gotta take the rest of the day off?" As usual, he was edgy about his cash-flow situation. The rent was due, the fridge was empty, etc., etc.

Ozzie drank some of his Coke, leaned across the table, slid his finger into Dean's brown paper lunch bag, tilted the bag towards him and peeked inside. Dean had another sandwich tucked away in there, a couple more rough-cut slices of white bread wrapped around another pound of meat, the whole thing glued together with some kind of purplish jelly-like substance. What else? Ozzie wiggled his finger, probing. A great big chocolate-chip cookie, must've weighed a quarter of a pound. A shiny green apple. A banana that had gone spotty. Dean hadn't bothered to wrap anything in wax paper. The food was all jumbled and mashed together.

Dean said, "You hungry? Want something?"

Ozzie pushed the bag away. He shook his head.

"Go ahead, help yourself. Take something."

As if that were advice Ozzie needed. He hesitated a moment, and then dug deep, pushed his hand down in there, swirled his stiff fingers around in the food, snatched the banana and squeezed it to mush, busted the cookie up into crumb-size pieces. He grabbed the apple, plucked it out of the bag, grasped it in his two hands and rotated his hands in opposite directions. The apple tore apart in a burst of sticky juice. He broke the two pieces into two more pieces, tossed one at the garbage can, a lazy, looping shot that fell a little bit short.

Dean watched him but didn't say a word.

Ozzie paced himself, took his time. He kept breaking the apple into smaller and smaller pieces, picked bits and pieces off it as methodically as a cruel child might pull the legs off an ant. Occasionally he hit the can, but usually he missed. Finally there was nothing left of the apple but a few small wet glops that lay there in the palm of his hand.

Dean said, "I guess I should've told you that you're supposed to eat it. People in China are starving, Ozzie." He'd tried to come across as ironic, but to Ozzie's ear only managed to sound whiny and petulant.

Ozzie smiled. "People in the downtown eastside are starving, last time I looked. Hell, there's poor people all over the city dropping like flies. So what? In my opinion, there's still way too many of 'em."

The linoleum all around the garbage can was littered with fragments of apple. Dean pushed himself away from the table and shambled over there in his scuffed workboots and baggy-ass jeans, unbuttoned pale-blue-and-soft-yellow plaid short-sleeved shirt. His chest hair gleamed healthily in the shaft of sunlight that came in through the open door. Muscles bulged all along the tanned length of his arm as he lifted up the near side of the garbage can and used his boot to sweep the mess under the can. He let the can drop with a clang that reverberated off the unpainted walls.

Ozzie thought, that's you in a nutshell, Dean. Tidy, in a pigshit-sloppy, half-assed, bone-lazy kind of way. Handsome, but about as intelligent as a wheelbarrow full of rocks. He drained the Coke, popped the tab on can number two. Squinting out the doorway at the dusty, sunlit yard, he saw stacks of cut stone, granite mostly, looming over wafer-thin shadows. A forklift crawled across his field of vision, past his gleaming, hell-red '56 Chevy short-box pickup. The truck's moon hubcaps and chrome trim had been polished to a mirror-bright shine, and the freshly waxed paint was so glossy it almost hurt to look at it.

Ozzie was a stonemason by trade. Dean, a first-year apprentice, had been working under him for three months going on four. In Ozzie's considered opinion, Dean was a man of moderate talent and severely limited intelligence. Not that Ozzie was complaining.

Dean glanced up at the clock. He said, "Hey, Ozzie. We got a job, or what?"

"Don't worry about it." StoneWorks was a medium-small company, family-owned. Mom answered the phone, Dad did the estimating. A trio of plodding middle-aged sons were, nominally, foremen. A daughter in her late thirties, plain as a tailgate, pounded the computer. Four guys worked in the yard, drilling and splitting and stacking the stone. Depending on the size of the job, anywhere from two to a dozen men prepared the sites, cleared away brush and trees, dug trenches, laid concrete foundations. The company employed one apprentice, Dean, and two journeymen stone-masons, Ozzie and a older, quiet-type guy named Bob. A couple of minimum-wage hulksters drove the flatbed trucks loaded with cut stone from the yard to the job, humped the rock from the trucks to the site. It was young men's work, hard work with sudden lengthy periods of unemployment, the kind of work that attracted footloose types who came and went.

Ozzie had worked for the company a solid eighteen months, nonstop, if you counted in a two-month December–January layoff. He was already a senior employee. Eighteen months was far too long to be rooted to one small patch of earth, but he could see an end to it, at last. He wasn't quite close enough to stick his greedy hand into the rainbow and watch his palm turn all those pretty rainbow colours, but he was getting there.

He brushed sun-bleached hair from his forehead, rolled the can of Coke across his sweaty skin. His pale green eyes were solemn.

Dean said, "Where we workin'? Down there on Third Avenue, above the beach? That one?"

"Yeah, that one."

"Holy shit! You shittin' me?" Dean enthusiastically slapped the table. He was about five-ten, maybe a hundred and seventy pounds. Short brown hair, wide brown eyes. No visible scars, not much visible education. Just your basic average-built guy.

He gnawed on the remains of his sandwich a moment or two, mulling the happy news, and then said, "Just so I know we ain't got our wires crossed, we talkin' about that big fake-barn-style house, got the pool out back, the twin sisters with the blonde ponytails, were wearin' them skimpy bikinis, from a distance you couldn't hardly tell what was bikini and what was skin . . . ?"

Ozzie resisted a sudden urge to corkscrew his fist into Dean's teeth, knock him on his unconscious ass and hope he woke up about fifty IQ points less stupid. He lit a cigarette, tossed the match on the floor. No wonder, with guys like Dean wandering around, that rich people paid a whole lot of money for towering walls of stone. The sisters were prime. Looking at it from Daddy's point of view, it'd be worth spending almost any amount of money to keep an amoral halfwit like Dean away from them.

He stood up, slapped stone dust from his jeans, flicked cigarette ash onto the table and blew a double lungful of unfiltered smoke at the ceiling.

"Let's roll, kid."

Dean, his face full of mashed banana, glanced at the big round-faced wall clock over the door. He chewed desperately. His throat rippled as most of the banana slid down the chute. He said, "It's only twenty-four minutes past twelve, and we didn't even start lunch until almost ten past." Cogs that were slightly out of sync threw off dull sparks as he struggled with the math. He said, "We got almost another quarter-hour, Ozzie."

Ozzie said, "Yeah, but I was thinking maybe the twins might take a dip in the pool, about now."

Dean's face lit up. The mere thought of those bikini-clad girls had turned him in an instant into a ball of fire. He swung his legs over the bench seat and stumbled to his feet and headed for the door, loudly sucking the last of the fruit from the gaps between his molars.

Ozzie revised his estimation of Dean's intelligence down to half a wheelbarrow full of rocks.

Absolutely hopeless.

And, for what Ozzie had in mind, dead perfect.

4

The sudden influx of deeply depressed detectives had chased all the usual customer-suspects out of the bar. Hours had passed, but the bar still belonged to the cops.

The homicide detectives, Jack Willows and Claire Parker, Farley Spears and Dan Oikawa, and Eddy Orwell and Bobby Dundas, sat huddled over sunny pitchers of beer, frothy glasses, overflowing ashtrays. Shrouded in smoke and ill will, a couple of Bobby's ex-pals from his recent vice-squad days leaned heavily against the bar. The constables who'd cuffed Fatboy had dumped their ill-fitting uniforms in favour of ill-fitting sports jackets, and were hitting on a near-sighted criminal psychologist who, Parker couldn't help but notice, had let down her dyed-red hair and rolled up her skirt and unfastened the top three buttons of her blouse the moment she'd left the courtroom.

Rumour had it the shrink was sleeping with both cops and that neither of them knew about the other. Nobody really wanted to know.

Parker sipped at her bar wine, an imported red that was far too young to have been allowed out. She glanced along the length of the smoky bar, to the lonely table where the Crown prosecutor and his team of skinny, underpaid lawyers were drowning their sorrows with bottles of Coors Light, a bowl of corn chips, separate tabs.

Orwell said, "Look at those guys, willya? Talk about cheap." Orwell's hard blue eye homed in on the Crown prosecutor, an emaciated, dour-looking scarecrow of a man named Gerald Kelly. Orwell said, "I ever mention I had lunch with Kelly, about six months ago?"

"You guys had a date?" said Spears.

"Fuck you, Farley. No, of course not. I ran into the stupid bastard at a deli, and he begged me to sit down at his table and eat with him. There was plenty of room at the table and I didn't have to sit too close to him, and there were no other seats available anyhow, because the joint was packed, so I reluctantly accepted his invitation."

"What deli was this?"

Orwell thought about it. "I dunno, I forget. What's the difference? Anyway, point is, I sit down, I notice he's got a free glass of water from the dispenser sitting in front of him, but no food. Then he makes me an offer to buy a quarter-share of my sandwich."

"Bullshit," said Spears.

"No, it's the truth. Told me I looked a little overweight. *Pudgy* was the word he used, the skinny little fuck."

"The man had a point, you got to admit," said Bobby Dundas, who was the only cop in the joint who hadn't loosened the knot in his tie, and knew it. He winked at Parker, who ignored him.

"Wanted half my dill pickle and a third of my potato salad," said Orwell. "Had it all figured out what it should cost, right down to the penny."

"Bullshit," said Spears again, but less forcibly.

"No way. It's God's truth, I swear."

"On what?" said Bobby.

"Your fat ass, cripple." Bobby went a little pale around the eyes, but Orwell was too far gone to worry about it. He raised his glass to his mouth and tilted back his head. His throat moved. All but an inch of beer vanished from the glass.

Bobby said, "My what? What'd you call me, mumble-nuts?"

Orwell flicked the remaining contents of his glass across the table. Beer splashed across Bobby's bronze-coloured suit.

Bobby gave himself a shake. In the calm but exasperated tone of voice you might use on a two-year-old, he said, "I wish you'd quit doing that, Eddy."

"Doing what?" Orwell poured himself a refill. Beer spilled over the top of his glass. He licked his fingers dry. Orwell's longtime partner, Ralph Kearns, had quit the VPD a little over two years ago. In the interim, Orwell and Bobby had worked two dozen homicides together. It was a union made in hell. Both men had desperately had wanted a divorce by the ten-minute mark of the first case.

Bobby Dundas was movie-star handsome, immeasurably vain, ruthlessly single. Like W. H. Auden's shop girls, he was often dressed in all his salary. Today he was wearing a new suit, a lightweight model in pure wool Teflon. He'd made the mistake of explaining to Orwell and the other homicide cops that the cotton had been dyed and then dipped in a vat of Teflon, baked in a high-temperature oven so the Teflon formed what he called "an invisible molecular shield" around the fabric. He'd claimed that liquid spills simply beaded up and rolled off, and that semi-solids like mustard or ketchup could be wiped away with a napkin.

Orwell had immediately begun field-testing the new miracle fabric, and he was still hard at it, abusing Bobby and the suit at every opportunity.

Bobby, slouched regally in his chair, was flanked by shiny aluminum crutches autographed by his wimp surgeon and those unfortunate nurses and the janitorial staff on his floor who had been unable to avoid him. Injured in an automobile accident a year earlier, Bobby had suffered through a slow recovery and then celebrated overly long and fallen down a flight of stairs and snapped both ankles.

"Getting back to Kelly," said Dan Oikawa. "What kind of sandwich was it?"

"Corned beef on rye would be my bet," said Spears. "Or maybe corned beef on corn."

Parker laughed and Bobby, frowning, glanced at her and won-dered what was so damn funny, but decided not to ask.

Orwell ran his hand up over the bridge of his twice-crumpled nose and across his abbreviated forehead, a lump of scar tissue that was a memento of his beloved wife, Judith, scoring a direct hit on him with a cast-iron frying pan. His blunt fingers heli-coptered over his close-cropped, wheat-gold hair. Lately, trying for a youthful spiky look, he'd been using a new brand of gel. He scrutinized the lacquer-like shine on his palm for a long moment and then said, "If memory serves, it was pastrami on rye."

Oikawa said, "Well, I don't blame you for being upset. That's a sloppy sandwich, it'd be real tough cutting it even reasonably exact."

"You cut, I choose," said Farley. "That's the way we used to do it when I was a kid, with chocolate bars or whatever, but usually some kind of candy. You cut, I choose; you cut, I choose."

"They still do it that way," said Bobby. "In fact, when the knife was invented, it became an even more popular method."

"Except, modern life, now it's I cut you and take it all," said Oikawa.

"Fuck you," said Farley, speaking directly to Bobby. Now that his buddy Ralph Kearns had resigned, slipped the VPD noose and slow-speed sprinted for greener pastures, Farley was the oldest detective in serious crimes. The oldest homicide detective. With Kearns gone, he felt vulnerable. Like he was gonna be the next cop who got sledgehammered, and there was a great deal less than sweet bugger-all that he could do about it. Except it was going to be a lot worse for him, because Kearns had jumped but he, Detective Farley Jason Spears, was going to have to be pushed. Pushed hard. He emptied his glass, wiped his upper lip and reached for the pitcher. Orwell got there first. He lifted the pitcher and condescendingly said, "Let me get it, Farley. It's kind of heavy."

Spears slumped back in his chair, exhausted.

Orwell said, "Anyway, Kelly. In the deli. We're sitting there, both of us munching away. He's got half my sandwich on half my paper plate, which he sliced up with his fucking pearl-handled switchblade. He's drinking the top half of my coffee. Slurp munch, slurp munch. Content as a whole fucking herd of cows. The knife's lying there on the table, pointing at me. What's he trying to do, intimidate me? I asked him, where's his wallet? He laughs, tells me it's in his back pocket but there's no point pulling it out 'cause it's got a fucking padlock on it, and he forgot the key. I can't believe it. I'm sitting there, my mouth hanging open. Fucking stunned."

"So what'd you do?" said Oikawa.

"What would you do?"

"Shoot him," said Bobby. "In fact, better late than never."

"My gun's in the trunk of my car," said Orwell.

"Shoot the trunk of your car," suggested Bobby.

"I heard Kelly was pretty cheap," said Oikawa.

"Cheap?" Orwell brayed. "Listen, the guy's so fucking tight-fisted he never learned how to masturbate." He glared benignly at Parker. "Excuse my language, Claire. Am I drunk?"

Parker smiled. "If you're looking for a volunteer breathalyser, forget it."

Orwell pushed back his chair, stood up, weaved elliptically, got himself approximately vertical. He spread his arms wide, as if to embrace all humanity. "I'm a happily married man and I want everybody to know it!" he screamed at the ceiling. "Except you!" he shouted, clutching at but narrowly missing a fishnet-stockinged waitress as she glided by.

Willows quietly said, "Sit down, Eddy."

"Okay, Jack."

Nearby tables shook as Orwell collapsed into his chair.

Bobby sipped his beer. Looking at him, he was a cucumber. Inside, he was a kettle on the boil. Steamed. The pressure building. If he pursed his lips, the resultant whistle would break every pint mug in the joint. The problem wasn't the suit. The Teflon really worked. Bobby had tested it with a smear of his own blood, when he'd cut himself shaving that morning.

No, the suit had proved impervious to all the beer and fruit and other junk Orwell had hurled at it all afternoon. The suit still looked as sharp as the day he'd bought it. The suit salesman had virtually guaranteed that the suit would be impervious to life's little spills. He had explained in mind-numbing detail that the wool had been given an extra twist at the factory, turning it into a "nervous fabric" that always wanted to return to its original shape. Bottom line, no wrinkles. And the pants had a bead of silicon under the crease, so they always looked sharp.

The problem was his creamy-white silk shirt, his fifty-dollar Italian silk tie. Bobby had tried his best to protect the shirt and tie with his suit jacket, but how could he be expected to maintain a status of full alert when he was surrounded by increasingly attractive women? The shirt and tie were taking a beating. They were a mess, a ruin. He resented it. Broken ankles or not, he was only one more spill away from dancing all over Orwell's stupid, beefy face.

Bobby glanced around. There wasn't a cop in the bar – with the possible exception of Claire Parker – who believed Fatboy deserved anything less than the death penalty. Gas him, fry him, stretch him or shoot him, whatever. Just put him down, put him in the ground. But, once a suspect or perp had been arrested, there was no death penalty. Sometimes, that could be a problem.

Willows, too, was thinking about Jimmy "Fatboy" McEwen. He'd been the primary on the case, had been there for every level of appeal, right through to the Supreme Court. At one point during McEwen's long and arduous journey he had been granted bail. Willows and Parker had learned from a snitch that McEwen was planning to flee the country, and had obtained sufficient evidence to that effect to convince a magistrate to revoke McEwen's bail. McEwen had been arrested in his kitchen as he prepared to dismember a roast turkey with an electric carving knife. As Willows had come into the kitchen, bulled his way through the splintered remains of the back door, McEwen had spun towards him, knife in hand. He'd been standing at the kitchen counter, to the left of the sink. Detective and murderer were suddenly close enough to reach out and shake hands. Willows was the tiniest fraction of a second away from shooting the teeth right out of McEwen's grimacing mouth when the knife clattered to the floor. Willows' chance to do what he considered the ultimate right thing had come and gone. And now Fatboy was free as a goddamn bird.

He drank a little beer. He was acutely aware that Parker was watching him, knew that if he made eye contact she'd signal that it was time to leave.

And she was right. It *was* time to get the hell out of there, away from the drifting smoke and aimless chatter, the sometimes vicious gossip, Bobby's mustard-proof suit.

The thing was, he'd had too much beer and it had made him feel gassy and bloated, a little sleepy. He needed a Cutty on the rocks, just one, a double, to put an edge back on his world.

He checked his watch. It was quarter past four. His daughter, Annie, would be home from school by now. He should let Parker take him home, ask Annie about her day, offer to help with her homework. But from now until half past six the streets would be crammed with rush-hour traffic, drivers at their snarliest. It was reason enough to delay their departure for a little while. If Parker offered to drive, and he knew she would, he'd smile and whisper in her ear that she drove him crazy.

He drained his glass and helped himself to the pitcher squatting in the middle of the table. Orwell was talking about Judith, again. What a wonderful woman she was, such a good mother to his kids. It had been almost six years since Eddy and Judith had first parted company, and in the interim she'd kicked him out and dragged him back at regular and frequent intervals. It was one of those special relationships. They couldn't live with or without each other. The latest split had ended when Judith had told Eddy she was six weeks' pregnant. He'd moved back that same day. Since then, the only significant change in their relationship that Eddy had remarked upon was the new sofa and matching love seat Judith had bought from Sears.

The fishnet stockings drifted past.

Bobby looked right past her, didn't even see her.

Willows, curious as to what had deflected Bobby's interest, turned and glanced over his shoulder. His inspector, Homer Bradley, moved implacably through the hilarity towards their table. Willows shifted a few inches closer to Parker, giving Bradley a little more room, as he eased his arthritic body into Dan Oikawa's recently vacated seat. Bradley acknowledged the detectives with a terse nod. He sat there, outwardly relaxed. In his late fifties and nearing mandatory retirement, Bradley was still a handsome man. His eyes were dark and calm. He had a copper's long hard nose and bushy black eyebrows, and for as long as anybody could remember, his thinning white hair had been combed straight back in a no-compromise style.

The table fell deathly silent. It was as if Bradley were a human vacuum cleaner, come to vacuum up every last syllable of conversation. His smile took in the assemblage. "I hope nobody objects to me stopping by for a quick one."

A flurry of muttered denials. Bobby Dundas' crutches clattered as he leaned forward. His voice was a degree too warm as he said, "A pleasure to have you with us, Homer."

Spears caught Willows' eye, raised an eyebrow. Willows almost smiled. Both cops were thinking along exactly the same lines – that Bobby had pretty big balls, to suck up so cravenly.

There was more, and worse, to come.

Bobby pushed away from the table, snatched up a single crutch, and made a production of limping over to the bar. He snagged a clean glass from the bartender and brought it back to the table, poured his superior officer a beer and put the glass down on the table within easy reach of Bradley's right hand.

Orwell shot Bobby an under-the-eyebrows look of utter contempt that was missed by no one at the table except Bobby and Bradley. Oikawa, on his way back from the stalls, was clearly staggered by the sight of Bradley sitting in his chair. Despite his rank, Bradley wasn't much good at bullshit or deception. Oikawa had recently fouled up a witness interview, and Bradley had let him know how he felt about it. Ducking his chin, Oikawa veered sharply towards the bar, where he unwisely tried to engage the duet of vice cops in idle conversation. The cops skittered away, warily eyed him with a mixture of suspicion and disdain.

Farley Spears said, "What'd you think of the McEwen verdict, Homer?"

Bradley shrugged. "The waiter's dead, and he'll be dead forever. Fatboy's alive, for now. Is that an equitable situation? I don't think so." Bradley sipped carefully at his beer. "Maybe you should've pulled the trigger when you had the chance, Jack."

"Pow!" said Orwell. "Case closed."

Parker, the renowned soft-hearted liberal, said, "I hope you guys are pulling my leg."

"I'll pull your leg any time you want," offered Bobby. He winked at Orwell, but Eddy wasn't anywhere near dumb enough to wink back.

"In fact," said Bobby, "I'll pull both of your legs at the same time, and make a wish, if you want me to."

Parker's face was pink, but devoid of emotion. Her voice was tight as she said, "Farley, would you move over a little, please."

Homer said, "Wait a minute. Let me get out of here." He rested his free hand lightly on Parker's wrist as he slowly drained his glass. Thumping the empty glass down on the table, he stood up and walked purposefully away.

Parker emptied her wine glass into Bobby's smirking face.

The bartender glared across at them through the pale blue funk. His mouth fell open but no words tumbled out. He told himself – and he was right – that there wasn't a bartender in the world stupid or gutsy enough to cut off a table of cops in a bar that was full of the bastards.

Bobby wiped his face with his hands. He said, "Did I *deserve* that?" He glanced anxiously around. "Maybe I better apologize."

"Don't bother," said Parker.

Bobby stood up. The pain in his ankles made him wince. He rested a hand on Farley Spears' unwilling shoulder. "No, I insist. I was out of line, Claire, but now I've stepped back over the line, and I promise not to cross the line again, and that's no line." He took out his gold-coloured rattail comb and ran it through his hair, sucked wine from the comb. A belch rattled his smile. He sat down. He said, "I think I'm gonna buy a Teflon hat."

Dan Oikawa reclaimed his seat. Stomping all over the bartender's feeble objections, he'd bought two fresh pitchers of beer, and a glass of red wine for Parker.

"Good man!" said Spears jovially. But the smile was wiped off his face when Oikawa handed him his wallet, and he saw that he was broke. Outraged, he said, "You spent all my money!"

"I thought you wanted me to."

"What're you talking about?"

"Your wallet was on the table. When I got up to take a leak, you pushed it right at me."

"The hell I did!"

"With your elbow. What'd you think, I picked your pocket?" Oikawa shook his head, slightly dismayed. "It was your round anyway, Farley. Jeez, it's been your round since 1985."

"Damn straight," said Orwell. He added, "I didn't even know the cheap sonofabitch *owned* a wallet."

Bobby was going to stuff Orwell into the bottom of a dumpster, one of these days. He rested his elbows on the table and concentrated on feigning enjoyment of the dimwit repartee.

Parker wondered what Bobby was thinking. Look at him. All smiles and chuckles, smiles and chuckles. She sipped her wine, turned slightly so she could study Willows from beneath her regulation-length eyelashes. She was pleased that he hadn't punched Bobby's lights out when he'd made his brain-dead remark about her legs. But at the same time, a part of her wished that Bobby was crawling around on the floor right this minute, looking for his caps. Listening in, she discovered that Willows was discussing the McEwen verdict with Spears. Or rather, Spears was discussing the case with Willows, and Willows was working hard at being a good listener. Parker drank a little more wine. All cops were good listeners. When they were being cops.

As she sat there, covertly looking at Jack, it came to her, imperceptible as the dawn, that it wasn't in his nature to let Bobby's remark pass, and that he must have something in mind for Bobby, something worth waiting for. Serious grief.

Well, okay. Let him do what he felt was required, as long as he didn't get caught. It wasn't as if Bobby hadn't stuck out his chin and asked for it. It wasn't as if Jack didn't have every right to belt him one. Almost every right. He and Parker were practically engaged, after all. Living together. Tossing and turning in the same bed every night. But. She still kept her rented apartment, and in three months she'd have to renew her lease, or walk. She had already decided that if it came down to it, she'd walk. Walk away from her apartment, Jack, her badge. She'd been spinning her wheels long enough. She wanted a husband, babies. All of that and nothing less.

Jack, sitting beside her, raised his arm as if to give her a proprietary hug. But he was at his most affectionate when there were no witnesses. He'd signalled the waitress.

Willows hadn't paid the woman much attention. Close up, he saw that she was young enough to be his daughter, old enough to be his grandmother. A do-it-yourself blonde, she wore her hair in a falling-apart French twist. Her neck was encircled by a black velvet collar studded with bits of coloured glass. Her abbreviated tank top was made of a material that looked like stretch Mylar. Raggedy fishnet stockings clawed their way up her pale legs and just failed to make it to the hem of her pleated black skirt. The lifeless, mechanical way she moved, Willows decided not to be surprised if she made a right-angle turn and there was a big key sticking out of her back. The woman looked down at him, looked right through him. A walking pharmacy, she was wired like forty miles of prairie fence. You could drop pennies in those eyes, the coins would keep on falling long past forever.

Willows decided he'd had enough to drink after all. He took Claire's hand and led her out of the bar, into the city's frazzled, crackly, splintered light.

Bobby Dundas stared at Parker until long after the door had swung shut behind her. More to himself than anyone else, he said, "I wonder where they're going."

"Somewhere you can't," said Orwell.

Bobby said, "Don't bet on it."

An hour or more earlier, Orwell had ordered a basket of chicken fingers and fries, thinking it wise to put something in his stomach before he started the long commute home. Now the food had finally arrived, along with paper tubs of plum sauce, cute little plastic bags of malt vinegar, a large plastic squeeze bottle of ketchup. Orwell snatched up the ketchup. Oikawa and Spears both went for the plum sauce.

Bobby flinched and cursed, twisted away.

Much too late.

5

Quitting time didn't come a minute too early.

Another day older and deeper in debt, Ozzie and his good buddy Dean washed away the dust of their labours with pints of draft beer at a bar on Marine Drive that featured non-stop strippers and, weirdly appropriate, no cover charge. More important by far, the joint had a satellite dish.

It was fight night. The dish provided a direct live feed from Las Vegas to the bar's wall-size screens. The evening's main event was a championship bout between a talented Canadian fighter named Billy "The Kid" Irwin and a top-ranked slugger out of Detroit who'd recently had his name legally changed to Muhammad something or other.

Ozzie said, "Yeah, Muhammad Opponent. Or, more likely, Muhammad Chump."

Muhammad looked good, had a well-defined body and no fat, except perhaps between his ears where it was not so easily detected. His manager advertised him as owning a record of fifteen wins and zero losses, but as the freshly shaved TNT sports jacket duly noted, most of those fights had taken place in small towns in Mexico that could only be reached by four-wheel-drive vehicle. As the fight progressed, it became apparent that Muhammad's arsenal consisted of one potentially lethal punch, a knockout roundhouse right. It was also clear that his corner's no-nonsense strategy was to allow him to absorb as much gruesome punishment as was required to put him in a situation where he might deliver that punch.

By the time the fight entered the third round, Ozzie was deep into his second pint. Muhammad had already been floored twice. In Vegas there is a mandatory eight count. Soon, for Muhammad, it would be the mandatory ten. The Detroit slugger's legs were wobbly. His eyes were made of the stuff of marbles. Ozzie offered Dean ten-to-one odds but Dean laughed him off. Their burly waiter dropped two more pints on the table, hovered expectantly. Ozzie ignored him. A little clock in the bottom right corner of the screen said there were eleven seconds left in the round. The waiter moved in, said the beer was $7.50. Ozzie nodded, kept his eyes on the screen. Why shouldn't the waiter be kept waiting? He was a waiter, wasn't he? Persistent, too. He asked Ozzie, did he want the beer or not? Ozzie reached for his wallet, fat with small-denomination currency.

The round ended with a flurry of action, Irwin cool, not a hair out of place. Ozzie watched with frank admiration as Irwin encouraged his opponent to drop his hands by administering several hard smacks to the kidney. That task accomplished, the head unprotected, he bounced a quick left-right-left combo off forehead, cheekbone, nose.

Muhammad staggered off in the general direction of his corner, flopped onto his stool. His arms rested on the ropes, always a bad sign. His head was low. Blood oozed from both nostrils. When he ejected his mouthpiece, his teeth flashed red as any vampire's. His left eye was horribly swollen, squeezing shut faster than a subway door. His chest heaved. Sweat poured off him in sheets. Everything about him shouted *loser*.

Ozzie paid the waiter, tipped him a dollar and incidental change. He lit a cigarette. "Know why you and me get along so good, Dean?"

Dean shook his head, his eyes still on the big screen, watching the babe in the pink bikini strut around the ring holding up a square of cardboard with a big black 4 outlined in some kind of glittery stuff, sequins . . .

Ozzie snapped, "Dean, I'm talkin' to you!"

Dean reluctantly looked away from the woman.

"The reason we get along so good," Ozzie said, "is real simple. Know what it is? It's because neither of us get along with anybody else."

Dean pushed the ashtray a little closer to Ozzie, a little farther away from himself. What Ozzie said was true. The truth. He'd moved to Vancouver eight months earlier, on the run from child-support payments more brutal than anything you'd ever hope to see up there on the screen. Still sleeping in the back of his station wagon, he'd bumped into Ozzie at an eastside bar, let him buy a few rounds and ended up telling him all his troubles.

Ozzie might've had wings sticking out of the back of his plaid flannel shirt. The guy was such an angel. He'd bullshitted his boss at StoneWorks into giving Dean a job, had loaned him a couple of hundred bucks, no interest. He'd let him crash at his apartment until he earned his first paycheque, and even helped him find a cheap furnished room in a house just off Main Street, only a couple of short blocks from a liquor store and a McDonald's. Such a nice guy, but he was friendless except for Dean. Which was fine with Dean, who'd never been much of a mixer. As Ozzie frequently pointed out, they were both pretty much loners, at heart.

"A loaner?" Dean had said touchily, the first time. "What d'you mean, 'cause I split from the wife and kids?"

Ozzie thumped him on the biceps, slugged him a shade harder than the occasion warranted. Putting him in his place. "A *loner*, asshole. A guy who'd rather be all by himself, than spend time in bad company."

Dean rubbed his arm, still not 100-per-cent sure why he'd been punched . . .

In the opening seconds of the fifth round, Billy Irwin took a low blow, a hard shot to what the TNT guy euphemistically referred to as "the groin area," or what might alternatively be called "the *groan* area." The referee separated the boxers, called time out, and instructed the judges to deduct a point from Muhammad's scorecard. Muhammad scowled fiercely, but his anger was a sham. The Detroit pugilist's foul strategy was intended to take the wind out of Billy's sails. Since he was being thoroughly pummelled anyway, the lost point was of no consequence.

Billy crouched down by the ropes. Fighters wore a cup, naturally, but blows to the nether regions could be so excruciatingly painful and debilitating that bouts were often stopped as a consequence of a single punch. Even so, Billy showed nothing. His face was calm, emotionless. He was clearly a man of guts and dignity, who knew how to handle himself. The cynical Vegas crowd applauded loudly as he stood up. The referee asked him if he was okay. The fight resumed.

Billy moved in, feinted with his right. Muhammad shifted to his right. A thundering left hook caught him on the point of his chin, snapped his head back at a near-impossible angle. A spherical cloud of sweat hung in the ring beneath the lights, as Billy's fists smashed Muhammad's ribs to splinters. He had caused the Motor City slugger to drop his arms again and now he hit him with a flawless overhand right. Muhammad sprawled, apparently lifeless, on the canvas. The referee started the count and then took a closer look, and called for the ring physician. The sound of the fight's last blow continued to echo throughout the room.

Game over.

Ozzie loitered over his third pint. Dean was working on his fifth. Ozzie lit up. He said, "It's almost a done deal, kid."

"What's that?" Dean's head came up, but not much.

"The groundwork," said Ozzie.

"Yeah? You serious?" Dean lowered his voice to a whisper. "We really gonna do it?"

Ozzie nodded. He'd been softening Dean up for months, using words to pound away at him, bring down his guard and set him up for the knockout punch, since the day they'd met. In the early rounds, he'd felt Dean out, got to know him, find out what he could do, was capable of. What buttons made him jump in what direction. How far he'd fall, if you pushed him hard enough.

Ozzie was planning a snatch. He was going to nab a stock-broker, a guy named Harold Wismer, who was a zillionaire. Ozzie was confident things were going to work out just fine, because this was his second kidnapping, and he had learned a lot from all the mistakes he'd made the first time out.

There was a post-fight interview, Billy quick-speaking and articulate. Then the screen went dark and the first of the strippers followed her breasts on stage. A blonde. The woman stood there, waiting for the DJ in his glass box to crank up some music. Losing patience, she started taking off her clothes without the benefit of a soundtrack. A pro.

Ozzie said, "There's some things I gotta do. I'll see you later, about eight. Okay?"

Dean's eyes flickered over the woman. Top to, uh, bottom. Ozzie aggressively mussed his hair. "Eight o'clock, Dean. Be there."

Dean nodded, transfixed by what he saw up there on the stage.

Ozzie turned his back on him, and walked away.

His one-bedroom apartment was a top-floor, no-view unit in a drab three-storey stucco on Twelfth Avenue, a few blocks off Cambie. The apartment was furnished with a table and two chairs he'd bought at Ikea, a couch the previous tenant had left behind, a queen-size mattress and box spring from Mattress City.

He'd bought the twenty-inch TV second-hand at a garage sale, paid cash for the VCR at A&B Sound. The pocket-size battery-powered tape recorder and audio and video tapes had been purchased at London Drugs. His intention was to copy snippets of film dialogue from the VCR to the tape recorder, and to stitch these short pieces together to make an irresistible demands note he could play over the telephone.

He'd rented a few of the movies he'd needed from Blockbuster Video but had to go down to Videomatica on Fourth Avenue to get most of his material, because he had a weakness for the older stuff, black-and-white films starring guys like James Cagney, men who knew how to deliver a gangster's lines. Not that he wasn't flexible. He'd used a single word from a television series called "Law and Order," added a few words sputtered by a pissed-off Donald Duck. Just for laughs, he'd even tossed in a line from Woody Allen's *Take the Money and Run*.

Using scissors and a glue stick and sheets of plain white paper and individual letters and words culled from magazines as disparate as *Playboy* and *Town and Garden*, he'd put together a cute little note that politely informed Mrs. Joan Wismer that, if she wanted to get Harold back in less than five pieces, it was going to cost her an arm and a leg.

He switched on the tape recorder and played the first of the messages, hearing it for at least the tenth time, still feeling it achieved a kind of horrific politeness that struck him as exactly right. Heartened, he turned on the TV, slid a movie he'd rented on a hunch, *Demolition Man*, with Stallone and Snipes, into the VCR. He hit the play button. He was putting together the last of the audio tapes. Stallone had such a wonderful cheese-grater of a voice . . .

While the credits rolled, Ozzie put on the kettle, dropped a teabag in a chipped white mug. Since Stallone films were mostly stuff blowing up, and not too much dialogue, he estimated he could zip through the movie in forty-five minutes easy. Once he found the word he was looking for, all he had to do was dub it from video to the portable tape recorder. If he got the work down before he left to pick up Dean, he could get the movie to Blockbuster on time, save himself a few bucks in late charges.

The kettle boiled. He made a cup of tea, tossed the steaming bag into the stainless-steel sink.

He checked his watch. A little over an hour until he had to pick up Dean for the gun run. He lit a cigarette and stretched out on the lumpy couch. All sorts of stuff was blowing up. Numerous fifty-gallon drums of gasoline, buildings large as a city block.

He used the TV's remote to crank up the volume until it was so loud it hurt, to ensure that he remained alert.

He smoked his cigarette, blew imperfect smoke rings through the steam rising from his cup of tea.

More stuff blew up. Windows exploded. Roiling orange balls of fire lit up the inky-black sky.

He was determined to get it absolutely right, this time.

The setup, the knockout punch.

He was going to yank Harold Wismer into the ring, knock him flat on his pudgy ass. Hit that fucking leech of a stock promoter so hard he wouldn't move a muscle, though the count climbed all the way to five million.

Ozzie lay there on the couch, watching the destruction with half an eye. Nothing moved but the steam from his tea and the smoke from his cigarette, as he waited for Stallone to say the magic "yo" word.

6

Jake's special chair was over by the window, where he could sit in it and look down at the city, enjoy the view, think about the pretty girls out there. The thing was, Jake was tired of the view, there was a draft coming up off the plate glass, and he was cold.

He told Marty he wanted to be moved over to the gas fireplace. Marty snapped his fingers. Steve and Axel lumbered over to the big bronze-coloured leather chair, squatted and grunted and hoisted it up a little higher than necessary. Jake had bought the chair the last time he'd visited Italy, way back there in '84.

That'd be 1984.

Axel's job, until there was a vacancy in the organization and he got a one-rung promotion, was to mind the back door, junk the junk mail, wash and wax all the cars except the Bentley, which was Marty's responsibility. Now he could add a second line to his résumé – furniture mover.

Marty watched carefully, ready to jump in and lend a hand, as Steve and Axel huffed and puffed the chair over to the fireplace until it was so close to the hearth there was barely room for Jake's legs. The chair weighed a ton, and the sweat was pouring off the boys by the time they got it exactly where Jake wanted it.

Jake kept his eye on a vein on Steve's temple that looked as if it was ready to pop, spray blood all over him, like that time back in New York City, they were taking Tony Brillo for a ride, poor Tony couldn't stand the pressure, pulled a blade and slit his own throat. Snuffed himself in Jake's immaculate new Cadillac DeVille that had an automatic transmission, AM radio, electric cigarette lighter, pure wool carpets. The DeVille's gas tank still registering full because the fuckin' car only had three fuckin' blocks on the odometer.

That fuckin' dimwit Tony. Thinking Jake'd blast him in a showroom-new 1936 DeVille. Turnin' the fuckin' vehicle into a fuckin' abattoir. Jeez, the damn car'd be worth a small fortune by now, if he'd held on to it.

Jake watched Steve's distended vein. With every heartbeat, the blood surged, a rising tide that vanished into Steve's sweaty hairline. The kid's face was the colour of a fuckin' chili pepper. He looked like he was gonna croak like a fuckin' frog.

Jake thought maybe he should have got out of the chair before he told them to move it. But he was as light as a bag of dry leaves. What did he weigh nowadays? Nothing. Maybe a hundred and five pounds.

Ninety, without the wrinkles.

He told Steve to go get himself a glass of water, come back when he no longer had the complexion of an overripe tomato. Steve beat it. Jake told Marty to tell Axel to turn up the fireplace as high as it would go. Axel waited for Marty's command, then jumped to it. Jake felt his temperature climbing. Maybe he wouldn't freeze to death after all. He looked out the picture window at the fabulous city. The sun was low on the horizon. A million windows reflected squares and rectangles of gold. The highrises sparkled like giant bars of gold. Kind of pretty, in a way.

Jake's stomach churned. As if he didn't have enough fuckin' problems, goddamn Steve had shot that fuckin' guy in broad fuckin' daylight. Squibbed him, what'd he confess, six times? For what? A fuckin' dog? A *nice* dog. But even so . . . Steve was clean, well-groomed and dependable. But the kid was dumb as a ball of mud. Had a little bitty dried pea rattling around in there where his brain was supposed to be. Jeez . . .

Steve came back in, looking better. Marty told him to take care of the Bentley, vacuum the car and wash it with a bleach-and-water combo, get rid of the blood, the doggie hairs . . .

"What blood and doggie hairs?" said Steve, flabbergasted that he was being trusted with Jake's favourite car.

Jake cast a weary glance at Marty. Marty was muscle *and* brains. An ideal combination. Jake was proud of Marty – a project that had gone right. He owed Marty's father and would never ever shirk from the promise he'd made him to do right by the kid.

Marty said, "I'm not saying there's any blood, or hairs of any kind, human or canine. What I'm saying is, if there's hair or blood, get rid of it."

Steve frowned.

Axel opened his mouth, and then shut it.

Marty said, "Just wash the car, okay? Do a good job. *Pretend* the car is covered in blood, okay? *Visualize* the blood, Stevie. *Imagine* it, and make it *real.*"

Axel said, "I haff the skills to do that."

Jake asked for a couple of fuckin' Tums, some fuckin' Pepto to fuckin' wash 'em down.

Marty took care of it, not trusting Axel with such a complicated task, anything that hinted at medicine.

Sitting there by the fire, not quite scorched by the heat, Jake drifted off, and dreamed of Italy. He'd been seventy-three years old at the time of his most recent visit. A relatively young man. A fuckin' sprightly tourist stud, if he did say so himself. What a time he'd had.

His head, wreathed in a thin halo of snow-white hair, lolled against the bronze leather of the chair. His mouth fell open. His blue-veined eyelids flickered. He was in a hotel room, with a woman. He took her into his arms. What a gorgeous young woman she was! Dusky, olive-skinned. Vine-ripened and ready to pluck. Her dark eyes were huge, liquid. Her black hair glistened. Jake had forgotten all his Italian except the swear words. Fortunately, though the woman's English was minimal, she had command of a few crucial phrases.

"Yes," Jake had said to all her smiling questions. "Oh yes," he said. "Yes! Yes! Yes!"

Jake dreamed through a spectacular sunset, and far beyond his usual dinner hour. He slept so long he missed a Barbara Walters special he'd been looking forward to all week. But it was okay, because Marty taped it.

In the kitchen, Steve and Axel squatted shoulder to massive shoulder at the butcherblock table. Hunched over their throwaway paper plates, they ravenously gobbled takeout pizza from Domino's, and guzzled Granville Island beer. Marty leaned against the refrigerator, eating but keeping his distance. Steve's hands were red and wrinkled. An odour of bleach rose off him. He had ripped the filtertip from a Marlboro cigarette and exhaled clouds of smoke between huge, half-moon bites of pepperoni.

Axel considered it improper to eat with his fingers. His knife and fork clattered incessantly against his dinner plate and front teeth with the sound of demented wind chimes. His greasy blond hair rose stiffly above eyes murky blue as windshield-washer fluid. From time to time he accidently stabbed himself in the chin or upper lip with the tines of his fork. Parallel flecks of blood spouted from the wounds. Soon he looked like a failed connect-the-dots experiment. He seemed blissfully unaware that he had mutilated himself.

Or perhaps he was blissfully aware that he had mutilated himself.

Marty, observing the carnage, sadly wondered, Are these Martha Stewart rejects my pals? Am I a bird of a feather?

Meanwhile, Jake dreamed and dreamed.

He dreamed of lace curtains, and skin smooth as silk, appetites long since dwindled, a longing of the heart.

He dreamed of how things were. Or might have been.

He dreamed a full moon that lifted silently up into the window, and tilted towards the lovers, and gilded them in silver.

Jake dreamed on and on and on.

What a wonderful time he had.

7

An Irish stew had been simmering in the crockpot since early that morning. Willows lifted the stainless-steel lid, shifted the stew around with a wooden spoon. It didn't look like much, but it sure smelled good. He turned as Parker came into the room. Claire had gone straight upstairs to shower and she was dressed now in a loose-fitting black cotton blouse, silvery-blue silk slacks. Her feet were bare. Her tousled jetblack hair was still damp. Jack's heart fluttered. He smiled and said, "Dinner's ready."

Parker smiled. "I know, I can smell it."

"Wine?"

Parker gave him a look of mild disapproval. "Not for me, Jack. I don't think I'm going to want another drink for at least a week." She disappeared through the swinging door that led to the dining room. Willows wondered what he had been thinking. The last thing he wanted was a drink. But lately, they'd habitually enjoyed a glass of wine with dinner. He supposed that in itself was not such a good thing. Through the swinging door, he heard Claire alert the children to dinner, Annie's sweet response and, a few moments later, Sean's rumbling denial that he was hungry.

Annie came into the kitchen, peered into the fridge. "Are we out of chocolate milk?"

"Unless you bought some." Willows ladled generous portions of stew into a trio of steep-sided bowls. "Give me a hand with

47

this, Annie." He handed her a bowl, carried the other two bowls past the swinging door and into the dining room, held the door with his foot until Annie had passed through. Where was Claire? He put the food down on the table and went back into the kitchen to fetch the loaf of French bread that had been warming in the oven.

From behind him Parker said, "I'll get it, Jack." She turned off the gas, swung open the oven door, and adroitly juggled the hot loaf onto a maple cutting board. Willows, who had been hunting everywhere for the bread knife, vented an exasperated sigh and then thought to check the knife rack for the second time. Aha!

Annie had made a tossed salad and set the table, arranging the place settings so Willows was sitting at the head of the table with Claire on his left and Annie on his right. He held Parker's chair for her, and sat down. His mouth watered. He reached for the elusive bread knife.

"Daddy!"

Willows paused. His daughter was glaring at him. She shut her eyes and bowed her head. Willows glanced at Claire, but she had already followed Annie's lead.

Sheila, Willows' estranged and soon-to-be-divorced wife, had been a lapsed Anglican. Willows thought of himself as a wide-eyed agnostic. He liked the idea of God, and slightly envied people who had a strong faith. On the other hand, he didn't know a hell of a lot of deeply religious homicide cops. Where was God when people went looking for the bread knife for all the wrong reasons? It was an easy question to ask. Too easy, maybe. But there was a fat book of corpses forever lodged in the private library of Willows' brain. Men and women of all races and creeds, children, infants in swaddling clothes. Every face owned a vivid full-colour page all of its own. He bowed his head.

Annie's voice was clear and pure, strangely musical. She said, "Give us this day our daily bread . . ."

Claire joined in.

". . . and forgive us our trespasses as we forgive those who trespass against us. Amen," whispered Willows, too quietly for anyone but himself – and God, if He was listening – to hear.

Grace finished, Annie ate quickly. Her brand-new boyfriend, Lewis, was coming over after dinner for a game of Scrabble, and to meet Willows and Parker. Annie wanted the table cleared before he arrived. She was going to bake some cookies, if there was time.

"Bake some cookies?" said Willows.

"Chocolate chip." Annie gave him a look. She said, "Lewis loves chocolate-chip cookies. They're his favourite."

"Mine too," said Willows. He spooned the last of his stew into his mouth, cleaned his bowl with a slice of bread, licked the last smacks of gravy from his fingers. He asked Annie about school, but she wasn't interested in small talk, no doubt distracted by the impending appearance of sweet-toothed Lewis.

Willows had known a kid named Lewis, once upon a time. Back in the days when he was pounding the streets. But that Lewis had been a snivelling, runny-nosed drug addict and part-time snitch, not an honours high-school student.

Even so . . . He said, "How old is Lewis, Annie?"

"Seventeen."

Parker said, "What's so amusing, Jack?"

"Work," said Willows.

Annie made a small sound of disapproval. She reached for Parker's bowl. "Finished?"

"Not quite," said Parker firmly.

Willows said, "Say now, I've got a great idea. When Lewis gets here, instead of slaving over a hot oven, why don't you suggest that we all drive over to McDonald's for dessert?"

Annie smiled sweetly. "Like that nice family in the TV ad?"

"We'll take the Ford. I'll turn on the fireball, and the siren."

Giggling, Annie said, "Forget it, Dad."

By the time Lewis bounded up the front porch, the rich scent of baking cookies permeated the house, the dirty dishes had been hurriedly stuffed into the dishwasher, and Parker and Willows had been tucked away in the den.

The only sour note, from Annie's point of view, was Sean. Her recalcitrant nineteen-year-old brother sat slouched on the sofa in his black jeans and black T-shirt, eating lukewarm Irish stew with his fingers. The cats, Barney and Tripod, sat on his chest, dining off his largesse. They were neutered male marmalades, almost identical in size and weight but easily distinguished from one another, as Tripod's left front leg had been amputated following a hit-and-run accident. The missing limb had no measurable effect on the cat's appetite, or feistiness. When Sean offered up a particularly succulent fragment of meat, the cat growled low in his throat, forcefully wedged his blunt head in front of Barney, and snatched the titbit from Sean's greasy fingers.

The doorbell rang. Annie shouted, "I'll get it!"

Willows turned up the TV. Parker rested her book in her lap. She said, "It's absolutely crucial that you hear that putt drop, huh?" She cocked her head as the front door was opened. A deeper voice, the voice of a seventeen-year-old male, thundered down the hall. Parker said, "I guess that must be loverboy."

"*Please* don't use that word," said Willows. Parker smiled, but he wasn't trying to be funny. He thumbed the mute button, frowned. Lewis' voice was a little *too* deep, in his opinion. The boy was telling Annie how much he liked her hair in braids and she was laughing, insisting she'd had her hair in braids all week long . . .

Willows suddenly realized the voices were closer, moving down the hall, zeroing in on the den. He turned off the television. Parker smiled at him, and held tight to her book. Annie appeared in the doorway. She said, "Lewis, I'd like you to meet . . ."

Lewis was, Willows soon learned, a recent immigrant from Taiwan. He was a tall kid, a shade under six feet, with a long, thin face, bright eyes. His thick black hair had been parted right down the middle, and was marginally shorter at the back than at the front. It hung over his eyes in a glossy black sheet. Thirty bucks minimum, thought Willows. A downtown cut, for sure. Lewis moved purposefully towards him, smiling, right hand extended. His nails were glossy with a clear lacquer. Willows stood. They shook hands. Lewis had very white teeth. A nice smile. He was casually dressed but his clothes were expensive, tasteful. The sort of clothes a high-end financial consultant might wear if he visited the office on the weekend. Willows noted the gold watch, diamond stud earring. Lewis oozed confidence. Seventeen, for sure. The car would be a BMW or entry-level Mercedes . . .

Lewis shook hands with Parker, said a few words about having looked forward to meeting her. He kept smiling as Annie took his hand and led him out of the den. Annie shut the door behind them. The latch clicked. Had the door been shut when she'd come down the hall to introduce Lewis? Willows wasn't sure. He didn't think so.

Parker said, "Seems like a nice kid."

Willows, still thinking about the door, nodded distractedly. Annie had never dated an Asian boy before. He didn't know why he should be surprised that she was going out with an Asian now. Fear of repression in Hong Kong, together with posturing by the Chinese military over the island of Taiwan, had resulted in the sudden influx of tens of thousands of Asians. Huge numbers of immigrants had settled on the West Coast, in Vancouver and the suburbs. At Annie's high school, the student population was 70 per cent Asian and climbing fast. A few years ago Willows had visited the school for a heart-to-heart with Sean's counsellor. Even then, Caucasian students had been a visible minority.

"What're you thinking, Jack?"

Willows shrugged. He turned the TV back on.

"That Lewis is Chinese?"

"No, not really." Eddy Orwell was a racist, though Willows had no doubt he'd vehemently deny it, and mean every word, if you cornered him. Willows had sometimes laughed at his jokes. Funny was funny. Wasn't it? Sure it was. But whenever Orwell started telling a racist joke, Dan Oikawa slipped away, found a reason to be somewhere else until the laughter had faded.

Parker said, "You sure?"

"Yeah, I'm sure." Willows took a moment to collect his thoughts, take a peek inside. People were people. The colour of a person's skin was the worst reason in the world to form an opinion about them. Case closed. But there was something else. He said, "What bothers me is that he's too old for her."

"C'mon! Really?"

"Annie said he was seventeen. I believe it. I'd believe eighteen, or even nineteen. Hell, the way the kid handles himself, I'd believe thirty. Annie's only fifteen, Claire. Two years is a lot of time, at that age."

Parker sat there, thinking. On the television, a nationwide chain store was offering cheap furniture at nothing down and no interest and nothing to pay for almost two years.

Finally Parker said, "Seventeen sounds about right to me. You can't blame him for being relaxed." She smiled. "If he'd been nervous, you'd be twice as suspicious."

"Ten bucks says he's got a BMW or Mercedes parked out front."

"Daddy's car."

"More likely it's the car Daddy gave him."

Maybe," said Parker. She checked her page and put her book down on the arm of the sofa. "Back in a minute."

Willows flipped channels in the meantime. When Parker returned, her smile was wicked. "BMW," she said. "Black, with a sunroof. Tinted windows, a personalized licence plate. Want to know what it says?"

Willows waited. Itchy, but not letting it show. Parker picked up her book, a paperback copy of Alice Munro's *The Progress of Love*.

Willows muted the sound on the TV. He sat there, staring blindly at the screen, then pushed himself out of his chair and went into the kitchen for a glass of water. Sean slouched against the Formica counter, drinking milk out of the carton. Willows said, "I told you not to do that."

Sean took the carton away from his mouth. He swiped at his T-shirt. Milk spotted the linoleum. He said, "I forgot." He took the carton in both hands and shook it rhythmically as he danced around the kitchen. "Relax, Dad. It's almost empty anyway."

Willows got the water bottle out of the fridge, a glass from the cupboard. For the past year, Sean had been employed as a clerk at a convenience store a ten-minute walk away.

Willows said, "You working tonight?"

"Midnight to dawn. The ghoul shift. Want a lottery ticket?"

"Not if it's going to cost me a dollar." Willows had heard lotteries described as a voluntary tax on the stupid, and tended to agree. Not that he didn't do something stupid, once in a while, despite odds against of approximately thirteen million to one. But what were the odds of Sean remembering to buy him a ticket, if he'd said he wanted one? Not much better. He said, "There's cold chicken in the fridge, if you want to make a sandwich."

"Thanks anyway, but the store's got a special on Snickers and Pepsi." Sean rolled his eyes to let Willows know he was kidding.

Willows drank some water. He reminded himself that Sean was basically a really great kid. He was just going through a hard part of his life, that was all. One in four kids who entered high school didn't graduate. So it wasn't as if he were all alone out there. Minimum wage was, at least, a wage. Sean had been working steadily for more than a year. A major accomplishment. If he smoked a little dope now and then, at least he didn't flaunt it.

Sean was looking at him, studying him. Willows thought about giving his son a big hug. But what if he was rejected?

On his way back to the den he took a quick peek into the living room. Annie and Lewis were sprawled out on the carpet, on opposite sides of a Scrabble board. Lewis' nails flashed in the light as he laid down a vertical line of five wooden squares, cutting through the middle of a nine-letter horizontal. He smiled at Annie with his perfect white teeth and said, "*Desire*, for eighteen points."

Willows lurched into the den. He collapsed into his chair. The TV screen was a blur of primary colours. A multitude of alphabets raced through his mind. Words formed and instantly exploded, in a shower of glittering letters.

Hug for a hundred points. *Kiss* for five hundred points. *Foreplay* for one thousand points. *Fornication* for a million points. *Pregnant* for ten zillion points.

Parker said, "You okay, Jack?"

"Last time I looked."

"Well, excuse me for asking."

The front door banged shut. Sean. Willows recognized the slam. It had been years since Sean had bothered to say goodbye. He wondered where in all the wide world his son was going. Was his destination a mall, party, his favourite street corner?

He told Parker about the Scrabble game, the *hug* and *kiss* and *desire* words, but not the *fornication* word.

Parker put the Alice Munro book back down on the sofa. She went over to the door and quietly shut it. She moved towards Willows, sat down on his lap. "How's that? Okay?"

"Fine."

Parker used her fingers to push back a lock of hair that had fallen across Willows' brow. "May I speak candidly?"

"About what?"

She kissed him lightly on the mouth, a fleeting kiss that came and went in the space of a heartbeat.

"Have you noticed anything odd about Annie, lately?"

"Like what?"

Parker leaned away from him, so she could look him in the eye. "Annie isn't a little girl any more, Jack."

"Christ! What's that supposed to mean? She's only fifteen!"

Parker kissed him again, lingered for a moment or two. "Lewis isn't the first guy she's dated, but the important thing is that he isn't going to be the last, either, not by a long shot. Maybe it's got something to do with the divorce rate, but people are marrying later, nowadays, if they marry at all. So you better get used to Annie bringing dates home, because it'll probably continue until she moves out of the house."

Willows studied the ceiling.

Parker said, "Tell you what. I'll have a talk with her. If Lewis is older than seventeen, I'll try to get her to drop him. Okay?"

"Off a high cliff," said Willows.

Parker laughed. "Want to know what his licence plate says?"

"No, I don't."

"You're not the least bit interested?" Parker wriggled around on Willows' lap, making herself a little more comfortable. Or maybe the point was to make him a little more uncomfortable. Between kisses, she ruthlessly teased him about the licence plate. But Willows refused to admit he was interested, and, as Parker continued to kiss him, it became increasingly obvious that he was telling the whole truth and nothing but.

His intransigence drove her crazy. And there was another thing. If he was really all that concerned about Annie's love life, shouldn't they lead by example, show a little restraint? Willows' fingers plucked at the buttons of her blouse. She was, literally, breathless. Pulling back, she took his face in her hands and cooled him down with a single lethal syllable.

Lewis' personalized tag said, HUNK.

8

Ozzie sat there in the pickup, hunched over the steering wheel, his neck craned so he could look up at Dean's lighted apartment window. He leaned back. The heel of his right hand thumped the horn and made it blare. It was five past eight. Where was the moron? He backed up, shifted into first and rode the right front tire up over the curb and on to the boulevard, for a better angle. He punched the horn a few more times. A guy walking his poodle gave him a look that, loosely translated, said, Please teach me to mind my own business by breaking my stupid neck. Ozzie was sorely tempted. As his bony fingers closed on the door handle, Dean's window darkened.

Encouraged, Ozzie resumed banging away on the horn. In less than a minute, the apartment's glass front door swung open. Dean trotted towards him, jacket in hand. Ozzie continued leaning on the horn until Dean had finished fastening his seatbelt. He backed away from the boulevard, the Chevy rocking on its springs as he came down off the curb. A streetlight fired red streaks of light across the truck's hood as they got under way. His cold eye on the tachometer, watching the revs, Ozzie said, "You're late."

"No shit. Now ask me how to lose weight fast. Take a dump. Now ask me a hard one. Got a hard one, Ozzie?"

Ozzie shifted into second, swung wide on the corner and lifted his foot briefly from the gas pedal as he speed-shifted up into third gear. He stomped it, accelerated all the way down the block and then downshifted into second. The Chevy shuddered from stem to stern. A few loose coins rattled across the dashboard. The exhausts crackled and popped, spat out bright orange sparks and sharp splinters of sound that ricocheted off the hard-edged urban terrain.

Ozzie yanked on the wheel and in the blink of a sphincter they were riding on the two right-side tires, the street – or maybe it was the truck – tilted at a terrifyingly unlikely angle. Ozzie stared calmly down at Dean from a considerable height as the truck arm-wrestled gravity, wobbled crazily and then sideslipped with a high-pitched, yowling screech of rubber towards a dinky, hapless Toyota Tercel that appeared to be roughly the size of a postage stamp.

Ozzie held on tight to the useless steering wheel, whooped and howled like a rodeo cowboy. His grin was so wide it looked like his teeth were about to fall out of his mouth. All Dean could think about was the likelihood that he was about to die, become involved in one of those situations he was always reading about in the paper.

But no, they were okay. The Chevy was back on all four tires, the Tercel rocking in their slipstream. Dean turned and peered out through the rear window at ten white knuckles and a stunned white face. The Tercel veered sharply towards the curb, decapitated a parking meter, hit the rear end of a large white car and stopped on a dime. The driver's face ballooned against the windshield. Dean was left with a hazy impression of eyeballs and teeth, and then the apparition whiplashed back into the darkness, leaving nothing upon the windshield but a freeform scarlet smear. Meanwhile the business end of the parking meter, a ten-pound chunk of steel and plastic and various alloys, rebounded off the sidewalk and shattered a plate-glass window. There was a brightly lit blue-and-white sign above the window. A logo and three words. Bank of Montreal. An alarm shrieked.

Dean said, "Oh man . . ."

Ozzie's manic laughter hissed and fizzled like hard rain on a high-voltage fence. He punched Dean on his bruised shoulder and said, "Worried about the parking meter? Hey, we didn't kill it, it'd already expired!"

But he was worried, though he didn't show it. Okay, so he was a little frustrated about waiting for Dean. Was high-risk driving the appropriate method of blowing off excess steam? No way. The flirtation with the Tercel had been a near disaster. Paint on paint, that close. Come the dawn, he'd have to get busy with a tin of wax and a spray can of fire-engine red, do whatever was required to bring his baby back to showroom condition. He had to contain his anger, let it accumulate and bear interest until the time was right to let it all out, release the storm.

He made a slow left on Twelfth Avenue. Now it was a straight shot east across town through gradually thinning traffic to the highway that would carry them, in not much more than three-quarters of an hour, to the border crossing at the sleepy little town of Blaine, in the home of the brave and the land of the discount cheese.

Dean said, "We really gonna do this?"

"Do it right," replied Ozzie. The oil pressure and temperature gauges were both in the green, the tachometer holding nice and steady.

The highway ran through a valley, across land flatter than Muhammad Opponent's nose. Every so often, far away in the distance but closing fast, there'd be a lighted intersection or a farmhouse or farmyard that was all lit up. These glimpses of the landscape triggered memories from Dean's prairie-boy past of drab fields, triple strings of barbed wire, sagging posts, determinedly picturesque barns inside of which small boys and livestock could frolic in a harmless sort of way.

They came upon a herd of a dozen or so black-and-white cows standing quietly in the lee of a spindly copse of trees decorated with hundreds of small white lights. The cows weren't doing much of anything. Their heads hung low. To Dean, it seemed as if they were doomed, and knew it, and were content somehow to intuitively realize their fate. The cows had positioned themselves so as to avoid any risk of an eye catching an eye. They looked vaguely embarrassed, like a clutch of strangers stranded but safe in an elevator that had foundered at ground level.

Large green signs with reflective lettering warned them that they were getting close to the border. The speed limit dropped catastrophically. There were only two lanes open, no lineup. Lights that alternated green and red informed the traffic when to approach the customs officer's bulletproof glass booth. Watched closely by surveillance cameras, the Chevy crawled up to a glass booth. The officer's grey uniform was wrinkle-free, the creases sharp. His Sam Browne shone brightly. There was no rust on his pistol. He leaned forward, but didn't rise up off his stool. "Where you going, fellas?"

"Just into Blaine," lied Ozzie.

"How long you staying?"

"Couple of hours."

"Both of you Canadian citizens?"

Ozzie nodded. Dean said yes. Headlights filled the truck's rearview mirror as a car pulled up behind them.

"Carrying any fruits, vegetables . . ."

"Nope," said Ozzie firmly.

"Nice truck." A fat gold ring glinted as they were waved forward.

Ozzie had visited Blaine many times. The place was all gas stations and asphalt. Here and there lurked a dimly lit restaurant or bar. Ozzie turned onto the I-5. The Chevy's steel-belted radials rumbled on concrete. Ozzie stayed just under the speed limit. In Washington State, a speeding ticket was worth a hundred bucks. Credit cards were deemed acceptable, but not cheques. Or rather, checks.

Forty-one minutes after they'd successfully negotiated the border, they cruised into the parking lot of the Bellis Fair Mall, a huge retail complex that had depended greatly on foreign consumers until the Canadian dollar had plummeted. There were plenty of cars in the lot, but most had local plates.

Ozzie parked in a handicapped zone. He popped open the glove box and retrieved a plastic tag, a blue wheelchair on a glossy white background.

Dean said, "Where'd you get that?"

Ozzie hung the tag from the rearview mirror. "When you get out of the truck, limp."

Dean gaped at him. His slack-jaw look, and he had it down pat.

"Just until you get inside the mall," said Ozzie. "Then you can walk normal again, okay?"

"And what a grand fucking relief that'll be."

Ozzie shut his door. He walked briskly towards the lights. Dean waited a moment, leaning against the truck's fender. Was he really expected to do this, play the cripple? He looked around. Nobody was paying any attention to him. That he noticed. Except Ozzie, of course. He pushed away from the fender, keeping his right leg stiff, not bending it at the knee.

Right away, as they entered the mall, there was the entrance to a multi-screen movie theatre on their left, and to the right a vast open expanse filled with white plastic tables and chairs for several hundred people. Beyond the theatre there were a dozen or more brightly lit fast-food franchises. The starving consumer had his choice of hamburgers, baskets of deep-fried chicken or French fries, pizza by the slice. Or, if you were in a more exotic mood, there was Chinese fare, or Thai or Vietnamese or Greek. It was almost closing time. People were milling around, looking mildly confused, as if they had an urge to spend some more money but didn't really *need* anything.

Dean focused on a group of black girls who were drifting with the crowd, moving slowly towards the exit, coming right at him. The girls were about the same age as the swimming-pool twins. But these girls were different. Not so self-conscious, more natural. Dean, twenty-four years old but looking younger in his jeans and

T-shirt, fresh-shaved face, wondered if he was too old for them. If he asked one of them did she care to sit down and eat some French fries with him, or maybe let him take her to a movie, how would she react? Would she point at him and laugh, or take him seriously? Dean thought about his wife and kids. The minute she had told him she was pregnant, she'd looked ten years older. Is that what he looked like, to these girls? Some guy who was ten years older than he was supposed to be?

Ozzie reached out, snatched at his sleeve but missed. He said, "Hey! Where you going?"

There was one of them stood out from the rest. A slim girl, her hair shoulder-length and frizzy, kind of wild. She wore a pale-pink shirt with a button-down collar, lemon-coloured cords, brown leather shoes with a bunch of holes punched in them so you could see her lime-green socks. Her metal-framed sunglasses were up there in her hair, the lenses reflecting light from the high ceiling. Dean noticed that her lipstick was the exact same shade of pink as her shirt. Now he had something he could talk about, a question to ask her, whether she bought the shirt first, or the other way around . . .

He walked straight towards her. She glanced up at him. He said, "I was just wondering . . ."

"Fuck off."

The words, spoken without heat or malice, left Dean reeling. He pressed his forehead against a Radio Shack plate-glass window. Inside, a pyramid of pastel radios were on sale at 50 per cent off list. But when you added up the exchange rate, sales tax and duty . . .

Maybe she was a lot younger than she looked. Or maybe he was a lot older than he felt.

He was yanked away from the window, into the solid mass of humanity that moved towards the exit. He turned and looked at the place where he had stood. A fog of condensation lay upon the glass.

Ozzie said, "What'd you say to her?"

"Nothing!"

"You come on to her, say something suggestive?"

Ozzie had a cop's come-along grip on Dean's arm. As he frog-marched him past the takeout franchises, the collision of all those exotic smells touched off a flood of saliva, a rumbling in his belly. His dinner had been a bag of salt peanuts at the bar on Marine Drive. It wasn't enough. Maybe after they'd done their business with Lamonica . . .

They stepped outside, and Dean immediately resumed his stiff-legged, sad-ass limp. People were staring at Ozzie, giving him outraged looks. He let go of Dean's arm. Dean straightened up and went back to walking normally.

Lamonica stepped out from behind a Ford Econoline. He shook Ozzie's hand in a complicated grip that went this way and that, involved the thumbs and then the little fingers. Ozzie struggled to keep up. Finally Lamonica gave him a big hug. Certain that Ozzie wasn't wired, he stepped back a pace, and bestowed upon Ozzie a glimmering, gold-toothed smile. Turning on Dean, he poked him in the chest with a bejewelled finger. "I seen you ask my kid sister for a date? Corel? Back there in the mall? You best be stayin' away from her, man. Corel a sweet chile, but she gots the STDs somethin' awful."

Ozzie and Lamonica had met by chance in a Vancouver bar a little over a year ago, Lamonica six feet and two hundred pounds of seasoned ex-con on the hunt for a mule, some po' white boy to drive an eighteen-wheeler loaded with shrink-wrapped bricks of Lasquetti Island marijuana across the border into felony-happy America. Ozzie had taken a pass. He and Lamonica had gotten along okay though, exchanged cards. When Ozzie needed to arm himself for his first attempted kidnapping, he'd gone to Lamonica. And now here he was, back again.

They walked past Dean's truck and across the lot, Lamonica charting an eccentric course, bobbing and weaving among the parked cars and minivans and pickup trucks. His gold Lincoln Town Car was parked directly beneath a burnt-out light. Behind them, there was nothing but highway and the music of the highway, cars speeding past in the velvet night, the shrill whine of all-season tires and the soft rush of punished air, and every so often the subsonic, heart-battering thump of a passing radio, or the sudden blare of a horn.

Lamonica wandered around, pointing his MagLite into nearby vehicles, startling black shadows and making them jump, the bright beam of light rippling across steering wheels, bucket seats, overflowing ashtrays, empty coffee cups, loose coins. A skinny black kid slouched low in the passenger seat of a black Mustang a few slots over. When the MagLite lit him up, he smiled and waved. Lamonica said, "You awake, Beebo?"

Beebo slouched a little lower, but kept smiling. In the harsh glare of the flashlight, his gums were a bleached pink colour, and his teeth glowed a pale, silky blue.

Lamonica, satisfied that Ozzie and Dean fully understood the situation, managed a devastatingly accurate Eddie Murphy imitation as he danced to the Caddy's rear end. He popped the trunk on three identical dimpled aluminum suitcases. Slapping Dean lightly on the arm with the flashlight, he said, "Open 'em."

The first suitcase held a loose jumble of sheathed hunting knives, mostly survival-type weapons with black Teflon finishes, serrated edges, blood grooves. The second suitcase was stuffed with a wide variety of revolvers, from hideaway snub-noses to great long Dirty Harry models. A few of the guns were finished in blue steel but most of them were stainless or nickel plate. The third suitcase contained semiautomatic pistols.

Lamonica's hand moved negligently. "You be desirin' a wheel gun I gots twenty-two and three-eighties, thirty-eights and three-five-sevens, a couple forty-four-calibre monsters, kill yo' average po-lice vehicle with a single shot. The semis, I got nine-mils and forty-fives. All of these guns been made in U.S.A. or a bona fide ally of this great country. They in guaranteed good working order. The new ones are brand new. The others been checked out, they good as new."

"You field-test 'em?" said Dean. Lamonica gave him a blank
look. Dean rephrased his question. "Try 'em out, go off somewhere
and shoot 'em?"

"I only shot a gun but two times," said Lamonica. "The first
time, I didn't know what the fuck I was doin', emptied the magazine. The second time, I aimed careful and shot but once. Bam!
That was it. Since then, I ain't had reason to pop no caps. I got no
use for guns, tell you the truth." Lamonica scanned the parking
lot. He slapped the MagLite into the palm of his hand.

There were three stainless Rugers, nine-millimetre pistols with
spare magazines. Model P89s. Ozzie took two of them.

"You breakin' up the set, man. Whyn't you take all three?"

"Don't need three," said Ozzie.

"You want bullets? Gun ain't no good without bullets, I got
some nasty mothafuckin' hollowpoints, Winchester Black Talons.
Those babies tear a man up pretty good . . . Some asshole gotta get
capped, might as well fuck 'im up real good, ain't that right?"

Ozzie nodded agreeably. But Lamonica wasn't paying any
attention to him. He had his calculator in hand and was pushing
buttons.

"The Rugers is three hundred apiece. You wants two of 'em.
Let's see now . . ." Punch punch punch. "Six hundred sound right
to you?"

"A little steep," said Ozzie.

"Thirty a box for the hollowpoints. I got five boxes. Let's see
what the magic thaing be sayin' is five times thirty . . ."

Dean sparked his lighter, sucked smoke into the basement of
his lungs. The nicotine hit him. His body quivered like an arrow
shot into a mighty oak. He sighed contentedly.

Lamonica's head was down as he concentrated on the calculator's tiny buttons. "So, what'd we say? Five boxes of Black Talons
at thirty a box?" Punch punch punch. He aimed his flashlight at
the calculator's screen. "Only a hundred fifty? Must be some kind
of mistake." He ran the numbers again, frowned. "Yeah, I forgot
the six hundred for the guns. Hit the *plus* button, I be okay. There

we go. Now the other button. Yeah! Yeah!" Lamonica's broad face alternately expressed unbridled joy and sheer horror. Sweat blistered his skin. He smiled. "Be lookin' at a grand total of seven-fifty, Ozzie."

Ozzie pulled his wallet, counted out eight one-hundred-dollar bills. He offered the money to Lamonica. "Got a fifty?"

"You want change? What am I, the Bank of America?" He blinked his flashlight. Beebo climbed out of the Mustang and shambled bonelessly over, looking concerned. Lamonica said, "Got a fifty, man?"

"Yeah, maybe." Beebo yanked on his T, exposed the tiniest belly button Ozzie had ever seen, and the butt of a chrome-plated semi-auto. He reached deep into the crotch of his pants, grunted as he fished around down there, finally came up with an inch-thick roll. "Sorry, man, alls I gots is hundreds."

"Gots no twenties?" said Lamonica. He frowned. "Ain't I seen a few twenties, in the heart of that fat roll?"

"I might gots some twenties, two or three."

"Fives?"

"What I do with itty-bitty fives? Wait a minute now. One five. I gots just the one."

"Singles?"

"Ain't I lookin'?"

Lamonica was punching buttons again. "My friend Ozzie needs a pair a twenties and the five, and . . . hold on now, this's getting awful fuckin' complicated . . . five singles."

"I ain't gots but three."

Lamonica considered the situation. A constant stream of headlights swept across them as hundreds of cars flowed out of the parking lot.

Dean lit a fresh cigarette from the stump of the first.

Finally Lamonica said, "Okay, seems to me like we approximately two dollars short. Beebo, how you fixed for change?"

Beebo told Lamonica he never carried any change, that it was too hard on his pants, and he didn't like the noise. He said, "You try sneakin' home late wit a pocketful a nickels and dimes, see where you get hit."

"What about you gotta make a phone call?"

"I breaks a bill at the bar."

"Then what?"

"I make the call . . ." Beebo saw where Lamonica was going. He said, "I leave the rest of the money on the bar. Or if I at a payphone, just throw it away, whatever . . ."

Lamonica eyed him, openly suspicious. "I never knew that about you, man. What other secrets you gots, that I don't know about?"

"Nothin' much." Beebo hesitated. "'Cept I been screwin' yo' wife, on Monday nights when you be watchin' football . . ."

Lamonica laughed until he stopped. He pointed at Ozzie. "You gets no fuckin' change, man." He waggled a hand heavy with gold at the trunk. "Help yo'self to a blade, take whatever you want and get yo' ass outta here." He jerked his head. "That Chevy, what kinda mileage you get? Pretty bad, huh?"

"Twelve to the gallon," said Ozzie, fudging a little.

"Lookin' at thirty-point-six miles to the border, that'd be about two-point-five-five gallons times a dollar thirty-two a gallon, return trip'd cost you about three dollars and thirty-six cents." Lamonica slammed the Caddy's trunk, narrowly missing Ozzie's fingers. He had spat out the numbers at lightning speed, off the top of his head. Smiling, he climbed into the Town Car and started the engine. Beebo sashayed back to his Mustang. The alarm chirped.

Eight hundred U.S. dollars lighter, Ozzie walked away with the two Ruger semiautos, spare magazines, five boxes of ammunition and a carbon-steel knife with an eight-inch blade and a genuine cowhide sheath.

Half an hour from the border, he exited the highway, turning onto a secondary road that wandered into the countryside. Dean asked him where in the world they were going. Ozzie cranked up the radio.

They drove several miles to a T intersection in the middle of nowhere that was lit by a single streetlight. Insects had gathered. Bats swirled in and out of the light. Ozzie pulled onto the lumpy grass, killed the Chevy's big v-8. He showed Dean how to load his pistol, told him to get out of the truck, explained how to line up the Ruger's sights.

Dean hit a bat with his second shot. Beginner's luck. Crouching, the two men examined the wildly flapping wings and the bloody strings of flesh that were all that remained of the creature's body. Dean let off a few more rounds, and might have obliterated a moth or two. He hit his intended target – the streetlight – with his twenty-third shot. The huge glass bulb bloomed like a nuclear crocus, and then the landscape was plunged into what might easily have been mistaken for eternal darkness. Jagged chunks of glass rattled on the asphalt but missed the truck, thank God.

Dean was pumped. Shrieking, he danced maniacally around the starlit intersection.

Ozzie climbed back in the Chevy, switched the lights on high-beam and swung the truck's blunt nose around on Dean. Dean kept shooting his new Ruger into the sky. He didn't seem to mind being in the spotlight.

Staring disdainfully at him through the windshield, Ozzie quietly said, "Enjoy yourself while you can, moron."

9

By the time the rising tide finally reached the ex-Rottweiler-owner's two-hundred-and-ten-pound corpse, the bullet-riddled body had settled deep into the gluey, toxic muck of Coal Harbour. The briny sea lapped at the dead man's heels, darkened the material of his jeans, soaked his leather jacket. Saltwater rinsed the blood from his mouth. Wavelets lapped at his dead, unseeing eyes. His hair swayed in the gentle currents.

The water continued to rise. It gurgled and chuckled against the cut granite stones of the seawall. Forty-odd minutes after it had first touched the man, he had been swallowed whole.

The hours crept slowly past, and the ocean continued to roll in, until finally, at high tide, the body lay under six feet of water. There was a brief period, slack tide, when the harbour was so quiet that reflected security lights from the nearby marina lay still as death upon the jetblack surface.

But soon the tide was on the ebb, tons of ocean pouring with increasing speed from the little harbour's gaping mouth into Burrard Inlet, and out to sea.

The ex-Rottweiler-owner's body shifted restlessly, as the currents worked at it. There was air in the lungs and the belly was full of fetid gas. Water flowed at right angles across the length of the body with increasing urgency. The leather jacket billowed like a sail. The corpse's hair stood on end. A hand rose up, puffy white

68

fingers splayed wide. The body shifted, rocked from side to side. The left leg came unstuck from the muck, and a flock of tiny bubbles scooted towards the surface. A few minutes later, the right arm lifted up. The body jerked and twitched as if tugged by invisible strings. The other leg came free, and then, reluctantly, the left arm disengaged from the muck. The corpse tumbled across the slime. It rolled over so it lay face up, and drifted slowly away from the shoreline.

With agonizing slowness, it began to rise towards the surface. Resurrection.

10

Sex was good. But sometimes the refreshing sleep that followed was even better.

The bedside phone rang at a few minutes past one. Willows snatched up the receiver. The hot-red numerals of the clock came into sharp focus. He spoke softly into the phone, listened quietly for close to half a minute, disconnected.

Parker had been sleeping on her side. She rolled over on her back, as Willows pushed away the sheets.

"Jack . . . ?"

Willows reached out for her. His hand touched her bare shoulder. He shifted his weight, moved towards her. He held her hand in his.

Parker said, "Jack, what is it?"

Willows took a deep, shuddery breath.

He said, "Sean. It's Sean. He's . . ."

Parker turned towards him. She reached out, and touched his arm.

Willows' voice broke. He sat there on the bed, concentrating, working hard to hold himself still, push back the shriek of anguish that was rising up inside him.

Parker threw aside the blankets. She said, "We'd better get dressed, Jack."

A decision had been made to transport Sean to St. Paul's, even though UBC Pavilions was marginally closer. The university was, relatively speaking, a violent-crimes backwater. At St. Paul's there was a much better chance that there'd be an emergency-room surgeon experienced in gunshot wounds.

By the time Willows and Parker arrived at the hospital, Sean was in surgery. All Willows could get from the duty nurse was that he'd been shot in the chest and that his injuries were not believed to be life-threatening.

In jeans and a black cotton sweater and scuffed sneakers – no shirt or socks – Willows strode briskly up and down the corridor outside the emergency room. His eyes ached. The corridor was too shiny, too bright. A trio of interns in signature short white lab coats walked by, laughing too loudly at a private joke. He wanted to snap their necks.

Parker had walked with him for the first half-hour or so, lengthened her stride to keep up with his manic pace as she constantly talked to him, tried to calm him despite her own mounting sense of desperation. Finally, exhausted, she abandoned the chase.

Willows continued to stride up and down the corridor. He was almost running. His skin had an unhealthy translucent quality. His eyes were fever-bright. The black sweater clung to his sweaty body. He asked Parker for the tenth time if they should have wakened Annie.

"She needs her sleep, Jack. For now, let her sleep."

The uniform who'd answered the first of the 911 calls dropped by as a courtesy. He was just a kid, not much older than Sean. Willows buttonholed him. Staring into the cop's tired eyes from less than a foot away, he cross-examined him at breakneck speed.

It was obvious to Parker that the cop didn't like the way he was being handled, that his initial sympathy was fast turning to whole-hearted resentment. "Back off, Jack," she said. "He isn't going to make a break for it." Willows blinked. He moved laterally, one small, reluctant step. Parker offered her hand and introduced herself. The cop's name was Ken Gregory.

Parker said, "You were first on the scene, Ken?"

"Yeah, right. Can we go outside for a minute, so I can catch a smoke?"

They walked down to the end of the corridor, through the old-fashioned wood-and-glass doors. Outside, several people stood close by, smoking. An elderly man cried softly into a young woman's arms. The grass in the area around the exit had been trampled to mud. Dozens of cigarette butts littered the ground. Gregory lit up. Willows stood where he could see through the glass panels of the double doors, into the building. If somebody came looking for him, he wanted to be found. He said, "Okay, what've you got?"

The cop shrugged, smoke leaking from his nostrils. "I took the call, the dispatcher had a robbery at the premises where your son works." He smiled apologetically. "Not that I knew that at the time. Anyway, the call came in around twelve-thirty. Armed robbery, shots fired. I arrived on the premises at twelve-thirty-three. Backup got there a few minutes later, a corporal named Bob Jennings."

Gregory sucked on his cigarette, exhaled. "Okay, so the store's empty. At least, we can't see anybody. We go inside, slow, take a look around. They got those big convex mirrors, for shoplifters. We use the mirror to check the place out. There's someone down behind the counter. On the floor. It's your kid. Excuse me, your son. Jennings calls it in. The paramedics are there in two minutes flat, stabilize your son, bring him here." He shrugged. His badge glittered in the light from the door. "That's all I can tell you, that I can think of."

"He was shot where, in the chest?"

Gregory looked startled. "No, the arm. His left forearm. Chest? No, there were eleven shots fired, nine-mils, the casings were all over the place, on the counter, cash register, the floor. But I'm pretty sure he was hit just the one time." Gregory frowned, taking it seriously. "Somebody said in the chest? I don't know, maybe. I guess I could be wrong."

Willows stared at the ground.

Parker said, "Thanks, Ken."

"Yeah, sure. The kid, he going to be okay?"

"He's going to be just fine," said Parker, more forcibly than she'd intended.

It was another hour before Sean came out from under the lights. The surgeon's name was Fisher. He had the body of a light-weight boxer, intense, dark brown eyes. He was losing his hair. There was a thin diagonal scar on his upper lip. He said, "Okay, he's off the table, we've got him in intensive, and he's probably going to be there two or three days, but he's out of danger."

"I want to see him," said Willows. He felt no sense of relief, only a mounting anger. He shoved his hands into his pockets.

"No problem," said Fisher. "He's still under the influence of the anaesthetic. When he comes out of it, he still isn't going to make a whole hell of a lot of sense, because he'll be heavily sedated. Earliest you can hope to talk to him, late tomorrow morning." Fisher turned away. "Third floor, they'll give you his room number at the nurses' station."

Willows said, "Wait a minute."

Fisher glanced at a big clock over the waiting-room doorway. "I've got to get back in there . . ."

"Sean was shot in the arm?"

"I'm sorry, I thought you knew that. The left forearm, yes."

"He was shot once?"

"At close range. The bullet smashed the bone, exited just below his elbow."

Fisher nibbled at the scar on his upper lip. He looked away, swallowed. "Your child has lost a considerable quantity of bone and tissue. Nerve damage was extensive, likely irreparable. I'm sorry to have to tell you this, but it's doubtful that he'll ever regain full use of his arm."

Willows stared at him, his mind in turmoil.

Fisher said, "That's really all I can tell you, at the moment." He stared hard at the clock. "Look, I've got to run . . ."

Parker thanked him for his time. She and Willows took the stairs to the third floor. Sean was in a private room directly opposite the nurses' station. A uniformed nurse, an attractive young woman with blue eyes and short, sandy-blonde hair, stood by his bed. She glanced up as Willows and Parker entered the room. "If you're hoping to question him . . ."

Willows never thought to ask her how she knew they were cops. He managed a grim smile. "He's my son."

The nurse moved away from the bed. She said, "Well, it looks as if he's going to be okay. Call me if you need me," and quietly left the room.

Sean lay prone on the bed, flat on his back. His eyes were shut. His legs were close together and his arms were close by his sides, as if he were standing at horizontal attention. His left arm was heavily bandaged. Willows wondered what the intravenous was feeding into him. Glucose. Antibiotics. Sedatives. Morphine, probably. He should've asked. He stepped forward, and gently rested the palm of his hand on Sean's forehead. The boy looked as if he'd been dipped in wax. He was breathing steadily. As Willows stared intently down at him, his eyelashes twitched, and his breathing faltered. Willows' thumb was on the red emergency button when Sean's breathing steadied. He sighed heavily.

Parker had let Willows have his moment alone with his son, but now she moved forward, and enfolded Sean's hand in hers.

Willows said, "Sit down, Claire. Relax, make yourself comfortable."

The room's solitary chair was shaped red plastic with a perforated back and sprawling tubular chrome legs. It looked like something that had broken loose from "The Jetsons." Parker's snap judgement was that, if she wanted to relax and make herself comfortable, the chair would be the very last suspect on her list.

Willows said, "I'm going to the crime scene, I'll be back in a couple of hours."

"No, stay here with me. And Sean."

Willows turned towards the door. Was he leaving? Parker said, "Jack . . ."

Willows flinched minutely. He cast her an uneasy, hunted look, and then hurried out of the room.

Parker started after him, hesitated, decided to abandon the pursuit. Let him do what he needed to do. Dr. Fisher had stated categorically that Sean wouldn't regain consciousness until the morning. What difference did it make to the boy where his father was? But on the other hand, what did logic have to do with compassion? Parker felt the anger boil up inside her, red-rimmed, hot as lava. In his present state, essentially a drug-induced coma, no one really knew what Sean's emotional needs were, or what he knew, or sensed. She was deeply disappointed in Willows. She believed he should have stayed, and kept vigil by his son's side, instead of indulging himself.

The elevator doors slid open as Willows reached the fire door leading to the stairs. Inspector Homer Bradley stepped out of the elevator and peered around, getting his bearings. Bradley wore a bright yellow Gore-Tex rainjacket over tan slacks, a dark-blue golf shirt. His Adidas running shoes looked brand new. Their eyes locked. Bradley raised his hand in greeting. Willows nodded. He yanked open the fire door and hurried down the stairs.

There was an unmarked car up on the sidewalk around the corner from the convenience store. A blue-and-white pulled away as Willows got out of his car. Spears and Oikawa stood by the open front door. The sidewalk in front of the store had been fenced off with wide, yellow POLICE LINE DO NOT CROSS crime-scene tape. The three-quarter rectangle of brightly coloured tape somehow reminded Willows of a boxing ring. Maybe it was the fact that Spears and Oikawa were standing diagonally opposite each other, as if in the lull between rounds. Spears was smoking. Oikawa had positioned himself so he was upwind. The detective looked mildly annoyed, but whether it was the smoke or something else that was bothering him, Willows couldn't say.

He heard the clanging of bells, electronic hoots and whistles, a cry of triumph. He recognized Bobby Dundas' voice, and, as he drew nearer to the store, caught a glimpse of him through the plate-glass window. Bobby was playing a pinball machine. Spears caught his eye, nodded. "Sorry about all this, Jack." He pinched the glowing coal from his cigarette, thriftily stuck the butt in his jacket pocket.

Oikawa muttered a few words of consolation. He glanced up and down the street.

Willows entered the store, Spears and Oikawa trailing along behind. He ignored Bobby Dundas, the flashing lights, the noise. Splashes of dried blood streaked the shelves on the wall behind the open cash register. A few coins lay on the counter, in a sea of black fingerprint powder.

Willows said, "Okay, what've we got so far?"

Spears and Oikawa exchanged a quick look. Spears said, "By the time we got here, the CSU guys had already left. The 911 call came from the pay telephone across the street, by the Chevron station. We talked to the Chevron employee." Spears consulted his notebook. "Brian LaFrance. Nice guy. Anyway, he remembered somebody standing by the bus stop out there, a 'dark figure' was the way he put it. That's about it. He was busy with customers, couldn't even say for sure whether he saw a man or a woman. We dusted the phone, got a couple thousand overlapping partials."

Oikawa said, "The Chevron guy heard the shot, thought it was a tire blowing. Stepped outside his little cubicle and took a look around, probably hoping for an accident. All he saw, there was a truck parked in front of the store."

A bell clanged stridently. Bobby said, "*Go, baby, go!*"

"What kind of truck?"

"Older-model pickup," said Oikawa.

"What colour?"

"He wasn't sure. Red, or dark brown, maybe even black."

Spears said, "It's hard to tell colours, Jack. The streetlights do weird things. His booth over there, the glass is tinted . . ."

"Anyway," said Oikawa, "he's back inside the booth, this's less than a minute later, he hears tires squealing, a vehicle accelerating down the street. He's busy with a customer, but as soon as he gets a chance, he takes another look outside."

"The truck's gone," said Spears. "Vamoosed. Vanished."

Willows said, "We should be able to nail that down, get an exact time on that, the gas sale, the truck leaving . . ."

Oikawa said, "We're working on it, Jack. Chevron can't get a copy of the receipts to us until tomorrow morning. We asked the kid, was it a cash sale or credit? He can't remember. We'll talk to him again, but right now we're going easy. We already grilled him once. He was totally co-operative. Believe me, we drained him dry."

"The responding officer . . ."

"Ken Gregory. A nice kid. He arrived, assessed the situation. On paper, he did it by the book. But the truth is, he barged right in there, no backup, just him and his piece. He drop by the hospital?"

Willows nodded.

Spears said, "Sean was only hit once, is that right?"

Willows nodded again. His face was drawn, pale.

Spears and Oikawa exchanged a quick glance. Spears said, "Well, he can count himself lucky 'cause there were spent casings all over the joint, eleven of 'em, all told."

"Prints?"

"Yeah, partials, plenty of them. The csu guys bagged 'em and took 'em to the lab . . ." Spears trailed off. He was having a hard time dealing with the look in Willows' eye, the desolate look of a man with too much to do and no way to get any of it done.

Willows said, "You retrieved the bullets?"

Spears said, "Not yet, Jack." He yawned. His hand came up to cover his mouth.

A sharp knife wielded by a CSU cop had cut numerous holes the size of his fist out of the drywall behind the counter. Willows had once told an outraged, under-insured store owner that the holes had been caused by wall gophers. That was a long time ago. He wasn't thinking about that now.

Oikawa said, "The rounds penetrated the drywall, insulation. A couple of them hit metal studs, but passed right through. We figure they must be inside the office of the insurance business next door."

The pinball machine clanked and buzzed. Flashing red lights stained Bobby Dundas' face dull red. He slapped his hand down hard on the sloped glass top. "God *damn* it!"

Spears said, "We can't get inside. There's a big sticker from one of the local security companies on the door, but they claim they've got no record he's a customer. We phoned the emergency number on the door, no answer."

Willows rubbed his bristly jaw. He searched his pockets for a dollar, tossed it in the open cash-register drawer, and helped himself to a Diet Coke from the cooler. "Where's the guy who manages the place, Sean's boss?"

"On his way over. We called him right away. He lives in Port Moody, told us it's going to take him the better part of an hour to get here."

Dan Oikawa checked his watch. "Any time now." Willows popped the tab on his Coke.

Bobby Dundas yelled, "Hey, Jack. Got any quarters?"

Willows turned and looked at him. He stared at him a long time, until finally Bobby caved in and said, "I'm all out . . ."

Willows turned back to Oikawa and Spears. He said, "Claire's at the hospital. Sean isn't expected to regain consciousness until the morning, but I should be there . . ."

The two detectives nodded vigorously, glad to be rid of him. Oikawa said, "Anything breaks, you'll be the first to know."

"Absolutely," said Spears. He patted Willows awkwardly on the back as he followed him outside. Spears' clumsy intimacy had led

Willows to believe he intended to share a secret, tell him something of crucial importance. His heart clenched up in his chest as he turned helplessly towards his fellow detective.

But Spears wanted nothing more than to finish his cigarette.

11

They'd been cruising around, come upon the convenience store. Dean was thirsty, wanted a soft drink. He jumped out of the truck before it had fully stopped or Ozzie had time to yell at him to pull his shirt over the Ruger.

When Dean tried to pay for his root beer, the kid reached for the sky. Dean was confused, then pissed.

Ozzie, looking through the window, saw the kid try to grab a handful of ceiling tile. He went inside. The way he saw it, an inadvertent robbery was in progress. No point wasting all that momentum. He told the kid to empty the cash register onto the counter, hand over the lottery tickets.

The boy did exactly what he was told, no problem. A nice kid, kind of twitchy, but basically co-operative.

He and Dean stuffed their pockets full of money and scratch-'n'-itch lottery tickets and went outside. The truck was parked just a few steps from the store's front door. Dean broke stride to light a cigarette. He turned and saw the kid was staring at them.

Doing what? Memorizing their faces? Dean ran back inside and started yanking the trigger. Rehashing in his mind how it had gone down, Ozzie's face twisted into a bemused smile. Jeez, he couldn't remember the last time he'd been that surprised.

And there was Dean coming back to the truck. Smoking pistol in hand, his eyes full of sizzle.

Ozzie got out of there quick enough to rip the treads off his all-season radials. The hammer was back on Dean's Ruger, the muzzle nestled in Dean's crotch. Ozzie instructed him to de-cock the pistol, told him to put the damn thing away before he shot his balls off like that guy did a while ago, had the fight with his girl-friend, got so wound up he forgot to take precautions.

Dean said, "He's right there in front of me, close enough to touch. That first shot's the hardest. I'm bangin' away, the air's full of smoke and thunder. All of a sudden the guy's disappeared, I can't see him no more. But then I see this big red splash on the wall, and I damn well know where he went."

"Straight to hell, huh?"

Dean gave Ozzie a shocked look. Nonplussed, but only momentarily.

"I lean over the counter. Sure enough, there he is. Blood all over the goddamn place. He's staring up at me, no blinks."

"Dead," said Ozzie, hoping it was so.

"I was gonna shoot him a few more times, just to make sure. But what was the point? I could see he was dead. Shooting a dead man . . ."

Ozzie said, "You'd have to be the sickest puppy in the litter, pull a stunt like that."

Dean shrugged. "Yeah, I guess so . . ."

Ozzie drove three blocks and then Dean asked him to pull over for a minute. Ozzie stopped the truck and Dean got out, staggered over to a white Honda Civic and threw up all over the hood. Ozzie jokingly asked him what it was that he didn't like about Hondas.

Twice more on the way home he had to stop so Dean could dry-retch at the side of the road. Dean's weak stomach made Ozzie wonder if he should take him out of the equation. But he'd spent a lot of time and energy recruiting Dean, putting him in the mood for the snatch. He *needed* Dean. For now.

When he dropped Dean off at his shabby little apartment, Dean took a moment to scoop his loose scratch-'n'-lose lottery tickets off the dashboard. Ozzie considered this a positive sign.

Trying for a solicitous tone, he said, "You gonna be okay, partner?"

Dean nodded weakly.

Ozzie said, "Pick you up at seven, buddy."

Dean ignored him, walked slope-shouldered down the sidewalk towards the brightly lit lobby of his apartment.

Ozzie yelled, "You win anything, I get half!" He drove home, parked, climbed the fire stairs and covertly checked the hallway. No heavily armed coppers lurked. He unlocked and entered, used the bathroom and then went into the kitchen, where he made himself a Kraft cheese sandwich. The sandwich hanging from his mouth, he cracked a Kokanee, and went into the living room and turned on the TV. Vanna White waved hello as he flopped down on the couch. Ozzie ate and drank. It had been a long and arduous but nevertheless wildly entertaining day. He drained the beer and went back into the kitchen for another. Sitting there in the truck, listening to Dean's nine-mil had got his heart pumping. Though he desperately needed a good night's sleep, he was wide awake, totally wired, lusting after the beautiful-but-mute Vanna.

But then, half an hour later, he was watching the opening credits roll on a film called *Aliens*, had dumped Vanna and was lusting after Sigourney Weaver. The film ran for hours and hours. At seven, the alarm clock kicked him in the ear.

And now here it was, ten minutes to noon, and he was so tired he could hardly think. He shifted the stone another quarter-inch to the left, stepped back and eyeballed the line. Straight enough. He sluiced sweat from his forehead with the back of his hand, walked slowly over to the pile of granite and studied the stones. He heard laughter and slowly looked up, his eyes glittering in the shadow of his Mariners baseball cap.

The twins had been basking in the sunlight on the far side of the pool, but now they were back in the water, splashing around in there, giggling and shrieking. Ozzie figured they were sixteen, maybe seventeen years old. Pretty damn young. Old enough to get him into plenty of trouble, though, and they sure enough knew it.

Every so often one of them would strike a model's pose by the side of the pool or on the diving board, glance over at the tanned and muscular men sweating over daddy's new wall, to see how they were taking it. Hard. The men were taking it hard.

During the ten-o'clock coffee break, one of them had smiled and waved at Dean, playfully invited him to take a quick dip.

Ozzie said, "Don't even think about it. The first step you take in that direction, your ass is fired."

Dean scowled. Beads of sweat trembled all over his lean and hungry face. He stared at the ripply blue surface of the pool. He licked his lips.

Ozzie said, "What kind of person are you? They're schoolgirls. That kid you shot last night? He could've been her boyfriend."

"Then she's in need of a replacement."

Ozzie said, "Not you, Dean."

Dean shrugged, neither agreeing or disagreeing. That's how they'd left it, unresolved.

Ozzie laid two more stones, good ones, and then pulled off his gloves and stuffed them in the back pocket of his jeans. He sat on the wall, straddling the warm rock. The morning hadn't gone too badly, considering the night that had gone before. He could already see the form the wall would take, what it would look like and the impact it would have on the terrain it enclosed.

He glanced at his watch. Five past twelve. The coffee-truck girl had promised she'd be there by ten past at the latest. The crew'd keep working until she showed up. Only Dean packed a lunch. The others ate whatever the coffee wagon brought them, and paid through the nose for the pleasure. Ozzie couldn't understand such wilful, shortsighted stupidity. What kind of idiot couldn't think ahead as far as his next meal?

The sisters stood by the pool in their skimpy, peach-coloured bikinis, laughing at something that had amused them. In the harsh sunlight of high noon, they could've been stark naked.

Ozzie swore, as he jerked back his hand and glared down at the bright line of blood that ran across the ball of his thumb. He'd sliced himself open on a splinter of rock sharp as a razor. He sucked at the wound, spat a gob of red onto the ground. Sucked and spat again.

The coffee truck bumped up over the curb, stopped on the boulevard in the shade of a maple tree. The crew dropped tools. Ozzie sucked more blood from his wound, spat one last time. Dean had wandered off by himself. He sat down with his back up against the trunk of a copper beech, one of a clump of beeches that were marginally closer to the swimming pool than to the job site. Ozzie went over to the coffee truck to get himself a couple of nice cold Cokes. Waiting in line, he listened to the other guys flirt with the woman who drove the truck, a brassy blonde heavyweight with a great big screechy voice. He watched the way she moved as she served the crew cold roast-beef sandwiches, cans of hot soup, soft drinks. He turned and looked behind him, saw one of the sisters talking to Dean, standing over him, smiling down at him, a slim brown leg provocatively cocked. The Cokes were a dollar and a quarter apiece. Ozzie took a can in each fist and walked purposefully towards Dean. He stepped hard. The heels of his boots knocked little frown-shaped dents into the earth.

The girl turned and strolled casually back to the pool as he drew near. The bikini had ridden up over her ass, and Ozzie was pretty sure she knew it, the way she was walking. He heard the coffee truck start up and drive away. He sensed that the crew was watching him. He walked into the beech tree's puddle of shade and then, making a statement, sat cross-legged on the grass with his back to the pool.

He popped a Coke.

Dean said, "Her name's Erika. I got her to spell it for me. Erika. Cute name, huh?" Dean had stripped off his T-shirt. Ozzie tried to see him from the girl's addled point of view. Dean had wide shoulders, a thirty-inch waist, a washboard stomach. His hair was clean. He had a nice smile, white teeth. Devils danced in his dark brown eyes.

"Her sister's named Monika. Erika and Monika. Double-cute, huh? The mom and dad are in Palm Springs until the end of the month. So the girls are all alone with nobody to watch out for them, 'cept for grandma. And she's half blind, deaf as a fire hydrant."

"Erika and Monika?"

"The reason they're all alone over there, haven't invited any friends over, they're hoping to make some new friends."

Ozzie's heart slumped against his ribcage.

Dean let his tongue fall out of his mouth. He panted like a dog.

Ozzie tilted back his head and drank the first of his two Cokes. Now he had one left. Simple. He said, "You and me and the mirror twins, is that the idea?"

"Yeah!" said Dean.

Ozzie popped his second Coke. Did Dean think Ozzie had made friends with him because he liked to double-date? The *plan*, they were gonna kidnap a guy. A wealthy, full-grown adult male. Grab him right out of the middle of his life. Ozzie knew from bitter experience that this would not be an easy thing to do, how easily things could go wrong. A crime this heinous had to be perfect. There was no room for error.

Five million. When he'd first mentioned the figure he had in mind, Dean had laughed so hard he'd spilled his beer. Ozzie pointed out you started high, negotiated down, not the other way around. He showed Dean articles he'd clipped that involved Harold and his various promotions. Oil, gold strikes, diamonds, copper. He showed Dean a colour picture, clipped from a national magazine, of Harold's three-million-dollar Shaughnessy home. Where in hell is Shaughnessy? asked Dean. They got in the truck, Ozzie drove him around, showed him the neighbourhood. Mansions. Curvy streets. Big trees. Shiny Mercedes and Jaguars. Not many BMWs, though. Too sporty.

Now Dean said, "At quitting time, soon's the rest of the crew's gone, they're gonna let us in through the back door." He grinned evilly. "Granny'll be takin' her nap. We'll come and go, she'll never even know we were there."

Ozzie stood up, careful not to spill his Coke. He dusted off his jeans, turned and glanced towards the pool. Sky-blue water, no bikinis. He turned again, and carefully studied the crew. Nobody was paying him any mind.

He said, "I got to do some more work on the tapes."

"It'll wait. What the hell, Ozzie. A chance like this . . ."

Ozzie nodded. An important part of him wanted to bounce his steel-toed boot off Dean's skull until he woke up and smelled the gravy. But a different part of him was reminding him it had been a long time since he'd had any fun worth remembering. Mulling over the possibilities, he turned again. Erika, or maybe it was Monika, stood on the diving board. She flexed her knees, lifted her lovely arms. She bounced, gaining altitude. His brain took a snapshot of her long, curvy, golden body in mid-flight.

Splash.

Dean smiled up at him, a look in his eye that was knowing and feral.

12

Willows was sleeping one moment, half-awake the next. He pushed himself out of the chair. His joints cracked. He steadied himself, and went over to the bed.

Sean's eyes were open, at last. He smiled weakly and said, "Hi, Dad," his voice hardly more than a whisper. He lay quietly on the bed, beneath a woven baby-blue blanket. The threadbare hospital sheets were not much whiter than his skin. His eyes were dark, and seemed far too large for his face. He moved his left arm an inch or two. Willows squeezed his hand.

"How're you doing, son."

"Somebody shot me."

"So I heard."

Sean's head rolled on the pillow. The tendons in his neck bulged unhealthily. "My arm . . ."

"It's still there, if that's what you're worried about." Willows squeezed his son's hand a little tighter. He said, "You're going to be just fine."

"I can't *feel* anything."

"It's the medication. If you could feel anything, it'd be pain."

"Crank me up."

"I'm not sure that I'm supposed to do that, Sean." Willows went over to the door, leaned into the corridor. There was never a nurse around when you needed one . . .

"I want to see my arm. All of it." Sean's voice was pinched, furious. Willows went over to the foot of the bed, pulled out the crank handle. He turned it clockwise and Sean's legs began to levitate. He reversed the crank, and the foot of the bed flattened out. Sean's upper body slowly levitated until he had assumed a sitting position.

"How's that?"

"Better. But I can't . . . I can't move my fingers . . ."

Willows smoothed out the bedding. He gingerly touched his son's fingers. He felt a trembling in his heart. He told himself to be strong. He said, "It's okay, Sean."

Sean began to cry. He wept silently, the tears streaming down his face.

"Can you see your hand?"

Sean nodded, still crying. Willows shifted the barely upholstered chair he'd borrowed from the nurses' station a little closer to the bed. He rested his hand on the boy's shoulder until he had cried himself out. Smiling gently, he said, "You really thought you'd lost your arm?"

"Yeah, yeah." Sean took a deep breath, let it out in a racking sob. He plucked at the sheet, wiped his eyes. "Sorry, Dad."

"It's okay. You've been through a lot, you were in surgery almost three hours. That's a lot to endure, but you came through it in great shape."

Sean nodded again. He shut his eyes, and turned his head aside. Willows sat there for a few minutes and then stood up, and went over to the window. The sky was clear. There was a brisk wind. Flags snapped. Scraps of paper whirled down the street towards the harbour. A woman waiting for the light to change pressed her hands against her thighs to keep her skirt in place. Willows turned back to the bed, rested his hip against the window sill. He had a strong dislike of hospitals, but believed it was a healthy reaction, given the atmosphere of serious illness, and death. After a few minutes Sean opened his eyes. He said, "Where's Claire?"

"Upstairs, in the cafeteria, with Annie. They waited until the lunch-hour rush was over and then went for a bite to eat."

"You told Annie about me?"

"Had to." Willows' smile was kindly. He said, "Face it, Sean. Sooner or later, she was bound to notice you were missing." Outside, on Burrard, a horn blared. The entire block was a quiet zone, but there were a lot of drivers out there whose reading skills were a little rusty. Willows listened to the hum of traffic, the dull, oddly distant roar of a city on the march.

"Shouldn't she be in school?"

"Not in my opinion. It's not every day her brother is shot in an armed robbery. This is a special occasion, Sean. Relax and enjoy it."

Sean shut his eyes again. He lay quietly for several minutes and then said, "D'you know something, Dad?"

"What's that?"

"You're a real hard-ass."

Willows nodded. He choked back the lump of grief that had risen in his throat, and fiercely scrubbed his eyes. When he was sure he had himself firmly under control, he told Sean that he loved him.

"You too, Dad." It had been years since Willows had told his fully grown son that he loved him. He couldn't recall the last time Sean had made a similar confession. He leaned against the wall, his hands in his pockets. Is that what it took – a bullet? By the time Claire and Annie came back from lunch, Sean had fallen asleep. Annie chose to stay with him while Willows and Parker went for coffee.

The hours drifted slowly past. There was a change of shift. The new nurse was a hazel-eyed blonde whose hair was caught up in a utilitarian bun Willows somehow found mildly wanton. The nurse smiled at Annie and Parker as she approached the bed. "Sleep is healing, but too much of it isn't good for him." She briskly patted Sean's pale cheek. "Rise and shine, handsome." Sean's eyelashes fluttered. He looked around, confused. She said, "Hungry?"

"Not really." Sean's voice was thick with sleep. He licked his lips. "Thirsty, though."

"Dinner's going to be here in just a few minutes. Mashed potatoes. Roast beef. Broccoli. There's Jell-O for dessert."

Sean said, "In the meantime, can I have a glass of water?"

"Of course you can have a glass of water."

"I'll get it," said Annie, hurrying to the sink.

The nurse smiled at her as she briskly straightened Sean's sheets, plumped up his pillow. "A volunteer. How nice. Would you be willing to help him with his dinner, if he needs it?"

Annie nodded solemnly. The nurse glanced quickly at Willows and then at Parker, assessing their relationship. She ran her fingers through Sean's rumpled hair, wished him *bon appetit*, and hurried from the room. Did Parker give Willows a faintly jealous look? He wasn't sure. The food cart rattled down the hall. A burly woman checked Sean's name against his chart, slid a covered plastic tray onto the wheeled table at the foot of the bed.

"I'm going to help him eat," said Annie.

"Good for you, dear."

An hour later, Parker drove Annie home via a pizza pickup at Domino's. Annie was emotionally exhausted. She'd been allowed to skip school, but still had to cope with her homework assignments. Life went on.

Sean had fallen asleep as soon as he'd finished eating. He slept quietly until soft electronic bells and a recorded message advised friends and family of patients that it was eight o'clock, and visiting hours were over.

"You leaving, Dad?"

"Maybe in a little while, if that's okay with you?"

"I'm tired."

"Yeah, I know. You should be. Feel like answering a few questions, before I leave?"

Sean said, "I knew we were going to get around to this."

"Would you rather have someone else interview you? Claire, or some cop you don't know?"

"No, it's okay. But I can't tell you much."

"More than you know, maybe. I'm going to start off with the toughest question of all, so brace yourself." Willows was acting in a dual role now. He'd had harsh words with Bradley, pressed him hard for the privilege of questioning Sean. It was important not to screw up. He took out his notebook and Bic pen. "D'you remember being shot?"

"Yeah, I remember."

"You were behind the counter when the shooter came into the store?"

Sean's nod was almost imperceptible.

"A man?"

Just the suggestion of a nod.

"Caucasian?"

"Yeah."

"Just the one guy? Can you describe him for me? Hair colour? How tall was he? Was he heavyset, or thin . . . ?" Willows held the pen like a dagger. He was getting ahead of himself. Was this a good idea? He told himself to take a deep breath, relax. Sean was staring up at the ceiling. His eyes were wet. His chest rose and fell a little too quickly.

Willows said, "If you'd rather do this later . . ."

"No. It's okay. Really. Just give me a minute, okay?"

"However long it takes, son."

It took a while. Willows occupied his mind by writing down the same list of questions, in the proper order, that he would ask any victim. When he had finished, he tried to make sense of the myriad sounds that came to him through the open window and noisy hospital corridor. The room was warm, stuffy. He went over and pushed up the sash a little higher, letting in more air. Down on Burrard, the trees that lined the street were absolutely motionless. Partway down the block on the far side of the street a flag hung limply.

Finally Sean said, "His eyes were dark brown. His hair was short, brown. He had a silver gun. I gave him everything he wanted . . . He left the store . . ."

"But he came back?"

"He saw me . . . I . . . I was looking out the window, looking at him so I could . . . He shot me . . ."

"Take it easy, Son." The Bic was skipping. It was almost out of ink. Willows couldn't recall a Bic ever running out of ink. He'd always lost them long before. *Fuck.* He searched his pockets. In his jacket he found a push-button ballpoint with a red barrel. A PaperMate, with the two hearts. He smiled faintly. "How old was he?"

Sean looked at him. A blank look. He shrugged. "Mid-twenties, maybe?"

"Do you remember what he was wearing?"

"A denim shirt. Jeans." Sean's breathing was rapid but shallow. After a moment he said, "He was wearing workboots. Old ones. The leather had worn through, you could see the steel toe-caps."

Willows wrote it all down, taking his time. "Okay, good. Can you tell me how tall he was? I noticed a police yardstick by the door. Did you . . ."

"He was just average. Not tall, not short . . ."

"You're doing really well," said Willows encouragingly. Sean's face was slick with sweat. His body twitched. The clear plastic bag that fed liquids into his arm was empty. The plastic had collapsed in on itself, fracturing the light. How long had the bag been empty? Willows' stomach was a mass of knots. What was he, father or cop?

He told Sean he'd only be gone a minute, left the room and hurried down the corridor to the nurses' station. The hazel-eyed blonde was on the phone, her posture suggesting an intimate conversation. She glanced up as Willows drew near, saw the look on his face and spoke a few brief words into the phone and hung up. Willows explained the problem, and she followed him back into the room, a look of concern on her face.

There was, as she quickly pointed out, still a double handful of liquid puddled in the bottom of the bag, more liquid in the plastic tube that ran down to Sean's arm. She gave Willows a professionally cool, infuriatingly reassuring smile. "This won't need changing for another fifteen minutes, but I'll be back before then." She turned her smile on Sean, and left the room.

Sean said, "Why don't you go home, Dad."

He'd spoken in hardly more than a whisper. Willows wasn't at all sure he'd heard him correctly. He said, "How's that again?"

"Go home, Dad. I'm tired, I need to rest." He shut his eyes and then, with a visible effort, opened them again. It took him a moment to focus on his father. He said, "You're tired too. Aren't you? You're all blurry . . ." He shut his eyes again. Willows eased into the chair. He watched Sean's chest rise and fall. The boy's breathing was deep and steady. He was young. He'd heal quickly. Willows yawned. He was a long way past exhausted.

He waited until the nurse returned, watched as she hung a clear plastic bag, plump with fresh goodies, from the stainless-steel stand by the bed. He collected his jacket, kissed Sean on the cheek and wished him goodnight, and stepped into the corridor. The ward was quiet. The nurses' station was deserted. There was no one in the visitors' room down at the end of the hall. He walked slowly to the bank of elevators, pushed the down button and waited. It was a little past nine. Behind him, the setting sun had touched thousands of acres of glass afire.

The parking-lot attendant took his money with a smile, and cheerfully wished him goodnight.

Willows drove the unmarked Ford almost all the way home.

Most people took a quick peek at Freddy whether they really wanted to or not. It was his clothes, the way he dressed. He'd often wished he had a nickel for every time a drunk asked him if he was colour-blind. The answer was always the same. "My eyes are perfect. My problem is I'm insensitive."

Tonight, Freddy was wearing black patent-leather pixie boots, silk pants in silver pierced through with threads of gold and black, a rainbow-coloured leather belt and a shirt with a gaudy "State flags" pattern. His personal favourite was Wyoming, with its profile of an albino buffalo with a bullseye painted on its flank. He also liked Montana's "landscape with lake," which a lot of people thought looked like Pac-Man. Mississippi and Georgia's rebels flags were ever-popular. Alaska's Big Dipper was a favourite with the ladies. The only problems with the shirt, from Freddy's point of view, were Maryland's weirdly distorted yellow-and-black checkerboard, and Rhode Island's "clock with anchor." Both flags tended to confuse the better customers, the drunks.

Freddy was polishing glasses when his absolutely worst customer came in the door. He mustered a smile. "Hey, Jack. How's it hangin'?"

"No complaints, Freddy. Nice shirt."

"Yeah, thanks," said Freddy as Willows strolled past him on the way to his favourite booth, down there by the pool tables, about as far from the bar as it was possible to get and still be in the building. Freddy left-handed a bottle of Cutty Sark from the glass shelf. He poured a fat double into a sparkling clean lowball glass, eased out from behind the bar and carried the drink down to where Willows sat with his back to the wall.

Freddy owed Jack. Owed him huge. During his younger days, Freddy had played the piano in just about every bar in town. He'd been a talented musician, but had a fatal weakness; he liked to wander his hands over strange women with even more enthusiasm than he tickled the ivories. The last professional gig of his life, he'd got himself mixed up with a local mobster's girlfriend. Eleanor. What a babe. Willows and his partner, Norm Burroughs, had chased Freddy's screams into a ratbag Gastown hotel, found him chained to a radiator with the bloody remains of his right hand stuffed into a churning blender.

The mobster had meant to blend away an even more crucial appendage, once he'd finished with Freddy's fingers. Freddy'd been so grateful to the two detectives for saving him that, when he opened his bar, he promised them free drinks for the rest of his life. Norm had passed away but Willows was still taking advantage. If you asked Freddy how he felt about it, a payback that had been going on close to ten years now, he'd tell you he was grateful for the opportunity to serve, and he'd mean every last word. But wasn't he entitled to experience a vicious little twinge of resentment, once in a while?

Like now.

He slid into the booth as he delivered the drink. "There you go, Jack. Cutty straight up, a double." He twisted his wedding ring around his thumb. "I heard about your kid. My sincere heartfelts."

Willows acknowledged Freddy's sentiments with a slow nod of his head. He picked up his drink and put it down again.

Freddy said, "So how's your daughter doing? What's her name – Annie?"

"Annie's fine," said Willows.

"Claire okay?"

Willows nodded. His look told Freddy he'd showed enough interest in Willows' personal life, and to abandon the interrogation.

Freddy said, "The cook's got nothing to do, he's back there playing solitaire, listening to the radio. Want something to eat? A shepherd's pie, or maybe a burger, some nachos with sour cream . . . ?"

Willows drank half his double. He drained the glass and put it down on the table.

"Another?"

"Please," said Willows.

The light in Freddy's eyes faded perceptibly. He had learned long ago that the more polite Willows was, the more inclined he was to drink heavily. Tonight, it looked as if he planned to stick around until the chairs were on top of the tables and the roaches came out to play. He said, "Be right back," and stood up and started towards the bar. He'd deliberately left the empty glass on the table, so it would be easy for Willows to keep track of his freeloading.

As if he cared.

A little over an hour later, Willows lifted his fifth double to his mouth and there was Parker, right in front of him, at confrontational, point-blank range. She sat down next to him, hip to hip. His words were a little slurred as he said, "Evening, Claire."

"Jack."

"Want a drink?"

"Not really."

Standing beneath the bright lights of the bar, Freddy waited until he had caught Willows' eye, then screwed up his face in a futile attempt to convey the message that he was not responsible for Parker's sudden appearance.

Parker's hands lay in front of her on the table. Willows put his glass aside, reached out and lightly touched her fingers. He said, "It's pretty late. I guess Annie's been worried about me . . ."

"Me too," said Parker.

13

Jake sat in his imported Italian chair, a mohair blanket over his skinny legs, listening with half an ear as Marty read to him from the city's two daily papers. Marty read the headlines first, got deeper into the articles when Jake roused himself and said, "Yeah, dat one." Marty would read until Jake lost interest, told him to move on. Steve drifted in and out as he tidied up the house. Axel stood by the window, his back to the room, stolidly scrutinizing the landscape.

At the moment, Marty was reading a front-page article that told the sad tale of an unarmed drug dealer who'd been sitting in his Jaguar minding his own business – dealing drugs – when he was shot in the chest and killed by a friend of a customer. No problem, except the customer was an undercover cop and the guy who shot him was wearing a uniform. The cops, hoping to protect their trigger-happy asses, immediately released the victim's petty-criminal record to the media. Indicating that, because he'd done a little time, they had every right to squib the poor bastard.

Moving right along, Marty informed Jake that the city was considering, at some vague indeterminate time in the future, reducing the allowed number of private-residence garbage cans from three to one.

"Fuckin' assholes!" screeched Jake.

"Right on!" yelled Axel, who was always looking to score points. Axel's relentless toadying turned Marty's stomach. It was as if the Teutonic Thug believed Jake could, if motivated, wave a magic wand and transform him into a reasonably intelligent human being.

Jake told Marty to write a letter of complaint to the mayor, copy all ten alderpersons, for his signature.

"Want me to use foul language?"

"By all fuckin' means."

Marty made a note in the little spiralbound book he kept in his shirt pocket. Jake paid a little under twenty grand in property taxes and fired off two or three letters a week to City Hall, an equal number to the Parks Board dolts. His letters were always vaguely menacing but never openly threatening. He'd had only one response, an anonymous computer-generated plea to clean up his language if he wished to correspond in the future.

Steve came in carrying a tray with Jake's lunch: a bowl of home-made Italian tomato soup, side plate of original-flavour Ritz crackers. Marty folded the paper and put it aside. He smoothed out Jake's blanket and motioned Steve forward. Steve rested the tray on the arms of the chair.

Axel turned his broad back to the window. He said, "Mr. Cappalletti, vould you like me to feed you?"

Jake lowered his head and sniffed at the soup. His eyes watered. He scrutinized his spoon.

Steve said, "It's clean, Jake."

"So you say, but dat don' make it so."

Jake turned the spoon every which way in the light until he was certain that it was spotless. He dipped deep into his bowl of soup, waited patiently until the spoon had stopped dripping. He carried it to his gaping mouth. He sipped, swallowed, reached out and whacked the newspaper. "Ain't nothin' in dere 'bout dat guy Steve squibbed?"

"Not a word," said Marty.

Jake dipped his spoon into the soup. He lifted up the spoon and emptied it into his mouth. A thin stream of soup ran down his chin. He sighed. Not enough oregano. Was there such a miracle in all the world as a thug who could cook?

He wiped his face with a linen napkin stolen from the Wedgewood Hotel. Marty had sewn his initials into the material with gold thread, and done a fairly good job of it. Pointing at Marty, his stiff index finger covered by the napkin, like a gun, Jake said, "Ya lyin' ta me 'bout dat guy Steve shot, I'll find out sooner a later. Cut out ya tongue an' feed it to Butch. Unnerstand?"

"Yes, I do," said Marty solemnly.

Jake had been a young man for a very long time. Fifteen, twenty years. All those women. He'd never fallen in love except that one time, when he had visited the Motherland. Even then, he wouldn't have admitted he was ready to marry the girl. Get engaged, maybe. So far as he knew, he'd never fathered any children. So, really, all he had was Marty. He said, "I ain't gonna cut ya, Marty. Ya know dat as well as I do. But if I find out ya lying, ya can't watch no TV for a entire week."

"Swear to God," said Marty, "I ain't seen a word about a shooting in the park."

Jake nodded, satisfied. He said, "Wha' time ya got?"

"Three minutes to eleven."

"I haff eleven sharp!" said Axel.

His arms were so hairy, all that curly blond hair, Jake wondered how he could see the dial of his watch. He nibbled at his soup. Not enough oregano. Too much salt. Add it up, maybe Steve was trying to kill him.

And what about Melanie. What about Melanie? She was late, or would be in a couple more minutes. He dropped the spoon into the bowl. A few drops of soup splashed onto the blanket. It looked like anemic blood. Jeez . . .

Marty said, "You okay, Jake?"

"Where's Melanie? Where's dat gorgeous broad?"

"Stuck in traffic, I bet."

"Be here any minute," said Steve. Jake waggled his fingers above the tray and Steve stepped forward and picked it up. He stood there, hovering. "I made lime Jell-O with miniature marshmallows in it, you're in the mood for dessert."

"Lime Jell-O!" hissed Axel, wide-eyed. He licked his sausage lips. "From ven I vas a child, I haff a great luff for Jell-O!"

Jake sneered. He leaned back. He closed his eyes. Steve and Marty exchanged a look that could have meant anything.

Jake said, "Where's my special li'l girl?" His eyes snapped open. The ambient temperature plummeted.

There was a hands-free Motorola in Melanie's leased Acura, and he knew she used it all the time, because he paid the bills, which were enormous. He jerked his head at Marty. "Give dat pretty li'l bitch a call."

Marty snapped his fingers.

Axel got to work on his cellphone.

Jake gave Steve a hot-eyed look. He said, "Maybe I'm gonna have me some a dat Jella after all. What flava ya said?"

"Lime."

"Harry Lime," said Marty.

Jake, a lifelong Orson Welles fan, smiled fleetingly. He said, "Okay, I'll give it a shot. Axel! Get ya ass inna kitchen, an' yank alla stinkin' mushrooms outta da Jella."

"Marshmallows!" said Axel. "Fluffy little clouds of delight!"

Jake pointed a spatulate finger, the curving, sharply pointed fingernail gleaming ivory-yellow in the light. "Don't fuck wit' me. Just do it." He glanced worriedly at Marty. "Am I allowed ta use dat phrase, or dey got it copyright-protected?"

Marty shrugged. His face was blank as an unglazed plate. What in hell was Jake going on about now? Not that he wanted to know.

14

The alarm woke Ozzie at seven sharp. He phoned in sick. The boss's daughter, Iris, reminded him that his crew was behind schedule, and strongly suggested he get his ass to work. Was this part of the plan? Ozzie didn't think so. He said, "Yeah, okay, half an hour." An hour later, the phone woke him again. This time it was Iris' daddy, Franz. Tension or anger had resuscitated his accent. He yelled at Ozzie to get up or get fired.

Ozzie said, "Fuck you *and* Iris. No, wait a minute, I'll pass on Iris."

His head ached from too much single-malt Scotch. His eyes stung from an overdose of chlorine. He had a bruise the size of his fist high up on his hip, from falling on the concrete apron of the pool. Why had his pratfall seemed so hilarious at the time? He went into the bathroom, urinated, gulped a quartet of Aspirins as he stood beneath the shower. Feeling marginally better – as if he were perched on the edge of his grave instead of lying face down in the bottom of it – he dressed in pleated black Dockers, a plain black shirt with dull black buttons, a black linen sports jacket, black silk socks and a pair of shiny black penny loafers. He examined himself in the mirror. The shoes pinched his feet, but this wasn't necessarily a bad thing, as he believed a person could see in his eyes that he was tormented, but not by what.

He straightened the shirt's button-down collar, fastened then unfastened the top button. He looked like somebody, but he wasn't sure who. He tried on the plain-lens glasses. Better.

He made coffee and drank two cups, sitting at the round maple table in the tiny kitchen nook. It was a sunny day. He had left his Ironman watch somewhere. He remembered taking it off and throwing it away, but the details were vague.

He poured another cup of coffee and went into the living room. If the VCR could be trusted, it was twelve minutes past ten. He pulled the drapes and watched television with the sound turned down to almost inaudible for a little more than an hour, until it was time to go. As he reached the door he thought to check his wallet. His face purpled. Monika or Erika or whichever one of them he'd ended up with had left his Visa card but pinched his cash. Thieving bitch!

In the bedroom, he rooted round in his bureau until he found the sock with his emergency wad stashed inside. He peeled off a quartet of twenties and a pair of fives, stuffed the much-diminished roll back in the drawer.

He took the elevator to the underground parking lot. His truck squatted gleaming under the fluorescents, aviator-style Ray-Bans sitting there on the dashboard, begging to be stolen. He unlocked the truck and got in and turned the key and the engine caught immediately, the sound of the exhaust rattling off the concrete walls. He drove out of the parking lot and slipped the Ray-Bans up on his nose where they belonged.

He turned on the radio and learned it was thirty-two minutes to twelve. He'd done his research. Harold Wismer always left his desk at twelve sharp and it took him, on average, a little less than five minutes to ride the elevator down to the lobby, cross the marble floor and push his way through the revolving door and take that first step outside. Add another ten minutes for the leisurely stroll to Janice's, the intimate French restaurant that was Harold's exclusive lunchtime domain.

Ozzie added it up. He had forty-seven minutes and counting to make it downtown, find a parking spot and get to the restaurant. Less if he hoped to catch Harold outside his building. It was going to be a squeeze, but he was pretty sure he'd make it.

The radio guy invited him to stay tuned for Nancy Sinatra's hit "These Boots Were Made for Walking." Hey, no need to ask.

As he made a left onto Oak Street, Ozzie tuned in the all-news station. A plane had crashed . . . He drove straight down Oak, hit the Granville Street Bridge on-ramp at speed, eased into the right lane, exited onto Seymour Street and, a few minutes later, parked the truck on the third floor of the Bay Parkade. He killed the engine and tilted the rearview mirror towards his face, pressed the false moustache firmly against his upper lip. Now he looked like Jon Voight. Or so he told himself. He leaned back against the seat, shut his eyes and stroked the little piece of hair. To his gently inquisitive fingers the moustache felt like a very small, recently deceased pet.

He strode briskly across the glass-enclosed elevated walkway into the department store, rode an otherwise empty elevator to the main floor. He hurried past a display of miniature imported totem poles, a booth where you could buy a thousand different kinds of lottery tickets, shiny glass cases full of cheap watches, a clutch of women wearing white lab coats and too much makeup. He faltered. His pace slowed. The women stood dull-eyed and passive at their stations, as if victims of some benign gas. Ozzie drew closer, until he was suddenly enveloped in a fogbank of perfumes. They *had* been gassed! And now *he* was being gassed! He trotted towards the Georgia Street exit, turned right as he left the building.

The streets were crowded. Clusters of runaway kids squatted on the concrete. Most of them looked pretty well maintained, for homeless people. They wore Doc Martens, leather jackets, complicated haircuts. A girl of about sixteen, one of the genuinely raggedy minority, made eye contact. She had bad teeth but a nice smile. She muttered a few words. Had she spoken in a foreign language? No, it was only that she had a very strong *Québécois* accent. In the national interest, and because she was cute, he slipped her ten dollars. The money galvanized her. Wide-eyed and smiling, she leapt to her feet and chased after him as if she might follow him to the ends of the earth. What did she want? He never found out. Between one step and the next she abruptly lost momentum, turned away from him as if he'd never existed.

There was a film crew working behind the art gallery, big white trailers lined up along the curb, an auxiliary cop moving traffic. Ozzie asked the cop what was being filmed. "X-Files." He followed the lens of the camera, peered at the actors. Where was Scully? He asked the cop what time it was. The guy gave him a look, pointed at the big clock on top of the Vancouver Block. But just then the foghorn on top of the Electra began to play the first few notes of the national anthem. It was high noon. He was running late.

Harold Wismer's offices were in a tower located in the 600 block of Howe Street. Ozzie loitered directly across the street from the entrance. Sunlight on the revolving glass door had turned it into a bronze-tinted mirror, so it was impossible to see inside. He waited. The door shot beams of golden light across the street as it spat out several young women, a couple of guys in suits, lots more women, another suit. Hardly anybody over thirty, that Ozzie could see. He shifted his weight from foot to foot, staying loose. People kept coming out of the building, dozens of them. The men wore black or dark-blue suits. The women wore colourful blouses, boxy jackets, short skirts. Nobody seemed particularly happy. When the stampede was reduced to a trickle, the door spun wildly on its axis, and flung a signature three-piece suit the colour of a ripe banana onto the street. Harold Wismer had made his move.

Harold was, as usual, all by himself. Not that he liked to eat alone. Tuesdays through Thursdays there'd be two or three of his crooked stockbroker pals at the restaurant when he arrived. Twice a week his girlfriend would be waiting for him at an intimate little table for two way at the back, with a view of the gas fireplace and the restaurant's tiny bar, the singing midget bartender with the pink hair, who wore a different colour pastel tuxedo every day of the week.

It hadn't taken Ozzie long to figure out the stockbroker crowd. They liked to think they were creative types, that they led exciting, risky lives. They craved a little weirdness, but it had to be weirdness that was predictable and easily controlled. If you catered to that need, you could make a fortune. A midget bartender with pink hair struck just the right note.

Harold crossed the sidewalk to the curb. He glanced up and down the busy street, shook a fat cigar out of a shiny aluminum tube the size of a small jet aircraft. He bit the end off the cigar and spat, lit up with a heavy gold lighter. A black Jaguar swept past, horn blaring. Harold shouted, gave the Jaguar the finger, cackled happily in a cloud of sunlit blue smoke.

His suit was a double-breasted model in a shiny material that could have been silk. His shirt was white as Tom Cruise's teeth, his mile-wide tie and the handkerchief that flopped limply out of his pocket like a miniature parachute were dark red, and had the sickly gloss of dried blood. His handmade banana-yellow shoes were exactly the same shade of yellow as his suit.

Harold stood there by the curb, smirking and smoking, visibly preening. There was nothing unusual about this – it was part of his routine. A trio of middle-aged men came out of the building. One of them spoke briefly to him while the others waited at a discreet distance. Harold broke into the man's monologue by raising his right hand in a traffic cop's gesture. He shook his head, no. The man backed away, smiling. He and his companions continued up the street.

Harold strolled towards the harbour. At the doorway to Janice's, he turned and flicked the remains of the cigar, almost a foot of good Cuban leaf, into the street. The door was opened for him. In he went.

Ozzie counted off a minute before following Harold inside. Where was Harold? A thin, bald man with a steeply sloped skull

sidled carefully up to him. Ozzie asked for a table for one. Did he
have a reservation? No, said Ozzie unapologetically. The dozen
unoccupied tables were reserved. Ozzie was told he'd have to wait
at least an hour.

Ozzie said that would be fine. Harold was down there by the
fireplace, with the woman. His girlfriend. The babe. Melanie. He
plunked himself down on a wooden chair by the door. If he
hunched forward, he had a clear view of Melanie and of Harold's
yellow back and his silvery hair that had been tied in a neat ponytail, like a little girl's.

The thin bald guy was watching him.

Ozzie offered him a twenty. "Maybe if I could have a beer . . ."

The man's sneer was thin as a trip-wire. Ozzie decided to come
back at closing time, one of these days. Wear his steel-toed workboots. Do the guy a favour, kick some sense into him.

Melanie wore a pale-green suit in a lightweight, clingy linen.
The skirt was very short, too short for the office. Her cream-
coloured blouse had tiny gold buttons and was open at the throat.
She leaned forward to say something to Harold. She was wearing a
black bra. Ozzie caught a quick glimpse, swell of breast. He wished
like hell he was close enough to hear what she was saying.

Melanie said, "I hate this place. You call it intimate, I call it
cramped." She sipped at her ice-water.

Harold stared hungrily at the lipstick kiss on the rim of her
glass. Harold had learned early on that you had to watch Melanie
very carefully at all times. The way she moved, her body language.
Everything she said, word and tone. She was a sweet girl, but she
had a weakness for irony. And like all women who had any spark,
she could be a real ball-buster. Sometimes, sensing that she might
be in a spiky mood, he'd listen too hard, keeping a wary eye open
for a sucker punch. Their relationship could be a grind, now and
then. Jeez, he was a lover, not a fighter. Quarrels, bitter recriminations, he could get all that stuff at home. But Melanie was worth
the aggravation. She was more than worth it.

Their drinks arrived, gin and tonic, rocks, for him, a glass of the house white for her. He said, "Here's to us, Melanie."

She smiled politely. They touched glasses. Sipped.

Harold would never have admitted to being in love. He wasn't even sure what love was any more. Was love a permanent state of temporary insanity? Or merely a deep and abiding infatuation? All he knew for sure was that he felt very strongly about Melanie. She was borderline too young for him, but aside from that small and unavoidable flaw, she was perfect. She knew where to shop, how to dress and undress. She appreciated good food, could hold her liquor. She was an experienced traveller, a great conversationalist. Lots of fun in the sack. Most important of all, for reasons he was confident had absolutely nothing to do with his personal wealth or power, she was absolutely and totally crazy about him.

Harold started to tell her about a recent acquisition, a property in Borneo so rich, you walked around for ten minutes, you'd be picking nuggets out of the tread of your boots. No kidding! He was explaining the deal's fine print when his salad arrived.

Melanie bent to her own plate, knowing from past experience that Harold wouldn't speak another word until he'd finished eating. She felt a small twinge of desperation as she wondered if he planned to take the afternoon off, invite himself back to her apartment for a nap. Hopefully not. Harold a couple of times a week was really all the Harold she needed. Or could stand.

She picked at her salad, caught the bartender's sparrow-tiny eye and pointed at her glass. He nodded, and she gulped down the rest of her wine and put her empty glass where he could easily reach it. His name was Bob, but Harold always referred to him as the midget. Well, that was Harold. She touched her tongue to her lips, wondering how her lipstick was holding up. The guy crouched on a chair by the cash register was still staring at her. Bob trotted towards her, his abbreviated legs pumping away, the tails of his tuxedo flapping. He looked like a fresh-hatched shrimp. He put her glass down in front of her and removed the empty, all the while peering at her cleavage. She said, "Thank you, Bob."

Bob asked Harold if he was ready for another drink. Harold nodded, but didn't look up from his plate. When Melanie had first met him, a little more than a year ago, he'd been on a diet. But lately his appetite had picked up and his self-imposed discipline had fallen by the wayside. He was drinking more, too. Lots more. Not that Melanie blamed him. He had about ten million reasons. Wine glass in hand, she glanced idly around. The restaurant had filled up. There wasn't an empty table in the place. She remembered the first time Harold had brought her here. She'd asked him what kind of people frequented the restaurant and he had put down his knife and fork and turned a fraction of a degree towards her, so he faced her squarely. Oozing charm, smiling across the table at her with his capped, fabulously white teeth and famous twinkling blue eyes, he'd reached out and gently enfolded her hands in his and said, "People like me eat here, Melanie. People who appreciate excellent food, the very best service. People who like to be recognized, made to feel valued, and welcome." In other words, the kind of people who routinely dropped a hundred-dollar tip on a sandwich and a couple of drinks . . .

The guy in the chair was still there, staring down at the carpet. Not that it was any of her business, but she wondered if he'd applied for a job and was waiting for an interview. More likely he was meeting someone. A woman? He glanced up, sensing that he was being watched. She looked away, and there was Harold.

Harold said, "You okay?"

She nodded. Her braised chicken and rice pilaf sat there, steaming. When had the dish arrived? Her wine glass was empty.

Harold jerked his thumb over his shoulder. "You know that guy, by any chance?"

"No, of course not."

Harold raised an eyebrow, let it fall. His plate chimed as the silver-plated tines of his fork penetrated too deeply into a chunk of beef.

Melanie, winging it, said, "I mean, I don't *know* him, but I've seen him somewhere, on TV, or the stage . . ."

Harold nodded. He sucked unmusically at a sliver of meat caught between his teeth. "They're filming 'The X-Files' behind the art gallery."

Melanie acted surprised.

But Harold was concentrating on his meal. He'd lost interest in the guy the moment he'd pigeonholed him.

She was tempted to take another peek, see if he was still watching her. But what if he was? Then what? She nibbled at her rice.

Was it possible the guy was working for Jake Cappalletti?

Maybe. But she doubted it. He didn't look the type. Too smooth, too bright. Besides, his clothes were all wrong. Jake had a strict dress code, and expected his gangsters to abide by it. Marty had to wear black, when he was chauffeuring Jake around town. But, otherwise, you worked for Jake, the only time you dressed in black was the day of your mother's funeral. Jake liked his staff to wear baggy corduroy pants in subtle earth tones of rust or moss-green, narrow belts of unbleached canvas or braided leather, plaid shirts from Eddie Bauer, baggy Harris Tweed jackets. Marty was the only thug on Jake's payroll who was allowed to wear a pinky ring, or stand around with his hands in his pockets and a toothpick hanging out of his mouth. But even he wasn't allowed to wear a fedora.

When they'd finished eating, Melanie risked another bold look. Gone.

Harold wiped his plate clean with a chunk of bread. He told her he wished like hell he could take the afternoon off, but it was crazy at the office, this Borneo thing was worth millions . . .

Melanie let her disappointment show. She stamped her pretty little foot, and told Harold he better not make a habit of teasing her, or she didn't know what she'd do. He pecked her on the cheek as they left the restaurant, told her she was sweet as a peach. Outside, he lit one of his stinking cigars, and stood upwind of her, pointing and yelling, until finally he'd got her a cab. Melanie stood still for a fleeting smack on the lips, a furtive grope. He told her he'd call. She told him he'd better. One last smooch and it was over. For now.

The cab pulled away. Ozzie, standing by the curb, used his mental powers to force Melanie to look at him as she drove by, but she must've been tuned in to a different channel. He jogged across the street. Harold's jutting ponytail made his beefy head look a little like a weathervane as he turned to stare at a young woman jogging past in shorts and a snug white T-shirt that said, "JUST DID IT." Ozzie shook a big cigar out of its aluminum tube. He walked right up to Harold, close enough to count his nose-hairs. He said, "Hey, buddy. Got a light?"

Harold made a snap decision that it would be less trouble to say yes than no. He dipped his hand into his pants pocket for his gold lighter, thought better of it and offered up the hot end of his cigar.

Ozzie put his hand on Harold's, helping him hold the big cigar steady. Harold didn't like that at all. He tried to pull his hand away and discovered he was no match for a muscular kid forty years younger than him. Ozzie said, "I see we smoke the same brand."

Harold looked startled, and then suspicious. Ozzie let go of his hand. He looked deep into Harold's eyes and then turned and strode rapidly up Howe Street towards the art gallery and film crew. Harold shouted after him, asked him if he was an actor. Ozzie stopped dead in his tracks. He spun around and jogged back to Harold, didn't stop until he'd bumped into him. Give Harold his due, he held his ground. Ozzie said, "Yeah, I'm an actor. A *baaad* actor."

Harold smiled uncertainly.

Ozzie waited until the smiled had died before he walked away.

15

Willows arrived in time for breakfast and stayed past lunch. He'd have stayed all afternoon and into the evening if Sean hadn't told him he was tired and wanted to sleep. All morning long, Willows had struggled against the urge to resume grilling his son about the robbery. Now the chance was lost.

There was a pay telephone in a little nook by the elevators. He dialled Parker's number at 312 Main, but she wasn't at her desk.

He tried Farley Spears.

Orwell picked up.

Willows asked him if he had any idea where Parker was and Orwell said he understood she was out working, but he didn't know exactly where. Or have any idea at all, actually. Willows asked Orwell to check his desk for the lab report on the bullets. Orwell told him to hang on. Spears' phone thumped on Spears' desk. Orwell was only gone a minute. He reported that ten bullets had been recovered from the insurance company's office – Black Talons. No one from the lab had left a message, yet.

Willows thanked him and hung up. He still had his hand on the receiver when his beeper vibrated against his hip. He dropped his last quarter into the phone and dialled the displayed number.

Parker picked up on the first ring. "Jack, where are you?"

Willows said he was at the hospital but just about to leave. Parker asked him how Sean was doing and he told her the doctors were satisfied with his progress, that he was healing rapidly.

"Get anything else out of him?"

"We talked about everything but the robbery. If he isn't ready to discuss it, I'm not going to push him."

Parker was pleased, and let him know it. She told him that she was at the Chevron station across the street from the convenience store, that she'd just been given a copy of the Chevron receipts from the night of the robbery. Brian LaFrance, the Chevron employee who'd been on duty when Sean had been shot, worked a split shift. He was there now. Willows told Parker he was on his way and would be there in twenty minutes, max. Parker mentioned that she'd also confirmed an informal at-home interview later that afternoon with the BC Transit employee whose bus had passed the station at the approximate time of the robbery.

Willows had said twenty minutes, but was slowed by a tangle of traffic on West Broadway. By the time he arrived, LaFrance's shift had ended and he was eager to go home.

LaFrance was twenty-seven years old, of average height, a little on the plump side. His sandy-blond hair was cut short. The eyes behind his oversize metal-frame glasses were standard-issue brown. He was clean-shaven, had a pleasant smile. When Willows offered him a ride home he gestured proudly towards an older-model Chevrolet parked at the far end of the lot. Parker admired the car, and suggested they sit in it while they conducted the interview. LaFrance mentioned that he'd already told the other detectives everything he knew. He had Farley Spears' card, Oikawa's card. He dug deep in his wallet and showed Parker Bobby Dundas' card.

Willows said, "Can I take a look at that . . . ?"

Bobby'd had his own cards printed. The paper was high-quality stock, glossy and smooth. The card superficially resembled a police-issue card, blue ink on a white background, the city crest in the top left corner and VANCOUVER POLICE DEPARTMENT in block letters in the top right corner, lined spaces at the bottom for the Officer's name and badge number, Incident number, the officer's 665 phone number and the Victim Services number. On the reverse of the card an uncredited quote had been printed in block letters:

"COMMUNITY POLICING IS THE POLICE
AND OTHER SERVICE PROVIDERS IN THE CITY
WORKING IN PARTNERSHIP WITH THE COMMUNITY
TO ADDRESS COMMUNITY PROBLEMS."

This was identical to the quote on Willows' or any other cop's card, but Bobby had replaced the city crest with his portrait – a colour head-shot. Willows wondered if the look on his face was intended to convey an impression of honesty and dependability. Was Bobby moonlighting in real estate? Willows offered the card to Parker, who glanced briefly at it, smiled, and returned it to LaFrance.

Willows told LaFrance that the boy who'd been shot was his son. LaFrance offered his sympathies. He led them to his car, unlocked, and slid behind the wheel. Parker got into the backseat. Willows sat up front. In response to Parker's question, LaFrance said that he had been employed by Chevron for eighteen months. He volunteered that he'd spent the previous five years travelling and working in Eastern Europe. Before that, university. He'd majored in history. Big mistake. Now he was taking computer and business-management courses, three nights a week.

Willows said, "Last night, at the time of the shooting, were you alone?"

"No, I wasn't." LaFrance's eyes skittered sideways to the pumps. He stared blankly at a picture of a man in a Chevron uniform who had a bluebird perched on his shoulder. The message, presumably, was that wildlife preferred Chevron exhaust fumes.

From the spacious backseat Parker said, "Brian, according to last night's sales slips, a cash customer, the only customer you had during a sixteen-minute span, pumped ten dollars' worth of gas at twenty past midnight. But you didn't ring up the sale until twelve-thirty-six. So what were you and your customer up to, during that time?"

"Sixteen minutes? You kidding me?"

Parker said, "Brian, listen to me. We've got a shooting on our hands, an attempted murder. Your girlfriend drops by, it's quiet, she talks you into spending a few minutes in the Chevy . . ."

"Look, I need this job. I mean, I really, really need this job."

A white Saab had pulled up to the pumps. A man in baggy, knee-length tartan shorts and a lilac sleeveless T-shirt got out of the car. LaFrance put his hand on the Chevy's door handle, but there was no need for his services. The Saab driver had inserted his credit card into a slot in the pump. It was a self-serve sale.

LaFrance turned back to Willows. He removed his glasses and wiped the lenses on the sleeve of his shirt. He put his glasses back on and said, "Her name's Beverly."

"She see anything?"

"No. At least, not that I know of. Not that she told me."

Parker said, "What's Beverly's last name?"

"Novik."

"Could you spell that for me?" Parker wrote the woman's name in her notebook, winkled her address and phone number from LaFrance. She said, "Is Beverly working?"

"She's a student. Are you going to phone her?"

"We'll probably just drop by," said Parker. She leaned forward, rested her hand on LaFrance's shoulder. "We'd like to surprise her, okay?"

LaFrance shrugged. He glanced at Willows, looked away.

Parker said, "Okay, you're out of the car, back at the cash register. You hear an explosion, what you mistakenly think is a tire blowing. You're curious, go outside, take a look around. You see the truck. Is that how it went, Brian?"

"Pretty much."

"Tell us about the truck. It was a pickup?"

"Yeah, a pickup. An older model, mid-fifties, maybe. With a rounded hood, split windshield. That's about all I can tell you, really. Like I told the other officers, I'm not even sure what colour it was . . ."

"Red or black, you said."

"Or orange, burnt orange." Brian was becoming agitated. He said, "I'm sorry, I'm really sorry. But I just don't know."

Willows said, "I don't understand, Brian. You're into cars. I'd have thought you'd be able to tell us exactly what year and model it was."

Brian grinned sheepishly. "I couldn't see that well. I took off my glasses when Beverly and I . . . When she left I forgot all about them, that I'd taken them off in the car."

Parker said, "Brian?"

"Yeah, what?"

"If you think of anything, give us a ring."

The bus driver, Ed Spinello, lived in a ramshackle clapboard house on East Sixty-First. The weedy, unmowed front yard was surrounded by a chain-link fence. Several plywood BEWARE OF DOG signs, wildly spray-painted red letters over crudely drawn canine jaws, hung from the fence by lengths of rusty wire. Mail was delivered no farther than the front gate, to a locked metal box.

Parker slipped her pepper spray out of her purse. Willows swung open the gate. A hinge creaked. Inside the house, several dogs immediately started barking. The detectives made their way up the steps. Willows knuckled the grimy door. A few moments later the safety chain rattled, and the door opened the width of a strawberry-shaped nose. Willows showed his badge. A dog squealed shrilly, there was the scuffling sound of claws on linoleum, and then the chain rattled again, and the door opened wide. A short, potbellied man wearing unbuckled motorcycle boots, wrinkled grey pants and a pale-blue shirt stepped outside. His hair was unkempt. He needed a shave. His complexion was sallow and his eyes were bloodshot.

Parker said, "Mr. Spinello?"

"Yeah, what d'ya want?" Spinello turned and lashed out with his booted foot. A dog shrieked. He slammed the door and locked it with a key that hung from a leather neck-thong. He sat down heavily on the porch's concrete top step and sighed. Willows put away his badge. He distanced himself from the bus driver as much as the cramped porch allowed. Spinello smelled like death in a hothouse.

Spinello's rheumy eyes focused on Parker. He said, "You here about my wife, Suzie?"

"What about her?"

Spinello tilted a hip, dug deep in his back pocket and produced a fat, shiny black wallet. He flipped open the wallet on a sheaf of photographs in plastic slipcases. Willows counted three Dobermans and a pair of pit bulls, before Spinello showed him a snapshot of a plump-faced, tangle-haired woman with small dark eyes, a sour downturned mouth. His beloved wife, Suzie. She'd vanished six months ago. He'd filed a report with Missing Persons a few days after she disappeared. Since then, nothing. He had no idea why she'd abandoned him or where she might have gone. He suspected foul play. He asked Willows if he was married, and Willows said no.

Parker's face showed nothing.

Spinello asked Willows if he could recommend a good private detective. Without pause, he asked Willows if he'd like to make a little extra cash.

Willows said, "Mr. Spinello, all that interests me right now is . . ."

"Hey, do I look stupid? I know why you're here! You don't give a shit about Suzie!" Spinello's voice dripped with contempt. He said, "I told the other cops everything I know. Which is nothing!"

In the space of a heartbeat, the bus driver had rotated a full 180 degrees, dropped his pants and given the detectives an unsolicited view of his dark side.

Parker said, "We'll try not to take too much of your time, Mr. Spinello. There are just a few questions . . ."

Willows said, "Can I see that picture of your wife? Suzie, is it?" He held the photo at an angle, to reduce glare. "A woman like that, I can understand why you'd want to get her back . . ."

Spinello glowered at him.

Willows tapped the picture with his thumbnail. He turned to Parker and said, "What about Ralph Kearns?" To Spinello he said, "Ralph quit the force about a year ago, went private. He's a good man, the best." He turned back to Parker. "Claire, d'you think Ralph might be able to give Ed a hand?"

"He'd be perfect," said Parker.

Spinello jumped to his feet. He went over to the door and unlocked it, raising a cacophony of snarls and barking. He glanced from Parker to Willows and back again. "You dimwits think you can bullshit me? I told you already, I didn't see nothing!"

The door slammed shut behind him. A dog howled.

Parker said, "Are you thinking what I'm thinking?"

Willows nodded. Parker was thinking that Spinello looked like hell, his Dobermans and pit bulls were full of beans, and his plump wife, Suzie, was missing.

Missing, or consumed.

Beverly Novik shared a two-bedroom apartment located on the corner of Hastings and Templeton, above a U-Frame It shop. A large framed print of van Gogh's "Sunflowers" stood on a small wooden easel in the shop's window. Parker pushed open a door to the left of the shop. The door had been painted bright blue with purple polka-dots. They walked up a narrow flight of stairs that would have required a rope and crampons if it had been any steeper.

There were two doors at the top of the landing, one on either side. Both doors were painted bright blue splashed with clumsy purple stars outlined in bright yellow.

Willows bruised his knuckles on a star. He and Parker waited quietly. The door at the bottom of the stairs hadn't shut properly, which was a lucky thing, because the ceiling light had burnt out. The low growl of traffic carried up the stairwell. Willows tried another star. He thumped the door with the side of his fist, and then tried the knob. It turned freely, but there was a deadbolt.

Parker tried the door on the opposite side of the landing. She was still knocking when the door opened a crack. It was dark in the apartment, and the face wasn't much more than a pale blur below dark, tightly curled hair. A dark eye glittered.

"What can I do for you?"

Parker showed her badge.

Willows said, "We're looking for Beverly Novik. Do you know her?"

"Impossible not to. She's the friendly type." White teeth flashed. "Hey, just kidding, don't quote me." The door clicked shut and then the chain rattled and the door swung wide. The man was in his mid-twenties, muscular, very pale. He was naked but for a towel fastened around his narrow waist. Parker wondered if he was a model. He indicated the murky depths of his apartment. "Beverly's behind the first door on your left . . ." He smiled at Parker as he offered his hand. "I'm Bill Dickie."

"Detective Parker," said Parker. She introduced Willows.

"Would either of you care for a glass of Chardonnay? I was just going to open another bottle . . ."

"No thanks," said Willows. He followed Parker down the hall, to the first door on the left. Watery light seeped through a bamboo curtain. An empty wine bottle glittered in the yellow glow of a trio of thick white candles that burned steadily on a table next to the bed. A woman lay on her back beneath the rumpled sheets. Her long blonde hair was dishevelled. She wore no lipstick or any other makeup. Her lips were slightly parted.

"Found her, huh."

Parker turned to Dickie. "That's Beverly Novik?"

"In the flesh." He winked at Willows. "Seductive pose, wouldn't you agree?"

The woman appeared to be sleeping. Parker said, "Is she all right?"

"Absolutely the best."

Parker gave Dickie a hard look. Dickie said, "Shall I rouse her from her sweet, sweet dreams?"

"Please."

Dickie went over to the bed, lifted up the sheets, slipped in next to her. Willows inadvertently caught a quick glimpse, head to toe, of Beverly Novik's naked body. Dickie kissed his girlfriend on the lips, whispered into her ear. His hands moved beneath the sheets.

Parker said, "Hey . . ."

Beverly Novik sighed contentedly, turned towards Dickie and put her arms around him and kissed him on the mouth.

Parker said, "Excuse me . . ."

She opened her eyes.

She pushed Dickie away, and screamed loudly.

Parker had her badge out. So did Willows.

The sheet fell away from Beverly Novik's breasts as she let loose with a roundhouse right that landed flush on her boyfriend's smirk.

Dickie left a trail of blood all the way into the kitchen. He dripped blood into the sink while Beverly used the bathroom. Parker and Willows loitered in the cramped living room.

Beverly came out of the bathroom wearing tight jeans and a tight black cashmere sweater that fell just short of her navel, brown suede sandals, no socks. She'd brushed her hair, put on some lipstick and a brave smile.

"You wanted to talk to me about the robbery?"

"Robbery and shooting," said Willows.

Beverly said, "Why don't we go over to my place . . . ?"

They followed her out of the apartment, waited on the landing while she fumbled with her keys. She unlocked the door and led them into an apartment that was a mirror image of Dickie's, but neater.

Beverly said, "I'm thirsty. Too much wine. Can I get you something to drink? Diet Pepsi . . . ?"

"A glass of water," said Parker, "would be nice."

Beverly led them into the kitchen. She poured glasses of bottled water for Willows and Parker, and leaned against the kitchen counter. Her profile was reflected in a chrome-plated toaster. Outside, traffic hummed like monstrous bees. After a moment she said, "What'd you think of Bill?"

"Handsome," said Parker.

"He's an artist. A sculptor. He's really talented, and *so* good-looking. But d'you know what I really like about him?"

"What's that?" said Parker cautiously.

"Unlike Brian, he doesn't smell like an oil refinery."

Parker smiled. "That must be nice." She handed Beverly her VPD card. "Tell us what you saw, last night."

"Not much. I was standing by the pumps when they drove up. The radio was blaring. Country and western. That Garth Brooks song with all the thunder sounds. That's what made me look up, the noise."

"You saw the truck?"

"It was old, but in really nice condition. There were two guys in it. The driver stayed behind when the other guy went into the store."

"Can you tell me what he looked like?"

"The passenger?"

"Both of them," said Parker.

"I didn't get much of a look at either of them, really. All I saw was silhouettes, because the store was all lit up. The guy who went inside was about average height, slim . . ."

"White?"

Beverly wrinkled her brow. She ran her fingers through her hair, then turned and opened the refrigerator door. She bent from the waist, and reached inside. She cast a sidelong glance at Willows, asked him if he'd mind opening her Pepsi.

He popped the tab.

She smiled and thanked him. "Sure you don't want one?"

He nodded.

"You can split this one with me, if you want."

"No thanks."

Parker said, "Let's get back to the guys in the truck. Can you tell us anything about them? Were they white?"

Beverly shrugged. "I think so, but I couldn't really say for sure. Like I said, all I saw was silhouettes. So they were black in a way, weren't they?"

Willows said, "D'you remember anything about the way the man who went into the store was dressed?"

Beverly sipped at her Pepsi, delicately licked her lips. "I'm sorry, but I couldn't actually be sure that he was even wearing clothes. Because, like I keep telling you, all I saw was silhouettes. But I do remember that the driver was smoking, because there were sparks when he flipped his cigarette into the street, and then a car went by and there were a bunch more sparks."

"The smoker. Did you see his face?"

"No, not at all."

"When the other guy got out of the truck, didn't a light go on inside the cab?'

Beverly thought about it for a long time. Or maybe she was thinking about Bill. Or Brian. Finally she said, "There wasn't any light."

"You're sure?"

"Yes, I'm sure. Or if there was, I don't remember."

Parker said, "Let me ask you again about the truck. Brian thought it might be red or black or even dark brown . . ."

"It was definitely red. And it had a kind of a thing that stuck out over the windshield, like an extension of the roof, a visor."

"Red, with a visor," said Parker, taking notes.

"Really bright, like Chinese Red lipstick." Beverly smiled at Willows.

Willows smiled right back at her, tooth for tooth. He said, "Would you mind coming downtown with us, look through a few catalogues, see if we can pin down that truck . . ."

Beverly said, "Anything you say . . ." She rolled the Pepsi can across her forehead. "It's hot in here, isn't it, or is it just me? Or is it this sweater?" She gave Willows a coolly appraising look. "D'you mind waiting a minute, while I change into something a little more comfortable?"

Parker said, "Go ahead, take your time."

Beverly put her can of Pepsi down on the counter. She hadn't stopped looking at Willows. Speaking directly to him, she said, "Back in a flash." As she strolled towards her bedroom, she lifted the sweater up over her head and tossed it on a chair, gave her long blonde hair a shake.

Parker locked eyes with Willows, silently dared him to look anywhere but at her. Willows wondered if Beverly Novik would take a moment to get dressed before she came back out of her bedroom.

Somehow he doubted it.

He concentrated hard on a mental image of Suzie Spinello.

16

Drifting along like a huge bottom-feeder, the corpse snagged on a coiled length of rust-bitten steel cable. The body pirouetted like a drunken dancer as the tide rose and fell. Finally it broke free.

It continued its solitary journey until it bumped against the underbelly of one of the many splayed fingers of the Coal Harbour Yacht Club. The cadaver lay there, belly up, blank white eyes staring up through a narrow crack in the cedar planks.

In time a school of perch happened upon the corpse. They hardly knew what to make of it.

The fish nibbled, and moved on.

17

Harold hung his banana-yellow suit jacket over the back of his black leather wing-chair with the gold-plated studs. He thumped down into the chair and wheeled it a little closer to his justly famous desk, a star-shaped slab of gold-plated stainless steel that was two inches thick and ten feet across. Even though the desk was hollow, it weighed close to a ton. Harold had a habit of rapidly pounding the desk with a rubber mallet whenever he felt the need to forcefully make a point. The sound the desk gave off was apocalyptic, reeked of doom. Intimidated by the hammer, and Harold's rage, and all that noise, the unfortunate objects of his little tantrums rarely failed to buckle under.

Harold buzzed Tiffany and told her he desperately wanted a double-shot latte double-desperate quick. The mountain of urgent messages that had piled up on his desk during the lunch hour was not much smaller than Vesuvius. He snapped his suspenders and got down to work.

Work, work, work.

At three minutes past five he speed-dialled his wife, Joan, and told her in syrupy, apologetic tones that the Borneo deal was driving him crazy, he'd be stuck at the office until at least eleven, eleven-thirty. Joan was sympathetic. Harold explained that a vital piece of machinery had failed, he was working with the team to get parts to the site, but the situation was complicated by a glitch with the telephone lines, or the satellite had malfunctioned, some kind of foul-up. He had no choice but to stick tight to his desk, keep trying to get through.

Poor Harold, said Joan.

He told her not to keep dinner, that Tiff had made him a pot of coffee and he planned to order takeout from Tim Hortons, so he'd be just fine, don't worry about him, but he had to get that Borneo beast under some semblance of control.

Joan asked him what time it was in Borneo. She asked him, wasn't it late, or the wee small hours of the morning? Wouldn't everybody have gone home to bed by now?

The time-zone query. God bless predictability. Harold told Joan she was absolutely right about the time, but that the unholy hour meant nothing to men who were looking at the kind of bonuses he'd promised, if deadlines were met. If Harold's delivery was a little stilted, it was because he was reading from notes he'd written in large, easy-to-read block letters on legal-size bond stationery.

Joan said she might give him a ring about ten, if he wasn't home by then. Harold said that would be fine, he looked forward to her call. He warned her that his stomach was bothering him. If he didn't pick up, don't fret, he was sequestered in the can.

Sequestered? Joan chuckled at his choice of words. Harold frowned. Better she'd been amused by his deliberate little joke about ordering out from Tim Hortons.

He abruptly told her he had a call, had to run. Joan blew him a kiss down the wire. She told him she loved him.

Me too, said Harold.

He left the office at six sharp, called Melanie from the car phone, as he exited the parking lot. Melanie picked up on the first ring, a habit he found endearing. He told her he was en route. Did she get the flowers?

Melanie lived at a condo Harold had bought as an investment, a top-floor corner unit in one of the new towers on the north side of False Creek. She'd left her door off the latch, even though he had a key. Harold shut the door behind him, and locked it, and there she was, offering him her mouth and a drink. Harold kissed her and drank half his rye and ginger and kissed her again, emptied the glass. As usual, she looked enchanting, even spectacular.

Melanie wore open-toed shoes with spike heels that elevated her to a point where she was only an inch or two shorter than Harold. Her dress was sultry, low-cut, vampire-red. Fashioned of a soft, clingy material that looked like crushed velvet, it clung to every delicious curve on her delicious body, and threw off dully glowing sparks of light whenever she moved, which was more or less constantly. Harold summoned up his creative energies. He told her she looked great. He told her he'd like to be sequestered with her.

Melanie smiled dreamily, and drifted away to freshen his drink.

Following the routine they'd established, Harold shed his suit and took a solitary shower. Melanie had laid out a change of clothes for him – a pale-blue shirt, tan slacks, a baby-blanket-blue cardigan, wheat-coloured linen jacket. The clothes were expensive but had been bought off the rack. Off the rack! Harold had a hard-earned reputation for flamboyant taste. The clothes were intended to lend him a certain degree of anonymity, when he was out on the town with his babe. But what a price to pay.

Melanie, knowing how he felt, told him he was a handsome devil. She fiddled with the knot of his tie, helped him get his ponytail centred, tied down at an angle that was jaunty but not too jaunty.

She handed him his drink. Harold slid open the wide glass door and they went out on the balcony, leaned against the rail. The balcony offered views to the south and west. Harold looked across False Creek at the drab, huddled architecture of the co-ops. The coops. Subsidized housing, on some of the most valuable land in the whole fucking city. Brilliant.

He studied the ranks of sailboats moored at a small marina in the shadow of the Granville Street Bridge. There were fifty or sixty boats down there, live-aboards, mostly. He had never seen any of those boats move so much as a single goddamn inch. It was as if they were chained in place, rooted to the spot. He tilted his ear to the low hum of traffic from three bridges. His critical eye roved across the sparkly blue water.

Melanie had made a reservation for seven o'clock at Monk McQueen's, a seafood restaurant on Granville Island. Melanie drove her leased Acura. The payments were a little under five hundred a month, but Harold, unaware she was double-billing, didn't begrudge her a penny of it.

It was warm enough to eat outside, on the deck with its view of False Creek, the marina, highrises. Not that Harold was the outdoors type, a lover of urban scenery, the endless parade. The only thing he liked about being outside was the chance to burn a cigar.

They finished dinner at eight-thirty. Melanie said she'd had a little too much wine, and insisted on taking a stroll along the waterfront before driving back to the apartment. They walked east for fifteen minutes, following the wide, meandering path along the seawall, until they came upon a wooden bench.

She asked Harold if he'd like to sit down for a minute. Harold was too winded to speak. He shrugged casually. Why not? He sat downwind of her, puffed on his cigar and idly watched the endless stream of lights that flickered across the city's bridges, listened with half an ear to the evening serenade of emergency sirens. Melanie was apparently in no mood for casual conversation. She seemed content just to be there, in his company. Fine. For now. Harold smoked his cigar down to the label and tossed it into the water. A gull dipped low to investigate the cause of the splash, flared away with an angry squawk.

Melanie stood up. Harold took his cue. By the time they'd walked back to the car he was breathing heavily again, dripping sweat.

She waited until Harold had fastened his seatbelt, then drove the Acura sedately back to the apartment.

Her apartment lit up at 9:27. She'd left the balcony door open a crack. She pulled the door shut. Ozzie's fingers were perched like the legs of a large albino spider across the frame of his binoculars. He adjusted the focus, had a sharp picture of her for a split second, and then she turned and vanished into the depths of the apartment.

Ozzie sat there in his truck, fuming. He rolled down his window and told an elderly man walking a Dalmatian that, if that ugly fucking mutt tried to piss on his fucking tires, he'd fucking rip the goddamn spots off it, and shove it right through that fucking chain-link fence over there.

The apartment went black. By the grim green glow of Ozzie's Timex, it was exactly 9:34.

Ozzie was still sitting in his truck, still fuming, when Harold left the building at 11:25. The Rolls crept through the city at or below the speed limit, as Harold drove back to his Shaughnessy mansion. Ozzie found Harold's habit of never signalling turns particularly annoying.

It was 11:57 by the Chevy's dashboard clock when Harold wheeled the Rolls' blunt nose into the gently curving driveway of his Balfour Avenue home. He'd made it home a scant three minutes before the self-imposed deadline he never missed, no matter what luscious incentives Melanie offered to the contrary.

Ozzie cruised slowly past the house. He was rewarded with a view of the garage door engulfing the Rolls. He cruised along Balfour, made a left on Selkirk. If there was a street in Shaughnessy that followed a straight line for more than a hundred yards, he'd never found it. Gleaming Volvo or Saab station wagons squatted in the driveways of many of the well-tended acre and half-acre lots. Ozzie had observed that these vehicles were usually driven by the family nanny. The home-owners tended to drive glossy Mercedes, Jaguars, the odd Lexus.

Everywhere Ozzie looked, the lawns had been recently cut, the gardens were trim. Flowers were abundant. Trees grew straight and tall. Houses in this neighbourhood were priced at anywhere between two and thirteen million dollars. As he idled his truck slowly down the tree-lined street, he thought about what it must be like to roll out of bed in a joint like that. Know that your world was in order and that everything was taken care of.

Dull.

He drove back to his apartment, slouched down on his grungy second-hand sofa, drank some beer and watched a little TV, and then went to bed.

The next morning the alarm woke him at eight. He lay there for a few minutes, scheming, then got up and had a quick shower, shaved. He dressed in black jeans and a black golf shirt, white socks and a pair of almost-brand-new black Reeboks with white stripes.

He left the apartment, drove to the Denny's on West Broadway, bought a copy of the *Province* from a metal box on the street, and went inside and was promptly led to a table near the window. He ordered coffee, a small glass of orange juice, scrambled eggs, sausages and pancakes, whole-wheat toast and extra peanut butter. The waitress told him she'd bring him a selection of jams and jellies, he could choose whatever he wanted.

Ozzie said he didn't want any jams, he didn't want any jellies. All he wanted was peanut butter. Lots of peanut butter. He leaned back against the plum-coloured upholstered booth and told her this was a special day for him, and he was starting it the best way he could think of, with breakfast at his favourite restaurant. The last thing he wanted was to eat his way through all that food and then have everything spoiled right at the last moment because of a lack of something as basic as peanut butter. Toast without peanut butter was like Bogart without Betty Joan Perske. The waitress eyed him. Lauren Bacall, explained Ozzie. Did the waitress have a special problem with peanut butter, an allergy, or something along those lines?

And could he have some coffee right away, please?

After breakfast, he drove home to find Dean perched on the concrete retaining wall in front of the building. Dean wore a dark blue windbreaker, mud-brown pants, taupe Hush Puppies. His hair was combed. He hadn't cut himself shaving. He looked up at the sound of the truck's engine but made no move to shift his ass off the wall.

Ozzie cut across the road and pulled up to the curb. He tapped the horn. Dean bounced a bright orange tennis ball, *fwap*, off the sidewalk. He reached out and caught it, barely, windmilled his arms as he struggled not to tumble off the wall. He had the look of a man who'd just wet his last pair of underpants. His face was as long as a train.

Ozzie said, "Nice ball. Where'd you get it?"

Fwap. Fwap. Fwap.

Ozzie pushed open the truck's door.

Dean said, "I took it off a dog." *Fwap.*

"Yeah? What kind of dog?"

Dean shrugged. Either didn't know or didn't care to talk about it. A small dog, Ozzie thought to himself. Ugly little yappety-yap cockapoo, one of those.

He said, "Somethin' wrong, partner?"

Fwap.

Ozzie eased down out of the truck.

Fwap.

He stepped onto the sidewalk. *Fwap.* Dean was like a spoiled little kid, refusing to speak up, answer a simple question. Ozzie snatched the ball out of the air, held it up in front of him and squeezed hard. The ball shifted into a shape that was somewhat less than spherical. He squeezed harder. The ball resisted him. He rolled it around in his hand, working the seams.

Dean said, "I phoned in like you told me to, first thing in the morning. Said I was sick. The bastard fired me. Fired me, Ozzie."

"Yeah?"

"I told him, 'Fuck you, asshole. I quit.' "

"So what's the problem?"

"Erika's got a private phone in her bedroom. On her own private line, so dad can't listen in? I gave her a call, asked her did she want to drive up to Whistler with us."

Ozzie stood rock-still. The tension flowed out of his hands and into his lean, dark-tanned face.

Bitterly, Dean said, "She told me she couldn't make it."

Ozzie resumed throttling the ball. He said, "Probably the first smart thing she ever said in her whole life."

"Told me she didn't want to see me ever again."

Ozzie laughed.

"Told me I was too old for her."

"But not too mature, I bet."

"So I tried Monika."

Ozzie looked at him.

"Left a message on her machine, told her to get back to me, if she was in the mood for a big adventure."

Ozzie said, "Get in the truck, Dean."

Dean put the palms of his hands down on the concrete and lifted himself easily off the wall, swung his Hush Puppies over the narrow strip of grass and onto the sidewalk. He started towards the truck. Ozzie waited until Dean had his back to him, then reached into his jeans and pulled out his knife, pushed the blade deep into the tennis ball and then put the knife back in his pocket. As he climbed into the truck he stuck the index and second fingers of both hands into the slit and yanked hard. The cut widened to a length of about two inches. He fitted the slit ball over Dean's nose. The ball stuck, clamped in place. Dean's face turned a shade of red that did not go well with the orange.

Ozzie slammed his door. He said, "Nobody likes a whiner." Dean lifted his hand to his face. Ozzie slapped the hand away. He said, "Leave that goddamn thing right where it is, until I tell you to take it off."

Dean took his time lighting a cigarette. He sucked smoke into his lungs, looked hard out the windshield.

The drive to Whistler took a little less than two hours. Coming into the village, it didn't seem like much at first. Metal-roofed houses high up there in the trees. A golf course. A few hotels, restaurants. The town looked like an elaborate set for a medium-budget movie. It had been three years since Ozzie had worked in Whistler, but it didn't seem to him that the place had changed all that much.

Dean said, "Why don't we get something to eat, maybe a couple beers . . ."

Ozzie drove past the village, continued north towards Pemberton for the better part of a mile and then crossed the highway and turned down a narrow asphalt road, past a sign carved in a thick slab of wood. GREEN LAKE. There was nobody behind them, no oncoming traffic. On either side, alternating every hundred feet or so, a narrow driveway vanished into scrub forest. Here and there a roofline took a bite out of the sky, or a window reflected a spear of sunlight through the spindly trees. It was very quiet. No dogs barked. No foolish birds sang.

Dean said, "How come there's no power lines?"

"Underground wiring," said Ozzie. It was weird, the things Dean noticed. Power lines. Easily victimized dogs. Under-age nymphets. They were getting close. He lifted his foot off the gas pedal. The truck lost momentum. He tapped the brakes. Was this it? He spun the wheel, hit the gas. The truck surged forward. They drove down a driveway that meandered unconvincingly through a stand of fir and cedar that suddenly gave way to half a football field's worth of uncut grass. On the far side of the lawn stood a shingled house with a red metal roof, red brick chimney.

There were no cars in the driveway, no toys in the yard. The windows were shut tight, the curtains drawn.

The netting that hung from the basketball hoop above the garage was in tatters.

A birdhouse with a roof made out of a rusty licence plate had fallen off its pole and lay at an angle in the dirt.

Ozzie cut across the driveway until the truck's left front wheel touched grass. He backed up in a semicircle, got them pointed back up the driveway for a lickety-split getaway.

Dean was perplexed. He said, "Where we going?"

"Wrong house."

Ozzie drove back to the main road, turned right. He made another right at the next driveway. This time, they drove down at least a hundred feet of road before the scrub trees gave way to another miniature clearcut. Or, yard.

The house was a full two storeys high, fashioned of peeled logs, with a hand-split cedar-shake roof. The mullioned windows were trimmed in hunter green. The local building code required a concrete foundation, but the cement had been faced with local river rock. The same stone was used in the house's three massive fireplaces and the several stepped retaining walls that led from the rear of the house down to the placid shore of Green Lake.

Ozzie parked in front of the detached log garage. He killed the engine, dropped the key in his pocket.

Dean said, "We here yet? What if somebody moved in since you checked the place out?"

Ozzie got out of the truck. As he walked down the artfully winding brick pathway to the front door, he separated the long-ago-stolen brass door key from the other keys on his chain. He took the porch steps two at a time, slipped the key into the lock and rotated it counter-clockwise, felt the deadbolt slide back. He pushed the door open and stepped into the big entrance hall.

An outsized sofa upholstered in a dark-green fabric had its back to him. On the far side of the sofa was the largest of the home's three fireplaces. Ozzie had built and faced that fireplace all by himself, almost. It had taken him six weeks of, to be truthful, not exactly backbreaking labour.

The fire was set, balls of yellowed newspaper tucked under a pyramid of kindling and split logs. There was no sign of smoke discoloration anywhere on the stones or the slab of granite that served as a mantel, and he felt a sense of quiet satisfaction. There weren't a whole lot of masons who could design and build a one-off fireplace, no specs.

The room darkened as Dean stepped into the doorway. Ozzie said, "Get rid of that cigarette. Wipe your feet before you come in. And leave the door open, air the place out a little."

A voice much deeper than Dean's said, "Yeah, okay."

Ozzie spun around so fast his heart lagged behind. Silhouetted against the door was a large man in a uniform, peaked cap. Ozzie stuck his hands in the back pockets of his jeans, fingered the haft of his knife. He told himself to be calm, inventory the situation. What he saw were epaulettes perched on broad shoulders. A tall black mass, outlined in rich midnight blue. Scattered bits of metal gleaming dully. He blinked rapidly as he waited for his eyes to adjust to the light. The way the guy was standing there, so erect, his hands on his hips, legs slightly parted, reminded him of someone.

That TV guy.

The bald TV guy. Not Telly Savalas, the other one.

Mr. Clean.

Ozzie's mind skittered every which way. Where was Dean? Hiding in the weeds, probably. Ozzie smiled, said hello. Moving cautiously towards the dim figure outlined in the doorway, he took solace in his experience with the tennis ball.

How it had seemed so tough but cut so easy.

18

Willows called the hospital from an East Hastings payphone. Sean's condition was still listed as stable. Willows was asked to hold for a moment. He stood there with the phone pressed to his ear, idly admiring the way Claire Parker's hair was backlit by the sun. The nurse was gone only a moment. She told Willows that his son was resting peacefully. He thanked her and cradled the receiver, passed the news on to Parker. He glanced up and down the sparkly street. It wasn't a great neighbourhood for restaurants. But then, Parker probably wasn't hungry anyway. He checked his watch.

Parker said, "Want to get something to eat?"

Willows managed to look mildly surprised. "You hungry?"

"Not really."

Cruising, they passed on several chain restaurants, and then came upon a mom-'n'-pop operation that Willows had driven by countless times, and never given a moment's thought. There was an OPEN sign in the window. Parker noticed that the glass was clean. Willows parked at the end of the block and they walked back. Gaudy clusters of yellow and purple pansies overflowed a flower box by the window. A bell tinkled merrily as Willows opened the door. There were three booths to his right, the cash register and a five-stool counter on his left. Nobody at the counter. Three men sat in the booth closest to the kitchen.

A voice from the back, somebody's grandmother, cheerfully said, "I'll be with you in a minute . . ."

Willows had a view of the backs of two heads, one of them bald. The third man, curly black hair, heavy black eyebrows, unshaven, a black sleeveless T-shirt, heavy gold chains, sat facing him. The man glanced at him, dismissed him, returned to his conversation. Parker walked over to the middle booth, and sat down. Willows would have preferred the booth nearest the door, but let it pass. Parker picked up a menu. Willows sat opposite her. He was facing the restaurant's entrance. The three men were directly behind him. Uncomfortable with the situation, he eased over so he was sitting at an angle to Parker and had his back to the wall.

A miniature jukebox, heavy chrome and marbled plastic, squatted by his elbow. He flipped through the available selections. Roy Orbison. Elvis. Jerry Lee Lewis. Ricky Nelson.

Grandmother came out of the kitchen carrying three heavy oval plates. Willows studied the order. A fat clubhouse sandwich, hamburgers, French fries, tidy domes of coleslaw. His mouth watered. He checked the menu to see if the restaurant was licensed. No such luck.

The woman who served them was in her mid-sixties. Her silver hair was piled up on her head like a towering, billowy cloudbank. Tarnished silver moons and stars dangled from her ears. Her pale grey eyes grazed like sheep in a field of lush green eyeshadow. Her long eyelashes were black and spiky as a picket fence. Her lipstick and nail polish were a lustrous flag-red. When she smiled, jagged fault lines bloomed all across her makeup.

Parker ordered a veggie burger with a side salad, Diet Coke. Willows chose a deluxe burger with cheese and bacon, extra onion. Fries. He decided to risk the coffee.

The woman smilingly assured them the food would be ready in a few minutes, and that she'd be right back with their drinks.

Parker waited until the woman was out of earshot and then said, "I meant to tell you, Jack, ballistics have got all the lands and grooves they need to make a comparison."

"Now all we need's the gun, and the guy who owns it."

The waitress arrived with their drinks.

Willows emptied a container of cream into his coffee. He sipped and flinched. Dabbing at his mouth with a napkin, he pushed the cup away.

Parker smiled. "That bad?"

"Toxic."

Parker popped the tab on her Coke and poured about half the can into her glass. "Spears ran the truck. Red, black, even burnt orange. He went back five years and came up with a big fat zero."

Willows nodded glumly. The descriptions they had of the men who'd robbed the convenience store were vague to the point of being useless. They had no usable prints, nothing much from Sean. All they had, really, was an unreliable description of the truck. An older model, with a rounded body shape and a split windshield. Willows believed his best hope, based on the shooter's highly irrational *modus operandi*, was that the men were drug addicts who would rob again and again until they were caught.

He delved deeper into the jukebox's table of contents. Little Richard. Chubby Checker.

The burgers arrived. Grandma banged ketchup and vinegar bottles down on the table. "Anything else?"

Willows glanced at Parker. He said, "We're fine for now."

The woman nodded. The man in the gold chains snapped his fingers and called for his bill.

Willows took a bite out of his hamburger. He chewed slowly. His face became contemplative. He put the hamburger down on his plate, reached for a napkin.

Parker said, "Something wrong?"

Willows deposited the partially chewed hamburger into the depths of the napkin. Something was wrong, all right. Very wrong. In all his life, he had never tasted anything quite so foul. He washed out his mouth with some of Parker's Coke.

Parker had cut her veggie burger in half. She put down her knife, pushed away her plate.

Willows examined his hamburger. The slab of meat, or whatever it was, had been thoroughly cooked. But the texture wasn't
quite right and the colour was all wrong. His stomach growled.
He sniffed gingerly at a French fry.

The waitress drifted past. She placed the bill on the table
midway between her two cop customers. "How're you folks
doing?"

"Fine," said Parker.

As they drove to the hospital, every payphone Willows passed
reminded him that he still hadn't called Sheila. His wife had a right
to know what had happened to her son. Why hadn't he called?

Sean was watching television when they arrived. He turned the
sound down but left the set on. His greeting was borderline surly.
Willows asked him how he was feeling. Sean waggled his fingers.
What did that mean? That the question was so simplistic as to not
deserve an answer? Willows took it that Sean had regained his
spirit, that he was on the mend. Obviously he still had a long way
to go. Willows reflected that when Sean was fully recovered, he'd
turn the sound *up* when his visitors arrived.

Parker said, "Has Dr. Fisher been around lately?"

"The great man. Busy busy busy." Sean fiddled with the television. "He said I'll be out of here before I know it. Whatever that
means."

"How's the arm?" said Willows.

"Numb, except when it hurts."

Willows nodded.

Parker said, "What're you watching?"

"A movie."

"What's it about?" said Parker.

"It's about this rich kid, he's about six years old. His dad's in
Europe, on a business trip. The day he left, the kid's mom was hit
by a car as she crossed the street. She's in a coma. Her purse was
stolen, and nobody knows who she is. The kid's nanny quit, eloped

with some guy. So he's all alone and this guy and his girlfriend break in, they break into the house. The kid tells them his story, he's been living out of the freezer for about a week now, and they decide to adopt him . . ."

"Kidnap him?"

"Not really. He's lonely. He thinks he's been abandoned. He hasn't got anything else going for him."

"No friends, or family?"

"He just moved from another city. Everything's still in boxes . . ."

Parker said, "Sounds interesting. Jack, why don't you see if you can find another chair . . ."

They watched the rest of the film, and then a half-hour situation comedy about a stranded alien who looked human but wasn't. A hospital volunteer, a candy-striper, offered Sean a glass of milk, his choice of cherry or lime Jell-O.

Sean managed to eat the Jell-O one-handed, without taking his eyes off the television's tiny screen.

Something was nagging at Jack.

Both 911 calls, the one from the Chevron station and the one that had originated at the payphone on the street almost directly in front of the gas station, had come in at virtually the same time. Farley Spears and Dan Oikawa had canvassed the neighbourhood in an attempt to find out who had made the payphone call, and come up empty.

But *somebody* had made the call.

Had Spears or Oikawa checked with BC TEL to find out if a call had originated from the payphone before or after the Chevron 911 call? Willows reasoned that whoever had called from the payphone might have been in the vicinity because he intended to make another, *non-emergency* call.

It was worth a shot. Willows sat there, mulling over possibilities, until the sitcom ended in another burst of taped laughter. Standing, he went over to the bed and awkwardly kissed his son on the cheek, and told him he'd try to get back some time in the evening. Sean asked him if he'd mind paying for the full television package, which included SuperChannel.

Parker unhesitatingly told Sean to order whatever he wanted. Right, thought Willows. What else could Sean do but read or watch television? He told himself to relax, take it easy. It was great advice, but not that easily followed. He wondered if he'd ever learn.

Oikawa's chair creaked as he leaned back. He cocked his head, leaned forward and then back again. The chair squeaked shrilly. Metal on metal. He leaned forward and then tilted the chair back. Yeah, right there. He sat upright and then gritted his teeth and tilted the chair slowly back, narrowed the range of motion to a few scant degrees. Squeak, squeak, squeak. He said, "Check with BC TEL, see if any calls other than the nine-eleven originated from the payphone at about the same time the nine-eleven was logged. If so, speak to the recipient or recipients. Is that what you're suggesting?"

Willows nodded.

Oikawa said, "Great idea, Jack. Why didn't I think of it?"

"You don't want to know," said Orwell from behind his desk.

"Not that you could tell me if I did," Oikawa shot back. To Willows he said, "We got nothing from the canvass. In fact, as you damn well know, we got nothing from nobody. How's Sean?"

"Good," said Willows.

Seeking a second opinion, Oikawa glanced at Parker.

Parker said, "Eating lime Jell-O, watching television . . ."

Oikawa smiled. "Don't tell Eddy, or we'll lose him to a self-inflicted wound."

"Tell me what?" said Orwell.

Oikawa leaned back in his chair, and fired off a volley of ear-grating squeaks and squeals.

BC TEL called back within an hour of Willows' inquiry. A call had originated from the Dunbar Street payphone seconds before the 911 call was made. The telephone company's records indicated a second call to the *same number* had been made directly after the 911 call was terminated.

The male operator asked Willows if he wanted the number.

"Please," said Willows. He repeated the number the call was made to and the subscriber's name and address to the operator as he wrote it all down, thanked him and disconnected.

Oikawa overheard the address as Willows read it back to the operator. He consulted his notebook. "Hang on a minute . . ." He pulled a beige file folder and flipped it open. "Yeah, here it is. Jay and Nora Parsons. The house is less than a block from the store. Jay was at work, but I talked to Nora. She wasn't even aware that a robbery had been committed. I asked her, don't you watch TV, read the paper? She told me she watched TV all the time, but not the news. Too depressing."

Willows checked his watch. He dialled the Parsonses' number and got an answering machine, hung up without leaving a message.

Parker said, "Nobody home?"

"Just the machine."

"Why don't we go home, see how Annie's doing, get something to eat and then drive over? Maybe somebody'll be home by the time we get there."

"Sounds good," said Willows. He felt a sharp twinge of guilt. He loved Annie so much, but a whole day could shoot past, dawn to dusk, without his giving her a moment's thought.

But when they arrived home, the house was empty. Annie had taped a note to the refrigerator. She'd been invited to dinner at Lewis'. After dinner he was going to drive her to the hospital to visit Sean. Later, they planned to go somewhere for a bite to eat. She'd be back by ten-thirty, and had a key.

Willows said, "I thought she had a ten o'clock deadline."

"She does," said Parker.

There was nothing wrong with Annie eating at Lewis'. There was nothing wrong with Lewis driving her to the hospital. There was nothing wrong with the two of them sharing a milkshake at

Bino's, or wherever. So, Willows asked himself, why was he so upset? He was still trying to work it out when he parked in front of the Parsonses' modest stucco home.

Jay Parsons answered the door. He scrutinized Parker's badge and then invited the two detectives into the house. Parsons was in his late forties, a tall, heavyset man with close-cropped reddish-brown hair, wet brown eyes. He was casually dressed in jeans and a forest-green shirt with buttoned flap pockets. He led the two detectives into the living room, indicated a sofa upholstered in pale-blue leather. "Sit down, make yourselves comfortable. Can I get you a cup of coffee, tea . . . ?"

"Thanks anyway," said Parker.

A television that was too large for the room flickered in a corner. Baseball, but the sound had been turned off. The sofa's matching loveseat was occupied by a white long-haired cat with glacier-blue eyes.

Jay Parsons rested his hip on the arm of a wine-coloured wing-chair. The table lamp cast the off-side of his face in dark shadow. Parker realized that Parsons was deliberately assuming a pose. Genial host, lord of the manor. The man in charge.

She said, "Is Nora home?"

"Excuse me?"

Parker smiled. "Your wife."

"Yes, of course." Parsons was visibly flustered. But why? He said, "It's her book-club night."

"What's she reading?" said Parker.

"I have no idea. Modern American fiction, whatever that means. Look, she spoke to Detective Oikawa yesterday afternoon. She told him that we don't know anything. She made it quite clear that she was speaking for both of us, do you understand?"

Willows said, "Who phoned you, Jay?"

Parsons gave Willows a sharp look. "What are you talking about?"

"Somebody called you from the payphone directly across the street from the store that was robbed," said Parker. "Whoever called you hung up, dialled nine-eleven to report the robbery, and called you right back."

Willows said, "It was late, past eleven. Nora was sleeping, wasn't she, when you got the call? Who were you talking to, Jay?"

Parsons' face collapsed. "You've got it all wrong."

"How d'you mean?" said Parker.

"You want to talk to Nora, not me."

The house was dark by the time Nora rolled in. She braked, flashed her high-beams at the unmarked Ford that was blocking her driveway. Willows activated the dashboard-mounted fireball. The light bloomed red, turned Nora Parsons' white Ford Escort the colour of diluted blood. Willows killed the fireball. He turned on the dome light and checked his watch. Quarter past twelve. Parker got out of the car and walked slowly over to the Escort. Nora Parsons rolled down her window. She appeared to be listening carefully. The Escort's motor died, and Parker walked through the twin beams of the headlights, around to the far side of the car. She opened the door and slipped into the car.

Willows found himself thinking about Sheila. Time zones. It was far too late to call her tonight, but he couldn't keep putting it off. He'd try to get through to her first thing in the morning.

He had filed for divorce months ago, citing irreconcilable differences. Sheila would want to talk about that. There were probably a lot of things she'd want to talk about. Discussions that wouldn't be easy, or pleasant. Not for the first time, he found himself trying to imagine her life in Mexico . . .

The Escort's interior lit up as Parker pushed open her door and the dome light came on. She got out, shut the door, walked briskly towards the Ford. The Escort's starter motor whined and then the engine caught. Willows leaned across the bench seat and opened the passenger-side door. Parker got in, shut the door and fastened her seatbelt. Willows yawned wearily. He put the Ford in reverse. He slammed on the brakes as the Escort shot past, no lights.

Willows said, "Learn anything?"

"Jay's been fooling around for years. Younger women, mostly. She was going to find a shabby little apartment somewhere, move out of the house and try to start all over again. Then she met Charles."

Willows pulled away from the curb. They drove slowly towards the end of the block. He made a right, hit the gas.

Parker said, "Charles has domestic problems of his own, apparently. He had an argument with his wife, drove across town, made the call, asked her to meet him. He saw the truck pull up in front of the store, a man get out and go inside. He heard the shot. Nora told him to dial nine-eleven, hung up on him . . ."

"We need to talk to Charles."

"That's right," agreed Parker. "But Nora won't give him up."

Willows smiled. Feisty Nora.

Parker said, "She's going to call him first thing in the morning, as soon as he gets to work. If he refuses to talk to us, she'll roll him over."

"Or go to jail," said Willows.

"That's what I told her."

Willows pushed Annie's door wide open, so the hall light would fall on her. Annie lay on her side, her lightly clasped hands by her face, as if she'd fallen asleep in the middle of a prayer. Willows eased shut the door and tiptoed back downstairs. Parker was in the den, curled up on the sofa. She'd switched on the gas fireplace. Willows asked her if she'd like a drink and she said no. He went into the kitchen and poured half an inch of Cutty Sark into a lowball glass, got ice from the refrigerator and went back into the den.

Parker said, "Annie okay?"

"Sleeping like a baby."

The gas fire burned silently. No snap, no crackle, no pop. Willows missed it all. What he didn't miss was the need to buy and store wood, split kindling, eat smoke.

Parker said, "Don't worry about her, Jack."

Willows toyed with his glass, made the ice cubes rattle.

Parker said, "Because there's no chance in the world that she'll turn out like Nora Parsons."

"Or Jay, either."

Parker smiled. She took the lowball glass out of Willows' hand, sipped delicately at the Scotch.

He said, "I'm going to call the hospital, make sure Sean's okay."

"You do that," said Parker. She handed his glass back to him. "Then what?"

"Straight to bed."

"Right," said Parker.

19

The cable guy had just completed a service call, happened to see Ozzie and Dean drive by, and stopped as a courtesy. His name tag said RICHARD. He was tall, about six-foot-two, a trim two-hundred-pounder. Blond hair combed straight back, hazel eyes with tints of gold. He knew for a fact that the cable had been cancelled about a year ago, but, if Ozzie was interested, he could offer him a reinstallation special, a very attractive package deal on SuperChannel, Disney, a trio of U.S. superstations. This limited-time offer was ending that very same day.

Ozzie waffled. He was just moving in, hadn't really had time to think about his entertainment priorities. . . . The company must've had some kind of incentive plan, because Richard pushed hard, told Ozzie and Dean all about the wonders of cable, what a great deal he was offering. Was he legit? Ozzie checked out the leather belt loaded down with screwdrivers and crimpers, other equipment he couldn't identify, but looked specialized. He asked Richard how long it would take to get the system up and running. Fifteen minutes, tops.

Really? That swift? Ozzie asked him if he'd ever met Jim Carrey. Who?

The comedian, starred in a movie called *The Cable Guy*.

The real cable guy, the genuine article, told him he'd never heard of Jim Carrey or the movie. He volunteered that he didn't get out of Whistler a whole lot. So, did Ozzie want his line hooked up, or what?

Ozzie figured, what the hell. All he'd have to do was sign a piece of paper. By the time the bill arrived he'd be long gone. In the meantime, free TV. Something to entertain Dean, when his brain was disengaged. He told Richard to go ahead, followed him outside and around the side of the house to a grey plastic box with wires running in and out of it. Richard popped the box's lid, fiddled around in there, muttering. He finished with the box, told Ozzie he had to do some work on the power pole out in front of the house. Climbed into his truck and drove away, was back in ten minutes.

Ozzie led him inside, let him turn on the TV. He stared down at the back of Richard's easily snapped neck as he crouched in front of the set, flipping through picture-perfect channels. "Charlie's Angels." "Baywatch." Ozzie signed the papers, his careful scrawl perfectly illegible.

When Richard had finally left, Ozzie and Dean roamed all over the house, checking it out. They decided to put Harold in the top-floor bedroom, at the front. If he gave them any grief, they'd stick him in the basement. There was a big freezer down there that he'd fit into real easy.

Back in the city, Dean sprawled on Ozzie's sofa, unscrewed the cap from a bottle of Kokanee. He tossed the cap out the open window, guzzled the top half of the bottle and assumed the position of a man who was wide awake, and listening with both ears.

"Hit it, partner!"

Ozzie pushed the tape recorder's play button. The machine hissed sibilantly. He fine-tuned the volume. James Cagney said a few terse words, and then an actress whose voice Dean failed to recognize added a short clip. The message in its entirety lasted eleven seconds.

Ozzie rewound the tape.

Dean said, "Cagney. Bogart."

"Yeah, and who else?"

Dean drank some more beer.

Ozzie said, "Bette Midler . . ."

"Bullshit."

"From *Beaches*," said Ozzie. "That bit where she . . ." He trailed off. Dean had forgotten all about him, was holding his beer bottle up to the light pouring in through the window. Ozzie watched him tilt the bottle into the light, give it a shake. Dean's eyes widened. He marvelled at whatever it was he saw.

Ozzie said, "Dean?"

"Yeah, what?"

"Nothing, forget it."

"Consider it done," said Dean. He drank some more beer, sighed as if something was bothering him but he couldn't decide what that something might be.

Ozzie went into the kitchen, wriggled his fingers into his unlined black leather gloves and scooped up an even dozen pre-addressed envelopes off the Formica counter. He fumbled in his pocket for his keys, shook them and made them rattle.

"Time to hit the road, buddy."

"Yeah, okay."

Ozzie listened to the sound of the beer racing out of the bottle, Dean's drawn-out belch, the hard thump of the bottle hitting the oak-veneer coffee table.

Twenty minutes later, Ozzie parked and locked the truck, led Dean down a scruffy alley and up a side street and two blocks along East Pender, to a car-rental outlet.

The woman behind the counter was in her early twenties, professionally bleached, slim, blessed with a dizzy smile sudden as a broken window. Ozzie said hello, rested his elbows on the counter and told her he'd phoned ahead, reserved a Chrysler minivan. He spelled out a name for her, nice and slow, that Dean had never heard of. A strange name, the name of a stranger. Mike Newman.

Ozzie's wallet was slim and brown, but Mike's was thick and black. Dean gave him a sideways look.

The woman tap-danced her fingers across a grimy keyboard, verified Mike Newman's full name and address, occupation. Because Mr. Newman had no credit card, she required two references. Or, if he owned a vehicle, his registration papers.

The woman asked Ozzie how long he had been working at his current job, and how long he'd had his current phone number.

Dean told her she could have his number too, anytime she wanted.

Strike one.

The woman smiled at Ozzie. She needed a $550 cash deposit. Ozzie pulled a fat wad of bills out of the black wallet. There were papers to be filled out, crucial details regarding insurance coverage and the proper use of the ashtray.

He signed on the dotted line.

Dean asked her if she'd like his autograph, told her he'd write his name on her anywhere she liked.

Strike two.

The woman handed Ozzie the keys, raked her fingers through her hair, hit him below the belt with another blistering smile. "Have a nice ride . . ."

"I'd love to," said Dean. The woman gave him a look that would have shrivelled a lesser man's balls.

Strike three. But at least he'd gone down swinging.

The van was down at the far end of the lot, parked in the shade of the neighbouring building. Ozzie had asked for a neutral colour, something that didn't make too bold a statement. He was pleased to see that the van was an instantly forgettable shade of green. He said, "What d'you get out of it?"

"Outta what?" said Dean. He lit a cigarette.

"Hassling women."

Dean looked at him. Smoke poured out between the words as he said, "What the hell are you talkin' about?"

"That woman back there."

"What woman?" Dean glanced back over his shoulder. He grinned. "Oh, her. C'mon, don't tell me you didn't notice the way she kept checking me out, running her fingers through her hair, licking her lips. Only reason I talked to her was I didn't want to hurt her feelings. You want me to be aloof? Sorry, but that just ain't me." He lit a cigarette. "Who the hell is Mike Newman?"

Ozzie shrugged. "Beats me."

"Where'd you get the wallet?"

"Off a guy was loitering in the wrong neighbourhood." Ozzie gave Dean a look. Like, where d'you get *your* wallets? He unlocked the van's door, slid in behind the wheel and leaned across the bucket seat to unlock the passenger door. Dean climbed in. The van seated eight. The glass, except for the windshield, was tinted black.

Ozzie drove to Harold's office, and punched the little button below the speedometer. A row of zeros popped up on the trip odometer. He noted the time and then drove in as straight a line as possible to Melanie's apartment, parked across the street and let the van idle as he located her balcony and pointed it out, so Dean would know which one it was.

Dean said, "With the bicycle?"

"No, not that one. Bicycle? Don't make me laugh. Two up. The white table with the striped umbrella. See it?"

"Yeah, I see it. We're not going up there, are we?"

"Not unless something goes wrong," said Ozzie, pissed. The reason he'd pointed out Melanie's apartment was because he wanted Dean to have some appreciation of the time he'd spent researching Harold, learning about the various aspects of his life. Why was Dean being such a hard-ass? He decided it must be jealousy. Dean was hot because the car-rental woman had ignored him, but flirted with Ozzie.

He told Dean about Harold's routine, how Harold liked to have a glass of wine, or whatever, before taking Melanie out to dinner.

Dean made immature remarks about where he'd like to take Melanie, if he ever got the chance, and what he'd like to do with her when he got there. Ozzie tuned him out. He remembered to check his watch, check and reset the odometer. He drove back to Harold's office on Howe Street. Same distance, similar elapsed time. He drove north on Howe to Pender, made a left and cruised down Pender until it merged with Georgia.

Dean said, "Where we going?"

Ozzie turned on the radio, found the all-news station and cranked the volume loud enough to discourage casual conversation. The light at Granville and Sixteenth was red. He tapped the brakes, came to a full stop behind a shiny black Mercedes. Next to him in the left-hand lane was a tan-coloured Mercedes. He thought how terrible a thing it must be, to be sitting snug and smug in your Mercedes-Benz, have Harold pull up beside you in his Rolls, turn you and your whole life into an abject failure in the blink of an eye.

The light changed. They drove up Granville for a few blocks and then Ozzie made a right. He loved these streets, these gracefully winding, silent, tree-lined streets. There wasn't a scrap of litter anywhere. No one leaned against a lamppost, smoking and spitting. He loved the tall green hedges and the walls of cut granite, the big houses with their complicated architecture, imposing porches, leaded-glass windows. His left hand draped limply across the top of the steering wheel, he told Dean everything he knew about Harold's routine on the nights he met Melanie, and when he was a good boy and went straight home to bed.

He made a few more turns and found himself on Balfour, travelling in the wrong direction. He turned into a gated driveway, checked the traffic and cautiously backed out.

Dean said, "You lost?"

A guy in blue coveralls and black gumboots was peering myopically at them. Ozzie waved. The guy didn't wave back.

A few minutes later, Ozzie pulled over to the curb and pointed out the tall boxwood hedge, the great big empty house that he knew had been slated for demolition or major renovations because the trees in the yard and on the boulevard had been boxed in with bright-orange plastic mesh. He pointed out the crumbling garage where they could park the van and not be seen from the street, wait for Harold to cruise past in the Rolls.

Dean said, "You said we were going to grab him at Melanie's, in the parking lot."

"That's right. But what if we miss him? What if there's somebody else in the parking lot when he leaves?"

"Witnesses?"

"Yeah, you could call them that."

Dean made a fist, stuck out his index finger and pulled back his thumb.

Ozzie said, "Shoot 'em? Is that what you'd do?"

"Shoot the men, keep the women," said Dean. "Pow!"

Ozzie drove a little way further down Balfour. He wanted Dean to see Harold Wismer's multimillion-dollar house, because he thought it might help him understand that he'd never have to work another day in his lazy-ass life, if they managed to pull the job off.

Dean liked the big wrought-iron gate at the end of the driveway. He told Ozzie he hated that black-enamelled aluminum crap people used nowadays.

Ozzie kept driving. The way he saw it, Joan would roll over and cough up the five million, or she'd dicker with him, try to save herself a few bucks. Either way was fine with him. If Joan balked at five, two would do the trick. Or even one. The important thing was not to get bogged down in negotiations.

Looking at the situation objectively, Joan had a third option. She could choose to ignore his warning, pick up the phone, call the cops. If that's what happened, he'd cancel the operation, lie low for another year and then start all over again.

Either way, Harold was deader than Bogart.

Dean, too.

20

Despite Willows' best efforts, the investigation into the shooting had already begun to tail off. Nora Parsons' boyfriend, once he had decided to co-operate, had told Willows and Parker the shooter's pickup truck was red, about the same shade of red as a fire engine. But that's all he had been able to tell them, other than to verify that there were two men involved in the robbery and that they were both white.

Willows was at his desk when his telephone warbled. He picked up, identified himself.

"Jerry Goldstein, Jack. How's your son coming along?"

"Fine," said Willows. Goldstein was a cautious man. He'd have checked with the hospital for an update on Sean before he risked asking Willows how he was doing.

"Glad to hear it," said Goldstein. He paused, shifting gears. "I might have something for you, Jack."

"Spit it out, Jerry."

Willows' voice was tight. Parker's metal desk butted up against his, nose to nose. He sensed that she was watching him, tuned in to his every gesture and every word.

Goldstein said, "A little over a year ago, there was a kidnapping that went all wrong. The victim was a stock promoter named Ronald LeGrand."

Willows hadn't been involved in the case, but he remembered LeGrand. One of his properties, a mine in the Northwest Territories, had netted him eight million dollars and never produced an ounce of gold. He'd been cruising the outer harbour on his yacht with his wife and child when he'd been snatched. A member of the crew had been shot and wounded.

The kidnappers had demanded five million dollars. LeGrand's waterfront home had been wiretapped, surveilled. His wife had agreed to pay the five million, but something – nobody ever knew what – had gone drastically wrong.

LeGrand had turned up in a suburban drainpipe six months later, with a bullet in his head. His widow had threatened to sue. The department had weathered a storm of negative publicity.

Willows said, "Yeah, I remember the case." There had been speculation, at the time, that the kidnappers had been burned by one of LeGrand's many dubious and ill-fated promotions, that LeGrand had been killed because they were more interested in certain revenge than a dubious payoff.

Goldstein said, "We recovered the bullet that killed him, Jack. It was a nine-millimetre hollowpoint, a Winchester Black Talon."

Willows was taking notes, his fingers tight on the barrel of the pen. Various brands of hollowpoints – bullets designed to mushroom on impact and cause maximum tissue damage within the target – were used by police forces across Canada but were not available to the civilian population. On the other hand, hollowpoints were readily available in Washington State, and the border was less than an hour from downtown Vancouver. But crossing that border could be a risky proposition. And criminals were notoriously slothful, and not particularly knowledgeable. To most of them, a bullet was a bullet was a bullet.

The Black Talon was a special case. The copper-alloy jackets on most brands of hollowpoints were not designed to cause additional tissue damage. The Black Talon's six sharply curved jacket petals were made of brass rather than the softer alloys, and had been specifically designed to rip and tear tissue as they spread wide to allow the lead core to expand.

Goldstein said, "The bullet that hit your son was a Black Talon. So were the bullets we recovered from the insurance office. They were all fired from the same pistol. Firing-pin and ejection marks indicate that the pistol was a Ruger. It isn't going to solve the case, Jack, but it's something to go on with."

Willows thanked Goldstein for his help. He disconnected, and brought Parker up to speed. They agreed that the next step was to inform Inspector Homer Bradley of the connection between the two cases.

Bradley's pebble-glass office was down at the far end of the squadroom. Willows knocked. Inside, papers rattled. A dimly perceived shape rippled darkly across the glass. The door abruptly swung open, banged against the frame. Bradley stood there, swaying slightly. After a long moment he said, "Well, what a pleasant surprise."

Willows said, "Got a minute, Homer?"

"Much longer than that, one would hope." Bradley waved them inside as he made his way back to his unusually cluttered desk. He sat down heavily on his chair, leaned back and contemplated the ceiling. He slurred his words as he said, "What's up, kids?"

Had Bradley been drinking, or was he suffering an adverse reaction to an unfamiliar medication? Maybe he'd had a stroke. Willows didn't know what to think. Maybe it was best not to think anything. He glanced at Parker, but she was studiously looking out the window. He told Bradley about Goldstein's call, the probable tie-in with the LeGrand kidnapping. Bradley didn't seem much interested in what Willows had to say.

Parker said, "We thought we'd pull the file, talk to the investigating officers . . ." She hesitated. "Homer, are you okay?"

Bradley nodded. He struggled to a more upright position in his chair, managed the bottom half of a blink. He smiled wearily, and then his head fell back against the chair.

"Christ!" Parker reached for the phone, but Willows stopped her hand. He moved around the desk and checked Bradley's pulse, then leaned over him until he was almost nose to nose. He stepped back. Parker's hand was still on the telephone. Willows said, "He's been drinking."

"I don't believe it."

"Gin," said Willows. He loosened Bradley's tie and turned off his desk lamp, tracked the telephone cord to the wall jack and disconnected the line.

Parker said, "What're you going to do, just leave him there?"

"He'll sleep it off in a couple of hours. What else can we do, hide him in a body bag? Look at him. He's too drunk to stand up by himself, much less walk out of here under his own power."

Parker didn't like it – but Jack was right. What else could they do? She hit the wall switch, killing the overhead fluorescents.

Returning to her desk, she asked Orwell if he remembered who'd worked the LeGrand case. Orwell put aside his pencil and shut the file he'd been reading. This was a trick his wife, Judith, had taught him. To always make a show of giving a woman his undivided attention. He locked his fingers behind his blond bowling ball of a head and leaned back in his chair at a precarious angle.

"Yeah, I remember the case. Ronald LeGrand. King of the sleazeballs. Guy was snatched, stuffed up a drainpipe. Ended up hosting a larva party."

Parker said, "Who was the primary, Eddy?"

"Ralph."

"Kearns?"

"Yeah, Kearns." Orwell massaged his head. His close-cropped hair was no more than half an inch long, his scalp the colour of an unripe peach. His blue eyes sparkled. He said, "Memory serves, Homer turned over Ralph's open files to Bobby."

Parker went back to her desk. Willows had already accessed the file number from records and was busy searching the legal-size beige cabinets that served as a bulky metal room divider. Parker sat down at her desk. Willows slammed a drawer shut.

"If you're looking for the LeGrand file," said Parker, "try Bobby's desk."

"I did. It's locked."

Parker said, "Eddy?"

"Yeah. What?"

"Where's Bobby?"

Orwell ignored her. He unscrewed the lid of a fat brown bottle and popped several large, off-white capsules into his mouth. He chewed energetically, swallowed, offered the bottle to Parker. "Wanna try one?"

"What are they?" said Parker.

"Glucosamine sulphate in a gelatine capsule, vegetable-grade magnesium stearate lubricant. Damn things are worth their weight in gold, healthwise. But they only cost thirty cents apiece, if you buy 'em in bulk."

"What are they for?"

"Arthritis, rheumatism."

"I didn't know you had a problem."

"Preventative medicine," said Orwell. "The social fabric of this great nation is in extreme jeopardy. You ask me why?" He rubbed his forefinger and thumb briskly together, like a crazy man desperate to light a fire. "Money. Is medicare going to be around in ten years? I seriously doubt it." Orwell shook the bottle. The pills rattled like snakes. He said, "We all gotta do what we can to stay healthy."

Parker said, "Let's have a look at those."

Orwell screwed the cap back on the bottle and tossed it underhand to Parker. She slid open the top drawer of her desk, put the bottle away, and locked it.

Orwell said, "Hey, wait a minute."

"Where's Bobby?"

"Dentist. I overheard him making the appointment. You know what Bobby's like. If he could find a way to avoid it, he wouldn't even tell himself what he was up to."

Orwell got his bottle of Windex and a fat roll of paper towels out of the bottom drawer of his desk. He picked up the largest of the framed pictures of his wife and children, sprayed the glass and wiped it clean. He said, "If you pay extra, you can get keys cut out of steel."

Parker said, "I didn't know that."

"Then, if you want, you can get the key magnetized."

Orwell hit the glass with another powerful shot of Windex. He said, "A magnetized key, you want to hide it . . ." He put the bottle of Windex down on his desk and shifted his telephone an inch to the right.

Parker went over to Bobby's desk.

Orwell pushed away from his desk and started towards the squadroom's self-locking door. "I'm outta here. Better, I never was here."

A shiny, silver-coloured key clung to the underbelly of Bobby's phone. Parker pried it loose with the aid of a straightened paper clip. Willows unplugged the phone's jack and walked down to the far end of the squadroom and dumped the phone into the waste-basket next to the coffee machine. Now it wasn't Bobby's key that was missing, it was his telephone. He stripped a handful of paper towels from a roll, crumpled them and tossed them in the waste-basket on top of the phone, together with the business section from yesterday's paper. He pulled the used filter from the coffee machine and shook wet grounds over the towels and newspaper.

"Nice touch," said Parker. The desk's centre drawer had a lock, and the box and letter drawers were both controlled by a second lock. Parker tried the centre drawer first. The drawer contained a box of coloured pencils, a daisy chain of brightly coloured paper-clips, a ball of rubber bands, a disposable camera, a chrome-plated nine-millimetre pistol magazine, breath mints, a back issue of *Hustler* magazine, and several ballpoint pens, including her missing Sheaffer.

Parker slid the drawer shut and locked it, unlocked the box drawer. The LeGrand file was as thick as a city telephone book. She pulled the file and shut and locked the drawer, went over to

Orwell's desk and turned his telephone belly up. She placed the key on the metal bottom panel.

Willows said, "How d'you want to split this up?"

"Right down the middle," said Parker as she replaced Orwell's phone. She smiled up at him. "Does that seem unfair?"

"Should it?"

"Sort of, since I read faster than you do."

There were fifty-three witness reports, all of them bound together by a thick green rubber band that still had a fair amount of bounce in it. Most of the reports were no longer than a paragraph, but a few ran into several detailed pages. Willows passed the reports to Parker. The file was still large enough to be daunting. He scanned the table of contents. His heart plummeted. The damn thing was going to keep him pinned to his desk for days.

Ralph Kearns and Farley Spears had caught the LeGrand case. Kearns had been partnered with Eddy Orwell at the time, but Orwell had organized a month's unpaid leave so he could try to patch things up with Judith, and his caseload had been dumped on Spears. But only Spears could help Willows because Kearns was no longer a cop; he'd opted for early retirement a couple of years ago.

But where was Spears?

Willows started asking around, and soon learned that the detective had scheduled a late-morning appointment with his dentist for an emergency root canal, and that he wasn't expected to return to work until the following morning. Willows wondered if Spears and Bobby both shared the same dentist. Strange, that they'd made appointments on the same day.

He looked up Spears' number, punched the numbers. Spears answered on the first ring. A television blared in the background. He apologized, and turned down the sound. Willows asked him how he was doing.

Spears said, "Terrible."

Willows explained that he was researching the LeGrand case, that it was possible the perps were involved in his son's shooting.

Spears said, "You read the file?"

"Not all of it. I was hoping you might recall the highlights."

Spears was silent for a moment. Finally he said, "Far as I'm concerned, there's nothing in there that's going to help you, Jack. Ralph and I worked our asses off, we never got anywhere on that case. LeGrand was crooked as a jar full of drunken snakes. We had fifty thousand suspects. His wife loathed him. Jeez, his own mother hated the bastard's guts. By our third day on the case, me 'n' Ralph decided if he wasn't already dead, we'd have killed him."

Willows said, "If he and his wife weren't getting along, why was she ready to pay to get him back?"

"Good question, so we asked her. She said five million was a drop in the bucket, compared to the kind of dough he was making. One night we were over there, she'd been drinking, told us she was going to stick it out another five years or until his net worth hit fifty million, whichever came first. Meanwhile, she's socking away a thousand a week in her private account. Her plan, she was gonna use the money to finance the most rabid lawyer in town, eviscerate her sonofabitch husband with a dull knife." Spears laughed. "The coroner released the body, she never bothered to pick it up. She sold the house and cars, emptied the bank accounts and bought a one-way ticket to the Grand Caymans."

"Any chance she was involved in his murder?"

"I didn't think so. Neither did Ralph."

"A happy ending."

"For her," said Kearns. "The city got stuck with the cost of LeGrand's cremation." He hesitated. "Something to think about, Jack. Whoever snatched LeGrand was very, very careful. He took no chances and he took no prisoners. As soon as he smelled cop, he stuffed LeGrand up that pipe."

"Okay, Farley. Thanks for your time."

Spears said, "Hold on, there's something else. We had wiretaps on LeGrand's office, the house. His wife only got one call. I forget the details, but somebody screwed up, the tape was destroyed. But the transcript's worth reading, it's kind of weird."

"How so, Farley?"

"The kidnapper had taped his message, what he wanted to say. But it wasn't him speaking. The tape was made up of little sound bites from different movies. A word here, a sentence there. There was a theory that somebody in the film business might've been involved in the snatch, but we never got anywhere with it."

The television blared. Spears had resumed fiddling with the remote control. Willows thanked him for his help, and hung up.

21

Jake sat in front of the big picture window with his feet up on the sill. Marty lounged against a wall, reading *Sports Illustrated*. He looked up from the magazine, thinking that it was uncharacteristic of Jake to risk giving a gunman such a clear shot at him. But then, Jake acted uncharacteristically more often than not, nowadays.

The window was double-glazed and it was warm and sunny outside, but Jake was suddenly aware of a draft, a cool damp breeze that slipped up the leg of his pyjamas. His mind twitched. Suddenly he was thinking the unthinkable. How had that happened? Must be something else he could think of to worry over, other than his fuckin' prostrate . . .

Random possibilities skittered across the surface of his brain like water striders on a stagnant, scummy pond.

Butch, curled up in a muscular horseshoe shape by the fireplace, vented a startled "woof!" Rolling over on her side, she banged her massive skull against the fireplace's brick surround. End of dream. She gave Jake a wounded look, as if it were all his fault, then shut her big brown eyes and lowered her head so slowly her operating system might have been hydraulic. She had the attention span of a mayfly. More often than not, she seemed to have very little idea of what she was up to even when she was wide awake. She'd already got her tongue stuck in the mail slot twice. She'd lost her footing and fallen down the stairs so many times even Marty had lost count. It was a wonder she hadn't broken a leg.

Butch's owner, the guy Steve squibbed. There'd still been nothing on TV, or in the *Province* or any of those other papers. What'd happened to the guy's fuckin' body?

Jake had told Steve, take a ride downtown and pick up some maps or whatever that explained the speed and direction of the local ocean currents. Steve was curious as to why Jake, who got seasick watching the Discovery channel, was interested in tide charts. In the smallest words he could dredge up, Jake explained that he wanted to work out where the body had gone.

Steve got this look on his face. What's Jake talking about? What body? Jake had felt a surge of pride. Maybe there was hope for him yet. His first hit, he'd already forgotten all about it!

A shiny beige car took the corner at speed.

Jake's heart missed a beat.

Melanie beeped the horn of her leased Acura that she was so proud of even though Jake covered the payments. The car's shiny front bumper nudged the security gate. Jake was shaken by a sudden gust of anger. He'd *told* her not to bump the fuckin' gate! He'd even explained that, although the gate looked like it would stop a tank, it was made of welded aluminum, and had a baked enamel finish that was susceptible to chipping.

Marty pounded down the stairs. He yelled at Axel to go back to sleep. The front door squeaked open. Marty sauntered casually down the driveway to the gatehouse. Melanie blinked her lights. Marty took his hands out of his pockets. He waved at her, then disappeared inside the gatehouse. A moment later the gates swung open.

Melanie burned rubber up the driveway. The gates swung shut. Marty trotted after her, eating carbon monoxide and relishing the taste, judging from the goofy smile that was smeared all over his face. He'd left the light on inside the gatehouse – but then, he didn't pay the electricity bill, did he? Probably wasn't even aware there *was* an electricity bill.

Marty accompanied Melanie upstairs. He said, "Here she is, Jake." He patted his thigh and whistled at Butch. The dog struggled to her feet. Marty hooked a finger under her collar and led her towards the stairs.

Jake said, "Where ya goin'?"

"Take a stroll around the yard, sniff the flowers."

Jake nodded. Butch yanked Marty headlong down the stairs. The front door opened and then slammed shut.

Melanie wore a snug-fitting diagonally striped black-and-white striped jacket, matching skirt. The suit was reminiscent of a dead barber pole. But, somehow, she looked sensational. Jake said, "Nice outfit."

"Thank you." She mock-curtsied. That light-headed girl had apparently forgotten to wear a bra. Vertebra crackled like breakfast cereal as Jake hastily averted his eyes. But for all the rest of that long day, the memory of what he'd glimpsed would chase him around the house like an insecure puppy. Staring fixedly at the carpet, he said, "You was supposed to check in a couple days ago."

Melanie stood motionless in a beam of sunlight. She was lit up like a movie star, and twice as beautiful. She rolled her eyes.

Jake didn't like that too much. Her playing at being independent, after all he'd done to her. Oops. Correction, after all he'd done *for* her. But what was the big difference, really?

Steve and Axel wandered into the room, loitered by the stereo. Jake said, "Yeah, what?"

"We was just wondering, you need anything?"

"Ya washed da cars?"

"We haff vashed der autos from top all der vay to bottom," said Axel. He snuck a bold look at Melanie that indicated he'd be honoured to perform the exact same service on her, any time she cracked her whip.

"Find somet'ing else ta do." Jake made a gun of his fist, aimed at the narrow space between Axel's foggy blue eyes. "And stop gawkin'! Melanie's like a daughta ta me, unnerstan'?"

Axel's chunky smile faded. Jake was an old guy, half a century past his prime. But there was still heat in his watery eyes, venom in his fangs.

For example, Steve had told Axel that, shortly after he'd started working for Jake, he'd driven him to an empty warehouse, driven the Bentley right inside. There were six hoods in there, watching over a bookie named Lalo Espinoza, who'd been skimming from Jake.

Jake and Steve got out of the car. Espinoza was sitting on the floor, his back to a wall, calmly smoking a pipe. Jake crouched. He looked the bookie in the eye and then spat in his eye. He said, "Strip him naked and pound him like veal." He told Steve to stand back a few feet, and watch. Then he climbed back in his Bentley.

The hoods used their switchblades to cut away Lalo's clothes. Five of them held Lalo down on the concrete floor while the other hood pounded him with a hard rubber mallet the size of a baby sledgehammer, the kind of mallet used in automotive repair shops to knock dents out of sheet metal. Lalo's screams echoed off the walls, so it sounded to Steve as if a whole bunch of Lalos were getting mushed. After about five minutes it only took a couple of hoods to hold the bookie down, freeing up four of them to pound away on him. Then, pretty soon, nobody had to hold him.

Steve told Axel about the six mallets constantly rising and falling, how the bookie's supine body was surrounded by a swirling pink mist.

The hoods took a breather. By then Lalo was unconscious. A hood ran his fingers over Lalo's bloody, bruised and broken body. He went over to Jake and verified that all the bookie's large and small bones had been smashed.

Jake said, "Shoot da lyin' bastad."

A volley of shots made Lalo's body twitch.

Steve got back in the car. Jake pointed at him, laughed. Steve looked down at his white shirt and saw it was speckled everywhere with hundreds or perhaps thousands of tiny red dots.

So when Jake turned his watery eyes on Axel and warned him off staring at Melanie, it took all Axel's powers of concentration to keep his bladder under control. He swallowed hard and said, "Jake, Marty yust drove off in der Bentley. Me and Steve could sweep the garage until he gets back."

Jake flicked his fingers at him. "Nah, ya betta stick aroun', I might need ya services. But no more oglin', or I'm gonna pull ya eyes outta ya head wit a pair a rusty pliers." He patted the arm of his chair. "C'mere, babe, put yaself down here nex' ta me, nice 'n' close."

Melanie's delighted laughter was a waterfall of liquid silver. Her hips churned as she strolled past Jake, circled around behind him so he lost sight of her, then circled back. She straddled the padded arm of the chair so she was directly facing him. Her skirt had ridden high up on her silky thighs. Her knees were level with his sunken chest.

Steve and Axel studied the ceiling.

Jake's nose twitched. He asked after her perfume.

"That's just me, Jake."

"Yeah?"

She toyed with the fringe of hair at the back of his liver-spotted skull.

He said, "Wanna drink?"

"Not really. Well, okay. I don't want to put you to any trouble. Maybe a glass of white, if there's a bottle open."

"Ya hear dat, Steve?"

"Coming right up, Jake."

"And gimme a Turkey onna rocks, while ya at it."

Axel said, "Iss der bartender here? Ya, he iss very tender!"

"Shaddap."

Steve scurried over to the big mahogany sideboard a carpenter pal of Jake's had converted to a liquor cabinet. He plucked a bottle of wine from the mini-fridge, uncorked and filled a glass, poured a quarter-inch of Wild Turkey bourbon into a lowball glass, added ice. He served the drinks with soft linen napkins stolen from the Sutton Place Hotel.

Jake tilted his glass against Melanie's. "Mud in der eyeballs."

"In their eyeballs," agreed Melanie.

Jake sipped and sighed, remembering the first pimp he'd buried, more than fifty years ago. Dennis, the chump from Chicago. He'd dug the grave himself. Soft ground, but it was hard work all the same. Late October, cold, raining steadily. He'd dig for half an hour or so, take out his tape measure, check his progress. Meanwhile, Dennis kept pleading for his life, making crazy promises God Himself couldn't keep. Jake constantly yelling at him to shut up, but he wouldn't. Or couldn't. Then he'd hit clay. Hardpan. It had taken him most of the rest of the day to get down another couple of feet. The light was failing as he'd rolled Dennis into his grave. Poor Dennis went *splat* as he hit the bottom of the hole.

He happened to land face up. He resumed screaming for mercy. More to shut him up than anything else, Jake flung a shovelful of muddy earth into his open mouth. Dennis had looked so surprised. So startled, and so utterly betrayed. Jake had hurried more shovelfuls of mud into his eyes . . .

He rested his splayed fingers on Melanie's thigh. "So, how's married life?"

"We're not married."

"I'm kiddin' ya. Teasin'. Harold bein' a good boy?"

"He does the best he can."

Jake nodded, not entirely understanding what she meant, but letting it go. He sat up a little straighter. Melanie adjusted the neckline of her blouse over the swell of her breasts. Paradise lost. Jake slumped back into the chair. Might as well be comfortable. He said, "Da situashun's unna control?"

"The dishwasher's been acting up." Melanie gave him a slow smile. "But that's about the extent of my problems, really."

"No crazy talk about a honeymoon, one-way trip ta da Bahamas, anyt'ing along dem lines . . . ?"

Melanie shook her head. A few drops of wine spilled over the rim of her glass and plummeted to Jake's lap. Jake willed her to go to work on him with her napkin. To no avail.

An associate had told Jake he knew a stock promoter, Harold Wismer, who'd had a deal go sour on him, was looking desperate. Jake had invited Harold over, told him he had some cash needed laundering. Harold, talking nonstop, had come up with a dozen wildly lucrative scams. Jake had introduced him to the backyard Dobermans, explained in gory detail what would happen to Harold and his entire family, generations past, present and future, if he tried to screw Jake around. Harold had turned so pale you could almost see right through him.

But he hadn't tried to back out of the deal. Jake, sucked in by the prospect of doubling or even tripling his net worth, had emptied his vault into Harold's lap. Harold had given him a time frame, and exceeded it. Jake was growing increasingly distraught. Pissed, even. Where were his triple-digit profits, or even his fuckin' original investment? Melanie was doing her best to find out. Or so she said. Jake looked down at his pants. The wine stains were the diameter of .45-calibre bulletholes.

Jake rattled his ice at Steve, who snatched the glass out of his hand and trotted over to the sideboard and was back with the refill in jig time. Jake sipped at his Turkey. He said, "Guy ain't been onna phone ta his travel agent, lookin' at pictures a palm trees, nuttin' like dat?"

"Believe me, you'd be the first to know."

Jake patted her knee. "No, baby. Ya my early warnin' system and *ya'd* be da first ta know. Thas why ya doin' wha' ya do. Excuse my Portuguese, but tha's ya fuckin' job."

Melanie slurped half her glass. Jake watched her cheeks bulge as the wine sloshed around inside her mouth. If she spat at him he'd do something awful, he just knew it.

Melanie's throat moved. She dabbed at her lips with her napkin. The front door was opened and shut. Butch's collar rattled as the dog came racing up the stairs, dragging Marty along behind as effortlessly as if he were a human-shaped helium balloon.

Marty took note of the whipped, chickenshit look in Steve and Axel's eyes. He let Butch get close enough to the chair to have a no-touch sniff at Melanie. Jake was crazy about Butch, but that could change quicker than the weather. Butch was a little on the rambunctious side. She'd already chewed up a couple of grand's worth of furniture, and had a tendency to knock stuff over and not even notice. It was kind of funny, when vases shattered. It hadn't been the least bit funny when, two days before, she'd knocked Jake flying.

The old killer had reacted instinctively. Screaming with fear and rage, he'd yanked Marty's pistol out of his shoulder rig. He'd fired three times before finally getting his trigger finger under control. The first shot drilled the fireplace mantel. The second shattered a picture Marty had always liked. The third and last shot punched a hole in the picture window.

Butch, sensing she was in mortal danger, hunched her back and messed the carpet.

First things first. Marty had retrieved and reloaded his pistol, got Axel busy cleaning up, and then put on a tie and jacket and followed the trajectory of Jake's last shot to the house across the street. To his untutored eye the house had several major design elements in common with the starkly white church that squatted on the corner of Cypress and West Twelfth.

The house was set a hundred feet back from the lot line, at the end of a gravel driveway. Nobody answered when Marty rang the bell at the gate. He climbed over the gate and walked down the driveway until the sound of the rock crunching underfoot started to get to him, then cut diagonally across the emerald-green lawn.

A family of bronze deer, an eight-point buck and a doe and a cute little speckled Bambi-type fawn, grazed in the lee of the rose garden. Marty thought it would be kind of neat if Jake'd shot one of them, but it was not to be. The house had an empty feel to it. The curtains were drawn. There were no cars in the driveway or newspapers on the porch, or any sign of life at all, that he could see. He followed a narrow, pink concrete sidewalk around the side of the house to the cedar-fenced and gated backyard. A shot from Jake's window would have gone straight down that same path.

Spring-loaded hinges squeaked discreetly as he pushed open the gate. He stepped into the backyard, eased the gate shut. The swimming pool was right in front of him, a perfect circle about fifty feet in diameter, which looked like a huge blue eye. On the far side of the pool there was a stand of bamboo, and hard by the bamboo a glass-topped patio table with white-painted tubular steel legs, four tubular steel chairs with pastel cushions. A long-haired wig lay on the table, limp as a freshly-skinned pelt. In the chair most directly facing the pool sat a naked, somewhat anaemic middle-aged man.

An open package of Player's cigarettes covered the man's genitals. An unlit cigarette dangled from his mouth. A dark green Bic disposable lighter and several loose cigarettes lay scattered on the tiles at his feet. The man's eyes were open. He seemed to be staring straight at Marty, squinting into the sunlight, the glare of the pool.

Marty saw right away that there was no point in introducing himself. He walked over to the table, tilted the man's head back. The bullet had left a small dark hole about an inch above the eyebrow. It had not exited the skull. The chair was clean. There was hardly any blood at all, nothing but a thin, dark red line that ran vertically from the fatal wound to the eyebrow, where it made a sharp left across the bridge of the nose and trickled into the eye.

A fly circled, slow as a blimp. Marty punched it to the tiles. Stepped on it and felt it crunch.

He took the cigarette from the dead man's mouth, lit up with the solid gold Ronson Jake had given him for his twenty-first.

The back door was open. He went inside. There was a foot-high stack of mail on a table in the entrance hall. The stamps on the envelopes at the bottom of the pile had been cancelled a little over two weeks ago. The machine in the den had spouted yards of fax paper. He checked the dates, read a few messages, deduced that the home's owner and his wife were on a round-the-world cruise, had been gone a month and weren't due back for another week or so.

He continued his exploration of the house. The dead man lived over the garage. His name was Tim Grant. His expired Irish passport was in the bottom drawer of his dresser. He was fifty-eight years old. Next-of-kin was his mother, Colleen Grant. There was a Belfast address. Poor Tim. A single guy, so far from home.

In an envelope hidden beneath Tim Grant's thin mattress, Marty found a plain brown envelope fat with hundreds.

He put the passport in the envelope and stuffed the envelope in his pocket.

He called a glazier he knew, who was a pal of Jake's. When darkness fell, he and Steve went back across the street, wrapped the corpse in a plastic drop-sheet and stuffed it in the back of Marty's '96 Pathfinder. Bright and early the next morning the two of them drove north for hours. Marty found a disused logging road, followed it deep into the bush. He stopped, slung Tim Grant's corpse over his shoulder and walked a quarter-mile into a clearcut. Steve did the spadework. The clearcut had already been replanted. The area would be logged again in about twenty years.

Back in the city, Marty had mailed the passport and cash across the green waters to poor Colleen.

Jake said, "Hey, where ya been?"

Marty blinked away the memory of the clearcut. He said, "Butch had an appointment with the vet to get his teeth cleaned. Guy called my cellphone on the way. Had to cancel because of an emergency. A cockapoo got whacked by a Jeep. I rescheduled for next week."

Jake frowned. "Butch gonna be okay till den?"

"Yeah, sure." Marty smiled. "Look at her, she's got teeth like a brand-new chainsaw."

Jake's hand slithered across Melanie's luscious hip. "Wanna stay for dinner, baby? Chow down ta a nice plate a Marty's special homemade ravioli wit a delicious fillin' a leeks, brazil nuts an' cashews?"

Melanie smiled across the room at Marty. Her long nails, red as chili peppers, stroked Jake's smooth skull. "Is he kidding me?"

"We're gonna start with cold zucchini soup," said Marty. "Followed by stuffed artichokes. Brown bread ice cream for dessert."

"Yeah?" Melanie licked her lips. She said, "You can cook?" She kept stroking Jake's bald head but held Marty's eye.

"I can cook up a storm," said Marty.

"Stay," said Jake.

"Okay, but if I drink too much, Marty's got to drive me home . . ."

Marty shrugged. "That'd be Jake's call, not mine."

Melanie swung her legs around, kicked off a sparkly high-heeled shoe and languidly rubbed her foot against Butch's chest. The Rott leaned into her. She took the dog's head in her hands, tugged at her floppy ears and then tilted up her massive jowls and blessed her with a lingering kiss. Butch's stubby tail swept the carpet. Melanie lifted up her flews and clicked a fingernail across her sharp white teeth.

Jake sat there, quiet but tense.

Marty and Steve and Axel stood around him in a semicircle. All of them trembling a little, like blades of grass in a hot and capricious wind.

22

Willows took the Ronald LeGrand file home with him. He plodded through it as he sat at the dining-room table. The big pot of water he'd put on the kitchen stove a quarter-hour ago had just reached full boil. The rich, mouthwatering scent of Annie's spaghetti sauce leaked out of the microwave.

In the kitchen, Parker dropped a thick handful of spaghetti into the pot, stirred it with a fork.

She popped the cork on a bottle of red wine.

Jack looked up from the file as she came into the dining room carrying the open bottle and two glasses. He shut the file and pushed it away from him, poured the wine and handed her a glass.

Annie, seated opposite him, looked up from her French text. She said, "Ronald LeGrand. File ninety-six dash eleven. Who is he?"

"A stock promoter."

"Was he murdered?"

Willows nodded.

"Can I look at his file?"

Willows shook his head.

"Just for a minute? If I promise not to look at the pictures?"

"Forget it, Annie." Willows sipped at his wine.

Parker said, "Chilean. Ten bucks. Like it?"

Willows nodded. He'd have preferred a Cutty on the rocks, but nobody likes a whiner. Plus, he and Claire had agreed without

173

wasting a lot of time talking about it that he was putting too great a strain on his liver, that it would be a good idea if he cut back a little. Unfortunately, they had very different ideas about what "a little" meant.

He drank some more wine, a measured, self-conscious sip. Parker put her glass down on the table untouched. She said, "Back in a minute."

Annie said, "Want some help with dinner?"

"No thanks, honey."

Willows put his own glass down. He followed Parker into the kitchen. "Anything *I* can do?"

"Slice the bread, if you don't mind."

There was a twisty loaf of French bread on the counter. Willows got the knife and cutting board and went to work.

Parker carried the spaghetti pot over to the sink, poured the spaghetti into a colander and rinsed it with water that had been brought to a boil in the kettle and left to simmer.

The microwave beeped. Willows abandoned the bread, went over to the microwave and swung open the door. Annie's sauce bubbled volcanically in a clear glass bowl.

Parker said, "I'll get that." She brushed past him and lifted the bowl from the microwave. Willows shut the door. What was it that he found so irresistibly sexy about crocodile oven mitts?

Parker said, "The bread, Jack."

Willows cut up a little less than half the loaf, arranged the slices on a plate and put the rest of the loaf into a plastic bag. As was often the case, he found these routine domestic chores oddly soothing.

Parker picked up two steaming plates and announced that dinner was ready. Willows trailed along behind her, carrying Annie's plate and the bread, feeling satisfactorily useful. They sat down at the table and Annie, as had become her habit, offered up a prayer of thanks. Willows listened to the words with half an ear. Should God receive a note of appreciation for the food on the table when Sean lay in the hospital, recovering from a serious gunshot wound? He guessed the key word was *recovering*. The prayer ended. He reached for the bread, snatched up the crusty heel. Devil take the hindmost.

As they ate, Willows and Parker took turns asking Annie all the standard questions about school, and received all the usual answers. As Willows mopped up the last of his sauce with his third slice of bread, he said, "How's Lewis? You two still an item?"

Annie gave him a cool look. "Excuse me?"

"The last few days, it's been Lewis this and Lewis that. Lewis, Lewis, Lewis. But tonight, nothing. I just wondered, what happened to him? Did a piano drop on him? Was he snatched off the planet by an alien spacecraft . . . ?"

Annie's face was pink. Willows faltered. He glanced at Parker, silently enlisted her aid.

Parker said, "Is something wrong, Annie?"

"He's studying for a chemistry exam."

"Aha!" said Parker.

Annie's fork clanged against her plate. "Why are you cross-examining me like this? Are you accusing me of doing something wrong?"

Parker's smile faded. Annie was genuinely angry; she looked as if she was about to burst into tears.

Willows said, "No, of course not." But why was she behaving like this? He reached out, intending to give her hand a reassuring squeeze. She pulled away, shrank back in her chair to avoid him.

Parker said, "We didn't mean to upset you, honey . . ."

Tears welled up in Annie's eyes. She pushed back her chair and fled wailing to her room.

Willows stood up. His paper napkin tumbled to the carpet.

Parker touched his arm. "Sit down, Jack. Give her a few minutes to compose herself. Then *I'll* go talk to her, okay?"

"Fine," said Willows. He was surprised to see he'd emptied his glass. He poured himself another, tilted the bottle inquiringly towards Parker.

"No thanks, I never drink and parent."

Willows cleaned up the dishes, scraped the leftovers into the garbage and ran the plates under the tap before putting them in the dishwasher. When he went back into the dining room for the glasses, Parker was no longer at the table. He lurked at the bottom of the stairs, listened for a moment to Parker's quiet murmur, Annie's bitter, grudging response. Dialogue. Slightly reassured, he went back into the kitchen, and finished loading the dishwasher. He turned the machine on.

He got down on his knees and prayed for Sean's continued recovery.

His bets hedged, he helped himself to the evening's last glass of wine and went outside and slumped into one of a pair of green Adirondack chairs crowded onto the back porch.

The clump of thirty-foot-tall white birch trees by the garage swayed gently in the evening breeze. Thousands of pale-green, spear-shaped leaves shimmied and shook. A robin trotted across the lawn almost directly below him. The bird stopped suddenly, tilted its head as if listening . . .

Barney, the marmalade stray that had sneaked into Willows' unmarked car and subsequently shouldered himself into Willows' life, slipped stealthily through the picket fence at the lane. The cat flattened itself against the grass and crept slowly towards the unsuspecting robin. The way Barney held himself indicated that he'd finally learned to hunt without jingling his bell.

The robin stiffened. It's beak jabbed at the lawn, withdrew. The bird had a firm grip on a large earthworm. But part of the worm was still fixed in the earth, and the worm wasn't letting go.

Barney crept closer.

Tripod, the most recent feline addition to the household, lurched along the peak of the garage roof and then angled clumsily down across the shingles towards the gutter.

The worm suddenly gave it up. The robin staggered a little. The leaves of the birch trees twitched and shivered. Barney hurtled across the lawn. The robin uttered a panicked shriek and rose up into the air with a wild beating of wings.

Tripod leapt. The cat's left front leg had been amputated, but his right leg was fully extended, claws unsheathed.

Willows was on his feet, shouting. The chair tumbled down the steps.

Barney screeched in shock and terror as Tripod thumped down on him. A blur of snarling, mottled orange resolved itself into two terrified cats speeding in opposite directions. Barney leapt over the neighbour's chain-link fence and vanished into a flowerbed. Tripod's claws scrabbled on the concrete walk as he tore around the side of the house. The robin had vanished, but for a few pale feathers that drifted across the lawn.

Willows searched for his wine glass and found it in pieces at the bottom of the steps. He hunted down the shards, carried them in his cupped hand to the garbage can by the lane. Somewhere not far off a radio played faintly. On the far side of the lane, the neighbour's laundry hung from a drooping line. Willows looked away, but too late. He found himself making idle comparisons. Claire had once inadvertently left the price tag on a pair of silk bikini panties, and Willows had marvelled at the cost. What, he wondered, would be the tariff on Mrs. Larson's spinnaker-size sweet nothings.

Smiling, he made his way back to the house, followed the drone of the television into the den.

Annie and Claire were watching "The Price Is Right." Parker made room on the sofa and Willows sat down beside her, with Annie on his left. Annie's eyes were red, but she gave him a nice smile, leaned her head against his shoulder for a moment, and squeezed his arm.

Bob Barker wanted to give away a speedboat, a trip to Mexico, a bright red car so shiny it looked as if it was melting.

Willows wondered what he'd look like when he was Bob's age, should he live that long. Not that he had any idea how old Bob was, though it seemed he'd been around since the birth of the picture tube. Bob had probably given away tens of millions of dollars' worth of cars and boats and trips to the Grand Canyon during his career as a genial game-show host. Maybe the secret to eternal youth was an abiding generosity of spirit.

Or genetics. Or a careful diet, moderate consumption of alcoholic beverages . . .

The contestants had to guess the value of a five-piece solid-oak bedroom suite.

The first contestant dithered, peered anxiously towards her friends in the crowd. "Five thousand!" she cried.

"Six thousand, six hundred and eighty dollars!" cried Annie.

"Seven thousand, five hundred," said Parker.

"Six thousand, six hundred and seventy-nine dollars and ninety-five cents!" said Willows.

Annie threw a cushion at him. "That's not *fair!*"

The bedside lamp on Parker's side had a fringed, saffron-coloured shade and a ten-watt bulb shaped like a candle-flame. She and Willows had bought the lamp at an "antique moderne" store in Seaside, Oregon, when they'd found that their hotel-room lights were more suited to reading small-print paperbacks than to making love.

Willows had knocked the lamp over a few minutes earlier. He reached across Parker and set it upright. Parker smiled up at him. He made as if to shift his weight and she put her arms around him, holding him captive. He settled a little lower, so they were touching all along the lengths of their bodies, but she was spared his weight.

Parker said, "Relax, Jack."

Willows felt the heat rising up off her. He tilted his head back so he could look into her eyes. Whenever they made love, Parker seemed to lose a good ten years. Her face softened, the lines around her eyes and the corners of her mouth faded and slipped away. It was like knowing her before he had ever had a chance to know her, when she was younger, blessed with a sweet and tender innocence unknown to cops.

He held her for a few more minutes, stroked her hair, ran his hand over her body and kissed her everywhere his mouth could reach. Finally he moved off her.

Parker snuggled into the crook of his arm. The swell of her breast pressed against his ribcage. She told him why Annie had been so upset at dinner.

Lewis had told Annie during lunch that he couldn't come over that night because he had to study for a chemistry exam. After school, Annie happened to see him with a blonde girl named Bev, who was in Annie's math class. She had followed them to a nearby coffee shop. Lewis had bought two large lattes. He'd sat down next to Bev and put his arm around her.

"Damn conniving Bev," said Willows.

Parker giggled. She said, "Annie marched up to the table and tipped Lewis' large latte into Lewis' cheatin' lap."

"Ouch," said Willows, who was in a post-coital, acutely sensitive mood.

"Lucky for Lewis, he was wearing one of those thick flannel lumberjack shirts outside his jeans, so he wasn't burned."

"Merely terrified."

"A woman scorned . . . ," said Parker.

Willows reached out with his left arm, and turned out the light. Parker snuggled a little closer. She said, "Tired?"

"Yeah, a little."

"Me too," said Parker contentedly.

When Willows arrived at 312 Main the next morning, he found a single pink message slip on his desk. The note was terse and to the point. He was to report to Homer Bradley's office the moment he arrived. There was an identical note on Parker's desk.

Willows knuckled the pebbled-glass door. Bradley crisply shouted at them to come in. Willows pushed open the door and stepped inside. Parker took a moment to adjust the collar of her blouse, and then followed after him.

Bradley sat at his desk. He didn't look up from his paperwork. He said, "Shut the damn door."

Parker shut the door, leaned against the frame.

Bradley finished writing, capped his pen and slipped it into the breast pocket of his uniform jacket. His thinning hair gleamed frostily in the overhead lights. He glared at Parker and Willows in turn.

"I fell asleep at my desk yesterday afternoon. When I awoke, at approximately twenty minutes past seven, I discovered that my telephone had been disconnected, that the switchboard had been ordered to reroute my calls to your desk, Jack, and that my office door was locked and that you had taped a handwritten note to my door informing all and sundry that I was out of the building, and unavailable." Bradley took a deep breath, held it for a moment, slowly exhaled. "What in hell possessed you do to such a thing?"

Willows said, "We were talking to you about the LeGrand case . . ." Bradley was staring at him, openly hostile. He said, "You don't remember?"

"Remember what, for Christ's sake?"

"You fell asleep in the middle of a sentence," said Parker. "We thought you'd had a stroke . . ."

Bradley stared at her in shocked disbelief.

Parker said, "Jack took your pulse. We smelled liquor on your breath. We thought . . ."

"That I'd been drinking?" Bradley was shouting. He lowered his voice to a harsh whisper. "You thought I was *drunk*?"

Willows said, "Not at first. We . . ."

"Hold it right there!" Bradley held up his right hand, palm out, as if claiming the right of way at a conversational intersection. He said, "I'm having a little problem with my arthritis. I'm taking painkillers, prescription drugs. I had one little drink with lunch. Obviously that was a mistake, a minor error in judgement. But I was *not* drinking on duty and I sure as hell do *not* have a drinking problem. Is that clear?"

"Absolutely," said Parker.

"In future, should you find me comatose at my desk, kindly assume that I am ill, not pissed. Act accordingly. Call the paramedics. Do *not* call a goddamn bartender!" Bradley was shouting again. He struggled to get himself under control. "Do I make myself understood?"

"Every word," said Willows.

"In that case, kindly get the hell out of my office!"

Willows held the door open for Parker, followed her out. He eased the door shut. The latch clicked. He said, "What time is it?"

Parker checked her watch. "Quarter to nine."

"Want to go somewhere quiet and have a drink?"

Parker gave him a rueful grin. "I hope you're kidding."

"Me too," said Willows.

23

Ozzie had forgotten to lower the blinds. The sun woke him early, but he managed to roll out of the sack and stagger over to the window and drop the blinds and fall back into bed without actually waking up. He slept until the ringing telephone woke him at just a few minutes past noon.

"Ozzie?" It was Dean. The shooter. He sounded excited, pumped. He reminded Ozzie this was the day they'd been waiting for. He pointed out that this special day was already almost half over. Was Ozzie sick or something?

Ozzie said, "I was up late, okay?"

"Wanna go somewhere, Denny's, get some breakfast?"

Ozzie said, "Forget it. Dinner, maybe."

He hung up and went back to bed, but the damage had been done. He was wide awake; there was no way he was getting back to sleep. He kicked free of the blankets, went into the bathroom, showered and shaved, washed his hair. He liked his hair cut short, but had let it grow the past few months, so it came down almost to his shoulders. As soon as he finished with Harold and Dean, he was going to get himself a military-style crewcut. Get his ear pierced, buy a gold hoop. Wear his Detroit Tigers baseball cap backwards. Create a whole new personality to go with his new look. Be a nice guy, someone gentle and kind, considerate.

In the kitchen, he made coffee, sliced a poppyseed bagel in half and shoved it into the toaster. Fucking Dean. The kid lacked patience, had to be kept on a real short leash, couldn't be depended on for more than a minute or two at a time. He became aware of a stream of dark-blue smoke rising from the toaster. The smoke alarm stuttered uncertainly and then broke into a full-bore scream. What a racket! As if the goddamn Three Tenors had kicked in the door for an impromptu sing-along. He burned his fingers trying to fish the bagel out of the toaster, desperately yanked the plug out of the socket.

He waved yesterday's paper at the smoke detector, trying to clear the air.

Nope, that wasn't going to work. He couldn't shoot the thing, either – too damn noisy.

He opened the living-room window and then went over to the door and yanked it open, and there was Thomas, the building's chubby gnome of a maintenance man, crouched low in the hallway.

Thomas stood there, master key in one hand and fire extinguisher in the other, a startled look in both his close-set eyes, vodka fumes leaking from his open mouth. Ozzie glowered down at him, thrust a *j'accuse* finger at him and shouted, "What're you, the bagel police?" Thomas flinched, and backed away. An ex-Hungarian, he'd fled his mother country back in the late fifties, when the Russkies invaded and the tanks started burning. The fifties were a long time ago, but he still suffered pangs of guilt. Ozzie had told him to let it go, that he was a man ahead of his time. It was the nineties. *When the going gets tough, emigrate.*

He went back to the TV, drank his coffee and munched on a charcoal-black bagel as he watched the last of the noon news.

The salmon were in trouble, again.

He watched a string of commercials, and then it was time for the sports update. He sat up a little straighter on the sofa. Who was this weird kid with no shoulders and a size-twelve neck, a two-dollar haircut and chirpy, overly cheerful voice? Nobody Ozzie wanted to know. He hit the remote's off button. The kid vanished in a burp of light. Zapped.

He was close to the bottom of his second cup of coffee when the phone started ringing.

Dean, again.

"Can I come over?"

Ozzie hung up. He put on a pair of latex gloves and went to work on the apartment with a roll of paper towels and a bottle of Windex. Starting in the bathroom, he wiped down any surface that might hold a fingerprint. By the time Dean arrived, he'd done the bathroom and the kitchen and was hard at work on the bedroom. He told Dean to sit on the sofa and watch TV, not to touch anything but the remote control. He finished the bedroom and started in on the living room. Dean was watching an old western, Dean Martin and a bunch of actors Ozzie vaguely recognized but couldn't name.

Ozzie wiped down the TV, playfully waggled his hands in front of the screen. He pulled both his sports bags out of the bedroom closet and filled them with his clothes and the few other belongings he felt it worthwhile to take with him: his shaving gear, clock radio, the Ruger and boxes of Black Talons.

Packed and ready to go, he pulled a couple of bottles of Kokanee from the otherwise empty fridge. He tossed a bottle to Dean and popped open the other.

The two partners in crime sat there at opposite ends of the sofa, Dean in his tight black jeans and tight black T-shirt, black leather belt and his new Doc Martens, Ozzie in battered Adidas sneakers, jeans, a baggy short-sleeved shirt in pale-blue cotton, his fogged-up latex gloves. They drank beer, watched the movie, passing the time. Dean smoked heavily. His posture was relaxed, but there was a tightness around his eyes.

The movie ended at three. Ozzie turned the sound up a notch before they left. He locked the apartment door and dropped the key and the latex gloves and empty beer bottles down the garbage chute.

Dean followed in the rental as Ozzie drove the Chevy out to the airport, and parked it in the long-term lot. They drove downtown in the rental, and then Dean wriggled his hands into a fresh pair of latex gloves and Ozzie drove around more or less aimlessly. Whenever they happened on a mailbox Dean mailed a photocopy of the patched-together ransom letter to Joan Wismer. In half an hour, they'd sent her a dozen copies. If Canada Post held to its part of the bargain, the notes would be delivered to the Wismer household about eleven-thirty the next morning.

But that would be then, and this was barely now.

Ozzie parked the van in a pay lot on Seymour, and they strolled over to Granville and paid eight-fifty each to watch the last hour of a gangster movie starring Bruce Willis.

As they left the theatre Ozzie said, "Can you imagine what it'd be like, being married to Demi?"

Dean, his face solemn and immobile, thought about it for the better part of a block. Finally he said, "No, I don't think so. But why would I want to? A woman like that, a movie star. She ain't real."

"What d'you mean?"

"She ain't *real*. She's a star."

"A star," said Ozzie. Not getting it.

"Besides, she's married to Bruce, and I like Bruce. He's a nice guy. You think I'd want to fool around with his wife, screw up his marriage? Forget that, man. Anyway, they got kids, and I hate kids. I already did the father thing, in case you forgot. It wasn't me."

"Good point," said Ozzie. Thinking, *moron*. They walked back to the van, and he tossed Dean the keys and told him about the Italian restaurant he wanted to try . . .

The restaurant was located on a corner, across the street from a place that sold discount Persian-style carpets, but was going out of business. Ozzie studied the menu taped to the inside of the window by the door, while Dean scrutinized passing women. Soups and salads were in the eight-dollar range, main-course pasta meat dishes twenty and up. Ozzie lifted a hand and peered though the plate glass. The joint was almost full, the men in expensive suits, the women wearing lots of jewellery, bright lipstick. A suit glanced up, happened to catch Ozzie's eye. They stared at each other until the guy remembered his soup was getting cold.

Ozzie grabbed Dean's arm and pulled him inside. There was a table for two by the far window. They brushed past a small sign on a tripod that said, "Please wait to be seated." Dean, a little intimidated by the restaurant's atmosphere, the ritzy classical music, all those obviously well-off people who were paying absolutely no attention to him, followed close behind as Ozzie made his way across the narrow room, pulled out a chair and sat. Dean stood there, not too sure about the situation. Ozzie stretched out his leg and kicked the other chair away from the table. "Sit down, make yourself comfortable."

Dean sat down.

A man in his fifties, balding, with a week-old beard, wearing pointy black shoes, tight black pants and an unbuttoned black vest over a crisp white shirt, strode briskly towards the table. His name was Rudolpho, if the shiny brass plate pinned to his vest could be believed. Ozzie pulled his roll, peeled off a hundred. He tried to cram the hundred into Rudolpho's pasty-white hand. The man flinched away as if the bill were a long-dead fish.

"I'm terribly sorry," he whispered, "but I'm afraid this table is reserved . . ."

"For us," said Ozzie. He peeled another hundred from the roll.

"Unfortunately, I'm afraid we have a dress code." The sweep of a limp hand encompassed the restaurant and all it contained. "As you see, gentlemen are required to wear a jacket and tie . . ."

"We ain't gentlemen," said Ozzie, peeling another hundred from his roll. "We're just guys. A couple of harmless, very hungry guys." He winked at Dean, licked his fingers and stripped another hundred from his wad.

Rudolpho was deeply offended. Pushing at the air with his hands, he propelled himself away from them, shuffled backwards across the dark carpet and vanished through the batwing doors that led to the kitchen. Three swarthy men dressed all in white pushed through the doors and into the dining area. The men had thick, hairy arms. Grim, European faces. The smallest discreetly wielded a meat cleaver.

Ozzie drove the van north on Granville to Broadway, made a right, drove past the blocky, bright-red neon letters of a Future Shop. He made another right and pulled into Denny's, parked in the handicapped slot and killed the engine. He hung his blue-and-white plastic handicapped tag from the rearview mirror. He reminded Dean that he limped.

Inside, the restaurant was crowded but not full, the air thick with the clatter of cutlery and conversation. Ozzie glanced around, categorizing the customers. Shoppers, lonely salesmen, the terminally unemployed. As far as he could see, he and Dean were the only professional criminals in the joint.

A woman whose style of walking hinted at a gene pool that was heavily dependent on waterfowl led them to a booth with a nice view of several other booths. Ozzie said, "We're okay like this?"

"Like what?" said the waitress.

"No tie, no jacket . . ."

"You got a shirt, shoes and socks? That's all we require here at Denny's, sir."

"And it's okay to sit here . . ." – Ozzie's gesture encompassed the booth's gleaming table, cushy seats, the quality stainless-steel cutlery, chrome-topped glass salt-and-pepper shakers, napkin dispenser – ". . . even though we got no reservation?"

"We don't accept reservations at Denny's, sir. Will you be having something to drink?"

"Got a light beer?"

"Coors?"

"Fine," said Ozzie.

The waitress turned to Dean.

Dean said, "You got a light beer?"

"Coors."

"Fine," said Dean. He lit a cigarette. The city had recently passed a by-law against smoking in restaurants and just about everywhere else, with the possible exception of school washrooms. He sucked smoke so deeply into his respiratory system that it would never find its way out again, then lifted his upside-down coffee cup from the saucer, squashed the butt in the saucer and carefully replaced the cup.

The waitress arrived with their bottled beer, glasses. She sniffed the air, glanced suspiciously around.

Ozzie said, "Why is it that, in every restaurant in this city, the only light beer you can buy is Coors?"

"Excuse me?"

"How come the only light beer you got is Coors?"

The waitress shrugged. She said, "You don't like Coors?"

"No, Coors is fine. Number one." He poured beer into his glass, dipped his tongue. He rubbed his stomach. "Mmmm, good!"

"Everything a beer should be, and more," said Dean.

Ozzie waggled a finger. "No, I think that's Budweiser."

The waitress had chewed a fragment of plastic off the tip of her pen. She put the fragment in her apron pocket. She said, "Would you like to speak to the manager? I could . . ."

Ozzie cut her off with a terse wave of his hand that made the napkins flutter and tremble. He said, "Gimme a well-done steak, a double order of hash browns, skip the vegetables."

"Same for me," said Dean. He smiled. "Bring us a couple more beers while you're at it, willya?"

"Coors Light?"

"Perfect," said Ozzie. He reached across the table and jovially thumped Dean on the shoulder. "I was hoping to treat you to a real nice meal, but you get something a whole lot better."

"What're you talking about?"

"A lesson in life, Dean. Now you understand what the difference is, between them and us. Nothing but money and clothes."

"I don't see your point."

Ozzie wiped his face with a paper napkin, looked at the napkin to see how much cleaner he was. Why in hell had he dragged Dean's stupid ass to an overpriced restaurant full of stiff faces poking out of expensive suits, a place with all the cheery atmosphere of a morgue, with a menu printed in a foreign language? He shifted on the bench seat, trying to make himself comfortable. His body felt as if it were corkscrewing into itself, wound too tight. Maybe he'd wanted to share the same kind of dining experiences that Harold and Melanie had enjoyed. Another nagging question: why had he asked Harold for a light, put himself in a situation where he might be remembered?

Was the pressure getting to him, was he starting to lose it? Maybe it was a good thing they were going to make the move, do the dirty deed. He had a strong feeling that if he'd waited much longer, he'd find he had waited a bit too long.

He looked down. The meal lay there in front of him, steaming. His mouth watered.

Dean's face was no more than an inch from his plate. His fork rose and fell, rose and fell . . .

Ozzie said, "The point is, I wanted to give you some small idea of what Harold's gonna do for us. Or, I should say, what his money's gonna do for us. How our lives are gonna change. For the better."

Dean slurped some beer. He nodded. Mouth full, he said, "The world's gonna be our oyster."

"Now you got it!"

Dean nodded. But the thing of it was, he was a prairie boy, and he didn't like seafood.

24

The ex-Rott-owner's corpse floated face up in the water. A dozen ghost crabs had hitched a ride. The eyes had gone. The ears were so badly decomposed that the gold earrings had fallen away. The grossly swollen flesh had assumed the colour and rubbery texture of an undercooked poached egg.

The corpse bobbed along in a light chop, on a course roughly parallel to the North Vancouver waterfront. A roving band of teenagers, believing it was a waterlogged bundle of rags, shot at it with air rifles until it was lost from view.

Not long afterwards, the swirling outflow of the Capilano River pushed the body away from the shoreline, into deeper and darker waters.

For several hours, it drifted on the diamond-bright ocean among the flotilla of small craft that sought the river's dwindling run of coho salmon.

Those eagle-eyed fisherfolk should have spotted the body.

Apparently no one did.

25

Joan finished the chapter and bent the page and put the book aside and turned out the bedside light. It was 11:59 by the digital clock on the night table way over there on Harold's side of their king-size bed. She plumped up her pillow and rolled over on her side. The diamond-encrusted Rolex Harold had given her on her fortieth birthday ticked quietly on her wrist.

The bedroom window was open a crack. She listened to the soft music of the wind moving through the leaves of the pink dogwood, and then her body stiffened as she heard the familiar sound of the Rolls turning into the driveway. She realized that she had been holding her breath in anticipation of Harold's arrival. She waited for the solid *thunk* of Harold slamming the Rolls' door shut, and then the car accelerated away, the muted throb of the exhausts lost out there, somewhere in the night. She was hearing things, letting her imagination run away with her.

She pressed down on the pillow so she could see the clock.

12:01.

But that was impossible, because Harold always got home by midnight and he was never, *ever* late.

She watched the numbers turn over until it was 12:15, and then turned the light back on and picked up her book.

Where was Harold?

She read for ten minutes and then got out of bed, slipped into her pink-and-white-striped terrycloth bathrobe and went downstairs. The driveway was empty. She unlocked the door that led directly to the garage, switched on the lights. Harold's BMW and her white Jaguar crouched low and elegant on the spotless concrete, the broad space between the two cars empty as empty can be.

She went into the living room and poured a half-inch of rye into a lowball glass. She got ice from the refrigerator's dispenser, jumped as the cubes rattled down the chute.

She was frightened. But why?

Because Harold was *never, ever* late.

Never!

She pictured him in the Rolls, driving through the city. Maybe, it sure as hell wouldn't be the first time, he'd had a little too much wine with dinner. Judgement impaired, he'd miscalculated his speed, run a light.

She pictured him slouched behind the wheel, half asleep. She saw, or almost saw, she *glimpsed*, as in a dream, the bulky, hunch-shouldered blur of onrushing metal speeding through the rancid orange glow of the streetlights.

Harold flinched, threw up his hands.

Joan pressed the cold lowball glass against her forehead. What if he came home and found her standing there, wide awake, drink in hand. Where would that lead? To a conversation neither of them wanted to endure. She freshened her drink and hurried back upstairs, slipped into the still-warm bed.

When he turned the corner and drove that last block towards the house he would see the light on in the bedroom window. But she'd hear the car turn into the driveway, and by the time he came upstairs the light would be out and she'd have turned on her side, her back to him, and she'd be sleeping, or at least she'd pretend to be sleeping . . .

She tried to read but the pages kept blurring, the words didn't seem to make any sense, and it was impossible to concentrate.

She had a terrible sense of foreboding. Harold was a long way from perfect, but through all the years of his infidelities he had always followed one ironclad rule. He was always home by midnight.

Always.

So, where was he?

Where was Harold?

Where in heaven's name was her husband?

What had happened to him?

Where was he?

Harold was late. He'd eaten too much roast pheasant, drunk too much wine. Melanie had told him to go easy. He'd advised her to relax and enjoy herself, live a little.

Back at the apartment, she'd gone straight into the kitchen to brew a pot of decaf. Harold, having lived a little too much, had fallen asleep on the sofa. He'd slept until she woke him, at quarter past eleven.

The rule was, and she knew it all too well, that he had to be out of there no later than eleven-thirty, home by twelve.

Why hadn't she wakened him earlier?

Melanie laughed out loud. One of the things Harold liked about her was the way she laughed, unrestrained but feminine. But tonight it seemed to him that her laughter had a hint of nastiness to it. He knew from hard-earned experience that when she was in the mood, Melanie could be a certified solid-gold, twenty-four-karat bitch.

She patted Harold's knee and reminded him that she was almost out of cigarettes and he'd promised to buy her a pack at the corner store before he went home. She suggested that, unless he intended to break his promise, he'd better get his fuzzy little ass in gear.

Harold checked the diamond-studded gold Rolex he'd given to himself on Joan's fortieth. He checked the VCR's clock. He turned Melanie's wrist so he could see the face of her Seiko. He leaned back for a view of the kitchen, the clock on the wall above the fridge.

Melanie said, "Come on, Harold. Up and at 'em. Drive me to the store and drop me off, I'll walk back to the apartment."

"At this time of night?" Harold reluctantly allowed himself to be pulled to his feet.

Melanie gave him a full-press hug. Harold put his arms around her and hugged her back, wandered his hands over her. She made a kittenish sound, a kind of mewing. Encouraged, he nibbled an earlobe. He said, "I was hoping we could fool around a little . . ."

"So was I," said Melanie, clearly a little frustrated. She broke free and moved towards the door. "Maybe you should go a little easier on the wine next time, okay?"

Harold was instantly contrite. "I'm so sorry, I really am." He stuck his hands in his pants pockets. Melanie gave him a coquettish look.

"What're you doing in there, Harold?"

"Looking for my keys."

She held them up, gave them a shake. The sterling-silver Rolls-Royce keyring glittered in the light.

"Follow me, handsome."

Harold sauntered along behind her. She knew him all too well. There *was* something going on down there. Maybe if he played his cards right . . .

Melanie locked the apartment door behind them. They walked hand in hand along the corridor towards the bank of elevators. Harold pushed the down button, and a few moments later the bronzed elevator doors slid open. He followed her into the elevator, pushed another button. His soft bulk eased her into a corner. He slipped his hands under her jacket. His fingers were full of cashmere, silk, flesh. He was up on the toes of his brown suede Rockports, his breath coming ragged and shallow. Lucky Harold, in Otis heaven.

The elevator doors slid open. Harold kept at her. The doors rebounded and started to slide shut, inexplicably sprang open again.

Harold struggled to get his hand under Melanie's skirt. She tried to push him away. His tongue lapped at her throat. He tasted her perfume.

Melanie screamed.

Harold fell back. Her eyes were wide. She wasn't looking at him. She was staring past him, at something behind him. She looked terrified. She had forgotten he existed.

His hands fell away from her breasts. He glanced over his shoulder, and gasped in shock and fear. Two men stood in the open elevator doorway. One of the men wore a black T-shirt, the other a pale-blue shirt. Both men wore jeans and black balaclavas and tight black gloves. Both were pointing guns at him. Large pistols, shiny as toys.

Ozzie said, "What the fuck are you doing here, Melanie?"

Melanie gaped at him.

Dean said, "What should we do with her? Should we shoot her?"

"In the blink of an eye, if she fucks with us." Ozzie cocked the Ruger's hammer, reducing the pressure required to pull the trigger from approximately nine to merely two pounds. As he adjusted his grip on his pistol, bolts of light were reflected from the stainless-steel barrel. He said, "Let's go, kids."

Harold shot his cuff. He said, "That's a Rolex. It cost me . . ." Dean slapped Harold's wrist with the barrel of his pistol. Harold yelped. His face, in Ozzie's opinion, indicated he believed he'd got exactly what he deserved.

Dean had parked the rented van directly in front of the Rolls. Everybody climbed inside. Ozzie pointed out a red plastic container of gasoline. He explained that, if Harold or Melanie caused any problems, they'd burn.

Ozzie tossed Dean fat rolls of duct tape in primary colours bright enough to make a rainbow blush with envy. Red tape for Harold's mouth, green for Melanie's. Then Ozzie held his pistol steady while Dean lowered a recycled brown paper Safeway bag over Harold's head. As Dean eased an identical bag over Melanie, he smiled and apologized for mussing her beautiful hair.

When he'd finished taping their hands, Dean said, "There we go, that oughtta do it." He stroked Melanie's arm. "Comfortable, honey?"

She made a small snuffling sound that could have meant anything.

"Good," said Dean, and clambered into the front passenger seat.

Ozzie started the engine. He put the van in gear and rolled down his window. As the van crawled past Harold's Rolls, he fired six times as quickly as he could pull the trigger. The first shot punched a hole in the windshield just above the rim of the steering wheel. The seat jumped as the bullet drilled into the soft leather upholstery. After that, it was all muzzle blasts and smoke, ear-splitting explosions, huge overlapping cobwebs in the Rolls' windshield.

Melanie was screaming. So loud. Hadn't Dean taped her mouth?

Correction. Dean was yelling, not Melanie. Ozzie's Ruger ejected to the right. A stream of scorchy-hot brass cartridges had hit Dean in the throat and tumbled down inside his shirt.

Now Melanie was making noise. Strange *murph!* sounds that were kind of unsettling. He swung at her with the pistol, missed. The van swerved dangerously. He shouted "Shut up, or you'll get the next one."

Dean said, "Hey, go easy on her. She's scared, that's all." He slapped the dashboard. "We got 'em, Ozzie! We got 'em!"

Speeding along the treacherous, black and twisty highway to Whistler, the radio playing, tires hissing on black pavement, a calming breeze rushing across his face from the partly open window, Ozzie thought about how easily Harold had allowed himself to be herded out of the elevator and into the van. The look on his face, disappointed but resigned, almost as if he'd been waiting for his cosy little world to come crashing down around him, a couple of hard-asses with guns to take him for a ride.

It crossed Ozzie's mind that maybe Harold had problems he didn't know about. Had Melanie somehow become inconvenient? Was it possible she was pregnant . . . ?

What if she were pregnant, blackmailing Harold, and he'd hired some muscle, a couple of frighteners? What if Harold mistakenly believed Ozzie and Dean were working for *him*?

Dean said, "What's so funny?"

"Why, was I laughing?"

"Snickering," said Dean. He lit a cigarette, blew out the match and tossed it on the floor. He gingerly rubbed his neck as he took a hard pull on his cigarette.

In the cigarette's soft orange light, Ozzie glimpsed the burn marks left by the spent casings. He said, "How's the neck?"

Dean grunted, indicating pain in a manly way.

Ozzie thought, *You ain't seen nothin' yet.*

26

Harold answered on the fourth ring. He told Joan he wasn't in at the moment, to please wait for the beep and leave a message, and he'd get back to her just as soon as he could.

It was a little past one in the morning. Joan had waited until then before losing patience and dialling her husband's private number at his Howe Street office.

The fact that he wasn't at his office meant nothing. He'd probably driven straight to his girlfriend's the moment he hung up on her. She decided to wait another hour, until two a.m., and then dial 911, and report him missing.

But when two o'clock finally rolled around, calling the police emergency number seemed an overly dramatic gesture.

She told herself Harold was just fine, that the Rolls would turn into the driveway any moment now . . .

She pictured a dark car running a red light. Sirens and flashing emergency lights. Pools of dark liquid on the road.

She imagined Harold in bed with his tart, drinking and laughing, having a good time at her expense.

She caught a glimpse of Harold in a body bag, his arms folded across his torn chest. His eyes shut forever, his heart stopped forever.

Her 911 call was logged at 2:31 a.m.

The dispatcher's voice was calm. "Ambulance, fire or police?"

Joan launched into a brief history of her marriage to Harold. All those years, and he *never* came home later than midnight. Had he been involved in an accident?

"Ma'am, do you have any reason to believe your husband is an accident victim?"

Joan patiently explained again that Harold never arrived home later than midnight.

"Did you wish to file a missing-persons report, ma'am? You'll have to wait seventy-two hours, if you wish to file a report."

Joan hung up.

The telephone rang immediately. It was the 911 dispatcher, calling to determine that Joan had hung up voluntarily and did not require an ambulance, fire or police.

Joan told her she was just fine, thanks. Her voice dripped with sarcasm as she apologized for any inconvenience she might have caused, said that she was hanging up now, if that was okay with everybody. She slammed the phone into the cradle and went downstairs and looked up "Hospitals" in the Yellow Pages. She tried St. Paul's and then Vancouver Hospital, University, St. Vincent's, Children's, Mount St. Joseph. What if Harold had driven out of the city? She phoned Queens Park, Richmond, Royal Columbian and Surrey Memorial. In half an hour she had tried every hospital in the lower mainland. When she finally hung up the phone, she still had no idea if Harold had been involved in an accident.

But if he had been in an accident, surely someone would phone her.

Unless . . . What if he'd been seriously injured, or even killed?

They'd send a policeman around to talk to her, and it would be a police car rather than Harold's Rolls that would turn into the driveway.

She turned on the porch light, dressed in loose-fitting grey slacks and a bulky black sweater.

At four o'clock and at a quarter and half past the hour, and at a quarter to five, she dialled Melanie Martel's number. Each time she called, she let the phone ring three times and then hung up and waited, her heart beating wildly.

At a few minutes past five, she hit the redial button again. But this time she let the phone keep ringing.

The answering machine picked up after the fourth ring. Melanie said she wasn't home at the moment, invited Joan to wait for the beep and then leave a message. In seductive tones, she promised to call right back, just as soon as she could. Joan slammed down the phone. The mini-blind was fractured by thin lines of pinkish light. She went over to the window and looked out. The sky to the east was a soft rose colour, the stars pale and fading.

She hit the redial button again, waited impatiently for the beep. All in a rush, she told Harold she knew he was there and would he please have the common decency to answer the phone and reassure her that he hadn't been in an accident.

She waited in vain, as the answering machine's tape hissed like an impotent snake, uncoiling from one sprocket, wrapping around another.

She shouted at Harold that she was fed up with his lies, that she wanted a divorce.

She told him she never wanted to see him again, except in court.

She took a long hot shower and went to bed, and lay there, fuming. At ten o'clock she tried the hospitals again, and then the police.

By noon she was half convinced that Harold had finally left her for the bimbo. When the mail arrived, an hour later, she was in the garden, pulling up anything that remotely resembled a weed.

Tossing aside her gloves, she hurried up the fieldstone pathway to see if there was a postcard from Harold. Or, as seemed more likely, a letter from one of his hotshot lawyer pals.

Mixed in among the cablevision and telephone bills and a rare letter from a schoolgirl friend who had long since moved to southern France, were several plain white envelopes with her name and address printed on them in an unlikely combination of letters and numbers. Studying the envelopes, she saw that the addresses were on separate pieces of paper glued to the envelopes and that none of them had a return address.

There were, in all, eight letters addressed to her that were identical in every respect.

She sat down on the sun-warmed top step and opened the first of the letters.

Inside was a photocopied ransom note that said:

Joan sat there, stunned, in shock. She read the note again and again, as the sun beat down on her, and the world went about its business. Finally she opened the other letters. All seven were identical to the first. She checked the postmarks. The letters had been mailed in the city the previous day.

She went into the house and mixed a small gin and tonic, and then went back outside and sat on the patio, in the sunlight.

Harold had been kidnapped. He would die if she didn't pay the people who had him five million dollars in cash, or if she called the police.

She sipped nervously at her drink. She told herself to be calm, and think things through. She knew Harold was in some kind of financial difficulty. During the past few weeks, a man who refused to identify himself had phoned incessantly, demanding to speak to Harold, shouting at her. Sometimes when Harold answered the phone, he'd just stand there, listening, not saying a word, his face grim. As soon as the call ended, he'd start drinking, drink himself insensible.

She'd beg him to talk to her, and he'd look right through her.

Once, the phone had rung as Harold was sitting down to dinner. The meal had grown cold as he'd stood there, ashen-faced. Finally he'd started talking, sounding frantic as he assured the caller that everything was under control, there was no need to worry . . .

As soon as he'd hung up, he'd burst into tears. Joan had attempted to comfort him, but he'd shut himself away in the den. She'd reheated his dinner. He'd had no appetite for anything but the bottle.

Sometimes the phone rang in the middle of the night, at two or three or even four o'clock in the morning . . .

Harold refused to explain the situation to her, allow her to share his grief and fear or to work with him to find a solution to whatever the hell kind of mess he'd gotten himself into.

Well, that was Harold. When things were going well, he'd bend her ear to the breaking point. When things were going badly, it was as if she'd ceased to exist.

She reread the ransom note for the tenth time.

Five million dollars. The enormity of the sum began to sink in. Harold had bank accounts all over town. A few she knew about. But she suspected there were many others that he kept secret. Was it possible he'd tucked away five million dollars in those mystery accounts?

Maybe all those phone calls were about the five million his kidnappers were demanding. Maybe the money was theirs in the first place . . .

Joan swallowed a mouthful of her gin and tonic. An elderly man walked slowly along the sidewalk, his small white dog running ahead of him, barking shrilly.

Five million dollars in cash.

It was an unimaginable amount.

But Harold, promoting hot gold strikes, fist-sized nuggets lying right there on the ground, had raised five million dollars in a single day. To Harold, five million was peanuts.

Joan found herself wondering about the bimbo. Melanie. What was she like? What kind of woman was she? She'd heard Harold speak to her once, on the telephone. The phone had rung and she and Harold had picked up at the same time. Harold had said hello and a woman had asked if she was speaking to Harold and Harold had said, "Melanie?" Joan had hung up immediately, hurried into the kitchen and noisily emptied the dishwasher.

Melanie had sounded young, sexy. On the basis of the few words she'd overheard, Joan pictured a slim blonde with big breasts and a narrow waist and long legs and absolutely no morals. She'd sounded, in those few words, like a woman who wanted all sorts of things and was used to getting every last one of them.

Joan found herself wondering if Melanie was involved in the kidnapping. Who better to set poor Harold up but his lover?

Five million dollars. The phrase came easier now. She lined up the numbers in her mind, all those zeros.

Of *course* it was possible that Harold had tucked that much cash away in his secret accounts.

Of *course* there were people who would do absolutely anything for that kind of money.

But if Harold had the money, and she let it sit there, made no attempt to retrieve it, and the kidnappers followed through on their threat and killed Harold . . .

Then she'd inherit the money, every penny of it.

Joan Wismer leaned forward in her chair. The old man and his dog had disappeared, vanished around a bend in the road. It was as if they had ceased to exist, or never existed at all.

If she tore up the letters and threw them in the garbage . . .

If she tore the letters into small pieces and flushed them down the toilet and disconnected the answering machine and packed a suitcase and drove to Seattle and shopped for a few days . . .

When she came back, Harold would be dead.

There was Harold, back in his body bag. His eyes shut forever. His heart stopped forever.

She would tell the detectives that she thought he'd run away with the bimbo. She'd tell them she'd been depressed, driven down to Seattle for a few days because she needed to get away from it all. Wasn't that a reasonable thing to do?

She'd be rich.

Five million dollars.

It certainly looked as if he hadn't planned to spend any of that money with her, didn't it?

Joan lifted her glass to her mouth, tilted back her head and shut her eyes. The ice had melted and the drink was watery, tepid.

But what if the people who had kidnapped Harold did murder him, and then decided to come after her?

Joan's mind was in turmoil as she went back inside the house to mix herself another drink.

27

Sheila and her new boyfriend liked to move around, but for the past year or so they had been living in Alvarado, a small town on the Gulf of Mexico. In one of her infrequent letters to Annie, Sheila had mentioned that Alvarado was an easy commute from Veracruz.

Annie had researched the town on the Internet, but hadn't learned anything of interest. She'd cross-examined Willows, who supposed the cost of living was low and the weather reliably pleasant. Studying his *Times Atlas of the World*, he'd found himself wondering why Sheila would want to live, even temporarily, in such a determinedly out-of-the-way spot.

There was a fax machine at the Alvarado post office. Sheila had given him the number, in the event of a dire emergency. She had advised him that the machine, and its operator, were frequently in need of repair. Should he have difficulty with the transmission, she had told him, wait a day or three and try again. Willows had composed and typed and then retyped a single-spaced one-page letter delineating Sean's injuries, current condition, state of mind and prospects for recovery. Parker, reading it, had complimented Willows on his unique style, which had been honed to a razor edge by thousands of tersely factual police reports.

"What's wrong with my style?" Parker's remark had put Willows on the defensive. He hadn't actually been aware that he had a style.

Parker rested her hand on his shoulder. She leaned over him, her thick black hair brushing his cheek. She said, "It's a little brusque, Jack. A little, I don't know, dry . . ."

"Dry? What's that supposed to mean?"

Parker said, "Formal. Try to loosen up, just a little. Think of Sheila's reaction, as she reads what you've written. She's going to be frantic, Jack. What you've written is a document, rather than a personal letter." It was clear from the expression on Willows' face that he still didn't get it. Parker tried again. "Think warmth."

"Warmth?"

Parker gave him a quick kiss. "Warmth."

Willows had spent as much time as he could spare reconstructing his fax. But no matter how he tried to alter the words, they always came out the same. Sean had been shot in the arm. His injuries were not life-threatening. He was recovering rapidly and would likely be discharged from hospital in the next week to ten days. His overall prognosis was excellent. He was in good spirits.

But there was no getting around the fact that Sean had suffered catastrophic nerve damage, and would require plastic surgery and months or perhaps even years of intensive therapy in an outpatient program. Worse, there was a very real possibility that he'd never recover the full use of his arm.

En route to 312 Main, Parker made a slight detour to the neighbourhood Shopper's Drug Mart, which had a post office at the back of the store. She waited in the car while Willows went inside. There was no lineup. Willows hesitated at the counter, pen in hand. How should he sign this . . . *document*? "Regards"? "Warmly"? "Best Wishes"? He finally settled on "Hope to hear from you soon, Jack."

The fax was sent without difficulty. Willows was charged a modest two dollars plus appropriate long-distance charges.

He wondered how things would go in Alvarado. He imagined a mob of excited, unruly children running down a narrow dirt track to Sheila's *hacienda*, the oldest of them waving the fax like a flag.

Or would his message gather dust on a shelf for days, until she finally dropped by to pick up her mail?

He bought a roll of breath mints before leaving the store, popped a mint into his mouth as he got into the car. Parker said, "Everything okay?"

"Yeah, fine. Want a mint?"

"No thanks." Parker put the car in gear and accelerated away from the curb.

Half an hour later, as Willows was getting into the day's paper-work, Dan Oikawa phoned to tell him that there had been a shooting in the parking lot of a highrise on the north shore of False Creek.

Oikawa gave Willows the address. He said, "No corpses, that we can find. What happened, somebody emptied most of a clip into the windshield of a Rolls-Royce. Late-model Silver Cloud. I'm no mechanic, but it looks to me as if the vehicle's been mortally wounded." Oikawa let the silence build, then added, "The reason I called, the CSU guys are tweezering chunks of nine-millimetre rounds out of the Rolls' body. So far, they're all Black Talons."

By the time Willows and Parker arrived at the crime scene, Oikawa had run the Rolls' tags past DMV and learned that the car was registered to Harold Arthur Wismer, of Balfour Avenue, in Shaughnessy. A "slim jim," a flexible length of steel that resembled a yardstick, had been used to unlock the car. Inside, the CSU had found a myriad of fingerprints, but no blood or human tissue or bone fragments that would indicate the car had been occupied at the time of the shooting.

Oikawa introduced Parker and Willows to the building's super-intendent, a man in his mid-fifties named Barry Holbrook, and then left to accompany the Rolls to the police impound yard. Holbrook gave Willows' hand a quick shake, lingered a fraction too long over Parker.

Willows said, "Is Mr. Wismer a tenant?"

"We got no tenants. This is a strata-owned building. Condominiums, not apartments. People own the units. Strata title. No rentals. It's against the by-laws."

Parker said, "Okay, fine. We'll do it your way, Barry. So tell us, did Mr. Wismer own a condominium in the building?"

"Yes, he did. Ten-zero-three. It's way up there on the tenth floor, a nice unit, with views to the west and south."

"Do you happen to know his occupation? What he did for a living?"

"Yeah, he was a promoter."

"What did he promote, Barry?"

"Stocks and bonds. He worked out of the vse. Gold and silver mines. I think he might've done a thing with giant pearls. Or maybe that was a pal of his, some other guy. One time only, I asked him for a hot tip. He laughs, grabs his crotch."

"His car's registered to an address in Shaughnessy. Was he living here, or did he just drop by from time to time?"

"Just dropped by, far as I'm aware."

"He needed a place close to the office where he could relax, is that it?"

"Yeah, you could put it like that."

Willows said, "How would *you* put it, Barry?"

"Mind if I smoke?" Holbrook lit a cigarette with a disposable lighter. He stepped away from the detectives, averted his head and exhaled with a rush. He flicked ash at the pavement. "Look, I'm only the super. I change the light bulbs, maybe if I'm feeling lucky I'll take a shot at a plugged toilet before I call a plumber. But that's about as complicated a situation as I'm gonna tackle. It ain't in my job description to stick my nose where it don't belong. You leave me alone, I'll leave you alone."

"Got a master key, Barry?"

"Sure, but you need a warrant, right?"

"Not necessarily," said Willows. He smiled. "Have you already been inside the apartment?"

"No, of course not."

"You don't think it'd be a good idea to take a look, make sure it wasn't just Wismer's car that got shot to pieces? What if he's up there bleeding to death?"

They rode the elevator to the tenth floor. Holbrook knocked several times, waited a moment and knocked again. Finally he unlocked and opened the door. Standing in the open doorway he called, "Mr. Wismer? Hello? Is anybody home?"

Parker brushed past him. Willows said, "Wait there, Barry. Don't even think about coming inside." He followed Parker into the apartment.

The drapes had been drawn. Parker found a light switch. Two empty lowball glasses squatted on the glass coffee table in front of the sofa. Willows turned on the kitchen light. The cupboard doors were shut. The countertop was clean.

In the dining room, there was nothing on the table but a subscription copy of *Details* magazine and an unopened telephone bill. The magazine was addressed to Melanie Martel, the bill to Harold Wismer.

Willows explored until he found the bathroom. He opened the medicine cabinet, worked his way through the contents.

Parker said, "Jack . . ."

He turned.

She crooked a finger.

He followed her into the apartment's single bedroom. Parker had opened the drapes, flooding the room with light. Sliding double glass doors led to a generous balcony. The carpet was ivory. The king-size bed's duvet had a pink floral pattern. The lamp on the single night table was in the shape of an angel, with a red shade and pink tassels.

The room smelled faintly of perfume.

Parker said, "I went through the bureau, top to bottom. There's nothing in there but cashmere sweaters and about a million dollars' worth of lingerie." She indicated the mirrored walk-in closet. "The closet's stuffed with designer clothing, but there's nothing that'd look good on you, Jack."

Willows smiled. "Harold's a cross-dresser?"

"I don't think so."

Willows unlocked and pushed open the sliding glass door. He stepped outside and glanced around. Another slider at the far end of the balcony gave access to the living room. Holbrook had been right about the view, which was spectacular. He went back inside, walked over to the doorway and called out, "Barry!"

Holbrook hurried down the short hallway. "Something wrong?"

"Tell us about Harold's roomie," said Parker.

"Who?"

"Melanie Martel."

"Right, Melanie. Nice girl."

"She lives here, does she?"

"Yeah, I guess so."

"Since when, Barry?"

"Five, six months."

"How long has Harold owned the unit?"

"Ever since the place was built, about three years ago."

"You've worked here all that time?"

"Since day one."

Willows said, "Step out on the balcony, Barry."

"What for?"

"So you can smoke. You worried I'm going ask you about Melanie and Harold, shove you off the building if I think you're lying?"

"No, of course not. But it's okay, we don't need to go outside, I'm trying to cut down."

"How many women have lived here, over the years?"

"Three."

"Three women, in three years?"

"No, it's not like it sounds, the new one's moving in as the old one's moving out. They don't stay that long, usually. Three or four months is about average. In between, Harold might entertain the odd overnighter, or a woman might stay a week or so. But that's about it."

"You said Melanie's been living here for the past six months?"

"Yeah, about that." Holbrook shrugged. "It ain't like I'm keeping a diary."

"How old would you say she is?"

"Mid-thirties, somewhere in there."

Parker said, "Did Melanie have any visitors, other than Harold?"

"Not really, no."

Was Barry lying? Parker couldn't decide.

"None at all?"

"Just Harold." Barry shrugged apologetically. "Sorry."

Willows said, "Ever put your ear up against Melanie's door, Barry?"

"I'd be out on my ass in a minute, I got caught doing something like that, listened in on private conversations."

Parker said, "Answer the question."

"The answer is no, I never put my ear on the door. I'd have to be crazy, risk losing a job like this for a cheap laugh. Forget it!"

Willows said, "You never overheard Melanie discussing Harold's personal wealth, or anything along those lines?"

"No, never. Like I already told you, I never heard nobody talking about nothing."

Willows thought Holbrook had probably concussed himself, banging his ear against Melanie Martel's door. But if he knew anything, he wasn't going to spit it out until Willows dangled him by one leg from the wrong side of the balcony railing.

And that wasn't going to happen, because Parker had warned him that the next time he pulled a stunt like that, she'd dump him.

The bell rang and Joan went over to the door and opened it without giving a moment's thought to who or what might be out there. A solemn young man stood in the sunlight next to a solemn young woman who, Joan thought, might easily be his wife.

She wondered if they were going to tell her the end was nigh.

The man offered her something. A pamphlet?

No, a badge.

Looking surprised was the easiest thing in the world. She said, "I don't know what you're doing here. They told me last night that . . ." She trailed off, her voice fading, the words swept away in a flood of uncertainties. Something terrible *had* happened to Harold, and they were here to tell her about it. She suddenly felt very weak, as if all the blood had been drained from her body. Oh God. Poor Harold.

Parker said, "Jack!"

But Willows was already there, steadying Joan Wismer, taking her weight and helping her inside the house. He helped her over to an ornate wooden chair by the telephone in the hall. The house was warm and stuffy. Parker left the door open. She glanced around. Money.

Joan Wismer sat up a little straighter. She toyed with the telephone's curly cord, looked beyond Willows to Parker. She said, "What's happened to Harold?"

"We don't know," said Parker.

"I don't understand." She glanced at Willows and then back to Parker. "What are you doing here? What do you want?"

Willows said, "Does your husband own a Rolls-Royce Silver Cloud with a vanity plate that says BRK R US?"

"You must know that's Harold's car. Otherwise you wouldn't be here, would you?"

Parker said, "The car was found in the parking lot of a False Creek highrise. Apparently Harold owns an apartment in the building that's occupied by a woman named Melanie Martel. Do you know Miss Martel?"

"No, I don't."

"Did you know your husband owned an apartment in that building?"

"Yes, I did."

"We're concerned for your husband's safety. We have reason to believe he may have been kidnapped."

Joan Wismer sat quietly by the telephone for the better part of a minute. Finally she said, "Why would you think something like that?"

Willows said, "His car was shot up. He's missing, and there's no obvious reason for his absence."

Joan said, "Was this woman, the woman you say was living in Harold's apartment, is there any chance she's involved in his disappearance?"

Parker said. "At the moment, all we can say is that she isn't in her apartment and we are unable to locate her."

Willows said, "Have you received a letter . . . ?"

"Absolutely not."

Parker said, "Anything at all that would indicate Harold is in trouble . . . ?"

Joan Wismer pointed a trembling finger at Willows. "I telephoned the police department last night, trying to find out what had happened to my husband! Nobody would help me! They told me Harold had to be missing for seventy-two hours before they'd even open a file! Three days! And now you . . ." Joan Wismer's eyes filled with tears. She struggled to maintain her composure.

Willows was tempted to explain that exceptions were often made to the seventy-two-hour rule when an officer stumbled across a bullet-riddled car, but let it pass in the interest of a less-spirited conversation. He said, "Mrs. Wismer, we're here to help you. That's our job."

"I don't care! I don't know what you're talking about! Get out of my house!"

Standing on the porch, Willows felt the shock wave as Joan Wismer slammed the door.

Parker said, "Must be nice, living in a neighbourhood like this. So leafy, and quiet, peaceful."

Willows smiled at her as he started down the front-porch steps. Joan Wismer was wound tighter than a forkful of spaghetti. He said, "Joan's been warned not to talk to the cops."

"Think so?"

"Yes."

"Me too," said Parker.

It was Willows' turn to drive. He unlocked the car and got in, reached across to unlock Parker's door. He started the engine and let it idle. "We need to talk to a friendly magistrate, secure a wiretap."

"Right," said Parker.

Willows released the emergency brake. He put the unmarked Ford in gear. "Know who else we need to talk to?"

"Tell me, Jack."

Willows began to softly whistle a tune Parker vaguely recognized but couldn't quite place.

And old Beatles tune. There it was, she had it.

Mister postman, look and see . . .

28

When they'd finally arrived in Whistler, Ozzie had parked the rented van in the log house's basement garage. Everybody sat tight while Dean, SnakeLight in hand, found a switch and turned on some lights.

Dean took Melanie's hand. Ozzie grabbed a handful of second-choice Harold. The four of them made their way upstairs to the main floor of the house.

Dean turned on more lights and then went back downstairs to fetch the groceries they'd bought in Vancouver. Kidnapping was surprisingly thirsty work. He popped the tab on a warm beer as he made his way back upstairs.

Ozzie made a quick tour of the house, reconnoitring.

Harold and Melanie stood mute in the living room. Harold was breathing hard and fast. His brown paper grocery bag collapsed and ballooned outwards with a faint rustling sound.

Ozzie was back in only a few minutes. He was pleased to report that the house was still empty and there was no sign of recent occupation.

Ozzie wanted to take some pictures right away, while Harold was still healthy, able to sit up straight and look like he was worth rescuing, no matter what the cost.

Dean guided Melanie to the couch, sat her down at one end and asked her in cloying tones if she was comfortable. No response. He patted her on the shoulder and told her she was going to be just fine.

Ozzie spun Harold around. He marched him two steps backwards and gave him a firm push that sent him sprawling across the couch, almost into Melanie's lap. He said, "Sit up straight."

Harold's fall had crushed the paper bag against his face. As Ozzie got the camera ready, Dean leaned over him and straightened the bag out as best he could. He said, "Hold it a minute," and hurried down to the basement, came back with a black felt pen. He drew a happy face on Harold's bag, a happy face with curly hair on Melanie's bag. Then he sat down between them and put his arms around them and pulled them close. Harold squeaked in fear, but Melanie snuggled up to him. Dean wasn't surprised. He'd checked himself out in the van's rearview mirror. He was one of those lucky guys who looked good in a black balaclava.

Ozzie backed up a foot or two. He crouched. He squinted through the camera's lens. The Happy Family, and their idiot son. He said, "Perfect. Hold it right there. Good. Okay now, say *cheese . . .*"

Dean shouted, "Cheese!"

The Polaroid's flash lit up the room.

Ozzie said, "Hold it a minute, nobody move. Dean, what's the point of sending Joan a picture of a couple of people wearing brown paper bags? They could be anybody."

"Right," said Dean. He drank some warm beer.

Ozzie unsheathed the hunting knife he'd got from Lamonica. He tossed the knife to Dean, fiddled with the camera as Dean turned to Melanie and carefully cut away the heavy brown paper. He leaned back, studied the results.

Melanie stared at him, at the Ruger sticking out of his belt. Dean said, "You got such pretty eyes . . ." The balaclava was itchy. He scratched his nose, and turned to Harold, sunk the blade of the knife into the bag and recklessly slashed upward. In moments the bag was in tatters. Harold, too, though the only cut he'd suffered was hardly a cut at all, just a thin red line that ran up the side of his pudgy face, jaw to eyebrow. Dean wiped away the blood with a piece of brown paper. He duct-taped Harold's mouth shut and then drove the blade of the knife into the coffee table, and leaned back and put his arms around their two victims.

Ozzie said, "Everybody ready?"

Dean squeezed Melanie's shoulder. "Ready, babe?"

Melanie nodded.

"Cheese!" yelled Dean again, a split-second too late.

Ozzie took a dozen pictures. The last was of Dean perched on Harold's lap, the knife at Harold's throat, the barrel of his Ruger screwed into Harold's ear. Harold's eyes were watery with fear. He looked like a bona fide victim, all right.

Ozzie slipped a fresh pack of film into the camera. Dean asked Melanie if she'd like to pose on his lap. Not for purposes of extortion, he hastened to assure her, but so she'd have a souvenir of their time together, something to help trigger a flood of sweet memories, when this particular time of her life might otherwise be lost in the distant past.

Melanie said, "Mrrph."

"Is that a yes?"

Dean groped her a little as she settled onto his lap. Her eyes smiled at him, and he believed her pretty little mouth was smiling too, under the tape.

Ozzie looked at them but didn't say anything. Dean said, "Cheese," and the room lit up again, bright as a muzzle flash. Ozzie tossed Dean the picture, a square of paper, black on one side and white on the other, that fluttered across the narrow space between them. Melanie held on to Dean in a casual sort of way as the image developed. Their bodies rose up out of the darkness as from a grave.

Dean gave her rump a friendly pat. He said, "You look great!"

"Mrrph," replied Melanie.

Dean said, "If I took off the tape, it'd hurt for a minute. But then you'd be able to talk to me, get to know me a little." He cocked his head. "Am I rushing things, going too fast?"

Melanie said, "Mrrph."

Dean put his hand to his ear. "'Scuse me, but was that a yes or a no?"

"Mrrmmph!"

Dean plucked at the short length of bright green tape that covered Melanie's mouth.

Ozzie said, "What d'you think you're doing?"

"Bestowing upon this luscious maiden the power of speech."

"Forget it."

"What's she gonna do, scream?" Dean stroked Melanie's cheek. "Who's going to hear her, Ozzie?"

"Me." Ozzie unzipped a duffel bag, tossed Dean a pair of glittery handcuffs. "Why don't you show her to her room?"

"Yeah, okay. I could do that."

Ozzie put the camera down on the coffee table. He snatched his knife out of the wood, slipped it into his belt sheath. He said, "Don't mess with her."

"Why the hell not?" Melanie tried to wriggle off Dean's lap but he held her close, shifted his grip so she could feel the hard bulge of his biceps against the swell of her breasts.

Ozzie's smile distorted his balaclava. "Because you're not the kind of guy forces himself on a woman, that's why."

"No?" Dean was wide-eyed with disbelief.

"Not yet. Maybe in a few years, when you've started to go to seed, lost your charm."

Dean threw back his head and brayed.

"In the meantime, I see you as a lover, not a fighter."

"You think I'd *force* myself on this pretty woman?" Dean had thought it over, decided he was mildly offended. He stood up, Melanie still cradled in his arms. The handcuffs rattled. He said, "C'mon, honey."

Ozzie told Harold to stand up. Harold was a little unsteady on his feet. Ozzie led him out of the living room and down a hallway to an open staircase. They climbed the stairs to the second floor. Ozzie was a little surprised to see that the door to Melanie's room was shut. He hesitated for a moment, listening, but heard nothing. Harold had wandered on ahead, and Ozzie had to step briskly to catch up. He guided Harold into his room, got him to sit down at the head of the antique queen-size brass bed.

The mattress sagged under Harold's considerable weight. Hell, *Harold* was sagging under Harold's weight. What did Melanie see in the guy?

Now, there was an easy question. Melanie saw the exact same thing in Harold that *he'd* seen in Harold – a fat wad of dollars.

Ozzie said, "Harold?"

Harold gave him a basset-hound look.

"Stay still," said Ozzie. He freed Harold's hands, tossed a pair of handcuffs in his lap. "One cuff goes around your right wrist, the other around the headboard. Make sure they're nice and tight."

Harold fumbled with the cuffs, managed to lock himself to the heavy brass headboard.

Ozzie said, "You got to go to the bathroom, there's a bell right there on the night table. Ring it. We don't get up here quick enough, there's toilet paper and a Rubbermaid bucket under the bed. You make a mess, you're stuck with it. Understand?"

Harold nodded.

Ozzie stood there, looking down at this man in the weird yellow suit who was entirely in his power. He crouched down so he could look directly into Harold's red-rimmed eyes.

"One more point, Harry."

Harold blinked. A tear rolled down his cheek.

"You co-operate, before you know it you'll be back at the office, gutting little fish. But if you fuck with me, you die." Ozzie pulled the Ruger, cocked the hammer and pressed the barrel against Harold's temple. A vein throbbed. He said, "I'll fire a bullet into your ear and stuff you in a culvert, and that'll be the end of you, Harold."

Harold was crying, making horrible sounds. Tears splashed out of his bloodshot eyes, down his purpled cheeks.

Ozzie stepped back. "You probably don't give a shit, but I'm gonna tell you anyway. I kill you, I'm gonna kill Melanie. You'll both end up in the same goddamn ditch."

He gently tapped Harold on the top of his balding skull with the pistol's barrel. "Do I make myself clear?"

Harold nodded. He gagged, choking on his grief. Well, who could blame him. He was dead no matter what, and probably knew it.

Ozzie walked out of the room, leaving the door wide open behind him. He strolled down the hallway. Melanie's door was still shut. He put his hand on the knob, hesitated, and then pushed open the door. The light was dim but he could make out a shape on the bed. He turned on his flashlight. Melanie lay on her side, facing him, her right hand cuffed to her left ankle. She blinked in the light. He shone the flashlight's narrow beam around the room. Wherever Dean was, he was somewhere else.

He said, "You okay?"

She nodded.

"Mrrmmph," said Ozzie good naturedly. He said, "Good night, sleep tight, don't let the bugs bite."

Melanie stared up at him. What was she thinking? He had no idea. He blew her a kiss and walked out of the room, shutting the door behind him.

Dean was downstairs, sprawled out on the leather couch with a can of beer balanced on his chest, watching country-and-western videos. He'd stripped off his balaclava. Ozzie pulled off his, shoved the sweaty, itchy thing in his back pocket. Dean said, "I sure like that Reba. She sings like a hard-luck angel." He drank some beer, belched. "We got the movie channel, too. *Demolition Man*. It's pretty good, but I already seen it about six times." Leather creaked as he twisted his body to look more squarely at Ozzie. Flickering light from the television turned his face various shades of grey. "You were up there with Melanie for quite some time. Make a move on her, did you?"

"She's too old for me. You want her, she's all yours."

"That's real generous of you, pops."

"But only if she's in the mood. Otherwise, leave her alone."

Dean drank some more beer. His brow was furrowed.

Ozzie said, "She's only a woman, Dean. The world's full of them, and they're all pretty much the same, aren't they?"

"You got that right."

"A guy like you, young and handsome, smart. You had a little cash in your pocket, you'd have to beat them off with a stick."

Dean grinned into his beer. He said, "And I got just the right-size stick to beat 'em with!"

Ozzie kept at him. "Melanie starts talking about how you and her could be a lot happier than you and me, you better shut her mouth real quick."

Dean waved away Ozzie's concerns. His eye was on a blonde songstress wearing a skintight sleeveless T, a white cowboy hat tilted at a rakish angle, jeans so tight it was like she was wearing nothing at all.

Ozzie wasn't finished. He said, "She starts saying bad things about me, grab yourself by the balls and give yourself a great big yank. Ask yourself if she's worth half of five million dollars."

"Will do," said Dean. The video ended. He drank some beer, moved on the couch so his body was angled away from Ozzie and more directly towards the television. Ozzie stood there in the doorway, wondering if he'd made his point. He watched Dean use the remote to flip through the channels, pause as he stumbled across Mary Tyler Moore arriving late to work because of a snowstorm. A fellow employee, Ted, a dead ringer for Harold's handsome younger brother, said something that triggered the laugh track.

Ozzie glanced over at Dean and saw that he was chuckling quietly, his face crinkled with mirth.

Strike two, thought Ozzie, who'd learned the hard way never to trust anybody with a sense of humour.

29

Sandy Beveridge was in her late twenties. Willows guessed her height at about five-four, her weight at one hundred and ten pounds. Her light-brown hair was cut short. She wore a sharply pressed pale-blue short-sleeved shirt and grey shorts, white socks, white leather Nikes. Her slim legs and arms were nicely tanned, the hair on her arms a fine, silky gold. The shirt had Canada Post flashers and Willows was confident that Miss Beveridge had at least one more button unfastened than regulations allowed.

Parker said, "What time did you deliver to the Wismer house, Sandy?"

"Uh, about one o'clock . . ."

"Did you notice anything odd about the letters you delivered?"

Sandy glanced at her supervisor, a tall, cadaverously thin man named James Wilkinson.

Wilkinson nodded encouragingly.

Sandy said, "Yes, I did notice something unusual. There was a lot more mail than I usually deliver to the Wismers. I thought there might have been a mix-up, so I checked as I went up the porch steps."

Parker said, "You wanted to ensure that you delivered the mail to the correct address?"

"Yes, that's right." Sandy toyed with a shirt button. She glanced at Willows and then back to Parker. "But there was something else.

222

The address was printed kind of weirdly. Letters cut out of magazines and glued to a piece of paper, to make words."

"Did you happen to notice a return address on the letter?"

"There was no return address. And there wasn't just one letter. I didn't count them, but I'd say there were eight or nine, altogether."

Parker said, "You're telling us Mrs. Wismer received up to nine envelopes with oddly printed addresses?"

Sandy nodded. "Yes, and they were all the same. Same printing, same-size envelopes. It looked as if the letters and numbers had been glued to a sheet of paper, and then photocopied." She smiled at Willows. "Not that I'm a detective."

Willows returned her smile. He said, "You're doing fine."

Parker said, "Did Mrs. Wismer come to the door when you made your delivery?"

"No, I put the letters through the slot in the door."

"You didn't see her at all, had no opportunity to see her reaction to the letters?"

"That's right. I've had the same route for about six months. When the weather's nice, she's often out in the garden. But I doubt if I've seen her in a week, maybe more." She snuck another peek at Willows. "She's a very nice person, very friendly."

Willows said, "What about her husband, Harold? Have you ever seen him in the garden?"

"No, never. I don't even know what he looks like."

"We'll be getting a warrant to intercept the Wismers' mail," said Parker. "We should have it by tomorrow. Mr. Wilkinson has said he'll do whatever he can to help us with our investigation. Can we count on you as well, Miss Beveridge?"

Sandy gave Parker a nice smile. "Yes, of course. Just tell me how I can help."

Bradley listened intently as Willows and Parker brought him up to speed. He toyed with an unlit cigar as he made the easy decision to seek a warrant to establish a wiretap on the Wismer residence. He told Willows he accepted his suggestion to assign Eddy Orwell and Bobby Dundas to the listening post. Willows almost smiled. Bobby would turn into a human pinwheel when Bradley gave him the assignment, but, as Willows had thoughtfully pointed out, Bobby's slowly healing ankle rendered him more or less immobile, so the back of a van was just the place for him.

Willows hadn't been back at his desk more than ten minutes when he took a call from a CSU cop named Larry Campbell.

"Jack, got a minute?"

"What's up, Larry?"

"On Wismer's Rolls, we got absolutely *nada*. Zip, Jack. Lots of prints, but the overlaps were all Wismer's."

Willows silently absorbed the information. Joan Wismer had refused to co-operate with the investigation, and so Campbell had taken it upon himself to gather a set of comparison prints from Wismer's office.

Campbell said, "The way we see it, the Rolls was so clean there's no doubt at all that Wismer was snatched on his way to or from his vehicle, but not while he was in it. Probably the car was shot up so everybody'd know what was going to happen to Wismer, unless the bills got paid." Campbell hesitated. He said, "You get anything on Melanie Martel?"

Willows said, "Her name popped up on the screen. She's got a couple of priors, early eighties. Nothing recent."

"High-end hooker, by any chance?"

"Larry, I'm amazed."

"Hey, she's a nice-looking woman, living large in Harold's expensive downtown condo, making herself comfortable on Harold's furniture, drinking fine wines out of his refrigerator. Don't tell me you didn't poke around in her closet. My wife'd die for clothes like that. Hell, she'd kill for clothes like that. Melanie's got no job. How can she afford all that stuff? Harold's doing the work for both of them. On his elbows."

Willows chuckled politely. From behind her desk, Parker gave him an inquiring look. He rolled his eyes.

Campbell said, "Think Melanie might've set him up?"

"We're looking into it."

"Well, it's been nice talking to you, Jack. Very pleasant. We going to see you at service, one of these days?"

"Maybe."

"God loves you, Jack. He loves you unconditionally and would welcome you into His arms if you could find it in your heart to take that single step towards Him."

"It's reassuring to know that, Larry."

Campbell said, "Don't be a wiseass, Jack. God has a wonderful sense of humour, but He'd rather be appreciated than poked in the eye with a sharp stick." Campbell disconnected. Willows cradled his phone.

Parker said, "Larry trying to recruit you?"

"I'm not sure."

Parker pushed aside a wrist-thick file. "Wismer's got a reputation as a high roller. He's made millions. Melanie's bank statements show a balance of slightly less than five thousand dollars. Snatching Wismer makes sense. But why bother to take her with him?"

"Maybe it was a package deal – two for one."

"More likely she was in on it, set him up for somebody else. A boyfriend, maybe. A woman like that, her looks, a geriatric like Harold couldn't possibly be the only man in her life."

"Are you suggesting that love doesn't conquer all?"

"I hope not," said Parker.

Willows said, "I think it might be a good idea to have another talk with Barry Holbrook, push him a little. It might not be a bad idea to take another look at Melanie's apartment, while we're there." Willows picked up a pencil, put it away in the top drawer of his desk. He wished he'd kept track of the number of pens and pencils that had levitated from his desktop over the years. Three digits, easy. He said, "If Melanie happened to be at the wrong place at the wrong time . . . Maybe they only took her along for part of the ride."

"You think she's dead?"

Willows shrugged.

They found Barry Holbrook on his knees in the open doorway of a third-floor apartment that had, as far as Parker could determine, a floor plan identical to Melanie Martel's tenth-floor unit. Holbrook dipped a yellow plastic scraper into a white plastic bucket of drywall filler. He forced the filler across a deep depression in the wall, used the scraper to smooth the stuff out.

"What they tell you, they had an armful of groceries, pushed the door too hard. More likely they're pissed off about something, boot the door instead of the husband." Holbrook waved the scraper at a round dent in the wall. "What the doorknob did, when it hit the plaster. Looks like a little bomb went off, don't it? A hole that deep, I got to fill it about halfway, wait a day or two for the goop to dry, fill in the rest of it, wait another day before I sand it down and paint it. And people bitch about the maintenance fees."

Willows said, "We need to get into Harold's apartment, Barry."

"No problem." Holbrook took a last swipe at the wall with the scraper, dropped the scraper into the plastic bucket of drywall filler and carefully placed the lid on the bucket. He said, "The lid ain't on good and tight, the stuff dries out, you got to throw it away." All wisdom expended, he picked up the bucket. "Okay, let's get out of here."

The elevator took them to the tenth floor. Holbrook unlocked Melanie Martel's door and stepped aside. The living-room curtains had been drawn; the apartment was dark. He said, "You okay by yourselves, or you want me to hang around?"

"We're fine – but don't leave the building."

Holbrook jangled his keyring. "Or what, you'll put out an all-points bulletin?"

Willows thought an all-*pints* bulletin might be more appropriate, but let it slide.

Parker shut the door in Holbrook's face. Willows pulled the drapes, flooding the room with light. Parker said, "I'll be in the bedroom, if you need me." Was she toying with him? Willows glanced up, half smiling. But Parker was already moving down the hallway.

He stacked the sofa's cushions on the coffee table and then plunged his hands deep into all the sofa's nooks and crannies. His search yielded a few coins, a ballpoint pen and a crumpled paper napkin.

Poking around behind the twenty-seven-inch television and stereo components, all he managed to do was tangle his fingers in the wires and cables.

He frisked a pair of wing-chairs upholstered in a shiny dark-blue fabric shot through with threads of gold, and came up with a handful of lint.

Parker came out of the kitchen drinking a glass of water. She crooked a finger. He followed her back into the bedroom. She sat down on the queen-size bed, hit the rewind button on the telephone answering machine. Willows took his spiralbound notebook from his jacket pocket. He searched for and found his Paper Mate pen. The tape hissed quietly as it ran from spool to spool. The machine clicked as the tape was fully rewound. Parker hit the playback button.

A male voice, ironic and grating, said, "Melanie, it's Marty. You there? Pick up the phone, sweetheart." There was a short pause. The voice said, "It's just past two. I gotta run some errands for the boss, drive down to that health-food joint you told me about, get the organic this, organic that. Gotta buy a couple free-range chickens, olive oil, garlic. Somethin' else, what is it . . . ? Oh yeah, I gotta bump a couple guys off." Ironic chuckle. "Tell you what – I'll call back in two, three hours. You gonna be home for dinner, sweetheart? Think about it."

The machine beeped. Same guy, essentially the same message. But partway into this one Melanie picked up.

"Sorry I took so long to answer. I was in the shower."

"Yeah?"

"Stark naked and defenceless in the shower," said Melanie. Bored, or pretending to be bored.

Willows kept listening. He and Parker sat there on the bed, close enough to touch but not touching, as the thirty-minute microcassette played one message after another. Harold Wismer called three times. He sounded as if he'd been drinking. Melanie's hairdresser reminded her of an upcoming appointment.

There was another call from the unidentified male. The free-range chicken guy. Marty, Willows assumed. He told Melanie he had the rest of the afternoon off, no plans. Melanie told him to come on over, make it fast.

Willows said, "Harold thought his plate was full, but all he was getting was leftovers."

"How crude," said Parker.

"Melanie's boyfriend, Marty. Listening to his voice, how old would you say he is?"

"Early thirties, somewhere in there."

"Younger than Harold, isn't he?"

The machine beeped for the last time. Joan Wismer's voice was angry, and then plaintive. Where was her husband? She wanted to speak to Harold. She became abusive. She started to cry. There was a long silence before she finally hung up.

"Much younger." Parker popped the tape out of the machine, slipped it into a clear plastic evidence bag.

Willows and Parker searched the kitchen and bathroom. Neither yielded anything of value. Willows checked his watch. The day was slipping past. He discussed the situation with Parker, and she agreed that it was time to take another shot at Barry Holbrook.

The super was in his apartment, watching television. Holbrook let them in, pointed his remote at the set and hit the mute button. He flopped down on a shabby brown corduroy sofa.

Willows said, "You lied to us, Barry."

"Excuse me?"

"You told us Melanie never had any visitors. Specifically, that she never had any male visitors. You lied to us. You obstructed a murder investigation. Barry, do you *want* to go to jail?"

"I didn't lie. It just skipped my mind. I forgot."

Parker said, "Forgot about who?"

"There was this guy. Marty. He comes around once or twice a week. Want me to describe him?"

Willows nodded.

"Okay, I'd say he's in his mid-thirties, about six feet tall, maybe two hundred pounds. Short blond hair. You watch NFL football?"

Willows nodded.

"That guy on Fox, Howie Long? He looks a lot like him. The hair, the big jaw, wide shoulders. The clean-cut type, except for the eyes. The way he looked at me, I might've been a bug."

"What colour were his eyes?"

"Brown."

"He have any tattoos, or scars . . . ?"

"Not that I noticed. Once he wore a gold earring in his left ear, a little motorcycle. I asked him about it, he said it was a Harley."

"How did he dress?"

"Casual. Slacks, sports jackets. Pointy-toe shoes . . . Something that might interest you – he carried a knife."

Willows said, "A knife?"

"Switchblade with a red handle. He was using it to clean his nails one time when he was waiting for the elevator."

Parker said, "What kind of car did he drive, Barry?"

"I dunno, I never saw a car."

Willows stared at him.

Holbrook said, "No car. Really."

Parker said, "Did Marty visit Melanie at any particular time?"

"Mid-afternoon, usually."

"What's his last name?"

"I got absolutely no idea. None."

Willows said, "Marty doesn't live here, but he comes and goes as he pleases. He helps himself to Harold Wismer's apartment, his girlfriend. He carries a knife. And now Harold's been kidnapped."

"You sayin' it's *my* fault?"

"Maybe if you'd done your job, nothing would've happened to Harold."

Holbrook turned the remote control over and over in his hands. "Miss Martel never caused me any trouble. Okay, so Wismer's paying the freight. Is that so bad? He's old enough to be her father, right? Maybe he *is* her father. I got to ask myself, is it really any of my business?"

Parker shrugged. "I don't know. Is it?"

"Wismer comes around regular, but not too often. What's Miss Martel supposed to do in the meantime? Be lonely?"

"When did you last see Marty?"

"Uh, it was yesterday. Somewhere around two in the afternoon."

Parker said, "Did you talk to him?"

"No, I didn't. Not a word."

Willows said, "He paid you to look the other way when he dropped by, didn't he?"

"What're you talking about?"

"What did it cost him, to keep your mouth shut? Not to say anything to Harold. To be discreet. A hundred a month, somewhere in there?"

Barry Holbrook's face and neck to his shirt collar turned red. He looked like he'd swallowed a sunset.

Willows pressed for details.

Marty was broad in the shoulder and narrow in the hip. He wore casual clothes. He had a lot of chest hair. He was clean-shaven. He was light on his feet. He smoked cigars. He had big, squared-off teeth that looked as if they'd been capped. When he smiled or laughed, you could see gold way back there at the back of his mouth. Lots of gold.

Willows asked Barry if he still had the card he'd given him. Barry said yeah, but Willows gave him another one anyway, pointed out his office number in the bottom right corner. He told Barry to phone him immediately, if Marty showed up.

Barry promised he'd make the call. But the look on his face, he was clearly worried about the ready-for-anything look that lurked in Marty's cool, uncaring eyes, the knife he carried in his pocket.

Willows decided to ask Bradley to put a uniform in Melanie Martel's apartment. He was certain that if Marty happened to drop by, he could count on Barry to look the other way for free.

30

Harold had adopted a glazed-eye look that was barely one small step above a coma. In other words, he'd made the adjustments necessary to cope with his reduced situation.

Poor Melanie was suffering badly, pining away.

In Dean's opinion most girls didn't mind being handcuffed to a bed and some girls absolutely loved it. Melanie was none of the above. Though she wasn't a whiner, she'd readily admitted that she wasn't exactly fascinated by the year-old issues of *Cottage Life* and *Country Living* that he'd scavenged from various downstairs coffee tables.

"I'm not much of a reader," she confessed to him.

"Me neither," he said, his friendly smile twisting the balaclava. He was thinking, okay, so she doesn't like magazines. What else can I do for her? He smiled down at her. He said, "What else can I do for you?"

"I'm claustrophobic."

Dean thought she was trying to tell him it was that time of the month. But all she wanted was to be let out of her tiny little room. Taken for a walk or whatever.

Dean flatly refused.

Melanie suggested he handcuff her to the big La-Z-Boy in the living room. If they tilted the chair back so the foot rest was extended, they could cuff her ankle to the metal support.

He assessed the risks and found them nonexistent. Melanie looked in pretty good shape, for a woman her age. But she sure as hell wasn't gonna run off with a La-Z-Boy chained to her leg.

Even so, he told her he'd have to think about it, and went downstairs and told Ozzie what she wanted.

Ozzie kicked the chair. He kicked it hard, and it moved about an inch. He said, "Okay, fine. Go ahead and cuff her to the chair, if it'll make you happy."

"It'll make *her* happy," said Dean. "Or, at least, less unhappy. She can watch TV. 'Days of Our Lives.'"

Ozzie was careful. The chair was situated a good ten feet from the TV, and that's where he insisted it remain, too far away from the set for Melanie to reach out and change the channel or fiddle with the sound. He wouldn't let her have the remote control. He pointed out that if they let her have the remote she could turn up the sound so loud that it might attract somebody's attention.

Dean wondered to himself why Ozzie didn't worry about her screaming.

As if reading his mind, Ozzie said, "You scream, I'll drag your cute little ass down to the basement, put a bullet in your head. Kill you. Understand?"

Melanie nodded. Her eyes wide, hair tangled in fragments of duct tape. Looking kind of tousled and sexy, vulnerable in ways that made Dean want to give her a gentle, reassuring hug that somehow turned into something else. Something passionate and wild. He told her they were going into the village to get some supplies. He paused at the door. Did she want anything? Ozzie damn near chopped his fingers off, he slammed the door so hard.

The drive into the village took about fifteen minutes. Ozzie parked in a paved lot an easy walk from the shops and hotels. He stood by the van for a moment, peering at the hundreds of well-dressed people who strolled idly in the sunlight, taking in the sights. Every last one of them, even the smallest child, looked as if he believed he was the only reason the world bothered to keep on spinning. What a wealth of smugness. Ozzie pushed the Ruger a little deeper into his waistband. "Think any of them are armed?"

Dean, alarmed, stood up a little straighter and glanced wildly around. He said, "Who're you talking about?"

Ozzie gestured vaguely at the crowd.

"Armed with charge cards," said Dean, relaxing. "Armed with fat wallets, and a solid line of credit."

They walked across asphalt and grass, into the village. The architects had apparently tried to give the place a high-Alpine, European look, but as far as Dean was concerned, they'd pretty much fallen flat on their faces. Whistler and Blackcomb combined had been North America's number-one ski resort for several years running. When the snow inevitably melted there was a nice golf course, trails for summertime hiking and biking. Lakes for wind-sailing and canoeing, fishing. Bears for the truly adventurous. But surely it was obvious to anybody who gave it a moment's thought that, despite all its attractions, Whistler was soulless as a bank. In fact, it *was* a bank, in that it had been designed as a final destination for money.

Ozzie took Dean by surprise when he suddenly made a sharp left and entered a restaurant's patio area. He sat down at one of the few unoccupied tables, his face to the sun. A small vase contained a long-stemmed rose. He leaned forward, sniffed mightily. He said, "Sit down, we'll get something to eat."

"I'm not hungry."

"Okay, something to drink."

Ozzie straightened his leg. A white resin chair skittered across the pavement. The chair banged against Dean's shinbone.

Dean sat down. The chair wasn't as comfortable as it looked, but it would do.

A pretty girl wearing a white T-shirt and grey suede shorts, bright red suspenders and lightweight hiking boots came smiling up to the table. Her hair was red, in short braids. Her eyes were bluer than the sky. She told them her name was Terry. She offered menus and a wine list, smilingly asked if they'd like something to drink. Ozzie thought she could be the next Vanna White, if Vanna ever decided to retire. He opened his menu. Ten-dollar burgers. Ouch! It was like being at Denny's, some time in the middle of the next century.

He said, "You got any champagne? Imported champagne?"

Terry bent from the waist, displaying a little cleavage. Her smile widened as she opened the wine list. Her scarlet fingernail tapped the plastic-sheathed paper as she pointed out the champagne list.

Ozzie said, "What's the most expensive brand you got?"

The finger moved, sharp nail sliding across plastic. In the 750-millilitre size, the Salon Blanc de Blancs, at a cool two hundred and fifty bucks per bottle.

Ozzie ordered an oysterburger and fries, the champagne. Two glasses. He told the waitress he wanted the champagne in an ice bucket, to keep it nice and cold. And that his oysters had to be cooked right through.

No problem.

Dean decided on a cheeseburger and a half Caesar salad.

"You don't want nothing to drink?" said Ozzie. Big laugh from Terry. Ozzie touched her arm, told her Dean was a lush, he didn't get some alcohol in him, he was gonna have a seizure any minute. More laughter. Ozzie stared hard as she walked briskly away from the table, through open French doors into the shadowy interior of the restaurant.

Dean loudly said, "Are you thinking the same thing I am? That girl's sure got herself a real nice ass. Five stars, man. She walked backwards, I bet she'd meet twice as many people."

Two tables away, a fork clattered. Ozzie turned and looked. A family of four. The guy still wearing his golf togs. A sweater that looked like a checkered flag, lime pants, spike shoes with tassels. The kids and little woman had been idling away the hours in the hotel pool; the kids still wore their bathing suits and the wife's hair was wet, combed straight back from her scalp. Ozzie caught the golfer's eye. He said, "Or don't you think so?"

The guy fired Ozzie's hard look right back at him, until his wife said something only he could hear. He shrugged, lowered his eyes and went back to his meal. Tough guy.

Dean took out his cigarettes, lit up.

Ozzie said, "Gimme one of those." He helped himself to the pack. He sneeringly blew smoke at the golfer, frowned as the breeze that was coming down the valley shredded his insult and carried it away in the wrong direction.

A guy in a gleaming white shirt, ironed bluejeans and brand-new white leather sneakers came towards them carrying a silver ice bucket nestled in a wrought-iron hoop welded to a wrought-iron tripod. Inside the bucket, ice rattled against the bottle of Blanc de Blancs.

Ozzie said, "Where's that babe Terry?"

The waiter smiled, shrugged. He offered up the bottle for inspection and, when Ozzie didn't respond, asked him if it was what he'd ordered. Ozzie took a close look at the label, nodded. The waiter stripped the wire and gold foil away from the bulbous cork and slowly eased it out of the bottle.

Ozzie said, "Don't spill any. We're talking dollars a drop, dude."

The cork pulled out of the bottle with a soft *pop*.

The waiter filled their glasses and stood back. Ozzie emptied his glass. He said, "Yeah, good."

The waiter poured him a refill.

Ozzie said, "So, where is she? Terry, the girl with the cute little shorts, fit so nice and snug. I say something that offended her?"

"I hope not," said the waiter.

Ozzie flicked ash on the table. "What's that supposed to mean?"

The waiter smiled. His teeth were almost as white as his shoes. "Enjoy your wine, gentlemen."

Dean made himself a private bet that they wouldn't see the girl in the suede shorts again. Wouldn't see *hide nor hair* of her, he told himself, and permitted himself a tiny smile. But, a few minutes later, there she was, her smile lighting the way as she brought their food to the table. She put Ozzie's oysterburger down in front of him, along with a little bowl containing three slices of lemon. She'd brought a small bottle of malt vinegar too, in case that's what he wanted, and a pepper grinder and a cute little bowl of ketchup for his fries. Ozzie imagined her pouring ketchup out of a Heinz bottle into that little container, her brow furrowing prettily as she concentrated on the task.

She avoided Dean's eye as she put his plate down in front of him.

Ozzie said he'd love a little fresh-ground pepper. He patted her hip as she moved away from him, towards the golfer's table.

They sat there in the sunshine, eating their overpriced burgers and drinking the champagne, Ozzie slouched low in his chair with the sun beating down on him. His brooding eyes in shadow but the rest of him brightly lit, his hair glossy and his dark-tanned skin sweaty and gleaming, muscles gliding this way and that with every move he made. He ate the last of his French fries and lit another of Dean's cigarettes. He tilted back his head. Smoke leaked out of his open mouth. He snorted hard, and sucked it back into his nose, recycling.

Dean said, "Want some dessert?"

Ozzie shook his head.

"Triple-layer chocolate cake, maybe a slice of peach pie . . . ?"

Ozzie forced a tight belch.

Dean lit a cigarette. Five left. He made a mental note to buy a carton, when they finally got around to the groceries.

"This is what it's gonna be like for us," said Ozzie, "when the money comes in. The easy life, Dean. The easy life."

Dean nodded, but felt glum inside. Two hundred and fifty bucks on a bottle of sneezes. He would rather have had a Heineken, no lie. The truth was, they were working stiffs, both of them. Lower-class guys. Was Ozzie really dumb enough to think two or three million dollars was going to make a dime's worth of difference to the person he was, the way he thought about things, his day-to-day life and the shitty way he lived it?

The bill came to just under three hundred dollars. Ozzie paid with six fifties, fanning them out on the table, laying them down

one by one. He waited a moment and then laid a seventh bill down
on the table, separate from the others. He told Terry that was her
tip, waved away her thanks, and then got up and followed her as
she went back inside the restaurant. Dean thought there was going
to be trouble, but all Ozzie wanted was a toothpick from the bar.
He told the bartender he was glad to see they had the kind he liked,
with a little twist of cellophane. The bartender offered him a
choice of red or yellow or green. Ozzie chose all three. He dropped
a ten on the bar and invited the bartender to buy himself a drink.
The guy thanked him. Ozzie laid another bill on top of the first
and told the bartender to buy Terry a drink, too.

Drug dealers, thought Dean. That's what they'll think we are.
Fucking dumb-ass drug dealers. Expendable guys from out of
town, intending to horn in on the local action, bite a piece out
of somebody else's tasty little pie. He made himself a small bet
that, if he turned around, the bartender would already be on the
phone. But would he be calling the cops, or the guy he moved a
little product for, now and then?

He spun on his heel and stared into the cool darkness of the
restaurant. The bartender was talking a mile a minute into a black
cellphone.

He had a sinking feeling in the pit of his stomach. He imagined his hamburger and the Caesar churning around down there,
in a lake of digestive juices, stomach acids and champagne.

Ozzie tugged at his arm. He said, "C'mon, let's go buy some
groceries."

The local supermarket was about a mile down the road. Ozzie put
Dean in charge of fresh vegetables and miscellaneous goods, and
strode off in the direction of the meat counter, to hunt up a few
pounds of T-bone steaks. At the checkout, he gave Dean a hard
time about his choice of frozen vegetarian pizzas, diet soft drinks
and even his choice of toilet paper. Dean told the girl he wanted a
carton of Player's Light. They, and everyone else in the lineup, had

to wait while she got a key from the assistant manager, so she could unlock the glass-fronted cabinet.

Ozzie paid from his rapidly diminishing roll of crisp new fifties and hundreds. He loudly told the checkout girl to keep the eleven dollars and fifty-eight cents change.

Dean hoped Harold's wife coughed up the five million pretty quick. For one thing, they had yet to plunder the liquor store, and he was concerned they might be running short of money. But it wasn't cash-flow problems that really bothered him, it was Ozzie. He seemed to think that the snatch was already a total success, just because they had Harold. It seemed to Dean that the tricky part – getting the money – was yet to come.

Back at the house, Melanie was stretched out in a seductive pose on the La-Z-Boy, watching "The Bold and the Beautiful." Upstairs, Harold snored with unabashed enthusiasm.

Ozzie jerked a thumb at the ceiling. "How can you stand that?"

Melanie said, "Believe me, he gets a lot noisier."

"Yeah?" Ozzie, his arms full of paper grocery bags, stared speculatively at her. "He does, huh? How much noisier, Melanie?" He smiled. "There's only one way for me to find out, isn't there? And I'm not going to try it, am I?" His smile broadened. "Harold better hope not, anyway."

The television discharged a burst of laughter. Those bold and beautiful actors were having a high old time. Melanie's pretty eyes drifted back to the screen.

In the kitchen, Dean put away the groceries, put the beer and wine in the fridge and then leaned against the stove and looked out through the French doors at the view. The lake was about fifty yards away. It was a fair-sized chunk of water, but nothing moved upon it. No canoeists or sailboarders. No swimmers. Not even a duck. Dean walked across the green tile floor to the French doors, slid back the deadbolt and pushed both doors open wide.

He stepped outside, onto the cedar deck. He took a deep breath. The air was hot and dry. He could smell pitch leaking from the trees.

He lit a cigarette, pinched the match between his fingers and let it drop into the narrow gap between the deck's planks.

He walked over to the railing, for a better view down the length of the lake. Almost directly below him, a man crouched low behind a bushy green plant. The man was very still. He wore cream-coloured slacks, a snug-fitting red T-shirt and a light-weight blue jacket emblazoned with the cablevision company's logo, a cablevision cap with the name RICHARD on it, sunglasses with purple lenses and heavy black plastic frames. His hair was close-cropped. His scalp was pink. An unlit cigar jutted from his small mouth.

Dean pulled the Ruger. He said, "Hey, you!" The guy looked up at Dean. Hot shards of sunlight flashed off the purple lenses of his glasses. Dean said, "Stand up."

Reluctantly, the man stood up. Dean leaned over the railing and swung at him with his pistol. Four pounds of steel and assorted high-tech alloys bounced off the guy's pink skull.

The man's mouth gaped open. The cigar fell onto the lawn. He reached up and yanked the purple sunglasses off his face and gave Dean a weird, undecipherable look.

Dean hit him again.

A line of blood sprang up across the guy's forehead. His knees buckled. He dropped face down on his cigar.

Dean trotted across the deck and down the stairs. He rolled the man over. Third-degree cigar burns. Where the Ruger had cut him, six stitches, easy. Dean patted him down. No gun. No badge.

He pried open an eyelid, wiped blood from his fingers. The man's eyes were pale brown. Correction, the left eye was brown. He pushed up the other eyelid. Okay, both eyes were brown. Or were they? The left eyelid had already slid back down over the eye, like a defective Venetian blind. Dean pushed both eyelids up and held them in place. Yeah, both eyes were brown. He rolled the man over on his side and yanked a wallet fat with cash out of his pants. He stripped away the cash and sent the empty wallet skittering far under the deck.

The man's pulse was faint, but steady. Dean grabbed a handful of red T-shirt and began to drag him across the lawn towards the house.

This was exactly the sort of unexpected development that control freaks like Ozzie went crazy over. With any luck, their unexpected visitor would keep him occupied long enough for Dean to make his move on Melanie.

31

Bobby Dundas lounged against the flank of the cube van. He wore a lizard-coloured suit, burnished gold shirt, immaculate chocolate suede brogues. Orwell, sitting in the van, could see Bobby in the rearview mirror if he tilted a few degrees to his left. There he was, a cigarette dangling jauntily from his mouth. Posing as if for a calendar. *HotCops.* Bobby lifted his hand, studied his fingernails. Not liking what he saw, he stuck a finger in his mouth, chewed, and spat. He drew deeply on his cigarette, exhaled a thin stream of smoke as he studied his newly trimmed fingernail.

Bobby was taking his third smoke break of the hour. For Bobby, time spent in the claustrophobic funk of the van was nothing but a break between smoke breaks. The motor-pool guy had forcibly warned them not to use the air-conditioner. Some kind of mechanical problem. Orwell was completely at home in the sauna-like atmosphere. Bobby, on the other hand, couldn't take the heat. Not that Orwell objected to Bobby slacking off. His partner's new cologne could have been called *Urinale.*

Joan Wismer's phone rang. She picked up between the first and second rings. She said only one word, "Hello." When it came to human emotions, Orwell's ear was made of sheet tin. Even so, he noticed that her voice was congested, as if she'd being crying.

At the beginning of his shift Orwell had honed the lyrics of his epic ground-breaking rap song, the song he'd been working on for months and months. It was tough work, writing what boiled down to nothing less than poetry. Especially poetry that made sense, and rhymed – sort of. Mentally exhausted, he'd decided to improve his mind with a little recreational reading. As Joan answered her telephone, he put aside his battered copy of Bill Watterson's *The Days Are Just Packed*, and turned up the tape recorder's volume just a tad.

Joan said, "Is anybody there?"

Orwell sat on the van's bench seat, the earphones clamped to his skull. The seat had lost most of its original upholstery. Somebody had padded the seat with a piece of quarter-inch-thick blue foam, but even so, Orwell's butt was causing him no little grief.

There was no response to Joan Wismer's query. Suspecting equipment failure, Orwell further adjusted the volume. His ears filled with a sound like air escaping from a high-pressure tank.

Joan said, "Hello? Hello? Is anybody there?" Her voice climbing the scales. Man, she was ready to snap like a frog's leg. She said, "Where's my husband? Is anybody there? Who is this?"

The headphones screeched. Startled, Orwell half-rose out of the seat, banging his head against the van's roof. Cursing, he lowered the volume. A voice he recognized said, "We're only in it for the money!"

Joan was silent.

A different voice, but instantly recognizable, said, "Five million dollars. Don't mess with me."

A third voice said, "Have it ready . . ."

A fourth voice said, ". . . tomorrow. Noon sharp."

"*Sharp!*" said a fifth voice.

"Or he dies," said the first voice. There was a sharp click. The line hummed.

Joan Wismer asked again if there was anybody on the line. Her voice trembled. She began to cry.

Pathos had never been Orwell's favourite musketeer. He wound down the volume until Joan's grief was barely audible. The call had lasted less than fifteen seconds. No chance of a trace. Joan was sobbing uncontrollably when she finally hung up.

Orwell rewound the tape, played it through as he dubbed a copy. There was a little dead air between the threatening phrases. As the voices spoke, he handwrote the transcript in the log.

We're only in it for the money. Edward G. Robinson.

Five million dollars. Don't mess with me. Arnold Schwarzen . . . How in hell did you spell the guy's last name? Orwell tried *Schwarzenegger.* Could that be right? It looked right. The tape had spun away from him. He rewound to the beginning, and played it again. Edward G., Arnold . . .

Have it ready. Orwell was stumped. He scrawled a question mark opposite the phrase.

Tomorrow. Noon sharp. He smiled. Had to be James Earl Jones.

Sharp! Brando?

Or he dies. Hmmm. Orwell chewed on his pen. The voices, urgent and shrill, skittered past as he rewound the tape a second time.

The van's side door slid open. Bobby's face was warmed by the burning coal of his cigarette, as he took a last deep drag. He dropped the butt and crushed it underfoot, entered the van and slid shut the door. "Got something?"

Orwell played the tape for the third time.

Bobby said, "Edward G. Robinson. I love that guy."

"He's dead," said Orwell.

"That's the way I like 'em – they don't put up so much fight. Arnie! How cute can one man be . . ."

Have it ready.

"Rutger Hauer," said Bobby, smiling. He laughed aloud when James Earl Jones delivered his line.

Sharp.

"Brando," said Bobby. "That fat fuck, that bloated watermelon, that rancid piece of cheese."

Or he dies.

Bobby eyed the on-board clock's digital readout. Fourteen-point-eight seconds. If they were lucky, they'd be able to narrow the call down to an area code. He said, "Jeez, who was that last one?"

"Beats me," said Orwell.

"Must make a nice change from beating yourself," Bobby observed. He shot his cuff, rewound the tape.

Or he dies.

"Paul Newman?" suggested Orwell.

"Fuck, no. Don't make me laugh." Bobby frowned. "Andy Garcia? One of the Baldwin brothers?" He rewound the tape and played it again.

Or he dies.

"Keanu Reeves?" said Orwell. "Or maybe Steve Reeves, or Steve Martin? Martin Short? Martin Borycki? Martin Landau?"

Or he dies. Or he dies. Or he dies.

Bobby snapped his fingers. "Got it!"

Orwell was sceptical.

"Peter Falk," said Bobby.

Orwell smiled. Not because Bobby was right, but because Orwell had finally learned what Bobby did in his spare time. Stayed at home and watched "Columbo" reruns on Arts & Entertainment.

Pitiful.

The Wismer phone rang again. On the fifth ring, Joan picked up. Hiss. Bobby fiddled with the sound. Orwell said, "There's a problem with the volume. You got to crank it to the max." He stuck his fingers in his ears. In a moment the van reverberated to the louder-than-life roar of a flurry of gunshots. Bobby screamed, "Jesus Christ!" His eyes bulged in his head. Tears of pain flooded his cheeks. Another volley of shots rocked the van. Shrieking, Bobby clapped his hands to his ruined ears and fell to his knees. A booming voice whispered "Gotcha!" loud enough to rattle the van's windows.

Orwell knew that voice, and believed he recognized the line. Demi Moore's husband, in *Last Man Standing*. Bobby scrambled to turn the volume back down to a normal level. But the call was over, and the line was dead.

Bobby said, "What the hell was that all about?"

"An equipment malfunction," said Orwell.

"No, I mean the shots. What's the point?"

"Joan's supposed to feel threatened, Bobby." Willows and Parker were staked out halfway down the block. Orwell wondered if he should tell them about the call. He decided not to bother. His cellular phone warbled. He unfolded. BC TEL had responded to his request for an automatic trace. He listened for a moment, muttered his thanks, disconnected. He made another note in the log.

"What?" said Bobby.

"The call came from out of town. Up north. Whistler. Pemberton. D'Arcy. Somewhere in there."

"That's it, that's all they got?" Bobby shook a cigarette from the pack, stuck the cigarette in his mouth.

"You ask me, I'd say they did pretty good, given the time they had, the duration of the call."

Bobby struck a match.

The Wismer phone rang again.

Robert Mitchum said, "Go ahead, spit it out."

"Help me!" shouted Harold Wismer.

The line went dead.

Bobby lit his cigarette. He said, "Jeez, who was that last one?"

"The victim," said Orwell.

"Right," said Bobby, laughing. He stepped out of the van and slid the door shut behind him. Orwell picked up *The Days Are Just Packed*. That kid Calvin. That tiger Hobbes. The van's door slid open. Bobby stood there, his hand on the shoulder of a kid wearing bluejeans, ratty black sneakers, a shiny red and blue shirt.

Bobby said, "Eddy, you order from Domino's?"

"What ya got?" said Orwell to the kid. "Two large with green peppers, olives, mushrooms and double anchovies, the twisty garlic bread, a six-pack of Diet Coke?"

The kid nodded.

Orwell said, "How much do I owe you?"

The segmented doors of the Wismers' triple-wide garage rose up into the rafters. Parker lowered her binoculars. She said, "Jack . . ."

Willows glanced up from his newspaper. He folded the paper and tossed it into the Ford's backseat. A few moments later, Joan Wismer's white '97 DeVille eased cautiously down the driveway. The garage doors slid shut. The Caddy's tires chirped like angry birds as Joan made a right and accelerated east on Balfour. Willows glanced in the rearview mirror. Dan Oikawa gave him the thumbs-up sign from behind the wheel of his unmarked Caprice.

The Caddy's brake lights flashed briefly at the corner of Balfour and Osler. Joan had run the stop sign. Willows gunned the Ford. The right front tire bumped across the curb. The front fender brushed the trunk of a large tree. Willows got the car straightened out and slammed the gas pedal to the floor. The Ford surged forward. Willows caught up with the Caddy as Joan waited for a break in the traffic at the corner of Balfour and Oak – a major artery. Joan made a left, heading downtown. Willows cut straight across Oak. Oikawa followed the Caddy as Willows activated the fireball, made a left on Laurel, drove a short block and made another left on Twenty-First Avenue, a hard right as he got back on Oak Street.

It wasn't as if they didn't know where Joan Wismer was going – they'd recorded her as she'd repeatedly phoned the Tenth and Granville branch of the Toronto-Dominion, and listened in as she finally got through at a few minutes past nine.

The manager's name was Bill Sheridan. Joan Wismer told him without preamble that she wanted to liquidate her RRSPs, term deposits, annuities, and anything else he could think of.

As a financial strategy for the nineties, liquidation was right at the top of Sheridan's list of undesirable tactics.

"Joan, you can't do that. Think of the tax repercussions. You'd take the maximum hit on your RRSPs . . ."

"Let me worry about that. Just do your job, Bill."

"My *job* is to protect your money, Joan. Yours and Harold's. Forgive me for asking, but is Harold aware that you intend –"

"Harold is otherwise engaged!" Joan snapped.

"I see . . ." Sheridan was clearly bewildered. His voice took on a guarded tone. "I wonder if it would it be possible to reschedule this meeting for a time that might be convenient to both of you . . ."

"I'll be there at ten sharp, alone." Joan had hung up before Sheridan could manage another word.

Traffic on Oak was moderately heavy. Willows swung in behind a black Jaguar ragtop driven by a woman whose blonde hair was cut so short it was hardly more than a gauze-like haze, a golden cloud that forever hovered above her head. Her driving was erratic, and Willows was careful to stay several car-lengths behind, even when the traffic slowed to a crawl. When they stopped for a red light, he examined her at his leisure. When she turned her head to glance at a passing cyclist, he saw that she wore sunglasses with oversized black lenses. The back of her neck and her hand on the steering wheel were dangerously tanned, the diamond on her ring finger bright as a mini-nuclear explosion.

Willows decided to buy a ticket on next Saturday's lottery. Maybe he'd get lucky. The odds were something like thirteen million to one, but somebody had to win. Didn't they? On the other hand, if somebody had to win, about thirteen million people had to lose. He glanced at Parker. Her hands rested quietly in her lap. He knew nothing about ring sizes. And anyway, he was getting ahead of himself, wasn't he?

Oikawa was on the radio, suggesting that he fall back, let Willows take the lead. Willows passed him in the block between Sixteenth and Fifteenth. He agreed with Oikawa's observation that Joan wasn't paying much attention to her rearview mirror.

Joan drove straight through to Granville. Given her destination, she'd taken a moderately circuitous but probably relatively
efficient route. This was a neighbourhood of upscale clothing
stores, banks, antique shops, art galleries. She drove across Granville and made a right-hand turn into the bank's parking lot.
Willows parked in the lane, in the shadow of the adjoining building. Oikawa pulled in behind him a few seconds later.

Joan Wismer got out of the Cadillac, used her remote to lock up.
The car's alarm beeped. She walked diagonally across the parking
lot, along the sidewalk and around the corner and into the bank.

Parker pushed open her door, walked back to Oikawa. The
detective popped a wad of gum. He said, "Think she's gonna rob
the joint?"

Parker smiled. "No, but I'd love it if she surprised me." She said,
"Jack wants to talk to Sheridan as soon as she's done with him."

Oikawa nodded. "Okay, I'll tail her home." He popped his gum.
"You don't play the market, do you, Claire?"

"Or the horses," said Parker. Walking back to the Ford, she
replayed the familiar phrase in her mind. *Play the market.* Lovely.

She and Willows sat in the Ford, thankful for the shade, for the
better part of half an hour. Willows was reminded of his days on
the robbery squad, where he'd come to believe that all cops really
did was keep the line moving, that the primary reason they were
allowed to put one villain away was to make room for his
inevitable successor.

Parker said, "What're you thinking about, Jack?"

"We should phone the hospital, let Sean know we won't be able
to drop by this afternoon."

Parker held her tongue. She said, "No word from Sheila?"

"Not yet."

A fireball-red Volkswagen Rabbit rocketed up the lane. Where
was Farmer Brown when you needed him?

Joan Wismer came around the corner, walking briskly. Parker
took note of the fact that she was not carrying a vault or an
overstuffed suitcase dribbling wads of cash.

Willows glanced in his rearview mirror. Oikawa looked very relaxed. His eyes were closed. His chin was on his chest. He'd stopped chewing. Had he fallen asleep, or merely died? Willows started the Ford's engine. He put the car in reverse and slowly backed into Oikawa's Chevy, jostling the car and making it rock on its springs. Oikawa's head rolled to the side. His mouth fell open. Had he choked on his wad of gum? Willows shifted gears, put five feet between the two cars and then shifted into reverse and goosed it.

Oikawa woke up cursing. Willows pointed at the white DeVille rolling speedily down the lane.

The Chevy's tires screeched as Oikawa's foot came down too heavily on the gas pedal. So much for covert surveillance. Willows comforted himself with the thought that it was only average driving. Par for the racecourse. He and Parker got out of the Ford and walked towards the bank.

Bill Sheridan was in his mid-sixties, an inch or two under six feet, no more than a hundred sixty pounds. He wore a dark-blue suit, plain white shirt, silvery-blue tie, shiny black shoes. His hair was white, a little on the longish side. He looked like a comfortably retired golf pro. His office had windows on two sides. The mini-blinds were a tasteful greyish blue, the carpet a darker shade of grey, the walls a subdued off-white. Willows introduced himself, and Parker. Sheridan offered a cautious smile. He shook hands and retreated behind his gunmetal-blue desk.

In strictest confidence, Willows told Sheridan that Harold Wismer had been kidnapped, and that the kidnappers were attempting to extort five million dollars from Joan Wismer. Sheridan absorbed the information without a flicker of emotion.

Parker said, "Did Joan Wismer come to you for a loan, or to make a large cash withdrawal, liquidate her assets?"

There was a small framed photograph of Sheridan's wife and children on his desk. Sheridan shifted the photograph so it faced him more directly. Not an attractive family, thought Parker. The banker said, "About six months ago, Harold sought my advice regarding short-term investment strategies. He informed me that he had a large sum of cash but that it was only available to him for a period of three months to a year."

"How much money are we talking about?" said Willows.

"Seven million, U.S. currency. Harold told me he'd rid himself of a large block of stocks. He was looking for 5 or 6 per cent, a nice safe return."

"Were you able to help him?"

"Yes, of course. Helping people manage their money is what I do for a living, detective."

"Where's the money now?"

Sheridan hesitated. His eyes strayed to the family portrait, as if he sought guidance from his wife. Or maybe the geeky kid with the bowl haircut and a million freckles. Finally he said, "Harold always kept a safety-deposit box, of course."

Parker said, "Yes, of course."

Sheridan cleared his throat. "Now he's got fifteen of them." He smiled. "Fifteen of the large ones."

Willows said, "Does Mrs. Wismer know about the boxes?"

"She does now."

"Does she have access?"

"Harold had arranged joint ownership. I've just given her the box numbers and keys."

"Does she know what's inside the boxes?"

"I assume so, since she spent the past twenty minutes inspecting the contents."

"Did she take any of the money with her, when she left?"

Sheridan smiled. "She might have stuffed her purse, I suppose. I don't know if you noticed, but she has a very large purse. Could she have spirited away a few thousand dollars? I should think so. But certainly not anything like the five million you've told me she requires."

Willows said, "What denominations are the bills?"

"Hundreds, in Bank of America packets of fifty. Brand-new bills with consecutive serial numbers. The money arrived in a

Brinks truck. We had to bring in extra staff to count it, packet by packet."

Willows gave Sheridan his card. "Call me the minute she gets in touch with you, or arrives at the bank. Or if anyone other than Joan attempts to gain access to those boxes. Or you think of anything."

Sheridan nodded thoughtfully as he accepted the card.

"Or if Harold makes contact," said Willows.

Sheridan's head came up. He looked startled. "Is that possible?"

Parker said, "Anything's possible. Isn't it?"

"I'm afraid not." Sheridan readjusted the family portrait so it was angled away from him. He said, "Perhaps you're thinking of our competitors."

32

Steve had vanished quick as a fart in a hurricane. Jake wanted to know why. Marty repeatedly dialled the car phone and "da idiot's" pocket cellular, but got no satisfaction. He had already searched Steve's private room above the garage, rummaged through the kid's sordid little bachelor life in a futile attempt to figure out what might have happened to him.

All he'd learned was that Steve liked to read about UFOs. Maybe he'd been abducted by an alien, one of those little grey men with pointy chins and great big eyes, Mr. Spock ears . . .

Marty glanced covertly at Jake. The old killer sat hunched in his chair by the gas fireplace, wrapped in a tartan car blanket, his slippered feet resting on Butch's warm and sturdy back. Jake's breathing was fast and shallow. He looked gaunt. Worried. Sandblasted. The lines in his face had noticeably deepened in the past few hours, sweat cutting fissures and gullies into the vulnerable flesh. Jake was no wimp, no whiner. He'd kept his mouth shut, but the eyes were the windows of even the most shrivelled of souls. Jake's pale and rheumy gawkers had showed the breadth and depth of his fear right down to the last inch.

Marty, peering into Jake's eyes, had been deeply shaken by the sudden revelation that Jake wasn't perched on the top rung of the ladder, that there were guys up there, hidden in the clouds, who wielded bigger mallets. If Harold had stolen Jake's millions instead of laundering them, Jake was liable to end up getting fed to his own Dobermans.

But, taking a minute to think about it, why should Jake be exempt from the immutable laws of nature?

Everybody belonged to somebody.

There was, theoretically, no biggest fish.

Marty crouched down in front of Jake and asked him if he'd like a nice glass of wine.

Jake stared right through him.

Butch growled low in her throat. Did the dog smell Marty's indecision, a dilution of his loyalty to Jake? No way, Marty told himself. And knew in his heart that his words were true. If Jake went down, Marty'd sink with him. Fuck Jake's creditors. Let them dig one grave, and toss him in first, so Jake'd have a comfortable bed to lie on!

His blood racing, Marty went over to the sideboard and poured himself an inch of Johnny Walker.

Jake, though his bar was being plundered, didn't even look up.

Marty downed the whisky and treated himself to another.

Eight million U.S. was a whole lot of cash. Close to eleven million, in domestic funds. But Jake was a wealthy man. He could absorb the loss and it wouldn't kill him, not quite. His main problem was that the bulk of his holdings were in foreign real estate. Jake believed in land, specifically waterfront. He owned tracts of undeveloped acreage in Florida and Texas and Mexico, bits and pieces of Italy and Greece. Jake bought with an eye on the long term. *Potential* was his second- or maybe third-favourite word. He was a man of vision, with an eye on the far side of the horizon.

In Marty's unspoken opinion Jake thought too far ahead, for a man his age. Even if he could take it with him, why bother? In hell, everything burned. Especially money.

But Jake had vaguely referred, from time to time, to the possibility of distant children. So maybe it wasn't himself he was thinking of. Anyway, the point was that, except for a few hundred grand in petty cash that Jake kept in numerous ten-thousand-dollar accounts scattered across the city, his wealth was essentially inaccessible.

Jake said, "Try 'im again."

Marty nodded, blinked rapidly. Try what? Steve. He hit the phone's redial button. He dialled Steve's pillaged room, his pocket cellular, the car phone. Ring ring ring. Defeated, he hung up.

Jake, feebly hopeful, said, "Busy?"

"It just kept ringing, Jake."

"Maybe he's takin' a piss."

Maybe. But a two-hander? Doubtful. Marty picked up, hit the redial. He pressed the phone against his ear and resumed listening to that ringing sound that probably meant Steve was down for the count.

Jake told him he'd maybe take a glass of wine after all. Spirits raised, Marty went into the kitchen and uncorked a nice Chianti, poured a glass about a third full, because Jake's hands were a little unsteady. He carried the glass back into the living room.

Jake said, "Where are we now?"

Marty frowned.

"Rings," said Jake. "How many fuckin' rings."

Marty had lost count. "A hundred twelve, altogether," he improvised. Lying like Burt Reynolds' rug.

Jake waved at him to hang up. A little wine sloshed over the side of his glass and splattered on Butch's head. The dog sighed.

Marty said, "All those mountains . . . Maybe he's in a valley, someplace there's no transmitters . . . Want me to drive up there, take a look around?"

"Forget dat," said Jake, glowering into the fire. Fucking Steve was a fucking idiot. He'd been told to watch Melanie's apartment, tail her if she went anywhere with the fucking broker. Harold. Suddenly Steve's on the phone, excited, telling Jake he's on the Sea-to-Sky highway, following a couple of guys in a van with a Budget sticker on the back bumper.

Melanie and the broker are in the van, tied up, wearing paper bags over their heads. The Rolls-Royce is back at Melanie's apartment, full of bulletholes, all shot up. Who are these guys? Pals of pals? Or independents? Jake mulled it over until his brain hurt. All he could think of was that he desperately needed an aspirin.

He had told Steve not to lose them, but not to get too close. Tricky orders. Too fucking tricky for dimwit Steve, presumably. Jake drained his glass, wiped his chin with palsied fingers. He should've known better but he hadn't known better. He was getting old. The big question, now, was whether he'd be given a chance to get much older.

"Marty?"

"Yeah, Jake."

"Ya still got dat piece a paper, wit' dat number Steve gave me, da plate number?"

"Yeah, I got it."

"Get da phone book, da Yella Pages."

There were seventeen Budget outlets listed in the book, but only six were located in the city. Marty started dialling. He tried the Chinatown location first, told the guy who answered the phone that a couple of pals had rented a van and left their car on the street for him to pick up, but they'd forgotten to tell him which outlet . . . The guy wanted a name. Marty told him there were five guys, he wasn't sure which one had signed on the dotted line, but he had the van's licence number . . .

Bingo. First pitch, and he'd pounded it over the bleachers. He thanked the man for his help, and hung up. Jake was looking at him. He said, "Michael J. Newman."

Jake scratched his nose. "Neva heard a him."

Marty fetched the white pages. He turned on a lamp, squinted. "There's a bunch of M. Newmans . . ." Marty's finger glided slowly down the column. He looked up, triumphant. "There's an M. J. Newman lives on East Sixth Avenue."

"Dere any udder M. J. Newmans?"

"Nah, just the one."

Jake peered into his wine glass. Marty went into the kitchen, came back with the bottle. He poured Jake a short one, put the bottle on the sideboard and leaned against the fireplace mantel, waited patiently for Jake to get his thoughts in order. Finally Jake said, "Okay, take a look. Don' walk inta a fuckin' ambush, unnerstand? Keep a eye open for da cops."

Marty said, "Okay."

"Ya wanna take Axel?"

Marty chuckled, shook his head in a lateral plane.

"Newman's at home, don't squib him till he gives up Harold. Marty, ya number-one priority's my bankroll. Dat's a lot a money, and I wan' it back. Every fuckin' penny. Ya gotta squib a couple dumb humps ta get t'ings squared away, so be it. But if I can't get my money wit'out lettin' some creep live what don' deserve ta live, dat's okay too."

"What about Melanie?"

"Who?" Jake smiled. "Jus' kiddin'. She's a nice girl." He studied his blood-red wine. "I always liked her. It turns out I don't see her no more, I'm gonna remember her fondly for a long time. Years, maybe."

Marty said, "Melanie's always liked you too, Jake."

Jake started to say something, thought better of it. His mouth clamped shut slowly and surely as a vice.

Marty stood there for a moment, giving his boss time to reconsider. But when Jake issued a death order, that was that. Marty walked out of the room, down the stairs to the main floor, out the front door. There was a wind coming up the hill from the ocean. The mountains on the far side of the water were a soft moss-green. A large flock of gulls, tiny specks of white that resembled hundreds of scraps of paper, were in hot pursuit of an incoming trawler. It made for a scenic view, but Marty knew the only reason the gulls were chasing the boat was because the crew were standing at the stern, eviscerating corpses and tossing the warm guts overboard.

Marty looked down at the city. He watched the city. Nothing moved, but he knew that everything was moving, nothing was still. The city was a goddamn highrise ant heap. There were a million people down there, all of them frantically scrambling to stay alive, all of them dying day by day. Or maybe that was just him on his way to work, being morbid.

Marty took Jake's white Land Rover Defender. Because he was packing iron, he drove at a steady fifty kilometres per hour and braked at every red light he noticed. The verbal abuse he received from other drivers was fierce, but no cops pulled him over, though they probably wanted to, suspecting he must be a DWI, to drive so cautiously. Snailing along, the drive to East Sixth took him almost half an hour. He parked a block from the building, fitted a bright-red wig over his close-cropped hair, put on a pair of glasses with thick black plastic frames and clear lenses.

He got out of the Land Rover, locked up.

Mike Newman's apartment was a top-floor corner unit in a square stucco box. The building dated from the fifties. There was no security system, other than a glass front door that automatically swung closed.

Marty climbed a threadbare waterfall of carpet to the third floor. He walked down the hall to 814. The door was locked. Deadbolted. He pressed the buzzer, heard it ringing inside.

He drew his Colt King Cobra .357 Magnum, the stainless model with the two-inch barrel.

His scalp itched. He scratched energetically, realigned the wig. The glasses slid down his nose and he pushed them back up again.

The buzzer raucously buzzed.

He stood there in the musty hallway with the revolver's muzzle in line with the seam of his pants. Except for the rasping buzz of the doorbell, the building was quiet. He had noticed that there were no cars parked out on the street and only a couple in the uncovered lot behind the building. The tenants in a place like this would be blue-collar types. With any luck every damn one of them would have gone merrily off to work, be someplace too far away to hear gunshots.

The Colt's weight tugged at him, enticed his body off the vertical. His palm was damp. He gripped the revolver so tightly his knuckles cracked.

The buzzer faltered, made weird clicking sounds, small electrical burps, and fell silent.

Marty banged on the door with the Colt. Each time he struck the door the gun's muzzle left a small semicircular dent in the mudbrown painted wood.

He pressed his ear to the door, put his eye up to the fisheye lens, even though he knew he wouldn't be able to see anything.

Correct.

He'd waited until it didn't make sense to wait any longer.

He stepped back, kicked hard. The door flinched away from the frame. Wood splintered around the lock. He kicked out again. The door flew open, banged against a wall. He followed the Colt into the apartment. The living room stank of cigarette smoke and beer. A tap in the bathroom was dripping at half the speed of Marty's heart. The bedroom smelled of cold sweat, introspective love.

Marty emptied the bureau drawers. Socks. T-shirts. Joe Boxer shorts, red hearts on a white background. A pair of almost-new bluejeans.

But where was Michael J. Newman?

Somewhere else.

Marty found a Blockbuster paycheque stub on the floor by the bed. He lifted the mattress, let it drop.

The fridge was empty but for a half-pound of butter, slab of bacon, a dozen eggs, a plastic jug of milk. He peeked inside one of several waxed cardboard containers of Chinese food. Noodles. He sniffed the milk. Yuk.

He phoned Blockbuster, asked for Mike Newman. The girl on the other end of the line sounded like she was about twelve years old. She told him Mike's mother was sick and he'd quit his job and gone back to Thunder Bay to be with her. Marty had never heard of Thunder Bay, got a quick geography lesson. The girl gave him an area code, 807, and phone number. He hung up, dialled the number. The guy on the other end said he was Mike's father. Marty asked if Mike had arrived yet and the guy said he'd been there a couple of weeks. Playing a hunch, Marty said he was a cop. Had Mike lost his wallet or had it stolen? The guy said yeah, lost it. He sounded pleased, and surprised. As if he hadn't much faith in the system.

Marty hung up, shut the door behind him when he left the apartment. There was no doubt in his mind that Michael Newman and Budget Car and Truck Rentals had both been victimized. He thought about how nice it would be if Steve had checked in by the time he got back to the house. But he knew it wouldn't happen, because nothing was that easy.

As he exited the building, he paused to hold the glass door open for a woman old enough and pretty enough to be his grand-mother. He'd expected the woman to brush past him. Instead, she gasped, brought her hand to her heart, stopped dead in her tracks and gave him a stricken look. In a trembling voice, she asked him if that was a real gun.

Marty looked down at the Colt. He noted the desperate way the woman clutched her purse.

He said, "Yeah, it's a real gun."

A few minutes and three long blocks away, he tossed the glasses and wig out the Land Rover's window. A mile or so down the road, he pulled the truck over to the curb. At the bottom of the purse he found a green rubber band wound tightly around a roll of bills thick as his thumb. Fifties, twenty of them. He sifted through the rest of the contents but found nothing of interest – unless you collected lint. He stuffed the cash in his pocket, powered down the curbside window and tossed the purse.

A thousand bucks. The only reason he had the money was because he'd been so tightly wrapped he'd forgotten to put away his gun.

Was there a lesson to be learned?

Jeez.

Marty sat there in the Land Rover, trying to make sense of his situation. Was he scared? No. Okay, what *was* he feeling? He settled on deep concern. But *why* was he deeply concerned?

Because he'd worked for Jake all his life. Not just his adult life, but even when he was a kid. Jake had always been the man. Solid as a rock. Totally in control. Daddy.

Marty flicked ash out the window. He worked it out, added up the years. He'd worked for Jake longer than he hadn't worked for Jake. More than half his life.

More than half his life, and what did he have to show for his labours? An interesting collection of scar tissue, courtesy of a spontaneous shootout with a low-level cocaine dealer, now deceased. Four gold crowns paid for by Jake's dental plan. Fifty-two thousand and change that he'd put away subsequent to unexpected bonuses such as the one he'd scored tonight.

He owned some nice clothes.

He lived rent-free in his garden-level bedroom with a nice view of the back yard. He ate well. Got to drive expensive cars at no cost to himself.

But he probably worked, when you added it up, about fifty or sixty hours a week. Hardly any of this was what you'd call serious gangstering. Most of it was pretty dull stuff. He still cooked weekends, when Maria was off duty.

What a situation. How grimly fucking pathetic.

It wasn't like he got a regular paycheque. Jake sometimes handed out money by the fistful, a thou or more at a time. But you could go for weeks and never see a penny. Worse, though he hadn't realized it until just this minute, Jake was no fun any more. When he'd first started working for the old man, they'd gone clubbing every night except Sunday. Partied till dawn, first-class all the way. No fucking lineups no matter which way you turned. Ringside tables. Complimentary champagne. Women falling all over you. Not the kind of girls you'd necessarily want to marry. But they were nice, most of them. The type who were always looking for a reason to laugh.

Marty bet that they were still out there, the next generation of them. Wild personalities. Girls with bright eyes and shiny hair, who never merely sat or stood but were forever *posing*. Doing their best to be better than they were, in every tick of the clock. Romantic girls. Girls who, if they ever bothered to ask what you did for a living and you said you were a gangster, toyed with their swizzle stick and whispered into your ear that it must be the most wonderful, wonderful life.

The only girl Marty knew any more who was like that was Melanie, and she'd been a pal of Jake's for close to twenty years. But just look at her now. In harm's way, due entirely to circumstances beyond her control.

But was there the slightest possibility that Steve and Melanie had relieved Harold of Jake's money, and then taken a hike?

Marty told himself the answer was no. He refused to believe it. Steve was young, and correspondingly foolish. That thing with the Rott owner, blasting the guy . . . *Squibbing*, Jake liked to call it. A marginally nicer word. When Steve had rashly pulled the trigger, he'd simultaneously yanked the rug out from under himself, labelled himself terminally expendable. If Steve had told Melanie what he'd done, she'd know he had no future. What if she took it upon herself to explain his fragile situation to him, suggested a course of action that would save his ass, make them both rich . . . ?

Marty pictured Steve and Melanie hunkering down in some cheap motel, getting romantic, hatching some seedy plot. No, wait. Melanie was a straight arrow. Wasn't she? He hoped to never find himself in a situation where Jake was shoving a rubber mallet into his hands, spittle flying as Jake yelled at him that truth was beauty and beauty was truth, so go ahead, what are you waiting for, pound the goddamn truth out of her!

The Land Rover had a powerful engine, but Marty drove home so slowly that he might as well have walked.

33

Willows half sat on the window ledge, watching Sean eagerly devour the pizza he'd just brought him from Settebello. Willows had just learned that Sean was making steady progress, but that no decision had been made as to when he might be discharged. Sean had been told about the connection between his shooting and the Harold Wismer kidnapping, the perforated Rolls. He'd listened intently as Willows told him about Harold's wife, Joan, and about Melanie Martel and her switchblade-toting boyfriend, Marty.

Sean finished one slice of pizza and started another. Willows told him about the superintendent of Melanie's building. Barry Holbrook. He explained why they suspected Marty was paying Holbrook a monthly retainer to look the other way, when Marty came to visit.

Sean finished the pizza. He yawned widely, and excused himself. He said, "You live an exciting life, Dad."

Willows smiled. "Wait'll I tell you about the paperwork, that's when things really go crazy."

"Yeah, I bet." Sean reached behind him to turn over his pillow, give it a shake and thump it with his fist. He said, "Dad, I'm tired."

"No problem, I should get going anyway."

"Say hello to Claire, okay?"

"I will."

Sean shut his eyes. Willows pushed himself away from the window. He went over to the bed, hesitated a moment, and then leaned over and kissed his son lightly on the forehead. Sean's eyes popped open. He looked surprised. For a split second Willows wondered if he'd already fallen asleep. He touched Sean's shoulder with the tips of his fingers, very lightly. "Sweet dreams, kid. See you in the funny papers."

Sean grinned up at him. "You haven't said that to me in about ten years."

"It's been a while since the last time I tucked you into bed."

Sean shut his eyes again, burrowed a little deeper into the blankets. His voice was muffled as he said, "Take care, Dad."

Willows lingered a moment, until he was satisfied that Sean's breathing was deep and steady.

The 312 Main squadroom was empty but for Parker, who sat at her desk sipping a hot mug of blackberry tea. She told Willows there was plenty of water in the kettle, if he wanted to make a cup. He speedily declined.

Parker said, "How's Sean?"

"Better and better. Making good progress. He said to say hello." Willows slung his jacket over the back of his chair, sat down.

Parker smiled. She drank some tea and put the mug carefully down on her desk. "Annie called."

Willows looked up from his phone messages.

"She's fine," said Parker. She held Willows' eye. She said, "Sheila's in town. She flew in this morning."

"No kidding." Willows noticed that his voice was curiously flat, almost as if he had deliberately suppressed any show of emotion. But he felt nothing, other than a sense of foreboding. Certainly he didn't feel elation, or a sudden sense of longing. No fire, not even a spark. He half rose from his chair and reached across his desk, picked up Parker's mug and helped himself to a small sip of tea.

"Good?"

"I've never met a blackberry I didn't like. Until now."

Parker checked her watch. "Annie phoned about an hour ago. Sheila's staying at the Davie Street Best Western. She told Annie she planned to spend the afternoon with Sean. She wants to pick Annie up at the house about five, to take her out to dinner. Annie said to call her at home if you had other plans." Parker looked directly at him. "Do you have other plans, Jack?"

"Not that I'm aware of. How about you?"

"I thought we might hang with Joan. Or, if she doesn't care for the pleasure of our company, loiter discreetly in the neighbourhood." Parker held the mug of tea in both hands. The mug was white, with red and orange and mauve lettering, a give-away from a Calgary radio station, 66CFR. "Calgary Flames Radio Calgary's Oldies Radio." She idly wondered how the mug had made its way to the squadroom. Via a circuitous route, no doubt. Usually things *disappeared*, not the other way around. She said, "Mrs. Wismer had lunch at home, alone, out on the deck. After lunch she phoned Eaton's, spoke to a clerk about the various brands of nesting luggage that were in stock. She used her Visa card to pay for a set of three green-and-black plaid nesting softshell suitcases – she told a clerk they had to be identical to a set she bought there a year ago. Russian dolls, the kind that fit inside each other? Like that."

"Green-and-black plaid?"

"She told the clerk she'd send a cab to pick them up. As soon as she hung up, she phoned Blacktop. Bobby intercepted the cab a couple of blocks from the house. There were three suitcases in the set. Bobby measured them, height, width and depth. "I could get every piece of clothing I own in the smallest of them."

"You *still* want a new leather jacket for Christmas?"

"I didn't get one last year."

"Gifts from the heart are rarely of a utilitarian nature."

Parker said, "Another thing. Joan got a phone call when she was at the bank. When the answering machine picked up, the caller disconnected."

Willows reached for his coat.

Bobby crushed his cigarette underfoot as the unmarked Ford turned the corner at the far end of the block. He saw that Parker was driving, and wished again that she'd grow her jetblack hair a little longer. He admired the pale oval of her face, her classic posture. Willows was slouched in the passenger seat.

Bobby sparked his gold Dunhill, lit another cigarette. The cramped interior of the surveillance van was driving him crazy. Worse, Orwell was thriving in there, every drop of sweat that leaked from his overdeveloped body a source of joy, to be celebrated with small yips of triumph, bursts of low, cackling laughter. Bobby believed sweat was a low-level blue-collar illness, something that should be avoided like the plague. But, except for his armpits, he was sweating now, sodden as a rainforest.

Parker pulled up behind the van, killed the engine. She and Willows got out of the Ford, strolled casually towards him.

Willows said, "How's it going, Bobby? You look *hot*."

"Yeah?" Bobby tried a cocky smile. His teeth felt as if they'd spent the night lying in a ditch. He said, "I'm fucking drenched." He plucked at his shirt. "I couldn't be any wetter if I'd just been baptized."

The two detectives brushed past him. Willows slid open the side door and he and Parker climbed into the van.

Parker said, "Kind of warm in here, Eddy."

"Yeah, well. Leave the door open, if you want." Eddy had been working on his rap song, churning out the lyrics. He shut his notebook and put it away in his pants pocket, glanced cautiously towards the open door. "Bobby's such an asshole. A woman happens to drive or walk by, it don't matter how old she is or what she looks like, he can't help himself, he's goes into his monologue, talks to her sweet 'n' low. You oughtta hear him. No, probably not. He's saying things . . . Man, I want to *arrest* him. He's like a sick and twisted cartoon, the way his eyes bulge, his filthy tongue falling right out of his mouth. And he's talking to these women like they're right there beside him, sitting in his lap, listening to every word. Guy's nuts. Plus, he's a whiner. Always complaining." Orwell smiled sheepishly at Parker. "Now I'm doing it, aren't I?"

"Doing what?" said Parker.

Orwell laughed.

Joan Wismer's phone started ringing.

Orwell stopped laughing.

Bobby hovered in the doorway, cigarette dangling from a corner of his cynical mouth, one eye weeping.

Joan Wismer picked up. She said, "Hello?" in a quavery, uncertain voice.

The caller neglected to identify himself, but even Orwell recognized the voice. Bogart, wanting to know if she had the money.

Joan said, "I'm working on it. It isn't that easy . . ."

"Just get it, baby!" Telly Savalas. The line hummed for a moment, and then fell silent.

Bobby, still lurking in the van's open doorway, said, "Didn't I read in *People* that Telly was dead?"

Orwell rewound the tape. Six seconds. Useless.

Parker climbed down out of the van. She motioned to Willows to follow her, walked a little way down the street until they had a clear view of the Wismer home.

She said, "The guy plays the tape, listens, waits for Joan's response. He's got to be wondering if she called the cops . . ."

Willows kicked a small stone, sent it skittering across the road and up onto the boulevard, where it was lost in the grass. Lost until someone went to work with a mower.

Parker said, "How did she sound to you, Jack?"

Willows thought about the few words Joan had spoken. *I'm working on it. It isn't that easy . . .* He remembered a movie about a kidnap victim whose wife decided she didn't want him back, that she'd rather keep the money. And there was another movie, a Mel Gibson film, about a father who'd turned the ransom money into a reward for the capture or death of the kidnappers. Joan knew about Melanie Martel, so she sure as hell had a motive for cutting Harold adrift.

They walked back to the van. Orwell played the tape again. Wrong. Willows couldn't pin it down, but Joan Wismer sounded absolutely dead *wrong*.

Parker agreed. Joan was up to something.

But what?

The Wismer phone began to ring. Eddy hastily cued the tape. Joan Wismer picked up.

"Be ready . . ."

"For . . ."

"Some . . ."

"Hard driving."

The last two words were sung by somebody with a twangy, hard-edged, country voice. Orwell recognized the voice immediately. Hank Williams, Jr., singing for "Monday Night Football." Discussing it, the cops found themselves agreeing that the unidentified voices had probably been lifted from television commercials. There were only a few key words. It would be easy enough, if you could stand *listening* to hours and hours of television, to work out a script based on what you'd collected on videotape. Running a feed from a VCR to a cassette tape machine was about as complicated as flushing a toilet.

Orwell rewound the tape and they listened to it again, all the way through, as hundredths of seconds rolled by on the recorder's digital readout. Orwell said, "I've got an idea."

"Better hold on tight," said Bobby, "'cause you'll probably never get another one."

"If we made a list of the movie soundtracks he used," said Orwell, "and took it to all the video rental outlets in the city, maybe we'd come up with a name."

Parker nodded. She said, "Even the small independents use computers to keep track of their records, create databases for their titles and customers."

Orwell fished around under the van's table until he found a battered, year-old copy of the Yellow Pages. In the city, there were nine Blockbuster and seven Rogers outlets. Orwell frowned. He said, "I'd've of thought there were a lot more than that . . ."

"Location, location, location," said Bobby, favouring Parker with a smile she'd have found seductive, if she'd been an iguana.

Orwell said, "There's dozens of independents. Plus a bunch of foreign-language and adult-video outlets."

A red light blinked on the van's grimy white plastic phone. Orwell picked up. BC TEL had not been able to trace any of the four most recent incoming calls.

Surprise, surprise.

An olive-green UPS van cruised slowly past, the tires making octopus sounds on the sun-soft asphalt. The van slowed and then abruptly turned into the Wismer driveway. Brakes squealed as it stopped opposite the front door.

"Now what?" said Bobby.

Good question.

34

Carried along on an ebb tide, the body drifted past Deadman's Island at a speed of less than three knots. The island had once been a sacred First Nations burial ground, but was now leased by the military. The water was flat and calm. Had any of the soldiers on the island happened to be looking for a body, they'd have found one.

Drifting parallel to the south shore of Stanley Park, the corpse slipped into the relatively open water of Burrard Inlet. There was a slight chop. The body lay face up, arms and legs spread wide. It jerked and twitched spasmodically, like a really ugly puppet on a very short string.

A gull described three gradually diminishing circles, flared its wings and splashed clumsily into the water a few feet from the body. The gull considered the dead man's ruined eyes, and licked its chops. Corpse and gull drifted side by side for several minutes, and then the gull lifted off, overflew the body and made a three-point landing on the bloated belly. The bird's weight caused the corpse to vent a rancid belch. The gull had a cast-iron stomach but was spooked by the sudden rush of escaping gas. Lifting awkwardly into the air, it flew away in search of fairer game.

Opposite Brockton Point, the current strengthened and the wind picked up. Soon the corpse was moving along at a brisk four-knot pace, trailing a perceptible wake. The wind grew brisker. The leather jacket's collar flapped softly. A few strands of hair twisted in the wind.

The corpse sailed on.

35

Marty was up at six. He showered, towelled off in front of the steamy mirror. Was his hair starting to thin, at the back? Hard to say. So say no. He powered up his Braun. The in-house phone warbled. Now what?

Jake was in the mood for a big bowl of Marty's infamous cowpoke chili for lunch.

But, first things first. How about some fuckin' breakfast?

Upstairs, in the kitchen, he wrestled a plastic bag of one-inch rounds of rattlesnake out of the freezer. He poured the chunks of rattler into a glass bowl, left it on the counter to thaw, then went to work on breakfast. In a few minutes, his special blend of Brazilian and dark French coffee beans were playing havoc with a quart of bottled water. As the coffeepot filled, he dropped a couple of slices of raisin bread into the toaster, poured a measured cup of Bran Flakes into Jake's favourite Pooh Bear bowl.

He opened a tin of prunes, ladled three of them into another bowl. The toast popped. He buttered it lightly, cut the slices diagonally. Then he fetched the newspapers off the sun-bleached porch, called Jake on the intercom and told him breakfast was ready.

Jake told him to come on up.

Marty put two mugs and the coffeepot and his toast and Jake's Bran Flakes and bowl of prunes, sterling-silver utensils and linen napkins pinched from the Wedgewood and a crystal jug of milk on an inlaid rosewood tray. He tucked the newspapers under his arm and picked up the tray and went upstairs and along the hall to Jake's bedroom.

The door was locked. He knocked. Jake buzzed him in.

Jake slouched low in his bed. He was wearing his Simpsons pyjamas, which he'd bought in the children's department at the Bay, cleverly avoiding sales tax. Bart and Lisa and the rest of the crew peeked mischievously out at Marty from the folds of cotton. Jake sat there, passive. His liver-spotted hands in his lap, fingers intertwined, his nails the colour of old ivory, cold lizard eyes focused on his big Panasonic TV. Jake liked to exercise his brain while eating. This explained why he always watched "Good Morning America" during breakfast. Or maybe not.

During commercial breaks, Marty read aloud juicy titbits from Malcolm Parry's "Town Talk" column. The journalist had written about a charity ball hosted by a city woman whose ritzy garden-supply shop was, if Marty had it right, a front for a high-end specialist brothel. Was Parry unaware of the nature of the woman's business? Or merely turning the other cheek? Yuk yuk. They talked about the brothel until Jake, abrupt as falling off a cliff, lost interest.

When they'd finished eating, Jake told Marty he wanted to take a bath, told him to fill the tub full of hot water. And to send Steve or Axel to the Safeway for whatever ingredients Marty required to mix up a big batch of his famous three-way chili.

Marty cautiously reminded Jake that Steve had vanished somewhere on the Sea-to-Sky. Jake slapped his forehead, miming despair. He wondered if Marty would mind doing the shopping. Marty suggested Axel. Jake thought that was a great idea.

Marty carried the breakfast tray downstairs. He loaded the dishwasher, checked the fridge and found it wanting, sat down at the table and wrote a grocery list. Two fresh whole chickens, a few pounds of stewing beef, ten large cans of kidney beans, chili pepper, onions. Also, Axel was going to have to drop by the liquor store, pick up a bottle of red wine, a couple dozen Coronas and a bottle of Wild Turkey.

The morning zipped by, as Marty laboured over a hot stove, drinking iced Coronas and tending to his famous cowpoke chili. Axel lingered in the background, occasionally darted forward to stick a finger in the pot. Marty swung at him a few times, missed. Axel was stupid, but he was quick.

He and Jake had lunch at a little past one. By then Jake was ravenous, had been turned by raw hunger from a sipper and a nibbler into a two-handed guzzler and slurper. What a disgusting racket. Marty rested his chin in his cupped hands and discreetly stuck his fingers in his ears. He and Jake sat at opposite ends of the long mahogany dining-room table. Ten feet apart, easy. But it was still too close. Marty hummed low in his throat, hoping to drown out Jake's munching in a flood of white noise.

He finished his Corona and opened another. Jake speared a chunk of rattler. He told Marty one beer was enough, since he was gonna be doin' some driving.

Marty said, "Okay." He put the bottle down on the table, pushed it away with the tips of his fingers.

Driving where?

There was no point in asking. By now, Jake probably didn't remember anyway.

Jake used an inch-thick slice of sourdough bread to wipe his bowl clean. He gestured at Marty's open bottle of beer. Marty pushed himself out of his chair, picked the bottle up by its neck between his finger and thumb, strolled down to the far end of the table. Jake pointed at his pint mug. Marty filled it one-third full. He put the bottle down on the table next to the mug, returned to his chair. Jake rinsed out his mouth with a sip of beer. He spat into his bowl, wiped his mouth with a napkin stolen from the Bayshore Hotel. "Dey only got four stars, but dat's quality fuckin' linen," he observed as he tossed the napkin on the table. He rubbed his belly. "Dat guy, moves da cellphones. Wha's his fuckin' name?"

"Arnold."

"Yeah, fuckin' Arnold. He still doin' bizness?"

"Far as I know."

Jake leaned far back in his chair. Wood creaked. There was a look on his reddening face of grim anticipation. Tendons stood out on his neck. His mottled hands gripped the edge of the table. He leaned back a little farther. Marty tilted sideways until he could see under the table. Jake's chair had risen up on its hind legs. Marty sat there, resigned. The old man's eyes widened as he gave birth to the first of what Marty knew from past experience would be an endless string of farts. The noise he made, a high-pitched shriek, was like a spinnaker bursting under intolerable pressures. The air vibrated. Jake's sunken eyes glittered.

He poured some more beer into his mug. The beer bottle's long neck rattled against the curved rim of the glass. Jake drank some beer. He farted again, loud as a shotgun blast. Marty's nostrils contracted involuntarily as Jake's awful stench hit him square on the nose. It was as if he'd been dropped from a great height into the main holding pond of a primary sewage treatment plant. His stomach twisted. Jake squirmed in his chair, his wizened face darkening, contorting.

Butch had come into the room hoping for scraps. Her claws raked the carpet as, whining piteously, she turned and fled.

Marty flinched as Jake fired another high-velocity round. Jeez, if he'd been fighting for the Iraqis . . .

Jake suddenly looked up. "So, Arnold. Da phone-meister. Look him up. Buy me a couple Motorolas. Two a dem."

Marty nodded. To speak required breathing, and he did not care to breathe. He stood up, stepped away from the table.

Jake said, "Ya okay fo' cash?"

Marty backed rapidly towards the stairs.

Jake frowned at him. "Ya okay?"

"Fine."

"Don't mind da stink of a old man's wind?"

Marty said, "What stink?"

Jake thought that was hilarious. It cracked him up. For a moment it looked as if somebody had thrown a rock through his face. Marty descended the stairs with all possible speed, chased by Jake's raucous, phlegmy laughter.

Marty took the Bentley. He revved the engine, put the enormous car in gear and mashed the gas pedal to the Scotchgarded pure-wool carpet. The Bentley's steel-belted Yokohamas squealed like a stuck pig. Fuck the mileage! Marty burned tread all the way down the driveway, accelerated past the gates and made a suicidally hard right onto the street. The Bentley heeled over, rose up on two wheels. A six-hundred-dollar hubcap whirled and rattled across the asphalt and was lost in a boxwood hedge.

The car weaved crazily back and forth across the street from curb to curb until, with all the grace of a drunken elephant, it finally crashed back down on all four wheels. Unperturbed, Marty ran a stop sign. Still reeling from the methane fumes, he was in exactly the right mood for a fiery head-on collision with a yellow bus full of special-needs children.

The way Jake treated him was fucking criminal. But it wasn't all Jake's fault, was it? He'd let himself slide. Over the years, he'd lost sight of himself and his lofty ambitions. By increments far too small to measure, he'd regressed into a toadying, fart-sniffing chauffeur, driving an ungainly circus act to the exact dead centre of nowhere.

But it is an ill fucking wind that blows nobody good. Slamming the palm of his hand against the dual airhorns, he terrified a gaudily dressed cyclist across the boulevard and into a stone retaining wall. The bicycle crumpled. It was no school bus, but it would do. The rider's sunglasses exploded in a burst of sharp orange splinters. Soft chunks of turf filled his mouth as he skidded face down and at high speed across a new-mowed lawn.

Marty laughed like a hyena. How true it is, that every mongrel has his day. If there'd been a moon, he'd have reached up, howling, and taken a great big greedy bite right out of it, and swallowed it whole.

36

Ozzie put four Hawaiian and four pepperoni frozen pizzas into the oven. The instructions on the back of the box said twenty minutes at 450 degrees. He set the alarm on his Timex Ironman, and slow-shuffled back into the living room. Dean, Dean, the Sex Machine, and his new friend Melanie were watching a TV quiz show.

Ozzie loitered, unseen, in the doorway. Losing patience, he snapped his fingers. The pop of flesh on flesh was sharp as a small-calibre gunshot. Dean looked up, startled. Melanie ignored him.

Ozzie said, "Get Harry."

"What for?"

Ozzie bristled. "Hey, while you and the golden bitch girlfriend sat there on your asses watching real-life cartoons, I was in the kitchen, slaving over a burning hot stove! So now I'm asking you, polite as peaches, to haul your lazy ass upstairs and drag Harry outta bed!"

Melanie said, "I'm not his girlfriend."

"No?" Ozzie turned on her, looked her up and down. "Whose girlfriend are you, Melanie? Harry's? You still chained to the loser?"

"I'm not chained to anybody." She gave him a look equivalent to spitting in his eye. "My God, what a way to put it."

Ozzie smiled. "How'd you like me to put it, Melanie?"

Dean said, "Hey, now . . ."

"You still here?"

"Yeah, I guess so. What does it look like?" Dean stood up, and Ozzie tensed as Dean walked towards him. But Dean kept walking, his elbow grazing Ozzie's shirt as he brushed past him. Ozzie watched Dean vanish from the head down as Dean climbed the stairs to the second floor.

When Dean had entirely disappeared, Ozzie turned towards Melanie and gave her a cool, knowing look. "You think you can mess with the kid's mind, fuck him up and turn him against me, don't you?" Melanie stared at him. He said, "Well, you probably could. But the first step Dean took in the wrong direction, I'd put a bullet in his addled brain. And then there'd be nobody around to care about you." He sneered at her. "Maybe that's what you want. A woman like you, the life you lead. Maybe you're so fucked up that nothing would make you happier than an unhappy ending."

"You don't know anything about me."

"I know *all* about you."

The short chain of Melanie's handcuffs rattled musically as she leaned back against the La-Z-Boy's cushions. She said, "Ever been married, Ozzie?"

"Not that I remember."

They stared at each other, neither of them giving ground. Time crawled by on hands and knees. Neither of them blinked. But when Harold and Dean started down the stairs, Ozzie was the first to look away.

Dean sat Harold down on the sofa, thrust a fresh copy of the *Province* into his hands. He told him to read the front-page headline and accompanying article, got the battery-powered Sony rolling.

Reading aloud, Harold said, "Chinese Dissident Claims Candu Reactor Used for Military Purposes . . ."

"Hold it!" Ozzie rewound the tape. He glowered at Harold. "What the hell's a Chinese dissident? Read about the runaway cement truck." He hit the recorder's play and record buttons. "Okay, hit it . . ."

280   Laurence Gough

"Runaway Truck Wreaks Havoc," said Harold flatly. He didn't have much of a delivery. No sense of drama. He squinted at the paper, peered anxiously up at Ozzie. "I can't read the rest of it without my glasses."

"What glasses?"

"My reading glasses."

Ozzie turned on Dean. "What'd you do with his glasses?"

"Tossed them out the window when I frisked him."

"Back there on the highway?"

Dean shrugged.

Ozzie mulled it over, thinking hard. Finally he said, "Okay, all we need is about five seconds. Dean, rewind the tape to the headline. I'll help Harold memorize today's baseball scores. You tape him when he's giving the scores, and then he tells Joan if she doesn't get the five million right away, he's deader than Babe Ruth."

"Sounds good to me," said Dean.

He cued the tape.

Ozzie said, "Mariners eleven, Oakland zero . . ."

When they'd finished the recording session, Dean fetched the pizza from the oven, Cokes from the fridge. Melanie was watching her figure. Not Harold.

When they'd killed the pizza, Dean took Harold back upstairs to his room and cuffed him to the brass headboard. Ozzie cuffed Melanie to the La-Z-Boy. Dean told her she might hear screaming, but not to worry about it. Then Ozzie and Dean went down into the basement.

Dean said, "Jeez, he's dead!"

"Nah, he's gotta be faking it." Ozzie had used most of a roll of yellow duct tape on their captive's ankles and hands and mouth. The guy had so much yellow tape wrapped around him he might've been wearing Harold's spare suit.

Ozzie hunkered down. He said, "The light's been on all this time. Don't tell me you didn't take a look around. Notice the freezer? That's where you're gonna end up in about thirty seconds, you don't wake up."

Steve opened his bloodshot eyes.

Ozzie said, "I'm gonna rip the tape off your mouth, so we can dialogue. Scream, it's freezerville."

He ripped away the tape.

The guy shrieked, a short, sharp cry of agony. Ozzie punched his face into the concrete. He showed him the Ruger.

"See this?"

"Yeah, I see it."

"What's your name?"

"Steve."

"What's this, Steve?"

"A gun."

"Tell me something. Would you rather be shot dead, or buried alive in that fuckin' freezer?"

"Neither."

Ozzie bounced Steve's head off the concrete. "If you had to choose, asshole!"

"Shot. But it has to be a flesh wound."

Ozzie stood up, went over to the freezer and flipped open the lid. He snapped his fingers at Dean. "Gimme a hand."

Ozzie got his hands under Steve's armpits. Dean took his feet. Steve went limp.

Ozzie said, "Okay, we're gonna pick him up and lay him across the top of the freezer so we only have to hold him a little, balance him so he don't fall in by accident."

Dean grunted, as he hoisted his end.

"Easy now . . ."

Steve lay there on top of the open freezer, in delicate balance, a gentle push away from the void. A thin, frosty-cold fog rose up from the freezer. Dean took a long step backwards but could still feel the cold reaching up at him, fingers like icicles plucking at him, wanting to pull him down. He shivered.

Ozzie rested his hand on Steve's shoulder. He rocked him towards the hungry belly of the freezer, pulled him back. "Steve, I'm gonna ask you some questions. Lie and you die. Where's your wallet?"

"It must be in the truck."

"The cable truck?"

"Yeah, the cable truck."

"It ain't in the cable truck, Steve. Dean looked, and he couldn't find it. He found the cable guy, Richard, wrapped up in about a mile of coaxial cable. But he didn't find your wallet."

Steve thought it over, considered the possibilities. He said, "Maybe it fell out of my pocket when I got slugged. Maybe it's outside, in the garden."

"By the sundeck?"

"Yeah, or somewhere in between."

"Between here and the sundeck?"

"Yeah."

"We already looked, Steve. No wallet."

Steve licked his lips. He said, "I'm cold."

"Think so? You ain't seen nothing yet."

Ozzie pushed and pulled, pushed and pulled. Steve glanced down, into the blue-white recesses of the freezer. He shuddered. "I just got paid. Two weeks, plus overtime. I had almost two thousand bucks in that wallet." His body convulsed. "Maybe . . ."

"Maybe one of us took it? Is that what you're saying, Steve? Me? You calling me a thief?" Ozzie had a fistful of Steve's T-shirt. He gave him a good shake. He pointed at Dean. "Or are you calling *him* a thief?"

Steve's face was pale. He shivered a little. Not much. The rising fog had turned the hair on the left side of his head silvery grey.

Ozzie said, "Who do you work for, Steve?"

"Jake Cappalletti." Steve's teeth chattered like a runaway castanet. He said, "I work for Jake Cappalletti."

"Never heard of him."

"Jake's into drugs, prostitution, gambling, the used-car market. He's a mobster, been around for centuries. He owns Harold Wismer."

"Yeah?"

"Wismer was laundering money for him."

"That's nice. Who the fuck is Harold Wismer?"

Steve shrugged. A fatal error, because Ozzie had just relaxed his grip on Steve's T-shirt. Falling, Steve straightened his legs and somehow managed to wedge his head into one corner of the freezer and brace his duct-taped feet against the diagonally opposite corner. There he stuck, fully extended. A horizontal man standing at rigid attention.

Ozzie leaned over him. He punched him in the stomach with his fist. Steve grunted. Tears froze solid on his cheeks. Ozzie hit him again, a quick left-right-left combination. Steve sagged. He twisted and squirmed.

Punch punch punch.

Steve screamed shrilly, a piercing wail that did not sound human. Ozzie held nothing back as he delivered a ruthlessly low blow.

Steve's face purpled. He folded up, and collapsed to the bottom of the freezer. Chunks of frost tumbled away from the icy walls. He kicked out at Ozzie with his bound feet. Ozzie slammed the freezer's heavily insulated lid.

Steve's husky screams seemed to come from miles and miles away.

Ozzie went over to the rough wooden stairs that led up to the main floor of the house. He was about ten feet from the freezer, but he could still hear, quiet as a memory, Steve's desperate cries.

He said, "Good insulation. Must be loud as hell in there."

Dean nodded. He looked shaken.

Ozzie climbed two steps. Louder. Would he ever fully understand the complex science of acoustics? No way. He descended to the concrete, lit a cigarette, dropped the smoking match to the floor.

Dean said, "I'm going upstairs."

Ozzie moved aside, giving him room to pass. "Don't mention Steve to Melanie, 'kay?"

Dean gave him a look. Partly resentment but mostly fear. Ozzie could live with that.

He was all ears, as he smoked his cigarette down to the filter. Steve's muted cries had faded to inaudible by the time he stepped on the butt. He checked his watch. Six minutes.

He went over to the freezer and stood quietly, listening.

Silence.

He placed his hand on the flat, enamelled steel lid. The metal vibrated minutely, but that was because of the motor, working to bring the temperature back down to minus twenty degrees.

Ozzie leaned over, pressed his ear to the lid.

Steve whispered, syllable by syllable, his desire to be let out.

Ozzie felt the blood fall away from his face. Jesus. He hoisted himself up on the lid, lit another cigarette. A few minutes later, he found himself idly banging his heels against the side of the freezer. Funny thing to do. What did Steve *think*, hearing that noise?

When he'd finished his second cigarette, he leaned over and pressed his ear to the freezer lid.

Nothing.

He released the catch and lifted the lid, to see what he might see.

37

Willows hated some aspects of surveillance. The wretched, unavoidable schoolboy sneakiness of it. He lifted the Zeiss binoculars to his eyes. The focus was wrong. By the time he had Joan clearly in view she was already turning away from the UPS driver, a padded envelope about the size of a phone book tucked under her arm. The front door banged shut. The UPS driver, jogging down the stairs, glanced back with a what-did-I-do-now look on his face.

A few moments later, the van cruised slowly past the police listening post. Parker started the unmarked Ford's engine, made a U-turn and followed the van to the end of the block before she lit up her dashboard fireball.

The van pulled over to the curb.

Parker got out of the Ford. She walked slowly towards the van, timing her approach so she and Willows arrived at the same moment.

The van's driver wore a drab brown UPS uniform, matching cap. He was in his mid-thirties, considerably overweight. He wore wire-frame glasses with undersized, peach-tinted circular lenses. His shirt pocket held five identical ballpoint pens. His stitched-on nametag said MILTON. He slid back the van's door and tilted his beachball face down at Willows and Parker.

"Hey, officers. What's up?"

Parker said, "Is that your shirt?"

"Yeah, it's my shirt."

"Then you must be Milton."

"Yeah, I'm Milton."

"What'd you deliver to the Wismer residence, Milton?"

"I dunno. A package."

"What kind of package?" said Willows.

"Small. About so big." Milton moved his hands. He wore no wedding ring.

Willows said, "Let's have a look at your manifest, Milton."

"I dunno if I'm allowed to do that."

"Okay, fine. Be obstructive. Call your supervisor. Tell him, the way things are going, you should be back on the road by midnight."

"No, wait a minute. What's this all about?"

"An opportunity to co-operate," said Parker, smiling.

Milton's belly shifted to accommodate the steering wheel as he leaned sideways. He offered a clipboard to Parker, and she took it.

Willows read the manifest over her shoulder. The package had been picked up at a Kinko's copying services outlet on Broadway. The customer's name was John Smith. He'd paid cash for the delivery, used the store for a return address. His signature was a terse, illegible scrawl.

Parker said, "What was in the package, Milton?"

"It's listed right there." Milton's oily thumb tapped the paper.

"I can't read that," said Parker. "Can you?"

"Not really."

"What's that other word?" said Parker.

"Fragile."

"Fragile?"

"Easily broken."

Willows said, "Like a nose, huh?"

Milton eyed him uneasily.

Parker said, "Did you get the impression Mrs. Wismer was *expecting* a delivery?"

"I dunno. Not that I noticed."

Parker returned the clipboard.

"That's it? Can I go now?"

"Fasten your seatbelt," said Parker.

Joan carried the package into the dining room. She put it down on the polished table next to a tall vase of pink roses. The package emitted a soft warbling sound.

She went into the kitchen, got a knife from the wooden rack, returned to the dining room and carefully sliced the package open. Inside, packed in plastic bubblewrap, was a small black cellular telephone. A Motorola. The phone had not stopped ringing. She flipped it open. She raised it to her mouth. She listened carefully, but heard nothing.

She said, "Hello?"

"Dat you, Joanie?"

"Who is this? Have you got Harry?" Her voice cracked. Tears blurred her vision. She struggled to control herself.

"Ya alone in da house, Joan?"

"Yes, of course."

"Dere's no cops in ya house, hangin' on ya every woid?"

"I'm not co-operating with the police."

"Dat's good. No offence, but d'ya want him back?"

"Of course I want Harold back!"

"How bad, Joan? Tell me somepin'. Is Harold wort' eight million to ya?"

"Eight million?"

A short pause. Laboured breathing. "Harry eva' mention a business associate a his, name a Jake?"

"No, he didn't." Joan gathered her courage. She said, "Have you got Harry? Because if you do, I want to talk to him. Right this minute. If I can't talk to him, then I'm not interested in talking to you."

Jake sighed wearily into the phone. He said, "No, I ain't got him. Did I hint udderwise? Lissen, what I got is resources.

You 'n' me, we both want Harold, but fo' entirely different but not conflictin' reasons. Unnerstan' what I'm sayin'? We can help each udder."

Joan decided not to hang up just yet.

Jake said, "Tell me, ya ever hoid of a woman name a Melanie Martel?" He waited for a response, but Joan was playing her cards close to her vest. He said, "Da t'ing is, Harry and Melanie's gone missin' simultaneous, an' I got dis awful feeling maybe Harry's reluctant to gimme back my funds . . ."

Joan sat down heavily on a reproduction Hepplewhite with spade-foot legs and a heart-shaped back.

"Now, I hope ya can unnerstan' why I'm dancin' around wit' dis t'ing, Joan. The precarious kinda situation in which all of us find ourselfs, for various different reasons . . ."

Jake sat there in his Italian chair, watching Marty thumb nine-millimetre rounds out of his Browning's magazine and into the palm of his hand.

He waited until Marty's hand was full of shiny bullets, and Marty had started to reload, then said, "No offence wit' regard ta ya matrimonial skills, but it ain't no secret to neither of us dat Harry and Melanie got demselves involved in one a dem crazy roman'ic interludes. Probably dat's why Harry decided not ta return da funds dat he owes me, 'cause he had investment plans dat weren't too fuckin' logical. 'Scuse me a minute? Whaddya say, Marty? Yeah, yer right. Sorry about da coarse language, Joan. I apologize. So anyway, whad I wanna know, ya really want him back? Or, bein' trut'ful, ya'd prefer him dead?"

Joan disconnected.

Jake redialled.

Joan counted thirteen rings, and then the instrument fell silent. But only for a moment. She shut her eyes, and tried to think clearly. Now, at least, she knew where all that money had come from.

Eight million dollars!

The phone started ringing again.

Joan picked up. She said, "Are you telling me that you'll help me find Harry, that you'll get him back for me, if I agree to return your money?"

Jake said, "I got a junior business associate, name a Steve, was keepin' a eye on Harry for me. Da t'ing is, Steve's supposed ta call in every couple a hours, and he's way overdue. Which ain't like him, as he's normally a punctual sort a person."

Joan said, "I'm listening."

"Last time I talked to Steve, he was tailin' Harry and da guys what snatched him up to da Whistler area. Dat big mountain where ya ski? But like I said, he ain't called in lately, an' it's got me frettin'. So I'm wonderin', does Harry have a place up dere, where he might've stashed my money?"

Joan said, "No, he doesn't."

"Ya sure about dat, Joanie?"

"Yes, I am." Joan was thinking clearly now, in a crooked kind of way. She said, "Harold doesn't have your money. At least, it isn't in Whistler."

"No?" Jake unwittingly packed a whole lifetime's worth of avarice into that single word, the one brief syllable. The old man's heart clenched up like a fist. His few remaining teeth grated together, and rumbled like stones. Hot juices dripped from his sagging jowls. His nostrils flared. What diminutive tinkling noises does a rheumy eye make, when it sparkles madly?

Joan heard it all, a cacophony of tiny unidentifiable squeaks and tremors that might have signalled the imminent collapse of a warehouse the size of a matchbox.

When Jake had collected himself he said, "So where's my money at?"

"My bank."

Jake said, "Da whole eight?"

"I didn't count it. But I can tell you that there are fifteen large safety-deposit boxes full of banded fifties."

"How much the kidnappers asking?"

"Five million."

Jake subtracted five from eight. He pictured himself lying face up on a cold concrete floor, rubber mallets pounding him into pink jelly. Ouch. Was Melanie a victim or an accomplice? Was she with Harold or was she with Steve? Could it be possible that she had somehow aligned herself with both men? Nah.

Who in his right mind would expect anybody in his right mind to cough up five million bucks for a dried-up turd like Harold Wismer?

Nobody, that's who. Unless . . .

Unless they knew Joan was sitting on eight extra-large.

Jake abruptly hung up. He slurped at his glass of Amarone Recioto Della Valpolicella-Massi. He peered myopically out the picture window. His trembling finger probed at the redial button.

Joan answered on the first ring.

Jake said, "Ya gotta gimme da eight. I know what yer maybe t'inkin', but dat ain't the way it's gonna be. It ain't a him or ya situashun. Unnerstan' whad I'm sayin' to ya, Joan? It ain't a him or ya situashun."

Joan said, "I don't . . ."

"Take da money outta da bank. Put it inna suitcases, garbage cans or whadever. Jus' get it. I'll call ya in a hour. One single hour. Be ready ta do whad I tell ya. An' don' forget, ya fuck wit' me, inform da cops or whatever, Harry gets took for a drive inna forest, he gets cuffed to a fuckin' tree and shot inna fuckin' elbows an da fuckin' kneecaps. Den no doubt he gets chewed ta death by wild animals."

"But . . ." Joan pictured bears ripping Harry to shreds. Disembowelling him, chewing off his ears. Eating him alive. She blinked away the horror. She said, "You don't even know where he is!"

"Yet," growled Jake. "But anyways, it ain't Harry what you should be worryin' about! 'Cause whad I'm gonna do, ya fuck wit' me, I'm gonna dispatch a couple a my fuckin' associates over dere wit' fuckin' rusty machetes!"

Joan gasped.

Jake was just getting started.

"Ya t'ink da cops can help ya? Not fo'eva! Ya t'ink ya can run ta da Bahamas or Paris or fuckin' Moscow? I'll find ya! I'll hunt ya down! And den my associate's gonna cut off ya fingers and ya toes! Cut off da rest a ya hands and ya ugly no-toes feet an ya arms at da elbows and den da shoulders! An' dat's just ta start! He's gonna cut off ya fuckin' legs! Ya nose! Ya ears an' eyelids, Joan! Ya eyelids! And den, but only if it's ya lucky day, he'll put ya outta ya fuckin' misery by choppin' off ya stoopid greedy head! Ya unnerstan' what I'm sayin' to ya? Ya gonna die a horrible fuckin' death!"

Joan mumbled something, she wasn't sure what. Groans of terrified acquiesence, rather than mere words.

"Have my money ready in one fuckin' hour!" screamed Jake. His spittle short-circuited the Motorola's innards. Bright sparks leapt from the instrument's mouthpiece to his saggy lips. The phone buzzed and hissed and rattled like an apoplectic snake.

Joan cried like a rainstorm.

Sensing that he'd made his point, Jake fuckin' hung up.

38

What had the UPS package contained? Another ransom letter? Graphic videotape of Harold on his knees, whining piteously? The ring finger of Harold's left hand, complete with wedding band? The possibilities seemed endless.

The two detectives strolled up the brick driveway and along the artfully winding sidewalk to the front steps. On the porch, Parker loitered while Willows leaned far out over the black wrought-iron railing and pressed his face against a window. The glass was clean but the view was limited. He leaned out a little farther, until he could see the oval dining-room table. On the table next to a vase of flowers squatted a small white box that lay like a misshapen egg in a nest of heavy brown wrapping paper and butcher's twine. A sheet of plastic bubblewrap reflected dozens of identical half-moons of soft white light.

Willows hooked the toes of his shiny black brogues under the bottom rail and leaned out another inch or two.

Behind him and to his left, the garage door rattled. The tail-lights of Joan Wismer's Cadillac flashed red. The car backed out of the garage, swung wide to face down the driveway.

Willows locked eyes with Joan Wismer. Had he not been so absolutely sure of himself and his place in the world, the look she gave him would have made him feel childish and ashamed. She gunned the Caddy and accelerated down the driveway. Shafts of sunlight glinted off the windshield as she made a hard left and rocketed down the street.

Parker started running.

Willows' left foot was caught in the railing. He tried to twist free. A jagged bolt of pain encircled his ankle. He said things he would not have wanted his mother to hear. Parker was yelling at him from the street. He knelt and untied the brogue's laces, yanked his foot out of the shoe and then pulled his shoe free of the railing. Parker was still yelling, but her voice had faded. He shoved his foot into the shoe, hurriedly tied the laces and ran towards her, ankle throbbing.

Parker unlocked the Ford and climbed in. Joan ran the stop sign at the end of the block, made a left. Parker started the Ford's engine. She fastened her seatbelt, glanced in the rearview mirror and saw Willows hobbling down the street towards her. She put the Ford in reverse and gunned it, laid down two fat black stripes on the asphalt. The neighbours were going to like that. Bradley too. Thou shalt not burn rubber. The Ford began to fishtail. Willows broke stride. He had the look of a man who wanted to jump in a minimum of three directions at once.

Parker eased up on the gas, got the car straightened out. She hit the brakes but was still rolling as Willows yanked open the passenger-side door and dove into the Ford. The door slammed shut. Willows buckled his seatbelt as Parker shifted gears, hit the gas. Willows reached behind him and adjusted his handcuffs so they didn't press against his spine.

Parker said, "What happened on the porch?"

"I got my foot stuck in the railing."

Parker smiled.

The Caddy had a two-block lead, but Parker was gaining fast. A large truck – a moving van – and a tight cluster of vehicles in front of the Caddy made it impossible for Joan to pass. She made a left on Granville. Willows said, "She's going back to the bank, to pick up the cash."

Parker nodded, agreeing.

The moving van signalled a left turn. Traffic came to a complete stop. Parker took her foot off the gas. Joan's lead had been cut to less than a block. She almost certainly realized she was being followed, but there was an off chance she didn't. Parker pulled the Ford in behind a red Volkswagen Jetta. The moving van started its turn. Parker was a little less than half a block away, but even at that distance she could see the "Two Small Guys with Big Hearts" logo painted on the side. The van completed its turn and the Cadillac surged after it, as if in hot pursuit.

Willows said, "Know what was in the package?"

"A telephone." Parker signalled a left turn.

He smiled. "When did you figure that out?"

"A split second before you did." Parker braked, waited for traffic to clear and then made her turn. A block away, the moving van signalled another left. The Caddy's brake lights glowed. She said, "D'you think the kidnappers have already set up a meet?"

"I wouldn't be surprised." Willows picked up the radio, got the dispatcher to patch him through to Orwell. "Eddy, Jack."

"Who?" said Orwell. He chuckled. "Just kidding. Aren't I, Bobby? Hey, Bobby!" Willows heard unidentifiable background noises, a radio softly playing. Orwell coughed. He said, "You requesting backup, Jack? Or would you prefer ketchup?"

Orwell's lazy but somehow manic laughter floated out of the Motorola's speaker.

Willows said, "Eddy?"

"What?"

"You okay?"

"Sure thing," said Orwell. But not quickly.

"Bobby there?"

"Yes and no. He's taking a . . . uh . . . nap."

Willows heard the whine of a starter motor, the surveillance van's engine catch. Orwell said, "Pedal to the metal." He coughed again, a long, drawn-out, series of racking spasms.

Willows said, "Eddy?"

"Over and outside," said Orwell.

Willows and Parker heard the shrill squeal of burnt rubber.

Orwell said, "Now we're getting somewhere."

He coughed again.

A horn blared.

Orwell said, "Uh-oh." He coughed. He said, "Oh my gosh."

His voice was distorted. It sounded as if he was broadcasting from inside a metal garbage can, as it was compacted.

The radio link fizzled and died.

Willows listened in as the dispatcher repeatedly called Orwell's number. A patrol car broke in. Orwell, slumped over the wheel of the cube van, had run a light without the benefit of his fireball or siren. He'd broadsided a large truck.

A moving van.

The driver, attempting to avoid the inevitable, had veered sharply away from the speeding surveillance van. The moving van overturned, spewing a houseful of miscellaneous furniture all across the intersection and nearby sidewalks. A blind passerby had the stuffing knocked out of him by queen-size mattress. His dog howled endlessly. A red corduroy beanbag chair burst on impact with a telephone pole, and sprayed its guts into the startled faces of a class of third-graders on a field trip. The thoroughly traumatized children wanted the whole world to know how terrified they were. The last victim was a corpulent off-duty BC Transit driver who'd suffered minor head injuries when he'd failed to outrun a camelback sofa.

Willows suggested that the moving van was now owned by two small guys with broken hearts.

Parker didn't think that was very funny, under the circumstances.

But she laughed anyway.

Joan Wismer parked her Cadillac in the lot behind the bank. Willows waited out a burst of cross-talk and then told the dispatcher he needed a backup car, another unmarked unit.

Joan popped the trunk and got out of the car, hauled a large softshell tartan suitcase out of the trunk and walked hurriedly around to the front of the bank and entered the building.

Parker drove forward about fifty feet, into a loading zone. She dropped the sun visor on the POLICE VEHICLE placard and killed the Ford's motor. They got out of the car, locked up, waited for a break in the traffic and hurried across the street towards the bank. Willows peered through the double glass doors. A woman in a teller lineup stared at him. Not Joan, though. He and Parker entered the bank. The woman continued to stare suspiciously at him.

Joan Wismer stood at the customer-services counter. She was facing away from them, speaking animatedly to a thin man with a receding hairline, pale eyes, coat-hanger shoulders. The man placed a file card down on the counter and offered her a pen. Joan signed the card with an angry flourish. Parker drifted away from Willows, who buried his head in a glossy brochure on mutual funds. The bank employee lifted a hinged section of the counter and held it for Joan Wismer as she passed through. His offer to carry her suitcase was summarily rejected. He trailed along behind, hurrying to keep pace, as Joan marched briskly towards the door leading to the basement vault.

The woman who'd been eyeing Willows was being dealt with by a teller. The teller was covertly studying Willows, as if memorizing his features.

Bill Sheridan's office door was open. The manager was working at his desk. Parker knocked softly on the door's pebbled-glass panel. Sheridan glanced up.

Parker said, "Got a moment?"

"Yes, of course." Sheridan half rose from his chair, settled back as Parker and then Willows slipped into his office. Willows stayed close to the door. He said, "One of your customers thinks I might be a bank robber. She's talking to the teller in the pink blouse."

Sheridan looked alarmed, then mildly amused. He got up and went over to the door, made eye contact with the teller and gave her the thumbs-up sign. As he returned to his desk, Willows eased the door shut until it was open only a crack.

Sheridan said, "What's going on?"

Parker said, "Did Mrs. Wismer call, in the past half-hour or so?"

"Not to my knowledge."

"But she wouldn't need to call ahead, would she, if all she wanted was to examine the contents of her safety-deposit boxes."

"That's absolutely correct."

Parker said, "Would you mind if we just sat here for a few moments, while Mrs. Wismer goes about her business?"

Sheridan hesitated.

Willows said, "You mentioned last time we talked that Harold's money is in your safety-deposit boxes."

"I take it you anticipate Mrs. Wismer effecting a withdrawal."

"A very large withdrawal," said Willows.

Sheridan nodded solemnly. He said, "I've tried to imagine what it must be like, to suddenly be snatched off your feet, have your life taken away from you, find yourself utterly helpless." He shrugged. "I hope things turn out for the best."

Willows looked out at the streetscape, divided by the Venetian blinds into parallel strips.

He wondered what had happened to Orwell.

A man walked up to the window. He stared at the glass for a moment, ran a comb through his hair and then wandered away.

Sheridan said, "Happens all the time. There's a reflective privacy film on the glass. People treat the window as if it were a mirror." He smiled wryly. "I suppose at times it would be fairly amusing, if I weren't a bank manager."

A few minutes later Parker said, "There she is."

Willows leaned forward so he had a better view out the partly opened office door. Joan Wismer was labouring under the considerable weight of three green-and-black tartan suitcases. She looked flushed. Her body was distorted by the suitcases' weight. Anything was heavy, if there was enough of it. Why should money be an exception to the rule?

A bank employee held the door open for her. Willows waited until she had stepped outside and then started after her.

The manager said, "What do you intend to do now?"

"Thanks for your help, Mr. Sheridan," said Parker as she followed Willows out the door.

In the parking lot, Joan slammed the trunk lid on the three suitcases, withdrew her key and got into her car. Parker and Willows walked with all due haste towards the Ford.

Dan Oikawa and Farley Spears sat in a pale-green Caprice parked nose out in the lane behind the Ford. Oikawa waggled his fingers. He turned and said something to Spears, but Spears didn't look up from his donut.

The two unmarked vehicles tailed Joan back to her house. Willows made a U-turn at the end of the block. By the time he'd come around, the Caddy had vanished inside the garage.

"Now what?" said Parker.

"We steal the cash, buy a couple of first-class tickets to someplace with a warm climate and easily corrupted politicians."

"Don't even think about it, Jack. Especially not out loud."

The green Caprice filled the rearview mirror. Oikawa got out of the car, walked towards them.

Parker rolled down her window.

Oikawa said, "You heard about Eddy and Bobby?"

"Yeah, what happened?"

Oikawa crouched down, rested his forearms on the door frame. "The van had a leaky muffler. Despite Orwell's objections, Bobby insisted on keeping the engine running so he could use the air-conditioner. The two of them sucked carbon monoxide all day long, dry-roasted their brains."

"But Eddy's okay?"

"Terminally embarrassed. Bobby broke his leg again. Neglected to fasten his seatbelt."

Fifteen minutes later, Joan Wismer's Cadillac swept down the driveway, made a hard left and accelerated towards the end of the block.

Parker started the Ford. She checked the gas gauge. Three-quarters of a tank. She pulled away from the curb. "If this is it, Jack, we're going to need at least three more units."

Willows reached for the radio.

39

Three sides of the booth were enclosed by dusty glass panels framed in brushed aluminum. The fourth side faced the oncoming traffic and had a folding glass door. The door was wide open, wedged in place. The bottom hinge was broken. The lower panel of safety glass had been fractured by repeated violent blows. Somebody's boot, somebody's head.

A semi rolled past, filling the booth with diesel fumes and dust, and the rich scent of hot asphalt.

Cuing the tape, Dean pressed the play button. He watched the counter run down to zero, and then hit the pause button. He tucked the recorder under his arm and picked up the receiver, listened for the hum of the dial tone. He dropped a quarter in the slot, dialled a 1 and then 604 and then Joan Wismer's seven-digit number.

Down at the far end of the line, the phone began to ring. Long-distance tolls from payphones were murder. Dean got ready to shovel in the quarters.

The phone kept ringing.

Where was she? In the can, most likely. Was this a cop trick? He hung up. His quarter dropped down the chute and he retrieved it.

Dean lit a cigarette. A more-or-less constant parade of Mercedes and BMWs and Jaguars cruised up and down the highway. He'd learned that there was all kinds of stuff to do in Whistler, even during the summer. You could ski up on the glacier. Play eighteen holes of golf. Swim. Go sailing or hiking or mountain-biking. Man, he couldn't wait to get back to the city.

A Mercedes zipped past and then a low-slung black BMW convertible flashed its turn signal, pulled off the highway. The Mercedes stopped in a cloud of fine grey dust that rolled away from the car and into the booth.

The car had a vanity licence plate – SNOCONE. The driver was in her early twenties, a lissome blonde. She wore black sunglasses, a black tanktop, and skimpy black shorts. Dean couldn't help wondering how she got all that leg into that little car.

She slid the sunglasses down her pert nose. Her lipstick was pink, her eyes an offshore green, her teeth white as uncut cocaine.

Dean thought she was nothing less than coronary-gorgeous. Struggling to maintain a degree of objectivity, he decided her teeth were too flawless, but otherwise she was perfect.

She said, "Are you going to be long?"

Dean gave her a king-size leer. "Long enough, sweetheart."

Still smiling, she spun the wheel and goosed it. The BMW's rear tires spat a wheelbarrow full of dust and gravel into the close confines of the phone booth. The woman gave Dean a good look at her middle finger. Scarlet nail polish. No ring.

Coughing and gasping, he staggered out of the booth. He lit a cigarette and stood there in the patchy sunlight, waiting for the dust to clear. An RCMP cruiser rolled by, but the cop behind the wheel paid him no mind.

Dean checked his watch. He'd fallen almost six minutes behind Ozzie's ridiculous tight-ass schedule.

He thought about Steve, in the freezer.

He trotted back inside the dust-choked phone booth, and redialled Joan's number.

There was a short pause, a series of distant clanks that sounded like somebody in a suit of armour falling down an escalator. Finally Dean's ears were filled with a ringing sound.

Joan's phone rang and rang.

And rang.

And rang.

Where the hell was she?

A sick feeling blossomed in the pit of Dean's stomach, crept furtively into the highways and byways of his intestinal tract.

Ring ring ring.

Dean lit a fresh cigarette from the stub of the last.

Ring ring. Ring.

Ring.

Where in hell was she?

Ring ring ring. Ring ring ring.

He hung up. His quarter dropped. He stepped out of the booth and walked blindly towards the rented van.

Somehow, he could still hear the telephone ringing. How could that be? He started the van's engine, turned in a tight circle and cut across the solid double, to the northbound side of the highway.

His stomach churned. Man oh man. Was Ozzie going to be pissed? He was going to be royally pissed.

A black BMW convertible with a blonde at the wheel overtook him at speed, sassily cut in front of him with no more than a few inches to spare. Dean's heart soared, but only for a moment. Identical-model BMW. Identical-model blonde. Wrong plates.

Dean flicked his cigarette out the open window, lit another. He'd never be able to forget the white-hot look that had raged across Ozzie's eyes a moment before he'd dumped Steve in the freezer.

No way Ozzie was dumping *him* into that freezer.

Or Melanie either, Dean decided on the spur of the moment. Starting to see himself, not a moment too soon, as one of the good guys. A guy who'd crunched a few toes but was finally learning how to dance.

He leaned back against the rental's bench seat. Who was he fooling? Nobody, not even himself. He was rotten to the marrow, doomed to stay rotten until the day somebody put him out of his misery. The ugly truth was that the caper had started to go wrong and he was looking for a way to bail out.

In his opinion Harold was nothing but a couple of hundred pounds of undercooked steak. But Melanie was different. The girl had looks *and* brains. Maybe if he told her he wanted out and was willing to take her with him, she'd take him by the hand and lead him to an exit.

40

It was a nice day, and it was going to be a busy day. A day that was just packed. How many nice days could be left to a man Jake's age? Not so many that he could afford to waste one. Not so many that he felt comfortable pondering the math.

Acting on Jake's instructions, Marty dialled an Italian deli on Broadway that Jake owned a piece of, as a result of a quick bet on a slow horse. Marty told the owner, Luigi or Mario or whatever the guy's name was, that Jake was in the mood for a deluxe wicker picnic hamper for two hungry people, and that it better be ready in ten minutes.

Axel wondered if he could come along for the ride. Smiling up at Marty with his gap-toothed, snaggly teeth, he said, "May I please come along for the ride, Marty?"

Marty said, "No."

He took the Land Rover, detoured en route to a liquor store to buy a case of Amarone Recioto Della Valpolicella-Massi. The '88, Jake had told him. The old man was awfully particular, for a guy whose taste buds were worn to a nub. Not that Marty blamed him. Jake was a liar and a fornicator and a thief and a killer. So, why shouldn't he enjoy himself to the best of his limited abilities, given he didn't have much time left in this world and chances were totally excellent that he was going straight to hell the minute the paramedics gave up on him?

Marty paid cash for the wine, tucked the receipt in his wallet. At the deli, there was no bill to pay, unless you counted being fawned over by a guy who'd apparently spilled a bottle of cheap aftershave all over his face.

Home again, Marty wheeled the Land Rover to the top of the driveway and found Axel and Jake waiting for him in the back-seat of the Bentley, Jake's scrawny body huddled under several cashmere car blankets. Axel was trying to trim his fingernails with a pair of wire-clippers. The Bentley was idling, the heater on full blast.

Marty put the wicker picnic basket on the seat beside him, ran the seatbelt in and out of the curved handle, so the basket wouldn't take a run at the burled walnut dashboard, in the event he had to slam on the brakes or crash a roadblock. He told Jake he was kind of warm. Feverish, actually. Would it be okay to turn down the heater?

Jake said no.

Crack a window?

Forget it.

Axel sat there next to Jake, rigid and silent, the thick, tight-curled hair on the expatriate's muscular arms matted with sweat. A slick wet sheen on his bleached and bony face, a waterfall of sweat tumbling off his nose.

Marty told himself, don't worry about it. Jake was tense. A little joke coagulated in his brain. He smiled into the black sleeve of his suit. Jake was beyond tense. He was almost past tense.

Who could blame him for being a little distraught, with eight extra-large hanging in the balance, the miserable crumbs of his life on the line.

Jake said, "Ya got dat Motorola ya bought offa Danny?"

"Yeah, Jake. Right here."

"Gimme."

Jake fumbled with a crumpled scrap of paper. His arthritic murderer's trigger finger dialled Joan's cellphone number one digit at a time.

Axel said, "You vant a hand wiff that, Jake?"

"Shaddap!"

Joan picked up on the first ring.

Jake said, "Hey, babe. It's me. Ya got my fuckin' cash?"

"I think so, most of it," said Joan. "I can't tell, exactly, I haven't had time to count it, but . . ."

Jake cut her off. "Ya skim a liddle offa da top, ya gonna wish ya wasn't quite so clever. I'm assumin' da cops know Harry's gone missin'?"

"Yes, they do."

"Ya got cops parked outside ya residence, sittin' in unmarked cars or delivery vans or whadever, drinkin' col' coffee outta paper cups, smokin' cigarettes and blowin' the smoke outta they noses?"

Joan knew a rhetorical question when she heard one.

Jake said, "Ya got my cash, put alla dem dollars inna trunk a ya Caddy dat's a yea' old, I unnerstand, and lookin' kinda lame?"

"Yes, I did."

"Okay, what ya gotta do now, ya gotta get inna car and drive away from da house, follow dis map I woiked out for ya." Jake rested the phone in his lap. He sniffed the air. "Chicken?"

"Roast beef," said Axel. "Good red meat, und plenty of it."

Marty glared at him.

Jake lifted the phone to his mouth. He said, "Ya inna car, Joan?"

"I'm just starting the engine."

Jake heard the roar of the Caddy's motor. He put his hand over the phone's mouthpiece. "Ya get da wine?"

Marty said, "Yeah, I got it."

"A nice bottle of Scharzhofberger Riesling Spatlese would haff been so vunderful tasty," said Axel.

"Shaddap. Dere's a full bottle in da basket?"

Marty nodded.

Jake leaned forward, patted Marty on the shoulder. Marty felt a sudden surge of warmth. He told himself not to get emotional, to stay calm. This was crazy, what they were doing.

Jake said, "Joan, ya onna road?"

"I'm just starting down the driveway. Now I'm turning on to the street."

"Okay, good. Dere's some one-way streets. I'm gonna send ya down 'em da wrong way, but if ya drive careful, ya'll do fine. Ya see any cars followin' along behind ya, dat ya recognize as been hangin' around ya street?"

"Yes, a green car, a large green car."

"Ya gotta nice voice, Joan. Real womanly an' smooth. Do like I say so I don't gotta mess ya up." Jake summoned up all his charm. He smiled into the receiver, and said, "Okay, Joan?"

"Okay," said Joan.

Jake glanced up, saw Marty watching him in the mirror. He put his hand over the telephone and gave Marty explicit directions as to where to drive and how to get there. Marty nodded. A red tide crept slowly up the back of his neck and vanished into his haircut. All those sweaty, painful, expensive hours he'd invested in tae kwon-do, karate, kick boxing and tai chi. The thousands of dollars he'd spent on combat shooting and related courses in the bitter cold hills of Montana and Utah, the snake-infested swamps of Georgia and Alabama. And for what – so he could wear plain black shoes and a cheap black suit and a white polyester shirt and a peak cap with a shiny brim, so he could grow up to be a fuckin' *chauffeur*?

Jake said, "Joan, get on King Edward, an' head east."

"Yes, all right. I have to turn around . . ."

"Take ya time, honey. Ya only gotta do dis once, so do it right. We don' wanna hafta do dat machete t'ing, do we, baby?"

Jake spread his palsied fingers wide. The phone dropped into his lap, making the blankets sag. He told Axel to get out his humidor full of Cuban cigars that would have cost him twenty dollars apiece, if he'd had to pay for them like a normal person. Axel used the wire-cutters to clip a cigar, sparked his lighter. Jake sucked in a lungful of smoke, exhaled. Marty was enveloped in a cloud of aromatic second-hand smoke.

Axel thought that was pretty funny.

The telephone squeaked.

Jake picked up.

Joan said, "I'm going east on King Edward."

"Okay, good. Take a right on Arbutus. Drive ta Forty-first an' take anotha right. Lemme know when ya hit Granville."

Jake sat there, smoking his cigar and looking out the green-tinted bulletproof window at his green-tinted world.

Marty shifted in his seat. Leather creaked. He said, "You really think she can lose the cops, Jake?"

"We haff no problems!" hissed Axel.

"Da cops got no choppa or we'd a seen it. Cars ain't no problem, I don't care how many dey got. Plus, me 'n' Joan got a deal woiked out, based on I'm gonna kill her, she fucks up."

Marty nodded. Sure thing, Jake. No chopper, no problem. Did Jake have any functioning brain cells left in his wizened old head? One or two, maybe. But definitely not three.

41

Joan had lived in the city most of her life, but she drove like the ultimate tourist; a stranger in a strange land who was unsure as to where she was going and how she ought to get there.

If there was anything at all about her driving that was consistent, it was her remarkable inconsistency. The Cadillac would keep pace with the flow of traffic for a few blocks, suddenly accelerate, navigate several abrupt lane changes and then an unsignalled left or right turn onto a side street, slow to a crawl or even come to a full stop.

Joan's police escort consisted of a single unmarked car on each flank, a third car keeping pace ahead of her and two more behind. From time to time the lead car would drop back, exchange places with one of the flanking or following vehicles.

After half an hour of this, Joan pulled into a full-service bay at the Forty-first and Granville Esso. She had the Caddy's tank filled with premium, the glass cleaned, the fluid levels and air pressure in all four tires checked.

Parker said, "Looks as if she's planning a good long run."

Willows agreed.

The Caddy burnt rubber just as the traffic light changed, narrowly missed the startled gas jockey, and ran the red against seven lanes of surging south- and northbound traffic. Brakes squealed. Glass shattered. Metal crumpled. Horns blared.

Willows blipped the siren as Parker drove up on the sidewalk, back onto the road, over bits and pieces of high-impact plastic and clouds of crunchy safety glass.

Oikawa's green Caprice filled Parker's rearview mirror.

The lead vehicle, a mudbrown Ford Crown Victoria driven by a traffic cop named Jamie Furth, had cut through a Toyota dealership and was half a block behind the Caddy, keeping pace. One of the flank vehicles had gone astray but was closing fast. The other unmarked flank car had rear-ended a burgundy-colour late-model DeVille. The DeVille's driver was described by several independent female witnesses as a blue-eyed, curly-haired redhead who was movie-star handsome. Add hot-tempered to the description, for the man had drawn a shiny semiautomatic pistol and shot out the police vehicle's front tires before vanishing down Forty-first Avenue in a haze of exhaust fumes and gunsmoke.

Was the gunfire another random act of aggression, or was the shooter a member of the snatch team?

It wasn't Willows' problem. All he had to think about was Joan Wismer and the tartan suitcases full of cash that were almost certainly in her Cadillac's spacious trunk.

Oikawa called in.

Joan had made a left on Oak. Willows and Parker had already fallen a full three blocks behind. Parker lit up the fireball. Traffic moved aside. She put her foot down hard on the gas, killed the fireball as they swung onto Oak and sped north towards the downtown core.

High-speed pursuit, no lights or siren. Parker was running on pure adrenaline. If she bowled over an unwary pedestrian, the press would crucify her.

The radio popped and crackled.

Oikawa said, "See me, Jack? Half a block up, curb lane. She's slowed to fifty and I'm right on her ass."

Jamie's Furth's Crown Victoria was in a holding pattern at the northeast corner of Oak and Thirty-third. Willows told Oikawa to fall back and let Furth take the Caddy as soon as it had passed the intersection.

At Oak and Thirty-third, Joan signalled a right turn and then made a sharp left. She drove east on Thirty-third past Cambie and into Queen Elizabeth Park. Furth dropped back a little as she drove slowly through the park's winding road to the asphalt lot over the reservoir at the park's low summit. Furth parked and got out of the Crown Victoria and walked towards the plexiglas dome of the Bloedel Conservatory. He contacted Oikawa via his walkie-talkie. There was only one road out of the parking lot. Oikawa waited.

Joan retraced her route, left the park and drove north on Cambie to Sixth Avenue. She cut under the bridge and turned left on Sixth.

She cruised sedately down Sixth to the Granville Street Bridge, swerved sharply into the curb lane.

By now the surviving police vehicles had traded positions a dozen times.

Oikawa said, "She just turned into Granville Island."

Willows ordered the other units to fall back. Granville Island was a very large cul-de-sac. Once again, Joan Wismer seemed to have deliberately boxed herself in.

Oikawa said, "Okay, she's stopped. She's talking to a guy wearing a black suit. Six-footer, short blond hair, orange-tinted sunglasses . . . Looks like that football player, used to play for the Raiders . . . Howie Long!" Oikawa's voice tightened. He said, "She just popped the trunk . . . The guy's got the suitcases, three of 'em, he's walking away, he's at the door of a pottery shop called Stone Pony. He's going inside . . ." Oikawa suddenly yelled, "She goosed it Jack, she's gone!"

"Follow the money!" yelled Willows into the mike.

But Oikawa was already out of the car, the heel of his right hand on the butt of his Beretta, the coffee and Tim Hortons donuts that had passed for lunch pulling at him like a thirty-pound anchor.

A short block away, the Caddy's brake lights flashed as it turned into an old flat-roofed wooden building that had been converted into a parking garage.

Oikawa's shoulder hit the shop's door hard, sent it crashing against a cleverly arranged stack of small wooden packing crates. Displayed on the crates were numerous important pieces by the area's most prominent artists. These works of art were as delicate as they were expensive. In a moment, the shop was filled with brightly glazed shrapnel. A chipped raku teapot rolled into Oikawa's path. He might as well have stepped onto a swiftly moving bowling ball. His feet went out from under him. He crashed headlong into the first of several parallel six-foot-high walls of glass shelving upon which hundreds of smaller pieces of pottery had been artfully arranged.

There was, predictably, a domino effect.

42

The bloated corpse drifted into the middle of the channel. Shortly past noon the massive, slowly rotating bronze propeller of a passing freighter caught it a glancing blow. The corpse's left arm, jacket sleeve and all, was rudely torn from the decomposing body.

The remains cartwheeled diagonally across the ship's broad and foamy wake, lonely hand rising and falling repeatedly, in manic salute.

An expatriate North Korean smoking a cigarette on the ship's aft deck made a snap decision not to spend his shore leave describing what he'd seen to a brutal police interpreter.

A quirk in the current pulled at the corpse and made it spiral into the depths. It hung suspended at a depth of twenty feet in a mottled green-and-black twilight, head down and almost motionless, the ruined shoulder socket trailing pink tendrils of flesh.

Then, imperceptibly, it began to work its way back to the surface.

43

Ozzie, unaware that Dean was about to piss off a strange blonde in a Mercedes-Benz *and* fail to get through to Joan Wismer, stood in the doorway waving a cheerful goodbye as the lamebrain drove off in the rental.

The way he stood there, muscular body tilted at a slight angle, splayed left hand perched on his hip and his right arm raised high, fingers flapping in the wind, he felt like some sicko pervert's idea of domesticity gone dreadfully astray.

The van passed from view behind a row of spindly evergreens. Ozzie went back inside the house, shut and deadbolted the door behind him.

He musically cried, "Ho-ney, I'm ho-ome!"

Melanie was watching TV. As always. The soaps. He sat down on the arm of the La-Z-Boy and put his arm around her.

She leaned into him, rested her head against him. She'd taken a shower a half-hour earlier, changed into a semi-translucent blouse and flower-patterned summer skirt Ozzie had found in a drawer. He hadn't been able to find a bra or panties, unfortunately. But Melanie was no slouch. She'd washed her sweet nothings by hand, in the shower, and put them on clean but damp.

Ozzie stroked her silky hair. They'd had a few intimate little talks, during those brief moments when Dean wasn't hovering.

Melanie had made it clear she was not overly attached to Harold, except maybe at the wallet.

She had indicated in ways that made it impossible to misunderstand that she preferred younger men. Men of approximately Ozzie's age.

He kissed her warm throat, felt the racy thump of her pulse beneath his butterfly mouth, the fast beating of her heart. He nibbled gently at an earlobe.

The problem was, she didn't want him to kill Harold. Or Dean, either. Ozzie told her not to worry, that he'd take care of the messy part. Melanie said it didn't matter who pulled the trigger, she'd be equally guilty in the eyes of the law. Where did she get all this stuff? From the soaps. Ozzie tried to laugh off her squeamish concerns. Melanie told him she felt the way she did because that was how she felt, and she wasn't about to change her mind.

Well, duh.

He trailed his hand across her shoulder.

Squeeze, squeeze.

He'd told her the mock-cable guy was trussed up in the basement. But not that he'd been stored in the freezer, turned into a human popsicle. He had a feeling that, if Melanie knew the whole awful truth and nothing but the whole awful truth, she might not be so receptive to his sly advances.

But what choice did he have?

Dead men don't stand up in court and point accusing fingers.

Dead men don't plea-bargain with tricky cops.

Dead men spill blood, but they don't spill the beans.

The way Ozzie saw it, those same rules applied to Harold. And he had plenty of excellent reasons for drilling Dean, too. Five million dollars split down the middle was exactly half of five million dollars not split down the middle.

Ozzie leaned into Melanie, let her take his weight. His fingers probed the bones of her spine, trailed across her ribcage, the rounded firmness of her hip, her thigh. He tried to make sense of his attraction to her, the reality of his feelings for her. She was a feisty woman. Snatched at gunpoint by ruthless men, she'd managed to stay rational, keep her cool. But once Joan paid out, he could have his pick of women.

So, why Melanie?

Maybe just because she was there. Conveniently located. He needed a partner. A special person to watch his back. Why not Melanie?

Maybe it would be cheaper, in the long run, to stick with Dean. Melanie was better-looking, but she was also a lot smarter. Dean's strong suit was his relentless predictability. You wanted to know what Dean was thinking, all you had to do was look at him.

Ozzie reached inside his shirt, found the handcuffs key.

He dangled the key in front of Melanie's eyes, moved it as if he meant to hypnotize her.

She gazed up at him with the hint of a smile.

He said, "Where would *you* like to go today?"

Her eyes were dark, serious.

Ozzie said, "You look kind of tired. Maybe you'd like to go upstairs with me, take a little nap."

Melanie leaned back in the La-Z-Boy, considering. She turned her body so she could look squarely up at him. "If I let you . . ."

Ozzie tilted his head. His eyes were bright.

Melanie said, "Are you going to let me live?"

"Cross my heart," said Ozzie. A split second too late.

Melanie stared at the television screen, a Ford Taurus commercial. She said, "Harold told me he'd buy me a white one, as soon as the lease ran out on my Acura."

Ozzie's hands flitted here and there. His breath washed hot and damp across her ear. He said, "Wanna go upstairs, Melanie?"

"I'd rather do it to myself with a dead trout."

Ozzie's hands fell away. His mouth sagged open. A dead trout? His imagination took a snapshot. Lack of discipline made him look at it.

Jeez.

He went into the kitchen and got a beer from the fridge. He looked out the window at the lake. He drank some beer. He consoled himself with the thought that, even if she had agreed to go upstairs with him, it'd be all over by now anyway. He checked his watch. Harold had been quiet all morning. Not a peep out of him since breakfast. He slammed the beer down on the counter and sprinted for the stairs.

Ozzie was pretty sure he'd left Harold's door wide open, after he'd delivered his morning cereal. But now the door was shut tight, and when he turned the knob and pushed, it didn't give an inch. He stepped back, kicked hard. The door trembled but held. He yelled Harold's name, told him in no uncertain terms what he'd do to him if he didn't open the door *immediately*. Harold was silent. He kicked the door repeatedly. Wood splintered. He put his fevered eye to a one-inch gap. The angle was all wrong – he couldn't see the bed.

Harold had listened in as Ozzie and Dean popped tabs on cans of beer down there in front of the TV. He'd heard them chatting about various news items – a downed jet in Venezuela, a random drive-by shooting and multiple deaths in Miami Beach. He'd listened carefully as they'd debated the best brand of audio tape, what to have for lunch and whose turn it was to cook.

He heard them chatting about what the mock-cable guy had looked like after twenty-four hours in the freezer.

Hard-bitten. By frost.

Yuk yuk yuk.

Harold listened in as Dean and Ozzie argued spiritedly about how many mock-cable guys it would be possible to stuff into a freezer.

Five mock-cable guys, they decided.

Five mock-cable guys or three-point-eight grossly overweight stock promoters.

Yuk yuk yuk.

Harold decided he wasn't going to just lie there, passive and helpless, while they worked their way around to killing him. He considered his situation for hours. How to escape? Finally it occurred to him that, if he couldn't break free of the bed, he'd take it with him.

It seemed, at the moment of inception, a brilliant idea. The heavy brass headboard and footboard were connected by a pair of six-foot-long iron rails that supported the box spring and mattress. The bulbous ends of the rails fitted into U-shaped slots. All that held them in place was gravity.

Harold waited impatiently for his kidnappers to relax their vigil. He spent a lot of time thinking about Joan. What if their positions were reversed? What if somebody had kidnapped her, threatened to kill her if he didn't pay millions in ransom money, but he *knew for a fact* that she'd been having one affair after another for years and years? What if he knew for a dirty fact that she owned an apartment where she kept her sexy boyfriends? Would he put his own life – his financial stability – at risk to save her?

No way.

With him out of the way, Joan would be independently wealthy, free to do whatever she wanted for the rest of her life.

Downstairs, there was silence. Was he alone in the house? Where was Melanie?

Harold decided that if he was going to make a break for it, there was no time like the present.

Ozzie backed up, charged. Wood splintered. Chips of glossy white paint skittered across the hallway's pine floor. The door abruptly collapsed. He spun sideways, stumbled, landed on his ass and rode a small carpet across the floor, bounced off a wall.

He saw as soon as the room came back into focus that Harold had taken a hike.

The mullioned doors leading to the balcony were shut, but even so, it wasn't too hard to figure out which way he'd gone. Ozzie yanked open the doors, rushed out on the balcony. Where was Harold?

Right there in front of him, close enough to touch. The blunt end of an iron rail turned Ozzie's ear to mush. His head snapped sideways. His brain rattled against his skull. His knees buckled. He fell against the balcony's wooden railing. The length of the iron hit him again, in the chest. He noticed that the sky was very blue, but off to the south there was a huge bank of fluffy white cumulus clouds. They were the kind of clouds you might see in a film about dreaming. The iron hit him again. The clouds vanished behind the roofline.

It was a twelve-foot drop to the cedar deck. Ozzie landed flat on his back. His head bounced off the boards repeatedly, but with diminishing force.

The sky was pink now, hazy and blurred. His eyelids were stuck in the open position. The sun burned him. He could feel his eyeballs dehydrating.

He tasted blood.

He tried to take an inventory of the damage he had sustained, but his body was beyond numb – it simply wasn't there. He wondered if he had died or was about to die. Had he slipped out of his corporeal body? Was it his spirit that was doing all the thinking? Was his spirit in a holding pattern, like an airplane waiting for clearance to touch down, or fly away forever?

The pink clouds evaporated. The sky turned blue. His vision cleared. Harold was leaning over the balcony, staring at him. Now he shuffled along the length of the balcony, the brass headboard glittering in the sunlight, throwing off firefly sparks of golden light. He carried the six-foot length of iron rail like a spear.

He raised the spear high above his head, took aim.

Ozzie found that he'd started breathing again. He sucked air deep into his lungs. His back was on fire. His legs ached. Both his arms felt as if they'd been ruthlessly broken. A lifetime of brawling had taught him how to accurately self-diagnose a concussion. He was, no doubt about it, concussed.

Harold's eyes bulged. His arm was a blur. He grunted with the effort, as he threw.

The iron rail, ten pounds of lethal metal, shot directly towards Ozzie. As he scrambled and clawed at the deck, his thought processes were about as complicated as those of an immature woodbug.

The iron rail caught him in the ribs. The sound that reverberated though his body was the sound of an hysterical grizzly rushing through a tight-packed stand of saplings. His ribs popped like corn in a microwave. From deep inside himself he heard a brittle splintering.

Harold was leaning over the railing, screaming at him.

No, *he* was doing all the screaming.

No, wrong again. It was *both of them.*

He advised himself to shut up. He reminded himself that five million dollars was worth all the pain in the world.

He gritted his teeth. He sat up, inch by agonizing inch. It felt as if he was falling apart, pieces of him breaking loose, tumbling into the void.

Where was Harold?

Back inside the house. Ozzie could hear him going down the stairs, the brass headboard banging and thumping against the walls.

He tried to work out what Harold would do when he made it downstairs, to the sundeck. Beat him to death with the headboard? Or take the Ruger away from him and shoot him to pieces?

Ozzie spat. A silky gobbet of blood sizzled on the deck. The Ruger! Where was it? Over there, not ten feet away. He spat again, spat a pink froth laced with bright scarlet threads that looked a lot like candy floss.

Maybe the situation wasn't so grim after all . . .

44

The cellular warbled as Joan drove into the twilight zone of the old wood-frame parking garage. The building was the size of a barn, and it was full almost to capacity, the cars parked in orderly rows. Rectangles of hard white light fell through large, glassless, chicken-wired windows. Joan picked up the ringing phone and said hello. Jake told her to use the remote, pop the Caddy's trunk. She did what she was told, glanced in the rearview mirror and saw the trunk lid rise up and wobble.

Jake told her to drive straight through to the far end of the building, make a right, and stop.

He told her to sit tight and wait patiently.

Not just wait, but wait patiently.

A man wearing a dark suit slipped out from between two cars, pushed the trunk lid all the way up and was lost from view.

Jake croaked into her ear, muttered further instructions.

Joan ignored him.

She disconnected, dialled 911.

The operator picked up on the first ring. Joan identified herself, first name and last. She tersely described her situation, gave the operator her exact location.

She reached out and adjusted the side mirror. There he was, standing directly behind the car. She was quite certain that, if she shifted into reverse gear and stepped on the gas, she could seriously injure or perhaps kill him.

She settled for consciously memorizing the man's description. He was about six feet tall, very muscular. His pale hair was cut very short and receding at the temples. He had tiny ears and wore mirror-lensed sunglasses that, as she watched him, he removed for a second in order to massage the bridge of his button nose. His blue eyes were small and close-set. A thick silver chain hung in a shiny loop from his back pocket all the way down to the knee of his baggy black pants.

Sensing that he was being watched, Axel glanced up. He scowled at Joan, and her heart raced. He reached deep inside the Caddy's trunk, pulled out two black-and-green tartan suitcases, one after the other. He glanced up at Joan again, bared his teeth and spun on his heel and was lost between the rows of parked cars. Joan heard running footsteps, turned and looked out the Caddy's back window.

There he was.

Axel lifted a suitcase high over his shoulder, tossed it through the ragged gap he'd cut in the wire mesh that covered the nearest of the windows spaced around the garage. He picked up the other suitcase and hurled it into the rectangle of light. Scrambling up on the hood of a car, he hooked a leg over the windowsill and hauled himself out of the building.

Joan sat there in the Caddy, fiddling with the seatbelt. All she had to do was take her foot off the brake and let the big car slide forward, make a quick right and she'd be gone.

She powered down her window.

A police car drifted slowly past the garage's exit, lights flashing. The cop looked right at her but apparently didn't see her.

The smaller of the suitcases lay on a patch of scruffy grass directly below the window. Axel landed on it feet first, bounced awkwardly. The damn thing was stuffed so full the sides were bulging. So Jake had been right about the woman paying up, and Marty had been wrong. Marty was such a fool. The larger suitcase was twenty feet away, at the bottom of a gentle slope. Axel yanked open the Bentley's front door. He shoved the smaller suitcase into the car and trotted briskly down the slope.

Jake stuck his nose out the open window and yelped at him to snap it up, be quick. It was good advice but Axel resented it anyway. The suitcase's handle had been knocked off. There it was, over to his left. Should he go and get it or leave it where it was? Leave it, he decided. The suitcase was fat and very heavy. He trudged back up the slope.

Jake, peering anxiously around, saw blobs of pink and pale-blue light flicker in the blank windows of the metal-clad building behind the Bentley. He heard a dozen car doors slam shut. His heart nose-dived into his churning stomach.

Axel scampered across the grass to the Bentley. He slipped and fell, scratched at the grass stains on the knees of his pants. His pants were ruined! He plucked a lump of mud from his shoe.

Now there were blobs of pink and blue light dancing on the walls of every building Jake could see.

Axel climbed into the car. He rested the suitcase against the steering wheel and slammed the door. He turned and smiled broadly at Jake. "Za mission haff been accomplished."

Jake said, "Get da fuck outta here, ya moron!"

"Yah!" cried Axel, beaming stupidly.

Jake said, "Da gas pedal's onna right, Axel! Let's roll!"

"We must haff music!" cried Axel. He turned on the radio, hit FM pre-sets until he'd tuned in the local country-and-western station. Jake had not stopped yelling at him. He peered anxiously at the smears of pink and blue on the wall of a nearby building. What did these pretty pastel colours signify? Something very bad, he feared. A black-clad ERT team scuttled across his field of vision. In the blink of an eye, they had come and gone. Axel hardly knew what to think. Had he seen a platoon of enormous ants? He pushed aside the big suitcase and cranked the radio's volume way past sensible.

An ERT sniper loped crouching across the flat roof of a tin-walled building. Five more ERT killers sprinted in single file across a narrow span of open ground between the parking garage and adjoining building.

Jake doubted he'd have seen them if he hadn't been looking right at them. Even then, it was a close thing. What now? He scratched his chin, and discovered a small area he'd missed with his razor.

He was an old man. He should've retired years ago, headed for Vegas or Palm Springs. Or even Reno. The smallest little city on earth.

He'd *known* what he should do. Why hadn't he done it?

Lack of foresight, imagination. Laziness, inertia. He had twenty reasons and each was as good – or bad – as the next.

Jake could hear more ERT guys off to his left, chattering like geese as they prepared to do him in. A patrol car eased into view. A loudhailer squawked. Jake screamed at Axel to turn down the radio. A bald cop with an old-fashioned handlebar moustache advised the occupants of the Bentley – that would be Jake and Axel – to exit the vehicle with their hands on their heads.

Jake sat there in the backseat, huddled and small, an old man whose life had taken a sudden turn for the worse. Axel was staring at him, waiting to be told what to do.

Jake said, "Get outta da car, Axel, an open da fuckin' door for me."

Axel said, "Okay, Jake. I do it now." He climbed out of the Bentley, and was buffeted by an angry, conflicting babble of incomprehensible voices. What a racket! He opened Jake's door. He offered Jake his hand.

As Jake exited the vehicle, Axel glimpsed the black bulk of the cellphone clutched in Jake's fist, and thought for a scrotum-tightening moment that it was a gun. Wasn't it likely that the ERTs, who were fifty yards away and blind drunk on adrenaline, would make the same mistake?

Axel snatched the phone out of Jake's hand. He turned to face the cop with the loudhailer. He extended his arm, offering the cop a clear view of the cellphone, showing him that he had nothing to fear but onerous long-distance toll charges.

They were in shade, and there was a strong breeze coming in from the harbour. Jake was cold. He muttered, "Fuck dis bullshit!" and turned his back on Axel and climbed back inside the Bentley.

Up on the roof of the tin-walled building, the ERT sniper moved the index finger of his right hand one-eighth of an inch to the west.

Axel dropped the cellphone. He heard a wet, splattering sound that reminded him of a sudden rainstorm, as bullet fragments and myriad small and large chunks of his heart impacted against the Bentley's gleaming sheet-metal flank.

He waited for the sound of the shot, but it never came. He dropped to his knees, sagged backwards against a gleaming chrome hubcap. His chunky blond head lolled forward. His chin bumped against his collarbone.

Jake flinched at the sound of the shot. The side window turned smeary pink. He said, "Wha' da fuck?"

Axel toppled sideways across the grass, limp and graceless as a two-hundred-pound sack of spuds. The blue had faded from his eyes. His tongue drooped. He tasted grass, and mud, and a warm liquid that was wet and salty. His pale face was no more than six inches from the convex, brilliantly polished chrome surface of the hubcap. He stared hard at his reflection.

Who could that ugly fellow be? he wondered, as he died.

In a moment there were cops swarming all over the car, hands clutching at Jake from all directions.

Axel was nothing but a dead punk, but Jake was known to them all. He was yanked out of the Bentley. His wrinkled old face was mashed against the steaming, viscous glass. He sniffed up the smell of Axel's blood, tasted of Axel's heart. He gagged, as a sour lump that might have been his soul welled up inside him and was caught like a sharpened stick in his throat. Somebody tried to break his arm just for the fun of it. Stiff fingers poked at him. Somebody took his wallet. Somebody else took his comb. His cigar was yanked right out of his mouth. His solid gold, diamond-encrusted lighter vanished into a bottomless pocket. His Rolex was stripped off his wrist. His flesh burned, where his diamond rings had been ripped from his fingers.

Somebody violently goosed him, and he jumped.

The cops howled with glee.

He looked down at Axel.

He'd seen a lot of dead guys, in his time. Guys that had been killed with large- and small-calibre handguns, rifles, sawed-off shotguns, a flare gun, a black powder muzzleloader. He'd watched guys die of suffocation, the murder weapon a plastic bag stolen from the produce department of the local supermarket. He'd known guys that had been meathooked, axed, stabbed with knives that were sharp, dull, pitted, rusty. He'd watched while a guy tied to a bale of hay was slowly cut in half with a scythe, seen another guy burn to death in a bathtub full of diesel fuel.

None of those guys were any deader than Axel.

Some of the guys he murdered had been close pals. Most of them were just guys. He'd hated or feared a select few of them so deeply it still gave him a migraine just thinking about it.

He felt nothing for Axel.

A fat bald guy was taking pictures. Unauthorized pictures. He crawled inside the Bentley and clicked off a couple more shots through the gore-streaked window. Jake snarled at him. The guy kept firing away.

A detective knelt down beside Axel, checked for a pulse.

A good-looking female cop flopped the largest of the suitcases down on the Bentley's hood. She worked the zipper, peered inside. Jake studied her face.

She reached inside, placed several bulky stacks of bills on the trunk and then said something to the detective who'd knelt by

Axel. A good-looking guy. Her partner. Jake noted the spark in his eye. Partner in more ways than one, maybe.

The woman spun the suitcase around so Jake could see inside. There were enough newspapers in there to wrap a whole lotta fish.

Jake said, "So, who da fuck're you?"

Parker introduced herself, and Willows.

Jake said, "I dunno what dis's all about. Ya dinks squibbed Axel. My chauffeur I imported alla way from East Germany. For what? Packin' a hot cellphone? He's got his air-brakes licence, can drive da big rigs, eighteen-wheelers. Dat's a talent! And you assholes pot him like he's a fuckin' mallard."

Parker said, "Where's Harold?"

"Who?"

"Harold Wismer. Where've you got him stashed, Jake?"

"I dunno know what da fuck yer talkin' about, if anyt'ing."

"His wife has received a number of telephone calls, demanding a five-million-dollar ransom. She packs two large suitcases full of newspapers and a little seed money, and delivers them to you. Why?"

Jake said, "I wanna talk at my lawyer."

Willows said, "Sure thing, Jake. But where's Harold?"

"Harold who?" said Jake. He glared evilly at a muscular, cheap-suited cop with short blond hair who had just accepted a light from another cop, who flicked the wheel of Jake's diamond-encrusted lighter and touched the flame to one of Jake's twenty-dollar Cuban cigars. Jake blinked, clearing his eyes. A dozen or more cops were standing around, smoking his cigars. Talking and laughing, having a good time. They'd cleaned out his humidor, the fucks. He watched, slack-jawed, as the fat photographer flicked mud off his cellular and casually punched in a twelve-digit number. A moment passed. The fatty's face lit up, his mouth moved. Who was the rotten fuck talkin' to? Twelve fuckin' digits was about as long distance as long distance could get.

Jake told himself to be calm. It wasn't even his phone. But theft of services was theft of services. He'd get Axel . . . No, Axel was dead. Okay, he'd get Steve . . . Come to think of it, where in hell *was* Steve? Gone. Okay, he'd get Axel . . . No, not Axel . . . Marty?

He decided it was time to hire some new help. There was no end of ambitious, just-barely-bright-enough guys out there, seeking employment. Steve and Axel types by the bushel-basketful.

The photographer sensed that he was being watched. He caught Jake's eye, smiled, waggled his stolen cigar. Jake thought he resembled a five-eighths-scale Winston Churchill. He said, "Hey, you! C'mere!"

The guy tried to wave him off.

Jake said, "I wanna buy a buncha dem pictures ya took a me. Whacha fuckin' name, anyways?"

The guy kept talking into the phone as he fumbled for his wallet. Jake had seen fatter wallets, but not many. A card was extracted. Jake took it. The guy's name was Mel Dutton. He told Jake to call him any time.

Jake said he'd appreciate it.

A bullet, scythe, plastic bag? Live burial? Jake decided that, as soon as he was clear of the cops, he'd get two or three of his newly hired domestics to pound Dutton's brains to mush, while another thug took souvenir Polaroids.

Like his fuckin' daddy used to tell him, irony was a dish best tasted cold.

45

Ozzie sat up.

The splintered ends of his broken ribs gouged his lungs. A chainsaw's whirling blade sliced into his skull. The stand of cedar and fir trees on the far side of the driveway were suddenly clearcut, and toppled sideways into the sky.

The lake tilted at a sharp angle. Acres of green water sloshed across the warped horizon.

Fluffy white clouds plummeted like stones.

A small brown bird flew vertically into the earth.

The log house spun like a top.

The sundeck tilted across all points of the compass.

A smoking fuse burnt down to nothing and Ozzie's head exploded in a fiery halo of flesh and bone. He sat there, hands clasping his pounding head as if to contain the powerful forces within, that threatened to burst his skull at the seams, and splatter his brains and all his low ambitions across the cedar boards.

From inside the house came the bumpety-bump of the brass headboard on the stairs.

The Ruger lay on the deck, halfway to the closed French doors. The muzzle was pointing directly at him. He began to crawl on his hands and knees across the deck. His ribs moved like the keys of a honky-tonk piano that had fallen off the back of a high-speed pickup truck. Splinters of bone ripped into his tender flesh. He whimpered.

A hinge creaked.

He squinted at the blank rectangular mouth of the open doorway. Harold cursed as he dragged the gleaming brass headboard out of the house. His face twisted as the thing sagged away from him, and he lost his balance and fell. The headboard clattered on the sundeck. Golden shafts of light were reflected off the metal and into the heavens. Harold got himself straightened out. He struggled to his feet. He looked awful. Terminally haggard. A middle-aged man teetering on the brink of instant antiquity. Clearly the cold Pop Tarts and lukewarm root beer he'd been guzzling for the past three days had not agreed with him.

Harold looked like a man who believed that his girlfriend had abandoned him for good reason.

Harold looked like a man who believed his wife had abandoned him for even better reasons.

Harold looked like a man who'd lost everything and missed every bit of it, and was determined to get it back right this minute, or die trying.

Hacking and spitting, Ozzie crawled slowly across the sun-warmed planks towards the Ruger.

He hooked his fingertips into the narrow space between two planks. He hauled himself forward another six inches.

Harold slung the brass headboard over his shoulder and staggered directly towards him, making noises that would shame a wild boar.

Ozzie's fingers grazed the muzzle of the gun just as Harold kicked him in the face. Retching, Ozzie fell back.

Harold bent and picked up the Ruger. His face was bloody. His knees and elbows were bloody. His Jockeys needed a wash.

Ozzie saw the look in Harold's eyes and knew his time had come. Well, fuck it. Live fast, die young. He plucked the handcuff key out of his pants pocket, shoved the key into his mouth. He swallowed.

Harold's face blossomed red as any rose.

Ozzie said, "Joan laughed in my face. Said she wouldn't pay a dime to save your ass. First and only time I spoke to her, she said she had a boyfriend named Steve, they were gonna buy a couple of one-way tickets to paradise." Ozzie worked up a nasty smile. "Look at it this way, Harold – at least you got what you deserved."

Harold's face fell apart like a cheap jigsaw puzzle. He lifted the pistol and, apparently, shot himself between the eyes and fell straight back, collapsed limp as a threadbare rug across the brass headboard. The thunder of the shot rumbled across the lake. A cloud of pale smoke drifted in the air.

Ozzie stared at the soles of Harold's dirty feet for the better part of a minute, then spat the handcuff key into the palm of his hand.

The key was dry as dust.

He nearly fainted as he pried the pistol out of Harold's clawed fingers. Harold oozed blood. His hair smoked. The bullet had cut a vertical furrow in his broad forehead. He lay there, attracting flies.

Ozzie staggered back into the house. He gathered himself, and shut and locked the French doors.

Melanie was watching television. He yelled at her to turn the damn thing off and then snapped off a shot that struck the Sony square between the shoulder blades. Thick chunks of glass bounced on the carpet. A line of evil-smelling purple smoke clawed its way out of the Sony's guts and wandered towards the cathedral ceiling.

Melanie still wouldn't look at him.

He heard the truck pull up beside the house. A moment later Dean came sidling into the house. He sniffed the air, frowned. His boots crunched glass. He glanced down, startled.

Ozzie said, "How'd it go?"

"Good," said Dean. His forehead rumpled. He took note of the smoking television and the way Melanie sat rigidly in the La-Z-Boy. He finally noticed the pistol in Ozzie's hand.

He looked past Ozzie, at the body lying on the sundeck. Harold chose that moment to sit up. His face was a mask of blood. He slowly raised his arm. He pointed accusingly at Dean.

Dean's mouth fell open.

Ozzie saw the fear in Dean's eyes. He spun on his heel and shot three times as quickly as he could pull the trigger. The bullets struck the glass panels in the French doors and carried away three perfect circle of glass. A hail of glass pebbles bounced across the deck. Ozzie shot into the door frame. He gripped the heavy pistol in both hands and lurched towards the ruined doors.

Blood poured from Harold's self-inflicted wound into his gaping mouth.

Melanie stared unblinkingly at the television's blank screen.

Dean's brain scrambled to work things out. Ozzie was pissed. The TV had been shot. Harold appeared to have already been shot. Now Ozzie was moving in for the kill.

Dean dwelled on Ozzie's likely reaction, when he learned that Joan Wismer wasn't answering her phone, and that Dean had heard on the car radio that the cops had killed one of Harold's kidnappers and captured another.

Dean hurled himself across the room. He swung hard, and accurately, his pistol's barrel laying flat the little whirlpool of hair at the back of Ozzie's skull.

Ozzie fell into the French doors. A sparkly shower of glass sprayed across the sundeck. Ozzie fell face down, but his nose broke the fall. The stump of an unlucky tooth was lost forever in the narrow space between two planks.

Dean confiscated Ozzie's gun.

Melanie yelled, "Hit him again! Harder!"

Dean hit Ozzie a few more times, striking at the base of his skull. Blood oozed from ruptured flesh. A clump of bloody, matted hair clung to the Ruger's front sight. Ozzie's head wobbled, and was still.

"Dump him in the freezer!" yelled Melanie.

Dean turned and looked at her. A dark shape, tucked away inside the larger dark shape of the La-Z-Boy. He moved towards her.

More calmly, she said, "Do Ozzie first, then Harold."

"Why should I?"

"Harold hid a million dollars in my apartment. Emergency money, in case Jake forced his hand."

"Hid it where, exactly?"

Melanie said, "First things first, Dean."

Dean shoved Ozzie's Ruger into his waistband. He dragged him over the chunks of glass and along the hall to the basement door, opened the door and watched Ozzie tumble ass over teakettle down the stairs, sprawl awkwardly across the concrete floor. A rivulet of blood leaked out of his broken nose.

Dean trotted down the stairs, flung open the freezer lid. Steve looked like Frosty the Gunman. His hands were raised above his head, his fingers wedged into a narrow gap between the top of the freezer and the bottom of the lid. Dean hoisted Ozzie up and over. He let him drop. Ozzie's falling body snapped Steve's frozen arms off at the shoulder. Dean threw up all over both of them.

Ozzie's eyes popped open. He looked, mostly, surprised. Dean turned as Melanie yelled at him to hurry up. What a voice that woman had.

Ozzie snatched Dean's Ruger out of his pants.

Melanie was still shouting.

Dean slammed shut the freezer's lid. He heard a muffled shot, and in that same instant, a ragged oval hole appeared in the top of the freezer. The bullet howled past his startled face. Ozzie fired again and again, quick as he could pull the trigger. Numerous ragged, gaping holes appeared in the freezer's white-enamelled shell. Shrapnel stung Dean's stunned face. He tasted blood.

It was suddenly very quiet. Dean counted the holes in the freezer's lid. Twelve. Or maybe thirteen. It was hard to say, really, because of the overlaps. He rinsed his mouth at the laundry basin and hurried upstairs, into a firestorm of complaints and recriminations.

Melanie, still shrieking, pointed outside, beyond the shattered door and gory sundeck.

Harold was about fifty yards away, dragging the headboard diagonally across the lawn towards a thick stand of evergreens. Dean yelled at him, and he redoubled his efforts. The headboard's stubby legs cut parallel gouges in the turf.

Dean hurried across the deck, climbed the rail and dropped to the grass. What did Harold think he was going to do, *escape*? Dean trotted across the grass. Harold had the wit to realize he wasn't going to make it to the woods. He veered abruptly towards the lake, lost his footing, and tumbled down the steep slope, the headboard skidding along on the grass behind him. A narrow strip of dirty yellow sand lay between the lawn and the water. He dug his heels into the sand, breaking his slide. The headboard caught up with him, thumped him on the shoulder. He plunged determinedly into the lake.

About ten feet from shore, the water turned from pale green to inky black. Harold seemed unaware of the sudden change in colour, or perhaps, stunned by his close encounter with a bullet, he failed to realize what it signified. He jogged through the shallows, trailing a foamy wake. Then, quick as a wink, he vanished.

Dean took a few hesitant steps towards the water. He craned his neck for a better view, but there was nothing to see but a rising haze of bubbles. He crouched low on his haunches. A fleet of fluffy white clouds flirted with the sun, drifted past the scenic, snow-capped mountain peaks, and were lost from view. A bird on the far side of the lake cackled insanely. He had counted off the seconds to just past a minute when a huge bubble of air ruptured the lake's placid surface.

Dean plucked a blade of grass from the lawn. He chewed the grass to a pulp and then stood up and stripped naked and strode into the water. In a moment he was hip-deep and the drop-off was right there in front of him. He shaded his eyes with his hands, and peered into the lake's shadowy depths.

Harold was down there, without a doubt. But Dean saw no shiny glint of metal, no soft gleam of waterlogged flesh. However deep Harold had sunk, it was more than deep enough. Dean surged back to shore. He dried himself with his shirt as he made his way back up the slope towards the house.

Melanie was waiting for him in the La-Z-Boy. She gave him a slow look, head to toe and all the way back up again. There was something in her eyes, a mica-hard glint. What did it signify? Dean couldn't pin it down but felt diminished nevertheless. He stood in front of her, naked but for the pistol in his hand. What was it he'd seen? Did she dare let him see it again? His wife had looked at him like that from time to time, until he'd put a stop to it.

He said, "Harold's dead. He drowned. Ozzie's froze to death down there in the freezer. You might as well know, the mock-cable guy, Steve, he's dead too." Dean scratched himself. "So I guess that just leaves you and me, Melanie." He smiled unconvincingly. "Things could be worse."

He unlocked the handcuff from the La-Z-Boy but left the other cuff dangling from Melanie's wrist. He told her he believed it would be safer if they waited until full dark before returning to the city.

There was, Melanie estimated as Dean took her by the hand and led her up the broad pine staircase to the bedroom, about four hours of light remaining in the day. Four hours. Two hundred and forty minutes, with nothing much for them to do but think of ways to make each other happy.

Her eyes were wet. A tear rolled down her cheek.

Marty was a nice enough guy but he was *always* late, and sometimes it just about drove her crazy.

Dean was no giant, but his body was ropy and hard. If push came to shove, she had no doubt she'd end up on the bottom of the pile. Four hours. That was a hell of a lot of foreplay. They reached the landing and started down the hallway to the bedroom. What she'd already come to think of as *her* bedroom. She saw what brute force had done to Harold's door.

She tried to think of an interesting topic of conversation, some clever distraction. Her mind was a blank. He turned her towards her room, ran his hand casually over the rising curve of her hip as she crossed the threshold. He'd put his gun down sooner or later, wouldn't he? If she kneed him or head-butted him, and snatched up the gun. . . . But could she shoot him, if she got the chance? She tightened her hands into fists, and told herself to be brave.

Four long hours.

She couldn't for the life of her imagine a honeymoon with Dean lasting a single minute longer.

46

The bedside telephone rang as Willows pried open a waxed-cardboard takeout carton of boneless pork. Sean picked up as Willows spooned a heaping portion of gluey sienna-coloured chunks of meat onto his paper plate. Willows waved the dripping spoon at Parker, who graciously declined. Ditto Annie, who was watching her weight for reasons neither Willows nor Parker could begin to comprehend.

Willows spooned steamed rice onto his plate, ripped open a tiny plastic bag of soya sauce. Sean pointed at his plate. Willows emptied the bag onto his son's rice. He shifted the narrow, rubber-wheeled hospital table so it was suspended above Sean's lap.

Sean was nodding into the phone, looking very serious. Finally he said, "Yeah, just a minute." Clamping his hand over the receiver, he told Willows it was Sheila.

Willows accepted the call.

His soon-to-be ex got straight to the point.

"It cost me a small fortune to fly all the way up here, Jack. I can only stay a few more days. Maybe it was naive of me, but I'd really hoped you'd be able to squeeze a few minutes out of your busy schedule to see me. I shouldn't have to remind you, but I am still your wife."

Willows felt the blood rush to his face. He said, "I left three messages at your hotel, Sheila. You could have got back to me."

"I tried. I left a dozen messages, Jack."

"Well, I didn't get any of them." Willows stabbed at a succulent chunk of pork with his plastic fork. He popped the meat into his mouth and chewed surreptitiously. Sean was staring at him. So was Parker. And so was Annie. He pointed at their plates, mimed eating.

Nobody moved.

Sheila said, "C'mon Jack. Don't lie to me. I could understand the office screwing up once or twice. But a dozen times? What about the message I left this morning?"

"What message?"

"The message on your answering machine!"

"When did you call?"

"A few minutes past eight. Why, what difference does it make?"

"I was out of the house by seven-thirty. I haven't been in all day. Believe me, Sheila, nobody's avoiding you."

Willows snuck another chunk of meat. It was delicious, even if it was bordering on lukewarm. He put his hand over the phone and said, "Eat up, everybody. Don't wait for me."

Parker took the lead. Sean and then Annie joined in.

Into the phone, Willows said, "Sean's just fine. He's coming right along, should be home in a few more days."

Sean held up two fingers.

"Day after tomorrow," said Willows.

Abruptly switching tracks, Sheila said, "Is Annie there?"

"Annie?" Willows lifted an inquiring eyebrow. Annie shook her head, made pushing-away gestures with her hands. Willows crossed his fingers and held them up for all to see. He said, "Annie's at home, as far as I know."

He helped himself to a square of lemon chicken.

Sheila said, "I'll be at the hospital in about an hour. I thought I might visit with Sean, and then you and I could have dinner together."

Willows nibbled at his steamed rice, popped the tab on a Diet Coke. He said, "I'd love to, but I can't make it." Wimp that he was, he added, "I've got a previous commitment."

"We need to talk about our divorce, Jack."

Willows was suddenly alarmed. After all she'd put him through, was she having second thoughts?

Sheila said, "Things are moving too slowly. I'd like to pick up the pace a little, if you don't mind."

He said, "Well, I'd be happy to do whatever I . . ."

"What exactly are you doing this evening, if you don't mind me asking. Are you working? Could we get together later, for a nightcap?"

Willows said, "I'm sorry, but . . ."

"I'm at the Best Western, in case you've forgotten. Call me in the morning, will you do that for me?"

Willows chewed hurriedly, swallowed. He said, "Yeah, sure." He sipped at his Coke.

"At nine," said Sheila.

"Nine," agreed Willows.

"Tell Sean I'll be there in about an hour."

"Will do," said Willows. But too late, because Sheila had already hung up. He told Sean that Sheila was on her way over, and that she was tired, and sounded a little distraught.

Sean held up a thumb-sized paper cup containing a small green pill. He said, "Don't worry about it, Dad. If things get too intense, I'll slip myself a mickey." He shook the cup and the pill rattled. "This little monster'll take about ten minutes to knock me flat for the night."

Willows thought, Great. I've taught my son to be a liar and a pill-popper, all in one easy lesson. As he and Annie said their goodbyes, Parker collected the used paper plates and dumped them in the garbage. Jack had bought far too much food; half a dozen of the waxed-cardboard boxes hadn't even been opened. Sean had learned that many of the long-term patients were eager for food that wasn't on the hospital menu. Parker would drop the unopened boxes off at the nurses' station on the way out.

She unhooked her purse from the back of an orange plastic chair, bent over Sean and kissed him lightly on the forehead. He smiled up at her. She said, "Call my beeper if you want anything."

His smile widened. "Have fun, Claire."

"If you insist."

"I do, I do."

She gave his hand a quick squeeze, and joined Willows and Annie at the door. Willows had promised to help Annie study for an upcoming biology quiz. Parker planned a leisurely shower, and then a hunt through the clothes closet for something prim and proper, but subtly seductive.

Eddy Orwell had organized a party at Freddy's Bar to celebrate the mostly successful conclusion of the Harold Wismer kidnapping. The promoter was still missing and probably dead, but Orwell had pointed out that the promoter didn't *deserve* a happy ending, since he was a morally corrupt, bloodsucking leech. All that mattered to Orwell was that the perps were in custody or in the morgue, and that Joan Wismer hadn't lost a penny of her inheritance.

But the real reason for the party was the arrest and certain conviction of Jake Cappalletti. For the better part of thirty years, Jake had been maiming and killing and extorting his way across the face of the city. There was hardly an officer on the force who didn't have the old man pegged for one crime or another. The fraud and vice coppers were particularly happy to see Jake fall. What had started out as a quiet little gathering of homicide dicks had quickly turned into a celebration for almost every detective on the VPD.

A dozen brightly coloured helium balloons floated at the entrance to the bar. Printed on the balloons in bold navy-blue and gold letters were the words, PRIVATE PARTY!

Freddy had hired a couple of guys from Beef, Inc. to guard the door. If you didn't carry a badge, you didn't get in.

Willows and Parker arrived late. The dull roar that spilled out the open door announced that the party was well under way. Oikawa had volunteered to pose as greeter. He introduced Willows and Parker to his fiancée, a tall, excessively blonde woman named

Barb Klinger. Barb giggled uncontrollably as Oikawa asked Willows and Parker if they'd heard about the huge RCMP drug bust that had just been thrown out of court.

Willows said, "Missed it, Dan."

Oikawa and Barb were drinking domestic champagne. Oikawa threw back his head and drained his glass. "Biggest bust of the century. Undercover Mounties, sailboats, a ton of coke. The case went all the way to the Supreme Court, and the decision came down this morning. The good guys lost on a technicality."

Barb refilled her glass.

Oikawa lowered his voice to a conspiratorial whisper. "The undercover Mounties? It turns out they weren't licensed by Disney!"

Parker took Willows' arm and they made their way to a table down at the far end of the bar, where Eddy Orwell and his wife, Judith, were sitting alone despite the mob. They exchanged greetings, and sat down. Judith said, "It's not that we're unpopular. Bobby and his bimbo were sitting with us, but Bobby kept making moves on me, and Eddy told him to scram."

"Hey, Judith, you wear a skirt like that, I warned you there was gonna be trouble . . ."

"You *hoped* there'd be trouble."

Orwell smiled grimly. The collision with the van had left him with two black eyes and a gap where his left front tooth should have been, but he was otherwise unmarked. He said, "Bobby's such a dink. One of these days I'm gonna . . ." He trailed off as Freddy arrived at the table with a tray crammed with bottled beer and mixed drinks.

"Going to what?" said Judith belligerently.

Orwell snatched a glass off the tray as Freddy put it down on the table. Freddy shot him a hard look. He doled out the remaining drinks.

"Double Cutty on the rocks for you, Jack. Another rum and Coke for you, Judith. Anybody hungry? We got a special on chicken wings . . ."

Orwell said, "We wanted something to eat, we'd go to a restaurant. We decide we want to die a slow and agonizing death, we'll order the wings."

Freddy rolled his eyes.

Judith said, "Come back in ten minutes with another round, 'kay?"

Freddy picked up the empty tray. Scar tissue on his nub of a thumb and his one-knuckle fingers glinted slick and shiny under the lights.

Willows glanced around the bar, looking in vain for Bradley. The inspector had said he might drop by for a drink, even though he'd never been fond of mingling with the troops.

Parker said, "How're the kids, Judith?"

"Pardon me?" Judith had slouched low in her seat. Parker realized Judith was already drunk.

"The kids. How are they doing?"

"Not too good, but it isn't *my* fault."

"What's that supposed to mean?" Orwell was an inexperienced drinker, and it showed.

Parker glanced up as Bobby Dundas hobbled towards her with the aid of a pair of aluminum crutches. He collapsed awkwardly into the booth. Parker had to be quick to avoid having him land on her lap.

The crutches clattered on the carpet. Bobby said, "Everybody having a good time?"

"We're having an absolutely wonderful time," said Judith. She elbowed her husband forcefully in the ribs. "Stop glaring, Eddy. It makes you look near-sighted."

Bobby tried to look down Parker's dress. He said, "I heard Cappalletti got out on bail." Bobby rested his hand lightly on Parker's shoulder as he leaned forward to make eye contact with Willows. "There's no justice, not in this fucking world. Right, Jack?"

Willows nodded tersely. He hated it when Bobby said something he couldn't find fault with. Jake had been questioned at length about his missing "associate," the guy who'd ducked into the Stone Pony, and vanished. Was that Marty? What was in the suitcases? A change of clothes, mountain of cash? The typical TV villain always waived his right to a mouthpiece. Jake had refused to say a word except under advisement of his lawyer, who happened to be the highest-priced sleazeball in a town stuffed to the rafters with high-priced sleazeballs. The lawyer had convinced a magistrate that Jake was old and feeble and probably suffering from the early stages of Alzheimer's. He'd argued that Jake was incapable of fleeing his home, much less the city or even the country. The gullible magistrate had granted Jake bail.

Would Jake skip? Probably not. At first glance, conviction looked like a done deal. But Jake's hammerhead lawyer had let slip a rumour that Harold Wismer owed Jake a lot more than the pile of newspapers and fifty grand that'd been in Joan's suitcase. The mouth insisted that the debt could be verified via a paper trail. He swore on his mother's urn that Joan had attempted to avoid her contractual obligations by setting Jake up for the snatch.

But where was Harold? Was he alive, or dead? Ask Joan, advised Jake's lawyer from the side of his mouth.

What had happened to Harold's girlfriend, Melanie Martel?

Where was Melanie's boyfriend, Marty?

Where was Steve, the kid who was responsible for washing Jake's stable of expensive imported automobiles?

Good questions, but Jake wasn't talking.

Axel Munsch had been packing a matt-black nine-millimetre Glock loaded with military-surplus hardball rounds – not Black Talon hollowpoints – when he'd been "drilled 'n' spilled" by the ERT sniper. The Glock had been stolen a year earlier during a break-in at the Quebec City *pied-à-terre* of a locally prominent separatist politician. How the weapon had fallen into Axel's hands was just one more question he was far too dead to answer. All that mattered to Willows was that there was no obvious connection between Axel and Sean's shooting.

Glancing around the crowded bar, he caught the eye of a robbery-squad cop named Pat Hickler. Hickler waved him over.

Willows advised Parker that he was going to go over and say hello, and Parker said she thought she'd join him. Hickler introduced them to his girlfriend, a red-haired woman named Sandra, who was a criminology student at SFU. Mel Dutton and pathologist Christy Kirkpatrick joined the group. Freddy was waylaid as he tried to slip by with a tray of drinks destined for a clutch of vice-squad cops. Kirkpatrick amused Sandra with a true story about a suicide who'd fired two shots, both of them instantly lethal, into his brain. Sandra was still trying to work out the puzzle when Orwell shouldered his way into the discussion.

Orwell had finished writing his lyrics and was recruiting volunteers to perform his rap song.

Sandra said, "Let's have a look at that . . ."

All three vice-squad cops volunteered. So did Kirkpatrick, when he'd put on his glasses and read the lyrics. Orwell tried to con Parker and Willows into singing along. Willows declined, but Parker accepted.

Orwell assembled the group into a short column, and told them to follow along, snapping their fingers and swaying, crying out "Yeah!" or repeating a line, according to the simple directions that accompanied the lyrics. The least drunk of the vice cops tried to drop out, but his buddies wouldn't let him. Orwell had brought along a portable tape player almost as big as the largest of Joan Wismer's tartan suitcases. He adjusted the bass and cranked up the volume.

All conversation instantly ceased.

Orwell slipped a black sweatband over his head. He handed identical headbands and pairs of impenetrably dark sunglasses with heavy black plastic frames to his backup singers. He put on his own sunglasses.

The thump of the bass and the percussive thud of drums shook motes of dust and unwary insects from the ceiling.

A vice-squad cop began to snap his fingers in time to the music. The others joined in. Spears of purple light flashed off the sunglasses. Orwell snatched a pint glass of beer off a table and drank it down in one long gulp. He tossed the empty glass into the crowd and shouted, "This's a little tune I wrote, called 'White Man's Rap.' Hope you like it, folks!"

There was scattered applause, all of it from Judith.

Orwell struck a pose. He thumb-jabbed his chest. His muscular body swayed and twisted. The words he'd laboured over so long and hard burst from him like chunks of white-hot metal.

I'm just a middle-class white
kinda average bright
Had it totally made
then suddenly I was afraid
fear as sharp as a knife
for my kids and wife
and nice green lawn
you cruise by in your car
take a shot and it's gone
you're somebody's nightmare
and I can see it
but I ain't gonna be it
gonna serve and protect
my cat named Fluff
and every last piece
of middle-class stuff
that's scattered all over my
   house
and all over my yard
if you try to take it
I would take it hard
so if you think
from violence I'd shrink
go ahead and try me
'cause I won't roll over and die
I bought a nine-mil baby

been down on the range
learned to shoot real straight
at anybody strange
so if you think
that you so bad
c'mon down to my 'hood
and I'll stitch you up good
lemme show you my scene
lemme make it clear
that a middle-class white
kinda average bright
with a new semiauto
in his fist
can give yo' life a brand-new
   twist
yo' boots and jeans and pre-
   stressed leather
ain't gonna protect you
from my kinda weather
so stay offa my block
or me and my pistol's
gonna roll 'n' rock
I'll blow out your tires
I'll shatter your glass
I'll shoot out your eyes
I'll puncture your ass

There was a raucous burst of applause as Orwell took his bow. It was impossible to say if the crowd was applauding the music or the end of the music. Orwell said something to his backup group that didn't go down well. One of the vice-squad cops took a swipe at him. Hickler grabbed the cop from behind and advised him to behave himself. Sandra shouted at Hickler that Orwell was reneging on his promise to let them keep their sunglasses.

Orwell easily slipped a sweeping roundhouse right. He countered with a wild left hook that caught Christy Kirkpatrick flush on the chin. The elderly pathologist toppled sideways onto a table crowded with thirsty cops and full pitchers of beer. The cops fell back in sodden disarray, upsetting another table, several additional gallons of beer and a few more hornet-tempered detectives.

Almost every cop in the bar rushed eagerly towards the growing fray.

A cop named Lambert bent to pick up an overturned chair. His intent was deliberately misconstrued. He was knocked flat and snatched up and knocked flat again.

An aluminum crutch thudded against a skull too thick to notice. A woman whooped a joyful battle-cry.

Freddy waved to Willows and Parker as they sauntered past him on their way to the door. Willows had his arm around Parker's narrow waist, and she was leaning into him, resting her head on his shoulder.

Freddy couldn't remember when they'd looked happier. He gave them a few moments to get clear, then speed-dialled 911.

47

Marty was a professional – a good soldier. Following Jake's plan, he had pushed in through the Stone Pony's front door, trotted gingerly past the glass display cases, and out through the back door. He was heartened to discover a battered dumpster exactly where Jake had said it would be. He tossed the empty tartan suitcases and Axel's favourite black leather jacket and Steve's mirror sunglasses into the dumpster and walked west towards the Kids Only Market at a pace a heartbeat slower than suspicious. Beneath the discarded leather jacket he'd worn a pumpkin-orange nylon windbreaker with a Grizzlies cap stuffed in the pocket. He smoothed out the cap and put it on, scrutinized himself as he strode briskly past a plate-glass window.

It was an excellent disguise. A minute ago he'd looked like everybody's idea of a mobster. Now he looked like a wilfully unsuccessful geek. Passing another window, he tucked in his chin and slumped his shoulders.

Jake had originally given the Stone Pony role to Axel. Who could blame him? Why would he choose to put Axel in a situation where it was just him and Jake and several million dollars? Marty had worked hard to convince Jake that not even Axel was moronic enough to try to scoot when he was weighed down by hundreds of pounds of money.

Besides, where would he go? Marty reminded Jake that he'd be waiting for them at the entrance to Granville Island, and that he'd be heavily armed, and that Axel knew it.

There had been a moment, just as they were approaching the point of no return, when Jake had locked eyes with Marty, allowed Marty to look deep into his wizened old soul.

Marty had been shocked to realize that the old man understood full well that his number-one hood had no faith in his plan. Jake knew all of Marty's thoughts. He knew Marty believed that Joan Wismer wasn't playing it straight, that there was a good chance the cops were going to take them out. It was clear from the look in Jake's rheumy eyes that he was fully aware that Marty had the best chance of getting away, if Joan had called the cops.

Jake had *smiled warmly* at Marty. He'd winked at him, and waggled his cigar. It was as if he were saying goodbye.

Marty's intention, now that he'd deflected at least a few of the cops from Jake, was to stroll briskly towards the Kids Only Market near the entrance to the Island, and buy a toy that merited a large bag. Bag in hand, he'd stand around looking like a proud parent until the Rolls showed up. At which time he would hop aboard, all set to blow a hole in Axel.

If the cops were in hot pursuit of the Rolls, he'd go straight to plan B, once he'd figured out what it was.

He hadn't walked a block when he heard a single rifleshot. The sharp crack of the shot made a flock of pigeons veer off course. The sound hit the enormous metal gridwork of the bridge and was torn to shreds and flung back, a tattered, much-diminished echo that sounded like a volley of small-calibre fire that had travelled a great distance.

Marty's heart lurched.

He should never have left Jake with that dumb fuck Axel.

Now what? He forced himself to keep walking. The second shot never came. He rounded a corner and there was the Kids Only Market.

He took his Rolls-Royce keyring out of his pocket. He slid a single brass key off the ring. As he walked past a gold-coloured Toyota, he tossed the keyring so it skittered beneath the car.

He hoped – he came close to praying – that Jake was okay, that it was Axel who'd caught the bullet. Either way, he and Jake were finished. He loved the old man but he wasn't about to let himself be dragged down by love. Not when he could fall so far.

A cab cruised past. Marty cursed and screamed, but the driver ignored him. Directly behind the cab was a white-with-blue-trim Chevrolet four-door with twin whip antennae, light bar, steel cage. The cop in the shotgun seat gave Marty a quick up-and-down. He said something to his partner.

Marty kept walking. Not fifty feet away a woman was bent over the open trunk of an older-model BMW. The car's engine was running. If the cops took an interest in him, he'd fire a quick five- or six-round burst through the side window and door of the patrol car, sprint for the BMW.

The patrol car slowed and then came to a full stop, brake lights flashing a hysteria-inducing red. Marty hesitated. The cop in the shotgun seat pointed at him. Marty spun the Grizzlies cap around on his head so the bill pointed sideways. He partially unzipped his pumpkin-orange jacket. The cop's gesture indicated he wanted Marty to step in front of the car.

For what – so they could run him over?

Marty was a fraction of a second away from drawing his pistol when he saw that the cops had stopped to avoid rear-ending the taxi. The taxi's rear nearside door was open. The driver waved at Marty, urging him forward.

Marty smiled at the cop. He pressed his forearm against his belt to stop his pistol from dropping down his pants, as he jogged light-heartedly towards the taxi. He climbed inside.

He reached out and shut the door.

The cabbie wore a rumpled plaid shirt with a frayed collar. He needed a shave, but it looked like it was a twice-hourly occurrence.

He dropped the flag and spat and accelerated down the pedestrian-clogged street. Mimicking the phrase that Microsoft had made tedious, he asked Marty where in the world he wanted to go today.

Marty dropped a crisp new fifty on the front seat. He told the cabbie he wasn't too sure, just yet. While he was thinking about it, would the guy please head in the general direction of the financial district . . .

The cabbie wondered if he was into stockades and bondage. No, that couldn't be right. He must have said stocks and bonds?

Not if I can avoid it, said Marty.

The elevator doors slid open and there she was, standing in her open doorway with some guy Barry Holbrook was pretty sure he'd never seen before, in or out of the building. Barry stepped out of the elevator and gave her a big welcoming smile. He said, "Hey, Melanie. The cops've been looking for you."

Melanie said, "Yeah, I know. But don't worry about it, because they found me."

Barry walked down the hallway towards her. Melanie's new boyfriend glanced incuriously at him. Chilly eyes, broad shoulders. Barry's hunch that Melanie had a weakness for cold-hearted fellas was reaffirmed.

Melanie said, "Did you hear what happened to Harold?"

Barry said, "Nope." He tried to look even more interested than he was.

"Me either," said Melanie. The boyfriend started laughing. Barry hesitated a minute, before joining in. The boyfriend got Melanie's door open. He dropped the key in his pocket and patted Melanie on the bum. Had she flinched? Barry wasn't sure. The boyfriend followed her into the apartment and shut the door behind him. The deadbolt thudded home. The safety chain rattled.

Barry still had the cop's card. Didn't he? He pulled out his wallet. There it was. Detective Jack Willows. Should he give the guy a call? He checked his watch. In the morning, maybe.

Dean gripped Melanie's arm. He told her to turn on the lights, all of them. He frog-marched her through the apartment.

Marty didn't blink his eyes when she turned on the bedroom light. He smiled at her from where he lay, on his side of the king-size bed Harold had squeezed into the little room.

She said, "I knew you'd be here."

"Did you?"

"Sort of."

Dean said, "Who're you?"

"I'm the guy who got here before you, and beat you to the punch. I'm the guy who took Harold's mad money, and I'm the guy who hid it where you'll never find it."

Dean showed Marty his Ruger.

Marty said, "What're you thinking, that you're gonna shoot yourself? Not a bad idea, but I've got a better one."

"Yeah?" Dean let Melanie's throat take the weight of the Ruger's barrel. He said, "What's she worth to you?"

"More than you could ever spend."

Melanie almost smiled.

Dean drew back the Ruger's hammer.

Marty said, "You shoot her, then what? I'm next?"

"Sounds good to me."

Marty smiled. He said, "Harold was the kind of guy who liked to hedge his bets. One egg, one basket." He said, "I'm Marty. What's your name?"

Dean stared at him.

"His name's Dean," said Melanie.

"You want a piece of Harold's egg, Dean? Or would you rather walk out of here with a pocketful of lint?" Marty sat up. Dean finally noticed the long-barrelled semiauto. No, the barrel wasn't all that long, the gun was equipped with a silencer. Marty said, "Or are you one of those suicidal assholes would rather not walk at all?"

Dean kept staring at him.

Melanie said, "Dean told me he's got a couple of kids, back on the prairies."

"Yeah?" Marty reached behind him to plump up his pillow. "What're their names?"

"Tiffany and Jodie," said Dean.

"A girl and a boy?"

Dean nodded reluctantly, as if the gender of his children was vital information he preferred to keep to himself.

"The girl pretty?"

Dean reluctantly nodded.

"Her mother too, I bet. What about Jodie? He as handsome as his daddy? Or are you in a position to know?"

Dean pointed the Ruger at Marty. "Hey, don't fuck with me! You think you can fuck with me?"

"Not even in your dreams," said Marty.

Melanie said, "He hasn't seen them for almost a year. Doesn't pay child support, write or phone or keep in touch in any way you can think of. He says otherwise, but I don't think he cares about them any more than if they were the neighbour's dogs."

Marty stared into Melanie's eyes, focused on her so completely that all the rest of the world fell away into the void. She stared right back at him, inviting him into her soul.

Her eyes asked him to think about when a guy like Dean would confess that he'd abandoned his wife and children.

Marty scratched behind his ear with his pistol. The made-in-Texas noise suppressor added half a pound to the gun's weight, about five inches to its overall length. He said, "Which is oldest, Jodie or Tiffany?"

Marty had put the question to Melanie, but Dean felt compelled to answer. They were his kids, weren't they? As he opened his mouth to speak, Melanie willed herself to relax every muscle in her body, went limp as a fresh-killed octopus, slid away and down from Dean, exposing his upper body. Dean could have shot her, but realized instinctively that it would be much wiser to concentrate on Marty. But Marty had already shot *him*, once, twice, and then a third time, in the area of his collarbone. The groans of anguish Dean made as the bullets bored into him were considerably louder than the noise of the shots, which had been reduced by the suppressor to a soft thump, remarkably similar to the sound of a feather pillow being forcibly punched.

Dean dropped his pistol. He sat down hard, fell against a wall. The three red spots high on his chest merged quickly into one.

Melanie sat down on the bed, on her front-row seat. Dean's chest turned red. Three streams of blood trickled down his chest and joined at his belt buckle to form a shallow pool of blood in the crotch of his pants. The wounds were bleeding at slightly different rates. Dean's eyes were open, but he didn't seem to be looking at anything in particular. Or anything at all, really. She said, "Is he already dead?"

Marty shrugged. "Not quite, but he's getting there. I shot him three times. It's got to hurt. Want me to call an ambulance?"

"Not just yet. Probably never." Melanie knelt beside Dean. She looked into his darkening eyes as she searched his pockets, found his cigarettes. She tilted her head towards Marty, brushed back her hair as he sparked his lighter.

He said, "I thought you'd quit for good, this time."

"Me too." Melanie exhaled a stream of blue smoke into Dean's face. He lifted his head an inch or two, and looked her in the eye. There was something about him that reminded her of a dog that hadn't been fed for a long time. But she was unmoved. She said, "How long is it going to take?"

"Until he dies?" Marty saw that Dean was watching him, listening hard. He said, "I dunno. He's bleeding to death. Maybe not as slowly as you'd think, because what you're seeing is only a small part of his problem."

"How d'you mean?"

"Look how pale he is. He's bleeding internally. I bet he's already got a bellyful of blood. But you just can't tell. He could last a long time, all night long, maybe."

"Good," said Melanie.

Marty wondered what Dean had done to her. He didn't want to know. He wondered if he should ever ask.

He said, "Where's Harold?"

"At the bottom of a lake."

"Steve?"

"In a freezer."

Marty indicated Dean. "He put him there?"

"Him an' his buddy, Ozzie."

"And where's Ozzie now?"

"With Steve."

Marty said, "I watched the six o'clock news. Joan looked me in the eye and swore up and down that Harold rented fifteen safety-deposit boxes but that they were all empty, except for one that contained fifty thousand dollars."

"She's lying."

"And very rich," said Marty. "Dean and Ozzie get any of it?"

"Not a penny."

Dean hadn't said a word or uttered the smallest sound. His chest and his pants all the way to his knees were soaked in blood. His mouth hung wide open. His eyes were all pupil. His face and hands and throat were ghostly white streaked with smudges of palest blue. He reminded Marty of a picture he'd seen a long time ago, of the aurora borealis.

Melanie said, "What're you thinking?"

"How deep was the lake?"

"Deep enough."

Marty said, "How deep?"

Melanie flicked ash at Dean. She nudged him with the toe of her shoe. "He said about twenty feet."

"Harold had something tied to him to hold him down, did he?"

"He was handcuffed to part of a bed."

Marty nodded, thinking about it. He said, "Twenty feet, that's not so bad. I could dive down, slip a rope around him, haul him back up."

Melanie said, "I don't mean to sound coarse, but why bother?"

"Maybe we could find a use for him. Revive him, sort of. Where's the lake, Melanie?"

"Up by Whistler."

Marty said, "Nice and cold up there. That's good." He crouched down and bent Dean's legs at the knees to keep the blood away from the carpet. He said, "Did Ozzie and Dean get Harold to make the usual pitch on tape, get him to speak into a tape recorder?"

Melanie nodded.

"Good," said Marty.

He touched Dean's throat just below the line of his jaw. Dean's body temperature had plummeted. He felt icy cold. His heart was beating quick as a hummingbird's – and by now was probably pumping about the same amount of blood. Talk about the living dead . . .

Marty wondered if he could find a use for Dean. And what about Steve and the other guy, Dean's pal, Ozzie? What small or large roles could they play in the drama to come?

Marty's imagination played across a darkening landscape. He had four character actors to choose from. Three of them were deceased. Pretty soon he'd have a quartet of corpses to strut and bow upon his stage, none of them drawing a penny's worth of salary.

Plus he had himself, and Melanie.

And Joan, who still believed Harold was alive.

Five million bucks.

Eight, if Jake could be believed.

He'd be risking everything. But that made perfect sense, since he had everything to gain.

Melanie said, "I'm going to take a shower."

Marty said, "Yeah, okay."

She hesitated, eyed Marty warily. It struck him that she'd been at least as badly wounded as Dean, and that he'd better keep that thought in mind for a very long time and maybe forever.

She said, "Would you mind washing my back?"

Marty picked up Dean's pistol. He ejected the magazine and racked the slide, tossed the empty pistol on the bed. He smiled warmly at her and said, "Be there in a minute."

By now Joan would be under the mistaken impression that her ordeal was over. Her resistance would be worn to a nub. She'd be ripe for the picking.

All he had to do was work out a plot that was feasible and find a way to exploit his pool of talent, write a few lines of convincing dialogue . . .

Melanie had shed her clothes on the way to the bathroom. The door was shut. The toilet flushed. Was she singing? Or crying? Water drummed on tile and glass as she turned on the shower. He gave her a minute to get settled, then pushed open the door and eased into the bathroom. Melanie was a dim shape, a pale wraith in the steam.

Marty said, "Honey, have you got a pen I can borrow, and some paper?"

48

Under blue skies and a gentle southerly, the outgoing tide swept the ex-Rottweiler-owner's body beneath the Lion's Gate Bridge and into the pleasingly sparkly but hardly pristine waters of English Bay.

The rising tide carried the corpse towards Third Beach. It bumped along the convex granite wall of the swimming pool that, only a few years ago, the Parks Board geniuses had filled with sand and covered with black asphalt, and called a "water park."

To the north there was a narrow strip of sand and an inhospitable jumble of low rocks that were home to tight-packed crowds of drab grey barnacles that resembled minuscule volcanoes.

At a few minutes past six in the morning, the eldest son of a Japanese family that was collecting seaweed for their city garden discovered a one-armed corpse in a tidal pool nestled between several large boulders, face down in the muck. With the exception of a deaf grandmother, all members of the family immediately ceased and desisted collecting seaweed.

There was a brief, heated discussion.

The eldest son was delegated to make an anonymous 911 call from the payphone located at the concession stand in front of the asphalted swimming pool.

The 911 call was logged at 6:13.

A unit was dispatched. The body was confirmed at 6:27.

Willows' phone rang at 6:31. He picked up on the eighth ring.
Sheila had arrived unannounced at a little before midnight. She'd
harangued him until well past two in the morning. He'd cracked
the seal on a bottle of Cutty as she drove away in her rented car.
He and Parker had finally gone back to bed at a little past three.
By then the level of Scotch in the bottle had sunk below the mid-
point of the label.

As Parker padded naked towards the bathroom, she wondered
aloud if she was in any condition to go to work.

Willows advised her not to worry about it. From what had been
said to him over the phone, he believed her first glimpse of the
body was going to turn her absolutely stone-cold sober.

It was obvious, even from a considerable distance, that the corpse
had been in the water a long, long time.

Willows and Parker approached slowly, from upwind. Willows
chewed on a mouthful of breath mints as he wriggled his hands
into a pair of latex gloves. A rusty chain led from a black leather
belt to a bulge in the back pocket of the man's ragged jeans.
Willows knelt, tugged gingerly and then forcibly at the chain. The
body twitched and shuddered as if it were alive. Willows shifted
his angle of attack. He yanked on the chain, but the wallet wouldn't
come out of the pocket.

Exasperated, Willows used his penknife to slice through several
inches of waterlogged denim, and then the leather belt. He eased
the wallet out of the ruined pocket. The chain rattled softly as he
took several quick steps backward, away from the stench.

The wallet was made of black leather. Willows pried it open.
Inside was a waterlogged half-inch-thick sheaf of thousand-dollar
bills, gold and platinum credit cards, a driver's licence.

He shut the wallet and balanced it on the corpse's swollen
buttock. He stood up. He handed Parker the driver's licence.

She glanced at it, smiled.

Fatboy.

MEMORY LANE

A WILLOWS AND PARKER MYSTERY

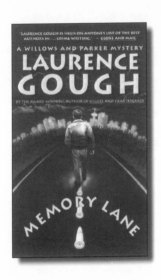

Ross's one good memory of the slammer was his friendship with Garret, in for robbery and murder. Now that Garret is dead, and Ross is out of jail, Ross and Garret's old girlfriend, Shannon, have gotten together. Are the two falling in love, or is Shannon hoping Ross knows where Garret stashed the loot from his robbery long ago?

Meanwhile, Willows and Parker are investigating the murder of a city police officer, who, it turns out, had an interesting sex life. Once again Gough brilliantly weaves together two taut plots as Willows and Parker race against the clock to prevent another murder.

"Gough twists the threads skillfully, tying up our attention."
– Saskatoon *Star Phoenix*

"Gough's accomplishment, once again, is his marriage of a tight plot and solid characters with mordant turns of phrase."
– Montreal *Gazette*

"Gough keeps the action moving right to the end and more than enough plot twists keep readers guessing."
– Margaret Cannon, *Globe and Mail*

0-7710-3437-7 • $26.99 cloth   0-7710-3404-0 • $7.99 paper

— HEARTBREAKER —

A WILLOWS AND PARKER MYSTERY

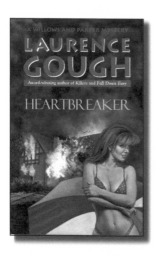

Shelley has it made: he's arranged his life in a way that affords him maximum comfort for minimum effort. He moves from one upscale house-sitting job to another, supporting himself with petty theft and the occasional job as a night-club bouncer. But a day on the beach turns sour when Shelley makes two crucial mistakes: he breaks into a car belonging to off-duty police detectives Willows and Parker, and he picks up a gorgeous beach-bunny named Bo.

Shelley is astonished at how quickly Bo worms her way into the most intimate details of his life – and equally surprised to discover that he's falling in love with her. Bo seems fond of Shelley, too. But Bo's former "business associates" want her back, and are eager and willing to do anything it takes to get her.

Meanwhile Willows and Parker are investigating the murder of a sleazy real-estate agent at a luxury penthouse condo, and, as the events in this fast-paced mystery bring everyone together, the results are – literally – explosive.

"This is the eighth and best book in the excellent series featuring the
Vancouver police team of Claire Parker and Jack Willows.
As always, Gough turns in a stellar collection of characters."
– *Globe and Mail*

"Mordantly funny ... moves at top speed."
– *Sunday Oregonian*

0-7710-3438-5 • $26.99 cloth   0-7710-3447-4 • $7.99 paper

KILLERS

A WILLOWS AND PARKER MYSTERY

It is mid-winter when the body of Dr. Gerard Roth is found floating in the killer-whale pool in Vancouver's main aquarium. Although he is known to enjoy tempting fate by swimming amongst the more dangerous mammals in the aquarium's collection, there are signs that he met his death at human hands. Detectives Jack Willows and Claire Parker are called in to investigate.

Meanwhile, feckless, unemployed actor Chris Spacy believes he actually witnessed Roth's body being dumped in the pool, but he's not exactly sure his blurred memory wasn't a drug-induced hallucination. With blackmail on his mind, he goes after the likely killer – an action that provokes further bloodshed, and complicates an already-murky case for the two detectives.

"Consistently entertaining ... another excellent hardboiled novel from the Vancouver master."
– *Ottawa Citizen*

"Laurence Gough is high on anyone's list of the best authors in ... crime writing, and if you want to know why, you don't have to look farther than *Killers*."
– Margaret Cannon, *Globe and Mail*

0-7710-3439-3 • $26.99 cloth   0-7710-3441-5 • $7.99 paper

FALL DOWN EASY

A WILLOWS AND PARKER MYSTERY

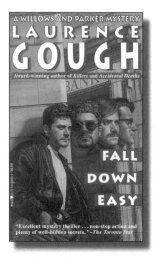

Greg is a cocaine addict, professional heartbreaker, weapons freak, a master of disguise – and bank robber extraordinaire. His latest heist, however, goes terribly wrong: a vicious fight ensues and a man is killed. Greg flees with the man's briefcase only to discover that it contains not, as he had hoped, money, but mysterious computer print-outs.

Willows and Parker are handed the investigation, and discover that the dead man was a plainclothes Panamanian policeman, in British Columbia for unspecified reasons. Are drugs involved, they wonder. And what about the bank manager and his beautiful daughter? Did they have personal dealings with the Panamanian? Complicating all this is Greg, the elusive thief whose chameleon-like ability to transform face and figure leaves Willows and Parker grasping to build up any sort of profile.

NOMINATED FOR BEST CRIME NOVEL
BY THE CRIME WRITERS OF CANADA

"An excellent mystery thriller ... non-stop action
and plenty of well-hidden secrets."
– *Toronto Star*

"One of the best crime novels of the season
– in Canada and anywhere else."
– *Toronto Sun*

"Compulsively readable."
– *Quill & Quire*

0-7710-3444-X • $26.99 cloth   0-7710-3443-1 • $6.99 paper